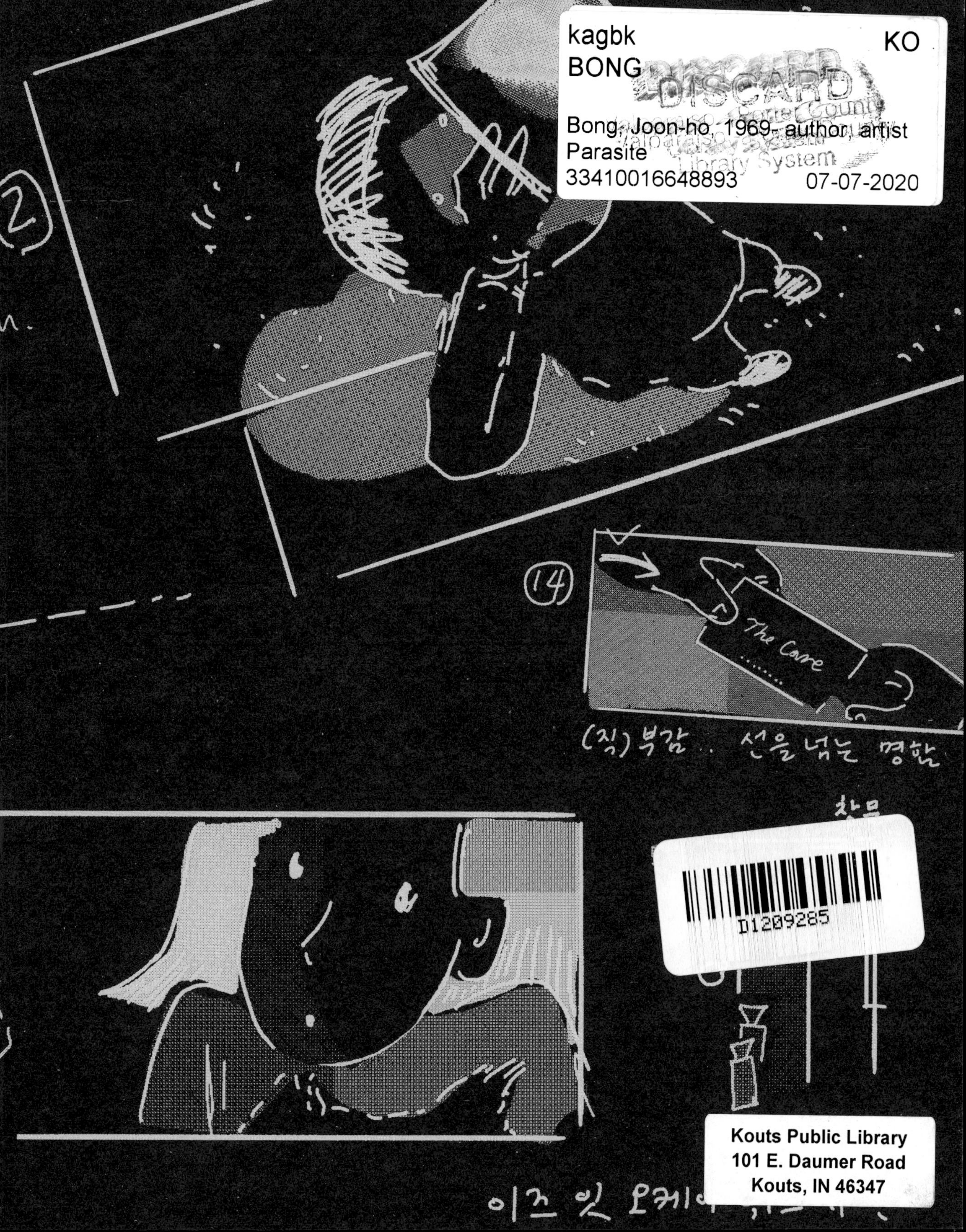
2
14
The Card
(직) 부감.. 선을 넘는 명함

PARASITE

A Graphic Novel in Storyboards

BONG JOON HO

GRAND CENTRAL
PUBLISHING

NEW YORK   BOSTON

Grand Central Publishing
Hachette Book Group
1290 Avenue of the Americas, New York, NY 10104
grandcentralpublishing.com
twitter.com/grandcentralpub

First Edition: May 2020

Grand Central Publishing is a division of Hachette Book Group, Inc. The Grand Central Publishing name and logo is a trademark of Hachette Book Group, Inc.

The publisher is not responsible for websites (or their content) that are not owned by the publisher.

The Hachette Speakers Bureau provides a wide range of authors for speaking events. To find out more, go to www.hachettespeakersbureau.com or call (866) 376-6591.

LCCN: 2020933681

ISBNs: 978-1-5387-5325-5 (hardcover), 978-1-5387-5327-9 (ebook fixed-format), 978-1-5387-1939-8 (ebook mobipocket), 978-1-5387-1937-4 (ebook PDF-format)

Printed in the United States of America

LSC-C

10 9 8 7 6 5 4 3 2

FOREWORD

Dear Reader,

I know many fine films are made without storyboards.

I've heard that the great Steven Spielberg doesn't often storyboard his films.

This book in no way purports that storyboarding is an essential shortcut to making good films. I actually storyboard to quell my own anxiety.

I only feel safe when I have all the shots of the day storyboarded and in my palm.

Whenever I go to set without storyboards, I feel like I'm standing in the middle of Grand Central Terminal wearing only my underwear.

But it would be misleading to say I only storyboard for my personal sanity.

The storyboards show in great detail how the shots will be constructed. They can be shot exactly as drawn and serve as valuable blueprints for the crew members. The finished film never deviates far from the storyboards, and this allows the crew to trust the process. Crew members who have worked with me in the past are especially aware of this.

The entire crew looks forward to receiving the day's storyboards in the morning. Once they do, they are able to concentrate their energy into achieving one specific goal. They are immediately able to tell what we are shooting that day and at which point in the story we are. And at that moment, the storyboards not only assuage my own fears but the crew's as well.

But then another fear begins to take shape inside me.

I begin to fear that shooting the storyboards frame by frame will result in mannerism. I fear that I've failed to capture the tiny sparks of spontaneity that were floating in the air of the set that day.

It would take a whole other book to explain this entire process in detail. But I'm sure some will be able to identify the small differences between the storyboards and the film—the exciting moments of fear and spontaneity that arose amidst the carefully and minutely storyboarded scenes.

Thank you.
Bong Joon Ho

CAST OF CHARACTERS

<table>
<tr><td>The Kims</td><td>The Parks</td></tr>
<tr><td>기택 (or 택) – Ki-taek</td><td>동익 (or 익) – Dong-ik</td></tr>
<tr><td>충숙 (or 충) – Chung-sook</td><td>연교 (or 교) – Yeon-kyo</td></tr>
<tr><td>기우 (or 우) – Ki-woo</td><td>다혜 (or 혜) – Da-hye</td></tr>
<tr><td>기정 (or 정) – Ki-jung</td><td>다송 (or 송) – Da-song</td></tr>
</table>

문광 (or 문) – Moon-gwang

근세 (or 근) – Geun-sae

민혁 (or 민 and 혁) – Min-hyuk

윤기사 (or 윤) – Driver Yoon

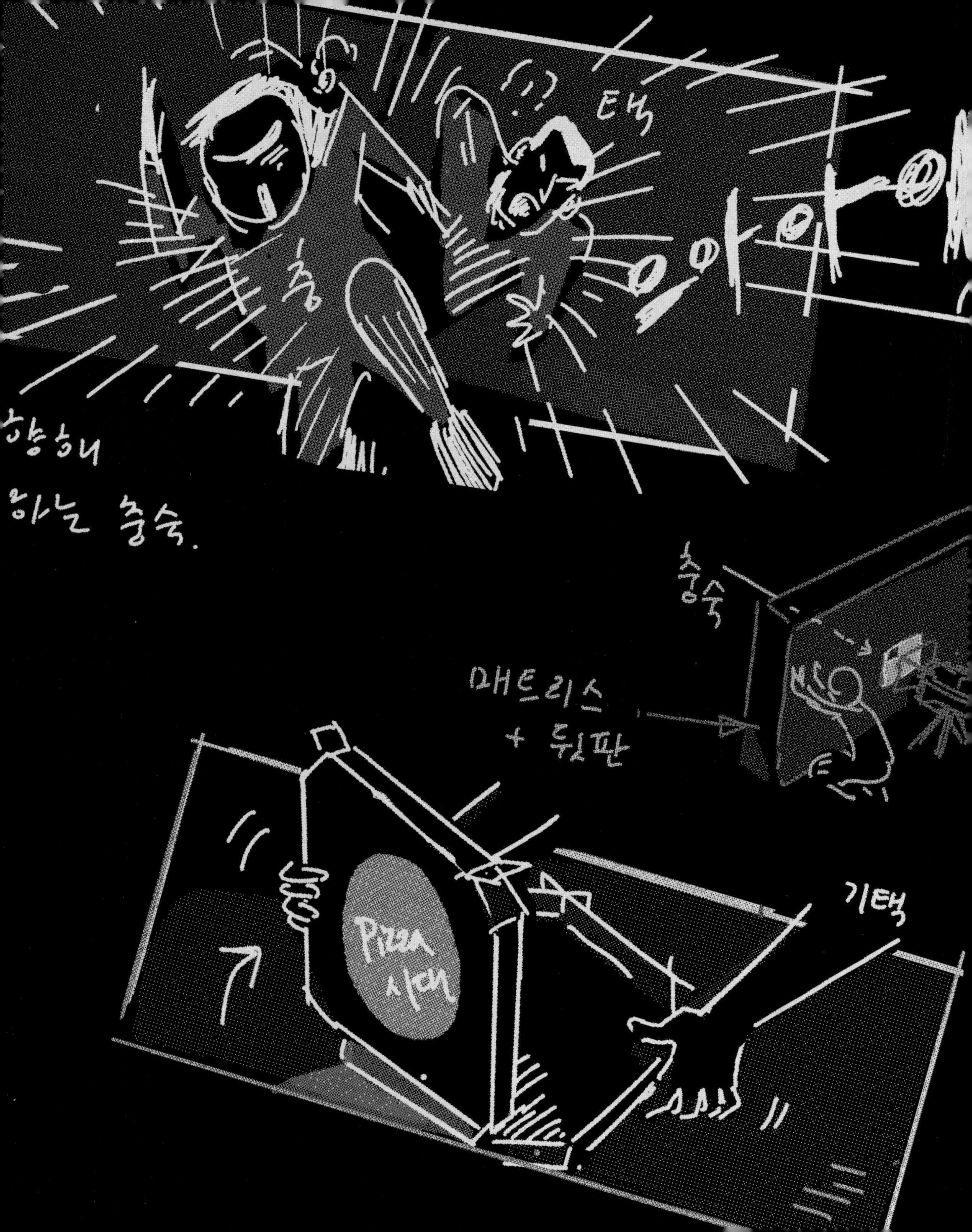

택
으아악
향해
하늘 충숙.
충숙
매트리스
+ 뒷판
Pizza
시대
기택

Part 1. A Graphic Novel in Storyboards

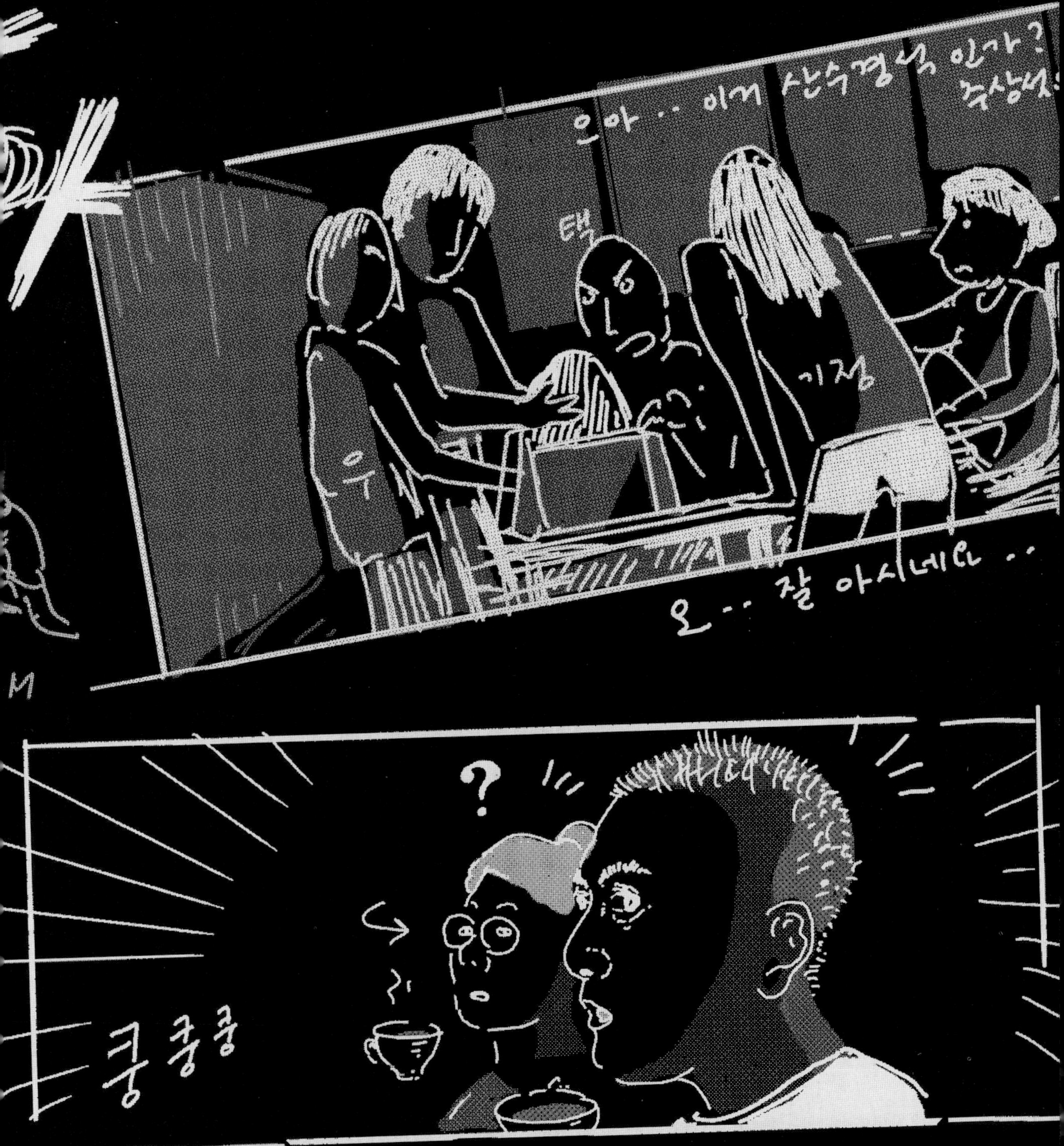
오아.. 이게 산수경석 인가?
택
기정
유
오.. 잘 아시네요..
쿵쿵쿵

기생충

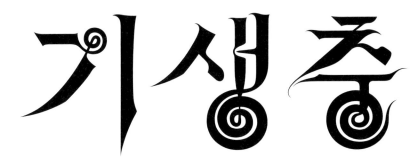

PARASITE

① Outside the window...
An alley slightly OUT OF FOCUS. Pedestrians etc.

"PARASITE" – The title comes IN and OUT.

Camera VERTICALLY DESCENDS...

White socks   Crane Down

Ki-woo's face –
looking at his cellphone.

② CAMERA – FIXED.
Ki-woo's POV:
Wi-Fi signals.

YUN&B 5GHz
iptime
U+Net6EF5

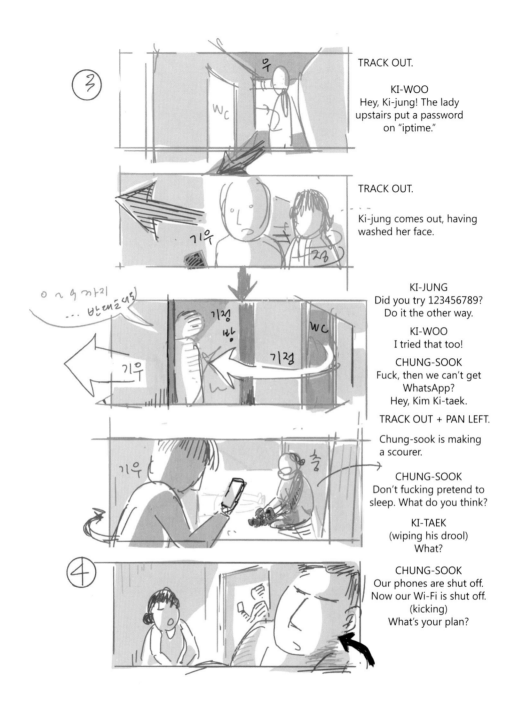

③ TRACK OUT.

KI-WOO
Hey, Ki-jung! The lady
upstairs put a password
on "iptime."

TRACK OUT.

Ki-jung comes out, having
washed her face.

KI-JUNG
Did you try 123456789?
Do it the other way.

KI-WOO
I tried that too!

CHUNG-SOOK
Fuck, then we can't get
WhatsApp?
Hey, Kim Ki-taek.

TRACK OUT + PAN LEFT.

Chung-sook is making
a scourer.

CHUNG-SOOK
Don't fucking pretend to
sleep. What do you think?

KI-TAEK
(wiping his drool)
What?

④ CHUNG-SOOK
Our phones are shut off.
Now our Wi-Fi is shut off.
(kicking)
What's your plan?

2

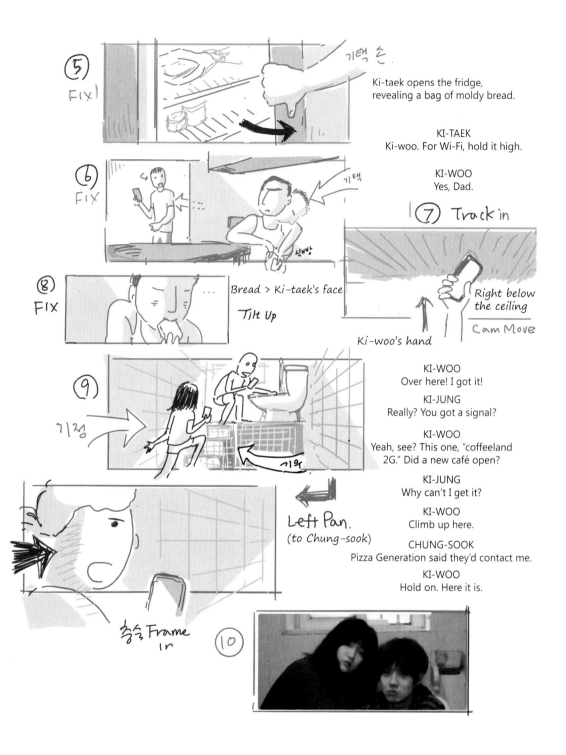

⑤ FIX

Ki-taek opens the fridge,
revealing a bag of moldy bread.

KI-TAEK
Ki-woo. For Wi-Fi, hold it high.

KI-WOO
Yes, Dad.

⑥ FIX

⑦ Track in

Right below
the ceiling

Cam Move

Ki-woo's hand

⑧ FIX

Bread > Ki-taek's face

Tilt Up

⑨

KI-WOO
Over here! I got it!

KI-JUNG
Really? You got a signal?

KI-WOO
Yeah, see? This one, "coffeeland
2G." Did a new café open?

KI-JUNG
Why can't I get it?

KI-WOO
Climb up here.

CHUNG-SOOK
Pizza Generation said they'd contact me.

KI-WOO
Hold on. Here it is.

Left Pan.
(to Chung-sook)

Frame
in

⑩

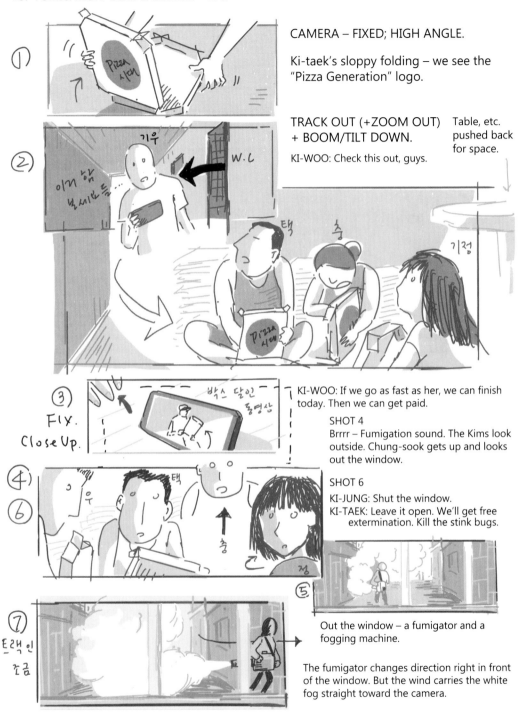

CAMERA – FIXED; HIGH ANGLE.

Ki-taek's sloppy folding – we see the "Pizza Generation" logo.

TRACK OUT (+ZOOM OUT) + BOOM/TILT DOWN.

Table, etc. pushed back for space.

KI-WOO: Check this out, guys.

KI-WOO: If we go as fast as her, we can finish today. Then we can get paid.

SHOT 4
Brrrr – Fumigation sound. The Kims look outside. Chung-sook gets up and looks out the window.

SHOT 6
KI-JUNG: Shut the window.
KI-TAEK: Leave it open. We'll get free extermination. Kill the stink bugs.

Out the window – a fumigator and a fogging machine.

The fumigator changes direction right in front of the window. But the wind carries the white fog straight toward the camera.

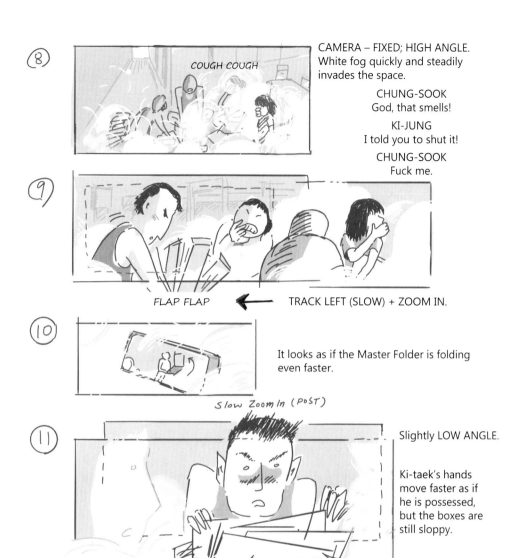

⑧ CAMERA – FIXED; HIGH ANGLE.
White fog quickly and steadily
invades the space.

COUGH COUGH

CHUNG-SOOK
God, that smells!

KI-JUNG
I told you to shut it!

CHUNG-SOOK
Fuck me.

⑨ FLAP FLAP ← TRACK LEFT (SLOW) + ZOOM IN.

⑩ It looks as if the Master Folder is folding
even faster.

Slow Zoom In (POST)

⑪ Slightly LOW ANGLE.

Ki-taek's hands
move faster as if
he is possessed,
but the boxes are
still sloppy.

Fog envelops the
area.

✓ RACK FOCUS (Ki-woo >> Ki-taek).
Slight ZOOM IN.

5

#4A

PEEPING

BACKGROUND.
Ki-woo sorts the boxes.
Ki-jung PEERS OVER
from the other room.

PIZZA SHOP OWNER
Take this one, for example. You call this a straight line? A quarter of them look like this. So 1 out of 4 are rejects.

RACK FOCUS to Ki-taek.

#4B.

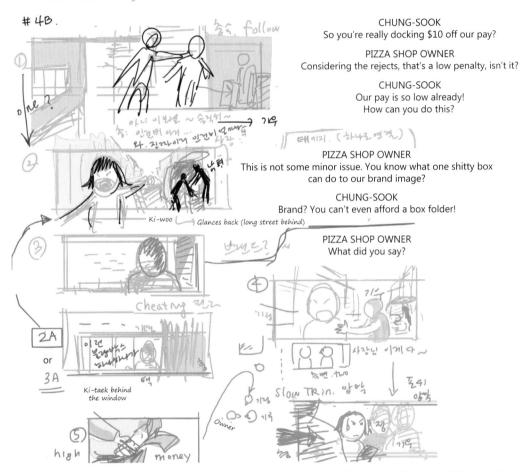

one?

Ki-woo — Glances back (long street behind)

2A
or
3A

Ki-taek behind
the window

Owner

high   money

CHUNG-SOOK
So you're really docking $10 off our pay?

PIZZA SHOP OWNER
Considering the rejects, that's a low penalty, isn't it?

CHUNG-SOOK
Our pay is so low already!
How can you do this?

PIZZA SHOP OWNER
This is not some minor issue. You know what one shitty box can do to our brand image?

CHUNG-SOOK
Brand? You can't even afford a box folder!

PIZZA SHOP OWNER
What did you say?

cheating

Slow TRin.

KI-WOO: This is all because of that guy, right?
PIZZA SHOP OWNER: What guy?
KI-WOO: Your part-time worker. He's gone AWOL, right? Just when the Love of God Church made a huge group order?
PIZZA SHOP OWNER: How do you know all that? Who told you?
KI-WOO: My sister knows the guy.
KI-JUNG: He's always been a bit strange. Got a bad reputation.

KI-WOO: Speaking of which, boss. We'll accept a 10% penalty. In return...
PIZZA SHOP OWNER: In return?
KI-WOO: Any thought of hiring a new part-time worker?
KI-JUNG: Ditch the guy you've got now. Just fire him.
The owner just stares at the smiling siblings. *Who the hell are these people?*
KI-WOO: Tomorrow I'll come for a formal interview. What time?
PIZZA SHOP OWNER: Wait, hold on a sec. Let me think about it.

#5. "SHOPLIFTING" NEIGHBORHOOD STORE

Ki-woo, holding a shopping basket, carefully goes through the merchandise.

Ki-jung, meanwhile, sneaks some groceries into her bag.

TRACK RIGHT.

She carefully checks on the OLD LADY.

FIX.

The old lady is oblivious, fixated on TV.
Ki-jung gleefully swipes groceries.

#6. "KING CRAB" NEIGHBORHOOD STORE - STREET

(1)

TRACK IN + Slight

BOOM UP.
TILT DOWN.

Once across the street
from the market,
Ki-jung shows off her
stolen goods.

HIGH
and then
TILT UP again.

KI-JUNG: Check this out!
KI-WOO: What did you...? (KI-WOO FRAMES OUT.)

TRACK LEFT.

(2)

KI-JUNG: (Follows Ki-woo) It's worth way more than $20. Right? Ooh, king crabs.
    Looks bomb.
KI-WOO: Too expensive.
KI-JUNG: Why don't you give me $20 and we say that you have paid for these.

Ki-woo doesn't see the logic. But he stops in his tracks and hands her $20 (in one $10
bill, one $5 bill, and five $1s).

(3)

KI-WOO: Make sure you pay them back when you get a job.
KI-JUNG: (scoffs) Aren't you Mr. Righteous. Stop worrying about them and worry
    about your own family.
KI-WOO: It's not that...
KI-JUNG: We're just helping the needy. Us. We're the needy.

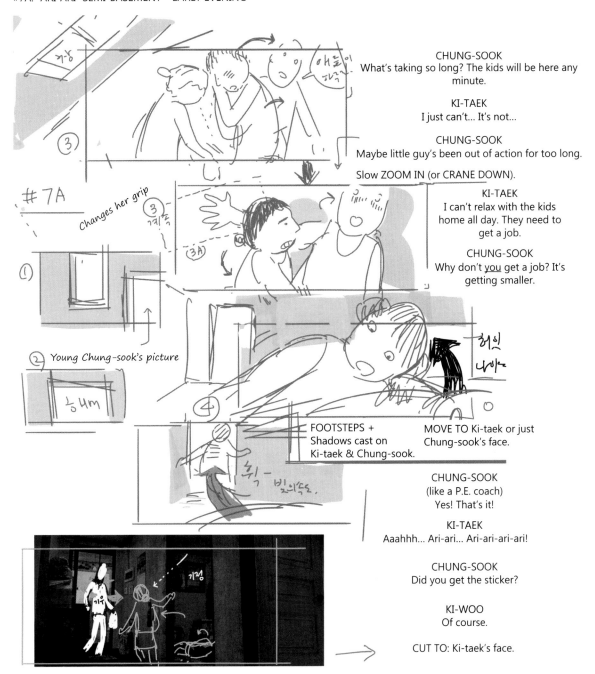

CHUNG-SOOK
What's taking so long? The kids will be here any minute.

KI-TAEK
I just can't... It's not...

CHUNG-SOOK
Maybe little guy's been out of action for too long.

Slow ZOOM IN (or CRANE DOWN).

KI-TAEK
I can't relax with the kids home all day. They need to get a job.

CHUNG-SOOK
Why don't <u>you</u> get a job? It's getting smaller.

Changes her grip

Young Chung-sook's picture

FOOTSTEPS +
Shadows cast on Ki-taek & Chung-sook.

MOVE TO Ki-taek or just Chung-sook's face.

CHUNG-SOOK
(like a P.E. coach)
Yes! That's it!

KI-TAEK
Aaahhh... Ari-ari... Ari-ari-ari-ari!

CHUNG-SOOK
Did you get the sticker?

KI-WOO
Of course.

CUT TO: Ki-taek's face.

#7B. "MIN-HYUK'S VISIT" SEMI-BASEMENT – EARLY EVENING

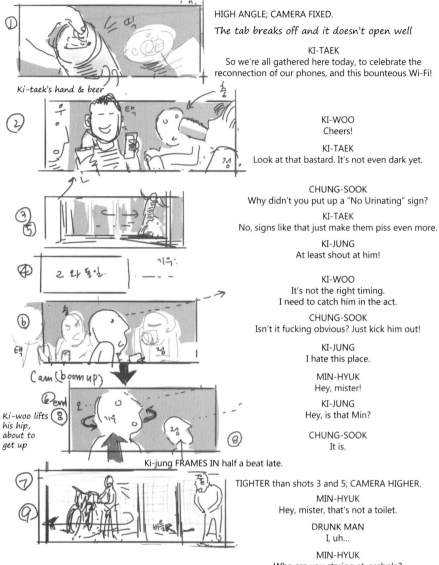

HIGH ANGLE; CAMERA FIXED.

The tab breaks off and it doesn't open well

KI-TAEK
So we're all gathered here today, to celebrate the
reconnection of our phones, and this bounteous Wi-Fi!

Ki-taek's hand & beer

KI-WOO
Cheers!

KI-TAEK
Look at that bastard. It's not even dark yet.

CHUNG-SOOK
Why didn't you put up a "No Urinating" sign?

KI-TAEK
No, signs like that just make them piss even more.

KI-JUNG
At least shout at him!

KI-WOO
It's not the right timing.
I need to catch him in the act.

CHUNG-SOOK
Isn't it fucking obvious? Just kick him out!

KI-JUNG
I hate this place.

MIN-HYUK
Hey, mister!

KI-JUNG
Hey, is that Min?

CHUNG-SOOK
It is.

(Cam (boom up))

Ki-woo lifts
his hip,
about to
get up

Ki-jung FRAMES IN half a beat late.

TIGHTER than shots 3 and 5; CAMERA HIGHER.

MIN-HYUK
Hey, mister, that's not a toilet.

DRUNK MAN
I, uh...

MIN-HYUK
Who are you staring at, asshole?

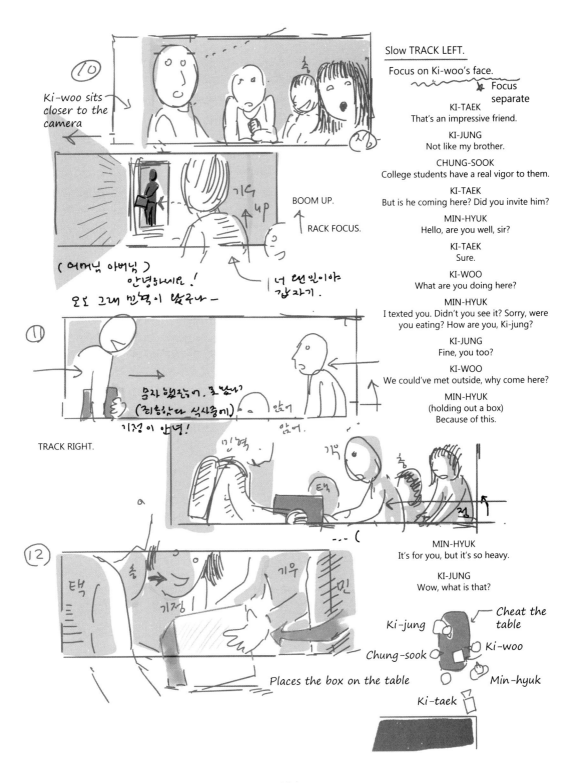

Ki-woo sits closer to the camera

⑩

Slow TRACK LEFT.

Focus on Ki-woo's face.

Focus separate

KI-TAEK
That's an impressive friend.

KI-JUNG
Not like my brother.

CHUNG-SOOK
College students have a real vigor to them.

KI-TAEK
But is he coming here? Did you invite him?

MIN-HYUK
Hello, are you well, sir?

KI-TAEK
Sure.

KI-WOO
What are you doing here?

MIN-HYUK
I texted you. Didn't you see it? Sorry, were you eating? How are you, Ki-jung?

KI-JUNG
Fine, you too?

KI-WOO
We could've met outside, why come here?

MIN-HYUK
(holding out a box)
Because of this.

BOOM UP.

RACK FOCUS.

(어머님 아버님)
안녕하세요 !
오 그래 민혁이 왔구나 —

너 면인이야
갑자기.

⑪

TRACK RIGHT.

문자 했잖니. 못 봤니
(죄송합니다 식사중에)
기정이 안녕!

앉어
앉어

MIN-HYUK
It's for you, but it's so heavy.

KI-JUNG
Wow, what is that?

⑫

택
종
기정
기우
민

Cheat the table

Ki-jung

Chung-sook

Ki-woo

Min-hyuk

Places the box on the table

Ki-taek

11

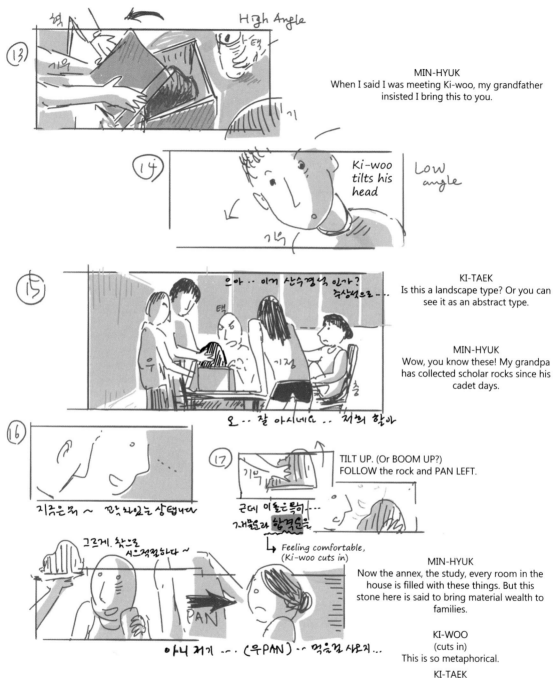

MIN-HYUK
When I said I was meeting Ki-woo, my grandfather insisted I bring this to you.

KI-TAEK
Is this a landscape type? Or you can see it as an abstract type.

MIN-HYUK
Wow, you know these! My grandpa has collected scholar rocks since his cadet days.

TILT UP. (Or BOOM UP?) FOLLOW the rock and PAN LEFT.

Feeling comfortable, (Ki-woo cuts in)

MIN-HYUK
Now the annex, the study, every room in the house is filled with these things. But this stone here is said to bring material wealth to families.

KI-WOO
(cuts in)
This is so metaphorical.

KI-TAEK
For sure. It's a very opportune gift. Please relay our deepest thanks to your grandpa.

CHUNG-SOOK
Food would be better.

① Fix. Wide. Ki-woo comes out of the store with fruits and soju in his hands. Min-hyuk cleans the table using wet wipes and makes sure it's spotless.

MIN-HYUK
Hey, thanks to that rock I saw your parents, they look healthy.

KI-WOO
They're plenty healthy, just out of work.

MIN-HYUK
Is Ki-jung taking lessons these days?

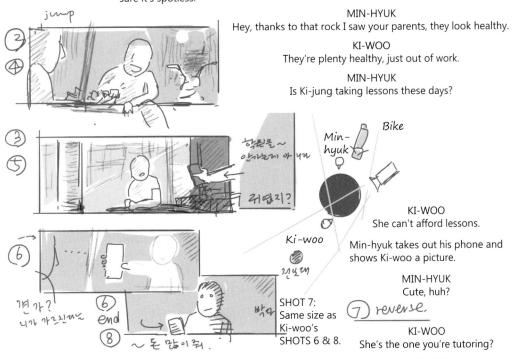

KI-WOO
She can't afford lessons.

Min-hyuk takes out his phone and shows Ki-woo a picture.

MIN-HYUK
Cute, huh?

⑦ reverse.

KI-WOO
She's the one you're tutoring?

MIN-HYUK
Park Da-hye. High school sophomore. You take over as her English tutor.

KI-WOO
What do you mean?

SHOT 7:
Same size as
Ki-woo's
SHOTS 6 & 8.

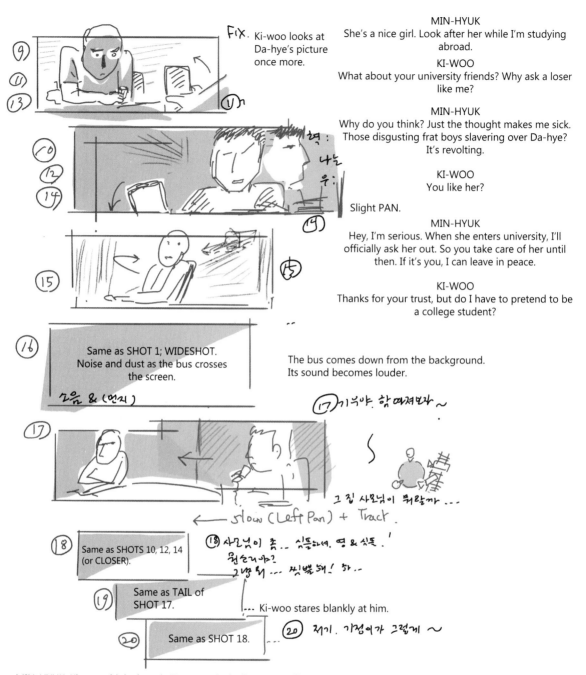

FIX. Ki-woo looks at Da-hye's picture once more.

MIN-HYUK
She's a nice girl. Look after her while I'm studying abroad.

KI-WOO
What about your university friends? Why ask a loser like me?

MIN-HYUK
Why do you think? Just the thought makes me sick. Those disgusting frat boys slavering over Da-hye? It's revolting.

KI-WOO
You like her?

Slight PAN.

MIN-HYUK
Hey, I'm serious. When she enters university, I'll officially ask her out. So you take care of her until then. If it's you, I can leave in peace.

KI-WOO
Thanks for your trust, but do I have to pretend to be a college student?

Same as SHOT 1; WIDESHOT. Noise and dust as the bus crosses the screen.

The bus comes down from the background. Its sound becomes louder.

Same as SHOTS 10, 12, 14 (or CLOSER).

Same as TAIL of SHOT 17.

Same as SHOT 18.

... Ki-woo stares blankly at him.

MIN-HYUK: Ki-woo, think about it. For years, including your military service, you took the university entrance exam 4 times. Grammar, vocabulary, composition, conversation... When it comes to English, you can teach 10 times better than those drunken college pricks.
KI-WOO: I guess so. But will they hire me? I'm not a college student.
MIN-HYUK: Just fake it. Don't worry, you'll have my recommendation, plus... How should I describe the mother...? She's a bit simple. (In English) *Young and simple.*
KI-WOO: Simple? What do you mean?
MIN-HYUK: Anyway, it's all good. I had fun there. Hey, you said your sister is artistic? Good at Photoshop?

#9. "INTERNET CAFÉ"

#9
Internet
café
①

OVERHEAD SHOT; CAMERA FIXED.

A mouse moves around dazzlingly.

②

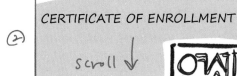

CERTIFICATE OF ENROLLMENT

scroll ↓

Computer Screen:
    "CERTIFICATE OF ENROLLMENT"

Cursor swiftly moves around the various Photoshop tool shortcuts.

> KI-WOO
> God, with skills like this, why can't you get into art school?

> KI-JUNG
> Shut up.

Ki-woo surveys the café.

> KI-WOO
> Take your time. We should hold off on printing until the place is clear.

③

④

CAMERA FIXED, SLIGHTLY HIGH; WIDE.

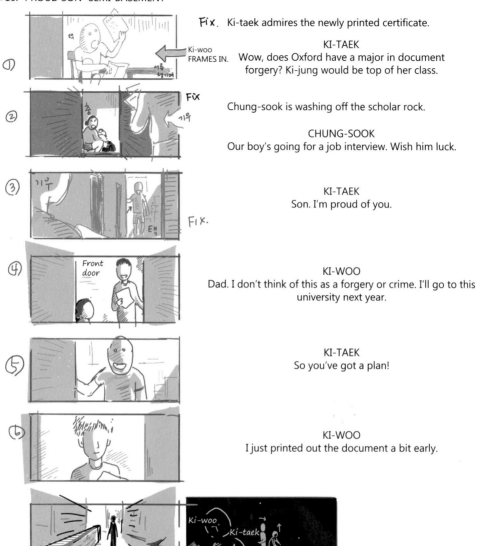

① Fix. Ki-taek admires the newly printed certificate.

Ki-woo FRAMES IN.

KI-TAEK
Wow, does Oxford have a major in document forgery? Ki-jung would be top of her class.

② Fix

Chung-sook is washing off the scholar rock.

CHUNG-SOOK
Our boy's going for a job interview. Wish him luck.

③ FIX.

KI-TAEK
Son. I'm proud of you.

④ Front door

KI-WOO
Dad. I don't think of this as a forgery or crime. I'll go to this university next year.

⑤

KI-TAEK
So you've got a plan!

⑥

KI-WOO
I just printed out the document a bit early.

⑦ Ki-woo walking down the alley from behind

Ki-woo
Ki-taek
Chung-sook

Ki-woo FRAMES OUT to SCREEN LEFT.
Ki-taek and Chung-sook are looking at him.
As the CAMERA PANS LEFT, we see Ki-woo walking down the alley shot from behind him.

#11. "THE HILL" RICH NEIGHBORHOOD – ROAD - DAY

① FIX.

② Ki-woo looks around as he walks up the Seongbuk-dong hill.

FRONT ENTRANCE

Seongbuk-dong
CG plate

③ Jeonju front entrance set.

TRACK LEFT >> Ki-woo FRAMES IN >> Follow Ki-woo PAN LEFT.

#12A. "FIRST VISIT ENTRANCE" RICH HOUSE ENTRANCE - DAY

#12
①

Jeonju front
entrance set.

Slight TRACK LEFT + RACK FOCUS.

Ki-woo

CLANK – the steel door automatically opens

FEMALE VOICE (V.O.)
Who is it?

KI-WOO
Madame? I'm here on Min's
recommendation...?

FEMALE VOICE (V.O.)
Oh right, come in.

#12B. "FIRST VISIT GARDEN" RICH HOUSE GARDEN - DAY

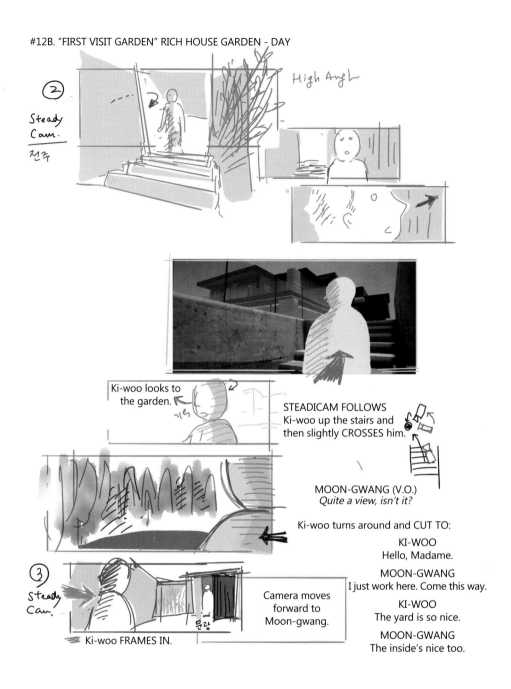

High Angle

② Steady Cam. 견주

Ki-woo looks to the garden.

STEADICAM FOLLOWS
Ki-woo up the stairs and then slightly CROSSES him.

MOON-GWANG (V.O.)
Quite a view, isn't it?

Ki-woo turns around and CUT TO:

KI-WOO
Hello, Madame.

MOON-GWANG
I just work here. Come this way.

KI-WOO
The yard is so nice.

MOON-GWANG
The inside's nice too.

③ Steady Cam. 문광

Camera moves forward to Moon-gwang.

Ki-woo FRAMES IN.

18

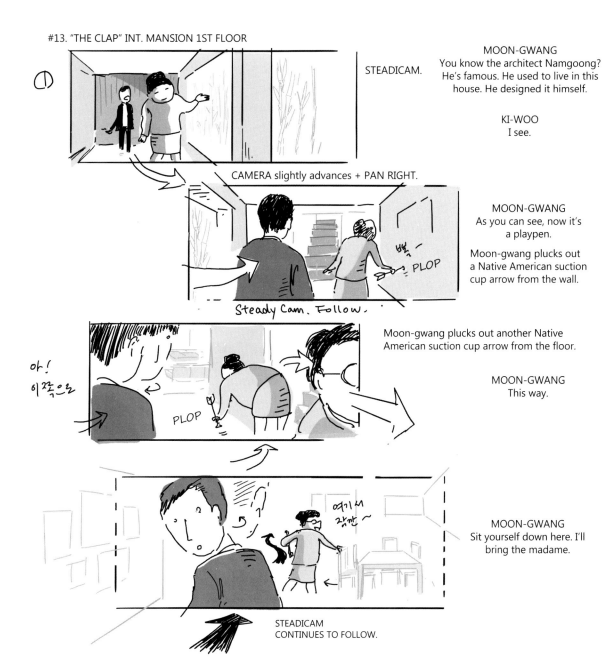

STEADICAM.

MOON-GWANG
You know the architect Namgoong?
He's famous. He used to live in this
house. He designed it himself.

KI-WOO
I see.

CAMERA slightly advances + PAN RIGHT.

MOON-GWANG
As you can see, now it's
a playpen.

Moon-gwang plucks out
a Native American suction
cup arrow from the wall.

PLOP

Steady Cam. Follow.

Moon-gwang plucks out another Native
American suction cup arrow from the floor.

MOON-GWANG
This way.

PLOP

MOON-GWANG
Sit yourself down here. I'll
bring the madame.

STEADICAM
CONTINUES TO FOLLOW.

②  Fix.

Moon-gwang exits and Ki-woo is left alone in silence. He quietly gets up and looks around.

There's some kind of AVANT-GARDE ART hanging on the wall. Next to it, he sees a typical Korean FAMILY PORTRAIT taken at a studio.

He turns his head as he hears Moon-gwang's O.S. voice from outside the window.

Ki-woo walks over to the window, overlooking the backyard. He sees—

③  Fix. High

CLAP

YEON-KYO dozing off at the patio table. English magazine on the table. Head tilted comically. Only her soft white neck is visible.

Moon-gwang walks over and CLAPS her hands loudly next to Yeon-kyo's ears.

MOON-GWANG: The tutor is here.
YEON-KYO: What do you think?
MOON-GWANG: I don't know, but
      he's handsome.

#14. "JOB INTERVIEW" MANSION – 1ST FLOOR KITCHEN

Slight move
+ RACK FOCUS.

YEON-KYO
I don't care about documents. Min
recommends you, after all.

Ki-woo listens quietly.

YEON-KYO
As you know, Min is such a *brilliant* human
being. Da-hye and I were quite happy with him.
Regardless of her grades. Know what I mean?

KI-WOO
Yes.

YEON-KYO
He was marvelous. So to be honest, we
wanted to stick with him through high
school. But all of a sudden he's going
abroad. Anyway, excuse me, but if
I can speak directly, if you're not up to
Min's level, then I'm not sure what
the point is.

Slow Track
+ Pan/
Tilt

THUMP - Moon-gwang places a cup of
coffee right in front of Ki-woo's face.

YEON-KYO
So anyway, what I want to say is, for
your first lesson today, do you mind
if I sit in? I want to see it *full time* how
you run your lesson.

KI-WOO
Uh...

YEON-KYO
(In English)
Is it okay with you?

이즈 잇 오케이 위즈 유?

21

#15A. "THE HIPS" MANSION – STAIRCASE (JEONJU BACKLOT)

FIX

Yeon-kyo climbs the stairs holding her dog.

Ki-woo follows after her.

FRAME IN from screen bottom

FIX

Living room is quiet.

Silent footsteps x 2

#15B. "THE HIPS" MANSION – 2nd FLOOR (DIMA STUDIO)

Very slow
TRACK OUT.

안성
2F 세트

Ki-woo looks around the 2nd floor.
He is led to Da-hye's room.

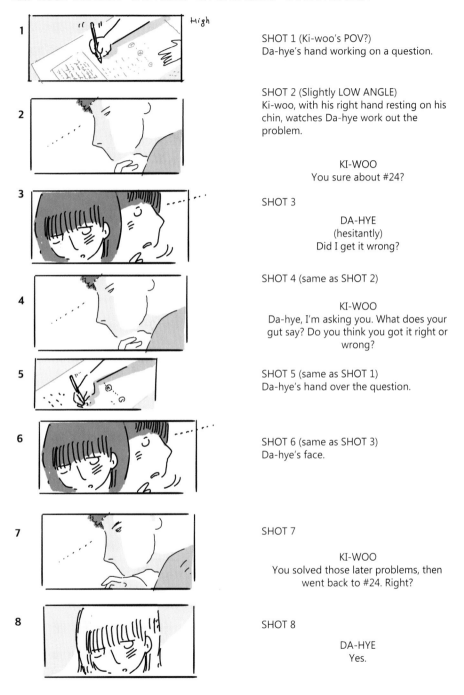

SHOT 1 (Ki-woo's POV?)
Da-hye's hand working on a question.

SHOT 2 (Slightly LOW ANGLE)
Ki-woo, with his right hand resting on his chin, watches Da-hye work out the problem.

KI-WOO
You sure about #24?

SHOT 3

DA-HYE
(hesitantly)
Did I get it wrong?

SHOT 4 (same as SHOT 2)

KI-WOO
Da-hye, I'm asking you. What does your gut say? Do you think you got it right or wrong?

SHOT 5 (same as SHOT 1)
Da-hye's hand over the question.

SHOT 6 (same as SHOT 3)
Da-hye's face.

SHOT 7

KI-WOO
You solved those later problems, then went back to #24. Right?

SHOT 8

DA-HYE
Yes.

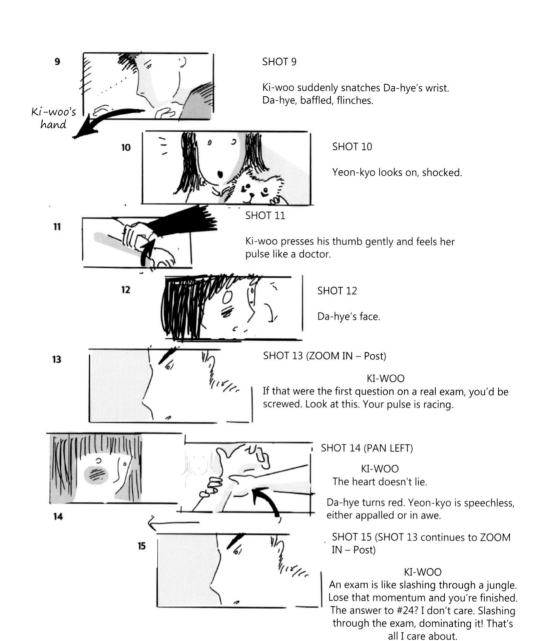

Ki-woo's hand

SHOT 9

Ki-woo suddenly snatches Da-hye's wrist.
Da-hye, baffled, flinches.

SHOT 10

Yeon-kyo looks on, shocked.

SHOT 11

Ki-woo presses his thumb gently and feels her
pulse like a doctor.

SHOT 12

Da-hye's face.

SHOT 13 (ZOOM IN – Post)

KI-WOO
If that were the first question on a real exam, you'd be
screwed. Look at this. Your pulse is racing.

SHOT 14 (PAN LEFT)

KI-WOO
The heart doesn't lie.

Da-hye turns red. Yeon-kyo is speechless,
either appalled or in awe.

SHOT 15 (SHOT 13 continues to ZOOM
IN – Post)

KI-WOO
An exam is like slashing through a jungle.
Lose that momentum and you're finished.
The answer to #24? I don't care. Slashing
through the exam, dominating it! That's
all I care about.

16

SHOT 16

DA-HYE: ...

17

SHOT 17

KI-WOO: What you need is vigor. Vigor.

18

SHOT 18

Stunned silence. Ki-woo finally releases Da-hye's wrist (as if to return something), revealing a round, pink spot where he had held her.

19

SHOT 19

Ki-woo looks over at Yeon-kyo.

SHOT 20

Yeon-kyo is completely floored.

21

SHOT 21 (CAMERA WORK: Ki-woo >> Da-hye >> Ki-woo)

KI-WOO

I know. You were angry. Frustrated. You worked so hard. Studied until your nose bled. But your scores weren't improving. You kept asking yourself, "What am I doing wrong?"

It hits something in Da-hye. Emotions swell, and her pupils tremble.

KI-WOO

I'm here to prepare you for the real thing. I'm not here to help you learn. I'm here to help you score.

#17. "MONEY ENVELOPE" MANSION – 2ND FLOOR – ROOM – EVENING (ANSEONG DIMA STUDIO)

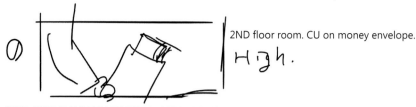

2ND floor room. CU on money envelope.

High.

#17B. "CHIMPANZEE" MANSION – KITCHEN – EVENING

CAMERA moves LEFT following Yeon-kyo as she descends the stairs and heads to the sofa.
>> CAMERA FOLLOWS Ki-woo in front of the audio system.
>> Moon-gwang FRAMES IN from BEHIND in between Ki-woo and Yeon-kyo.

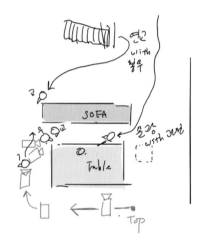

YEON-KYO
So I'll pay you this time each month. 3 classes a week, 2 hours each, okay?

KI-WOO
Yes.

YEON-KYO
As for the fee, I was going to pay Min's rate, then I added a bit for inflation.

KI-WOO
Thank you.

As Ki-woo puts away the envelope, Moon-gwang brings over a fruit plate – she's
noticeably friendlier.

YEON-KYO
How about a proper introduction? Da-hye's tutor, we'll call him Kevin.

MOON-GWANG
Mr. Kevin! If you feel like snacking during your lesson, just call me.

YEON-KYO
If you need anything, ask her. She knows this house better than I...

THUNK. A PLASTIC ARROW flies in and hits Moon-gwang's shoulder.
When Ki-Woo looks over – It's a boy in a Native American costume about to
shoot another arrow. This is DA-SONG (10).

YEON-KYO
Da-song, stop it!

Da-song continues shooting. Moon-gwang is used to the antics. She picks up an
arrow and rubs it in her armpit.

MOON-GWANG
(playfully)
Armpit attack!

DA-SONG
No!! It stinks!

TRACK RIGHT.
BOOM DOWN.

OUT OF FOCUS:
Ki-woo, Yeon-kyo
Moon-gwang

SWOOSH SWOOSH – arrows whip by and Yeon-kyo
makes a fuss. Moon-gwang charges towards Da-song.

YEON-KYO
I'm sorry, did he startle you?

KI-WOO
How cute. His name's Da-song?

YEON-KYO
Yes, our youngest. Da-song, come say hi!
This is Mr. Kevin!

Da-song doesn't care for Yeon-kyo. He is focused
on the battle with Moon-gwang.

YEON-KYO
This is an Indian arrow. I ordered it from the U.S.
From last year he's been an Indian fanatic.

KI-WOO
Indians? He's got a fanboy personality?

26

Da-song and Moon-gwang pass by in B/G OUT OF FOCUS.

YEON-KYO
Well, he's eccentric and easily distracted, he can barely
sit still! So last year I enrolled him in Cub Scouts, hoping
he'd learn moderation and focus.

Behind Yeon-kyo, Da-song and Moon-gwang's battle amps up.

YEON-KYO
But look. He's even worse. His scout leader is an Indian
fanatic, maybe that's why.

KI-WOO
The Scouts have roots in American Indian culture.
It's a good thing.

YEON-KYO
Were you a Cub Scout, Kevin?

KI-WOO
Sure, I'm a Scout by nature.

AHH – Da-song hoots O.S. firing up for the final blow.

YEON-KYO
Look how fine you turned out. What's wrong with him?
Da-song is an artist by nature. Look at this painting.

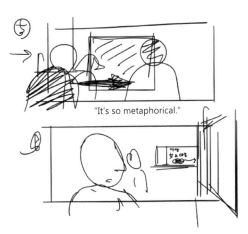

"It's so metaphorical."

Ki-woo takes a look at the picture that Yeon-kyo is
pointing at. A strange AVANT-GARDE PICTURE hangs
next to the family portrait.

KI-WOO
It's so metaphorical. It's really strong.

YEON-KYO
Strong, right? You've got an eye for this.

KI-WOO
It's a chimpanzee, right?

YEON-KYO
A self-portrait.

Awkward beat. We HEAR Da-song and Moon-gwang
continue to battle it out in the background.

KI-WOO
Sure enough! The perspective of a young artist
eludes understanding. Or perhaps it's Da-
song's expressive genius...

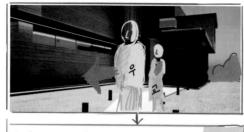

Steadycam. Back.

YEON-KYO
Anyway, we've been through so many art teachers.
None of them lasts even a month. And Da-song is just
so hard to control.

Ki-woo is about to descend the stairs, but stops in his
tracks.

KI-WOO
Just a moment, Madame.

YEON-KYO
Yes?

end.
Low.

High. Fix (by steady cam)

KI-WOO
Someone just came to mind. What was her name? That girl from
Girl's Generation. The one who launched a jewelry line.

YEON-KYO
Jessica?

KI-WOO
Right, Jessica... She was in the same
art school as my cousin. What was her
Korean name? Anyway, after studying
applied arts at Illinois State University,
she returned to Korea.

YEON-KYO
Illinois... tell me more.

Low. Fix

#18B. FRONT ENTRANCE – GARAGE - BACKLOT

Ki-woo &
Yeon-kyo
open the
gate and
come out.

Steady Cam.
Back.

Jeonju front gate set +
Seongbuk-dong
CG plate

KI-WOO
Her teaching is unique, but she knows how to handle
kids. She's got a special reputation in her field.

KI-WOO: But even though her methods are unique, she can
help kids get into good art schools.
YEON-KYO: Now I'm really curious. What is she like?
KI-WOO: Would you like to meet her? Though I heard she's
in high demand...

#19. "HAIR SALON" HAIR SALON - DAY

CAMERA FIXED.
RACK FOCUS.

KI-JUNG
Why Jessica? So tacky.

KI-WOO
It has a nice ring to it. Anyhow, she's a nice lady.

FIX

KI-WOO
Young. Not the brightest tool in the shed. But the money is good, and most of all, she's a "believer."

Ki-taek CROSSES THE SCREEN, handing out the corndogs

FIX. Wide.

CHUNG-SOOK
She's religious?

KI-WOO
No, it's just, she tends to trust people rather easily.

The Kims become thoughtful.
Ki-taek breaks the silence.

KI-TAEK
She sounds like a great lady!

KI-WOO
Right?

CHUNG-SOOK
Yeah.

①

Ki-woo is about to ring the doorbell when Ki-jung STOPS him.

②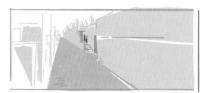

Pan·Tilt

Slight TRACK IN.

KI-JUNG
Jessica, only child /
Illinois, Chicago /
Classmate Kim Jin-mo /
he's your cousin.

Ki-jung's finger pressing the doorbell

③ CAMERA FIXED.

The DOORBELL RING echoes throughout the otherwise quiet neighborhood.

JESSICA JINGLE (Extended)
Jessica, only child / Illinois, Chicago /
Classmate Kim Jin-mo / He is your cousin /
UNICEF job interview / Kyunggi High broadcast /
G-Dragon follower

Daddy is retired / Yachts in Busan all day long /
Mommy is a professor / and LASIK specialist / (or Mommy is an attorney / makes 2 mil a year)
Christian name Rebecca / Big fan of Paella /
But not a fan of lie

Art gallery part time / Backpacking junior year /
Haiti was a calling / Meeting young kids /
Child psychology destiny / also art therapy /
Kids super specialist

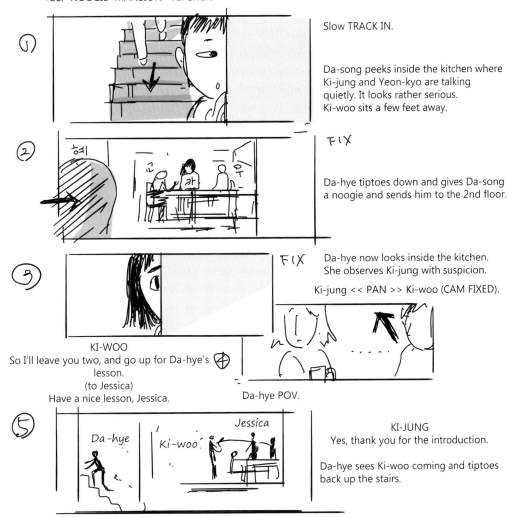

① Slow TRACK IN.

Da-song peeks inside the kitchen where Ki-jung and Yeon-kyo are talking quietly. It looks rather serious.
Ki-woo sits a few feet away.

② FIX

Da-hye tiptoes down and gives Da-song a noogie and sends him to the 2nd floor.

③ FIX

Da-hye now looks inside the kitchen. She observes Ki-jung with suspicion.

Ki-jung << PAN >> Ki-woo (CAM FIXED).

④

KI-WOO
So I'll leave you two, and go up for Da-hye's lesson.
(to Jessica)
Have a nice lesson, Jessica.

Da-hye POV.

KI-JUNG
Yes, thank you for the introduction.

Da-hye sees Ki-woo coming and tiptoes back up the stairs.

⑤ Da-hye   Ki-woo   Jessica

31

#22. "FIRST KISS" MANSION – 2ND FLOOR – DA-HYE'S ROOM - EVENING

Da-hye hurries back to her desk and pretends to work on her worksheet.

The door opens and Ki-woo enters.

> KI-WOO: So we'll start with #38?
> DA-HYE: Kevin?
> KI-WOO: Yeah?
> DA-HYE: Did you know that Da-song is faking it all?
> KI-WOO: Huh? What do you mean?
> DA-HYE: It's all a show. Acting like a genius, that 4th-dimension stuff is all fake. An artist cosplay.
> KI-WOO: Da-song?
> DA-HYE: You know that thing, when he freezes and stares at the sky, as if struck by inspiration.
> KI-WOO: So he's walking along, then he stares at the clouds for 10 minutes.
> DA-HYE: So you know what I mean? He gives me the creeps. He pretends that he can't live a normal life. Makes me want to puke.
> KI-WOO: So Da-song is pretending… But what's that got to do with your studies?

Da-hye pouts as Ki-woo suddenly shifts to tutor mode.

> DA-HYE: Well, I'm just saying.
> KI-WOO: Sure, so in that sense, what you told me about Da-song was very interesting, so let's write about it in English. And be sure to use the word "pretend" at least twice.

Ki-woo, the master tutor, skillfully steers the conversation back to the lesson. Da-hye still has something on her mind. She puts down her pen.

> DA-HYE: Then, can I ask you a question?
> KI-WOO: Sure.
> DA-HYE: That teacher Jessica. Is she really your cousin's classmate?

Ki-woo is caught off-guard. He disguises it with a smile.

> KI-WOO: What do you mean?
> DA-HYE: She's your girlfriend, right?

Ki-woo finally relaxes and laughs. He looks at Da-hye – all worried and serious. She is charming.

> KI-WOO: No way… I just met her today.
> DA-HYE: Jessica's really pretty, isn't she? Aren't you interested?
> KI-WOO: You saw her? Sure, she's pretty. She's a beautiful woman.
> DA-HYE: I knew it. So you *are* interested.
> KI-WOO: Da-hye… If you were a perfect ten, Jessica would be a six, maybe six-point-five?

A cheesy line, but Da-hye smiles, pleased. She suddenly grabs Ki-woo's wrist under the desk. She presses it gently, feeling his pulse. A bold and unexpected move.

Ki-woo quietly stares at Da-hye. Slowly, their lips converge. A soft and gentle kiss carries on until they HEAR FOOTSTEPS coming up the stairs.

> KI-WOO: Let's study.
> DA-HYE: Yes.

SHOT #1 (STEADICAM)

YEON-KYO
Please understand that my boy has trouble keeping still.

KI-JUNG
I understand.

STEADICAM: Moves FORWARD.

The door opens and Yeon-kyo and CAMERA ENTER to find the boy lying on the floor with a toy arrow stuck in between his butt.

Yeon-kyo, embarrassed, tries to read Jessica's face.

YEON-KYO
Da-song! Da-song, get up! Come on, Da-song! In your butt...

KI-JUNG
Madame, please leave us.

YEON-KYO
What?

KI-JUNG
I never teach with a parent in the room.

STEADICAM: Keeps advancing.

TILT DOWN.

The arrow shakes strangely to the rhythm of his buttocks.

#24A. "SCHIZO" – MANSION – KITCHEN - EVENING

#24

①

②

Slow TRACK IN.

TICK TOCK. Yeon-kyo nibbles on nuts in the quiet kitchen. The dog licks Yeon-kyo's face, which is a mix of agony, worry, and curiosity.

> MOON-GWANG
> Madame? Want some plum extract?

> YEON-KYO
> What?

> MOON-GWANG
> It's mixed with honey. To ease your tension.

> YEON-KYO
> Yeah, that would be great.

Moon-gwang turns on the light before walking down the stairs.

③ #24B. "PLUM EXTRACT" – MANSION – STORAGE BASEMENT - EVENING

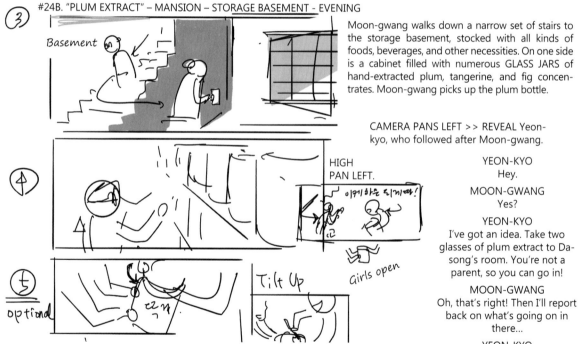

Basement

④

HIGH
PAN LEFT.

Girls open

⑤

optional

Tilt Up

Moon-gwang walks down a narrow set of stairs to the storage basement, stocked with all kinds of foods, beverages, and other necessities. On one side is a cabinet filled with numerous GLASS JARS of hand-extracted plum, tangerine, and fig concentrates. Moon-gwang picks up the plum bottle.

CAMERA PANS LEFT >> REVEAL Yeon-kyo, who followed after Moon-gwang.

> YEON-KYO
> Hey.

> MOON-GWANG
> Yes?

> YEON-KYO
> I've got an idea. Take two glasses of plum extract to Da-song's room. You're not a parent, so you can go in!

> MOON-GWANG
> Oh, that's right! Then I'll report back on what's going on in there...

> YEON-KYO
> Why didn't I think of it earlier?

Yeon-kyo's hands holding the plum bottle and Moon-gwang's hands twisting the cap >> TILT UP to their faces.

34

⑥ Moon-gwang and Yeon-kyo STOMP their way back up the stairs with cups of plum extract. Yeon-kyo is startled to see—

⑦ Ki-jung and Da-song are already inside the kitchen.

Slow TRACK-IN.

Track Out

⑧
YEON-KYO
So you're done already?

⑨ Ki-jung is holding Da-song's picture. Da-song stands politely behind her.

KI-JUNG: Madame. Come sit next to me.

YEON-KYO: Sure.

KI-JUNG: Da-song, go upstairs. Hurry up!

⑩ Slow TRACK IN + TILT UP/DOWN.

Yeon-kyo and Moon-gwang are stunned to see Da-song obediently bowing and heading upstairs.

KI-JUNG: Da-song just painted this.

Yeon-kyo is nervous. Ki-jung clocks Moon-gwang peeking over Yeon-kyo's shoulder.

KI-JUNG: I'd rather speak with Madame alone.
YEON-KYO: Oh, but she is...
KI-JUNG: No, leave us.

Yeon-kyo's voice falters at Ki-jung's ice-cold demeanor. Moon-gwang stares at Ki-jung before walking away.

KI-JUNG: Madame, I told you I study art psychology and art therapy?
YEON-KYO: Yes.
KI-JUNG: Did anything happen to Da-song in first grade?

35

Quick pan (telephoto) **+ TRACK**

Yeon-kyo yelps, but then covers her mouth.
Her hands tremble.

KI-JUNG
To be frank, before I decide whether to take
on Da-song, I need to hear about this.

YEON-KYO
That's hard for me to talk about right now.

Cam. Spin OVERHEAD SHOT.

KI-JUNG
Never mind, then. The lower-right region of
a painting is called the "schizophrenia
zone." Psychotic symptoms often reveal
themselves here. Look here. Da-song
painted this unusual shape, right?

YEON-KYO
I see.

Yeon-kyo suddenly looks up from the drawing and stares at the large framed picture on the wall.

YEON-KYO: Over there, it's the same! It's the same, right?
KI-JUNG: Yes, that's correct. A similar shape in the same zone. You see it now?

Yeon-kyo nods fervently. Guilt-ridden, she sobs.

YEON-KYO: I've stared at that painting at every meal! But I had no idea.

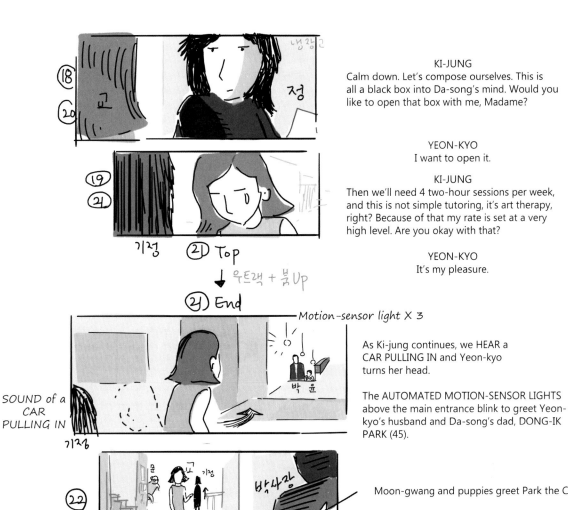

KI-JUNG
Calm down. Let's compose ourselves. This is all a black box into Da-song's mind. Would you like to open that box with me, Madame?

YEON-KYO
I want to open it.

KI-JUNG
Then we'll need 4 two-hour sessions per week, and this is not simple tutoring, it's art therapy, right? Because of that my rate is set at a very high level. Are you okay with that?

YEON-KYO
It's my pleasure.

Motion-sensor light X 3

As Ki-jung continues, we HEAR a CAR PULLING IN and Yeon-kyo turns her head.

SOUND of a CAR PULLING IN

The AUTOMATED MOTION-SENSOR LIGHTS above the main entrance blink to greet Yeon-kyo's husband and Da-song's dad, DONG-IK PARK (45).

Moon-gwang and puppies greet Park the CEO.

Three puppies pass Ki-jung's feet.

25

Track In.

박
교
교
교
윤
문

YEON-KYO
(wipes off her tears)
Honey, Da-song's new art teacher is here.

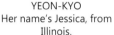

Yeon-kyo >> TRACK BACK.

26

박

YEON-KYO
Her name's Jessica, from Illinois.

27

성
교
동익

Track In.

YEON-KYO
(In English)
Jessica, this is Dong-ik.

KI-JUNG
Hello.

Only the lower class are left downstairs (what about the puppies?)

홀로
계단 오르는
박.
뒷모습

29
별도
shot

DONG-IK
Thank you for your help. Class is over?

YEON-KYO
Yes, just finished.

DONG-IK
Driver Yoon. Are you free? Then give her a lift, okay? We don't want her going down alone at night, right?

28

우리 다송이
잘 부탁
드립~

윤
박
교
홍

교
홍
교

① LOW.

②

Slight PAN + RACK FOCUS.

③
⑤

④
⑥

⑦

Slight PAN.

⑧

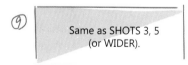

⑨

Same as SHOTS 3, 5
(or WIDER).

DRIVER YOON
Miss Jessica? Shall I drive you all the way home, then?
Which neighborhood?

KI-JUNG
No, that's fine. You can just drop me off at
Hyehwa Station. Thank you.

DRIVER YOON
I don't mind if it's far away. My shift is finished,
anyway.

KI-JUNG
I'll get off at Hyehwa.

DRIVER YOON
Looks like it's going to rain. Ride the Benz,
not the subway.

KI-JUNG
I'm meeting my boyfriend at exit 3 of Hyehwa Station!

DRIVER YOON
Yes.

The car bumps.

Yoon's smile disappears. He quietly turns
the steering wheel.

Ki-jung ponders as she stares at the back of
Yoon's head.

NOISE can be heard from out the window. A car
accident.

Two cars are parked, and the drivers are arguing.
Driver Yoon turns his head and looks out the
window.

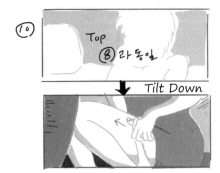

Top

⑧ 라동의

Tilt Down

While Driver Yoon looks out the window, Ki-jung swiftly starts to roll down her underwear.

⑪

Same as SHOT 9

Driver Yoon returns his gaze to the road straight ahead.

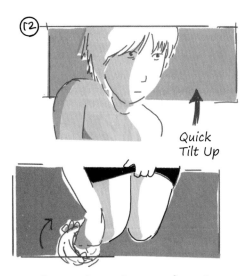

Quick
Tilt Up

Pulls out the underwear from her feet and coils it around her hand

⑬ Driver Yoon, unaware, steals a glance at Ki-jung.

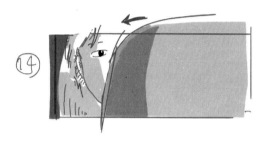

⑭ Through small gap in between the front passenger seat and her window, we get a glimpse of Ki-jung's face and her eyes sparkle.

#26. "DRIVERS' CAFETERIA"

STEADICAM PULLS OUT.

STEADICAM TRACK RIGHT.

STEADICAM
move

KI-JUNG
Dad, when you worked as a driver, did you drive a lot of Benzes?

KI-TAEK
Benzes? Not then, but I did when I worked as a valet.

CHUNG-SOOK
Sure, after the chicken place went bust, before the Taiwan cake shop, in that 6-month window?

KI-TAEK
No, it was after the cake shop went bust.

KI-WOO
We're moving to the next stage already?

KI-JUNG
I set a trap in the Benz. We'll see if he takes the bait.

KI-WOO
Then we're diving right in. Wow, this is so metaphorical. Look, Dad, we're eating in a drivers' cafeteria right now!

KI-TAEK
Right, a drivers' cafeteria! Eat as much as you want, kids.

CHUNG-SOOK
You didn't even pay for it, they did!

KI-TAEK
Son, have some more. Eat up!

KI-WOO
Yes, Dad.
(to Ki-jung)
What did you do to that woman yesterday?

KI-JUNG
What?

KI-TAEK
She was freaking out.
Saying she was so
moved, you put her in
shock.

KI-JUNG
Fuck, I don't know! I googled "art therapy" and ad-libbed the rest. Then suddenly she's weeping. Crazy bitch, I couldn't believe it.

A paper DROPS.

Dong-ik's POV.
HIGH ANGLE (almost OVERHEAD SHOT)
Ki-jung's underwear slides out from the seat

Dong-ik picks it up.
And catches a glimpse of Driver Yoon.

↑ Underwear

Dong-ik's POV:

Back of Driver Yoon.

Car SHAKES in darkness.
Dong-ik looks serious.

TILT DOWN.

Dong-ik SLIPS the underwear into his jacket.

TRACK LEFT.

: Dong-ik's head

원의었어?

Yeon-kyo springs up from dozing

Dong-ik rushes up the stairs. He passes the blinking motion-sensor lights and stomps toward the kitchen.

He waves his hand to invite Yeon-kyo and she comes after him.

YEON-KYO: Is something wrong?

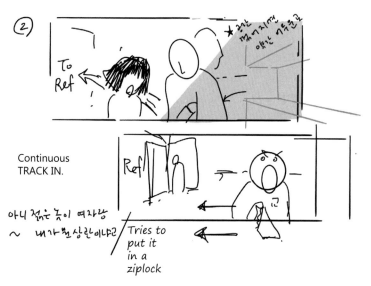

Continuous
TRACK IN.

To Ref

Tries to put it in a ziplock

Dong-ik begins as he turns the corner.

> DONG-IK
> Are kids upstairs? Is the housekeeper out? Honey. This was under my car seat. Driver Yoon is such a scumbag.

Dong-ik pulls out the panties. Yeon-kyo gasps, shocked and speechless. Dong-ik heads to the fridge.

> DONG-IK
> Don't you pay him well? Is he saving up by not paying for a motel?

Dong-ik opens the refrigerator.

> YEON-KYO
> He must be a pervert. He likes it in the car. In his boss' car! I'm sorry, honey. I didn't know he was this kind of guy.

> DONG-IK
> A young guy's sex life is his own business, that's all fine.

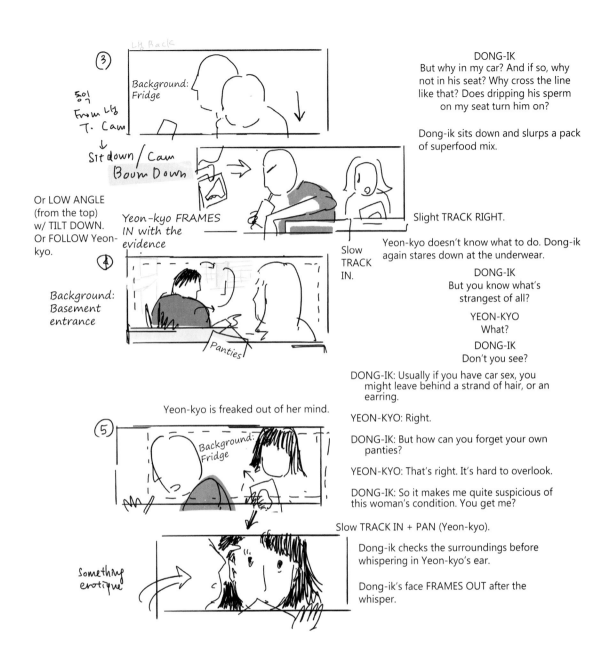

③ Lly Back

Background: Fridge

50/07
From Lly
T. Cam
↓
Sit down / Cam
Boom Down

Or LOW ANGLE (from the top) w/ TILT DOWN. Or FOLLOW Yeon-kyo.

④

Yeon-kyo FRAMES IN with the evidence

Background: Basement entrance

Panties

DONG-IK
But why in my car? And if so, why not in his seat? Why cross the line like that? Does dripping his sperm on my seat turn him on?

Dong-ik sits down and slurps a pack of superfood mix.

Slight TRACK RIGHT.

Slow TRACK IN.

Yeon-kyo doesn't know what to do. Dong-ik again stares down at the underwear.

DONG-IK
But you know what's strangest of all?

YEON-KYO
What?

DONG-IK
Don't you see?

DONG-IK: Usually if you have car sex, you might leave behind a strand of hair, or an earring.

YEON-KYO: Right.

DONG-IK: But how can you forget your own panties?

YEON-KYO: That's right. It's hard to overlook.

DONG-IK: So it makes me quite suspicious of this woman's condition. You get me?

Yeon-kyo is freaked out of her mind.

⑤

Background: Fridge

Something erotique

Slow TRACK IN + PAN (Yeon-kyo).

Dong-ik checks the surroundings before whispering in Yeon-kyo's ear.

Dong-ik's face FRAMES OUT after the whisper.

45

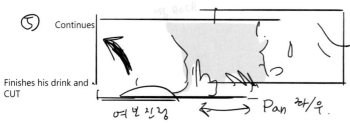

⑤ Continues

Finishes his drink and CUT

여보진경 ← → Pan 좌/우.

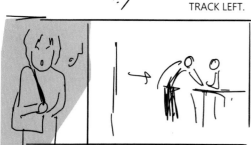

⑥

TRACK LEFT.

REVEAL Ki-jung.
Bigger?

⑦

YEON-KYO
Oh my... meth or cocaine?

DONG-IK
Shh! The kids...

YEON-KYO
What do we do? What if anyone finds white powder in your car?

DONG-IK
Calm down, *relax.*
For now it's just supposition. A rational guess.

Dong-ik gets up to throw away his drink and CAMERA TRACKS LEFT to reveal –

Ki-jung standing on the stairs with her bag, listening to the conversation.

DONG-IK
But no need to call the police. Still, for a busy man like me to ask, "Why are you fucking in my car?"

YEON-KYO
Exactly.

DONG-IK
So instead... Can you just invent some bland excuse to let him go? No need to mention panties or car sex.

YEON-KYO
I understand. We don't want the neighbors gossiping about the Parks' driver getting fired for car sex.

기정 Climbs the stairs and turns around and CUT.

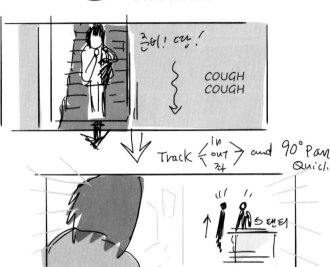

홍이! 대! COUGH COUGH

Track ⟨ in / out / 최 ⟩ and 90° Pan Quick

아나씨! Slightly TELEPHOTO?

DONG-IK
Exactly. We don't need to stoop to that level, do we?

YEON-KYO
But what if he goes online and accuses us...
What if he goes online and announces to the
whole world that he was unfairly fired by a
famous tech CEO?

DONG-IK
Just give him a good severance.

Ki-jung listens to Parks' conversation as she
walks down the stairs. She steps loudly so
the Parks can hear.

Yeon-kyo leaps out of her seat. Dong-ik
quickly hides the underwear and puts on an
awkward smile.

KI-JUNG
Hello!

YEON-KYO
So class is finished? How was
Da-song today?

47

#29A. "JESSICA NICE" MANSION – BACKLOT

STEADICAM BACK or DOLLY OUT.

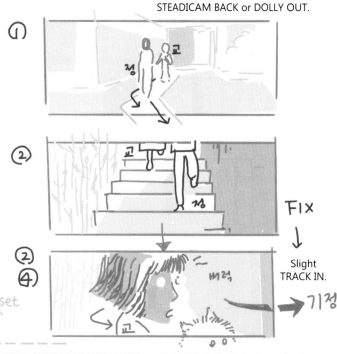

FIX
↓
Slight
TRACK IN.

#29B. "JESSICA NICE" MANSION – FRONT DOOR-GARAGE BACKLOT

STEADICAM BACK.

#18 - ④ 와
동일한 Cam.Move.

YEON-KYO
Jessica, the last time you came, our driver gave
you a ride, right?

KI-JUNG
That's right.

YEON-KYO
This may be an odd question, but nothing
happened then?

KI-JUNG
No, I went straight home.

YEON-KYO
Good, good. (relieved) That's good to hear.

KI-JUNG
He was very nice. I told him to go to Hyehwa
Station, but he insisted on driving me home.

YEON-KYO
That jerk! He took you home late at night?
Revealing where you live?

SHOT 2: Begins with FIXED CAMERA
then slight TRACK IN at the tail. SHOT 2
continues onto SHOT 4.

KI-JUNG
No, I got off at Hyehwa.

YEON-KYO
Oh, good girl. Very good.
(In English) *Jessica nice...*

KI-JUNG
Did something happen with him?

YEON-KYO
(opens the gate)
He won't be working for us anymore. A slightly
shameful incident. You don't need to know the
details.

KI-JUNG
But I'm surprised. He was so gentlemanly and
cool.

YEON-KYO
Jessica, you're too young and innocent! You
have a lot to learn about people.

YEON-KYO
That's true. They drive better, have better manners.

KI-JUNG
My father's brother had a driver just like that. Mr. Kim.
He was so congenial and nice. I used to call him
Uncle when I was young.

YEON-KYO
You know a man like that?

KI-JUNG
Yes, he was so mild-mannered. Oh, but my relatives
relocated to Chicago. I wonder if Mr. Kim's free now?

YEON-KYO
I'm really interested! Could I meet him?
I don't trust anyone now. I only trust
someone recommended by a person
I know well. But if you've known him
so long, I'd feel much more at ease.

Slightly HIGH ANGLE.

Moon-gwang walks within earshot and overhears the
conversation. Her curiosity is piqued.

The dogs wag their tails and swarm Yeon-kyo.

KI-JUNG
Do you really want to meet him?
(In English) *Are you serious?*

YEON-KYO
(In English) *I'm deadly serious.*
This chain of recommendation is best.

She makes a strange hand gesture.

YEON-KYO
How should I describe it? A belt of trust?

49

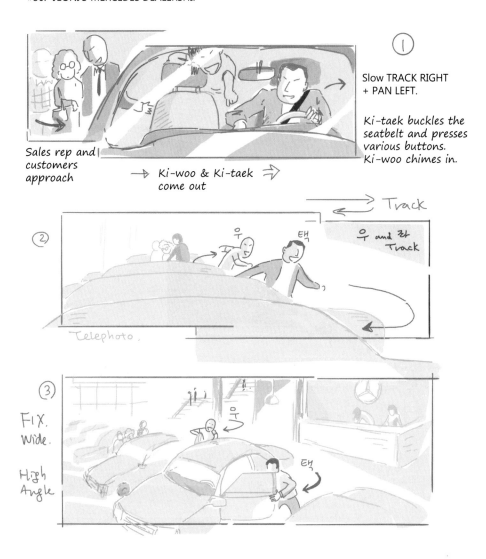

Slow TRACK RIGHT
+ PAN LEFT.

Ki-taek buckles the
seatbelt and presses
various buttons.
Ki-woo chimes in.

Sales rep and
customers
approach

Ki-woo & Ki-taek
come out

Track

우 and 잘
Track

Telephoto.

FIX.
Wide.

High
Angle

Fast TRACK LEFT.

TRACK LEFT.
>> Arrive

CAMERA FIXED.

Dong-ik greets Ki-taek with his eyes and signals at him to sit and wait.

Dong-ik looks up at the other side of the glass, where Ki-taek, in a suit, is sitting in a chair waiting patiently to be seen.

DONG-IK: (mouthing) "Sorry. I'll be right with you."

KI-TAEK: Don't worry, sir. (mouthing & gesturing) "Take your time."

VFX Comp.

Ki-taek sits awkwardly in a big office full of people.

Dong-ik and his team continue to work. (OUT OF FOCUS)

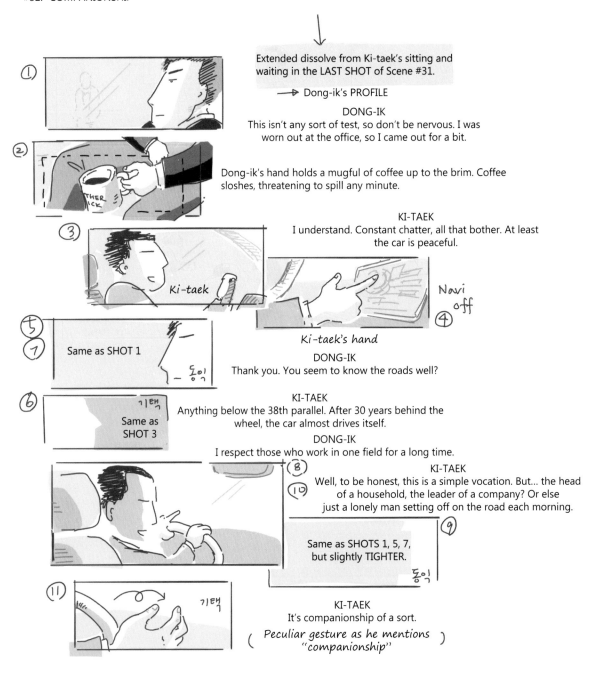

Extended dissolve from Ki-taek's sitting and
waiting in the LAST SHOT of Scene #31.

→ Dong-ik's PROFILE

DONG-IK
This isn't any sort of test, so don't be nervous. I was
worn out at the office, so I came out for a bit.

Dong-ik's hand holds a mugful of coffee up to the brim. Coffee
sloshes, threatening to spill any minute.

KI-TAEK
I understand. Constant chatter, all that bother. At least
the car is peaceful.

DONG-IK
Thank you. You seem to know the roads well?

KI-TAEK
Anything below the 38th parallel. After 30 years behind the
wheel, the car almost drives itself.

DONG-IK
I respect those who work in one field for a long time.

KI-TAEK
Well, to be honest, this is a simple vocation. But... the head
of a household, the leader of a company? Or else
just a lonely man setting off on the road each morning.

Same as SHOTS 1, 5, 7,
but slightly TIGHTER.

KI-TAEK
It's companionship of a sort.

(Peculiar gesture as he mentions
"companionship")

52

⑫ Dong-ik stays quiet.

⑬
KI-TAEK
So that's how I've approached each day. The years sure pass quickly.

Ki-taek turns the wheel, making a smooth left turn.

⑭ Dong-ik keeps his eyes on his mug.

DONG-IK
Sure enough, your cornering is excellent.

⑮ Dong-ik's POV.

High Angle

↑

Dong-ik keeps his eyes on coffee SLOSHING in his mug.

#33. "FOX" MANSION 1ST FLOOR STAIRS – KITCHEN - NIGHT

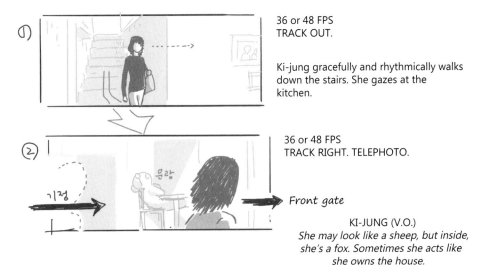

36 or 48 FPS
TRACK OUT.

Ki-jung gracefully and rhythmically walks down the stairs. She gazes at the kitchen.

36 or 48 FPS
TRACK RIGHT. TELEPHOTO.

Front gate

KI-JUNG (V.O.)
She may look like a sheep, but inside, she's a fox. Sometimes she acts like she owns the house.

#34A. "HISTORY OF MOON-GWANG" MANSION – DA-HYE'S ROOM - NIGHT

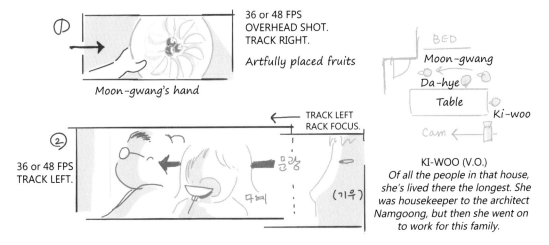

36 or 48 FPS
OVERHEAD SHOT.
TRACK RIGHT.

Artfully placed fruits

Moon-gwang's hand

TRACK LEFT
RACK FOCUS.

36 or 48 FPS
TRACK LEFT.

BED

Moon-gwang

Da-hye

Table

Ki-woo

Cam

KI-WOO (V.O.)
Of all the people in that house, she's lived there the longest. She was housekeeper to the architect Namgoong, but then she went on to work for this family.

Slight TRACK RIGHT.
36 or 48 FPS

Ki-woo's
POV.

Moon-gwang's face as she
quietly closes the door.

TELEPHOTO.

#34B. "HISTORY OF MOON-GWANG" MANSION – FRONT OF 2ND FLOOR DISPLAY CASE - NIGHT

TRACK LEFT. 남궁현자 선생의~

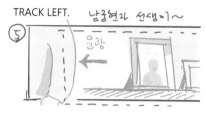

KI-WOO (V.O.)
*When the architect moved out, he
introduced this woman, "This is a great
housekeeper, you should hire her."*

2nd floor display case. Moon-gwang's body
crosses the screen against Namgoong Hyunja's
Architectural Grand Prize Award

#34C. "HISTORY OF MOON-GWANG" MANSION – 2nd FLOOR BATHROOM

Dong-ik enjoying a bath in the
2nd floor bathroom tub.

#35. "PIZZA GENERATION"

Serves Pizza

(Fix)

① Slight PAN + TILT.

③ Slight TILT.

④ Fix.

CHUNG-SOOK
So she survived a change of ownership.
KI-WOO
She won't give up a good job easily.
KI-JUNG
To extract a woman like that, we need to
prepare well.

KI-WOO
Right, we need a plan.

The Pizza Shop Owner cuts the pizza in
the background and carelessly sets
the pie on the table.

CHUNG-SOOK
Hey, how about some more hot sauce
here?

The Owner picks up a
hot sauce from the
other table and
TOSSES it in front of
Chung-sook. Chung-sook
mouths "bitch."

Ki-woo studies the hot
sauce. He SQUIRTS two
drops on a blank napkin,
as if testing for something.

KI-WOO (V.O.)
So according to what Da-hye told me—

OVERHEAD
SHOT.

#36. "FORBIDDEN FRUIT" MANSION – DA-HYE'S ROOM - NIGHT

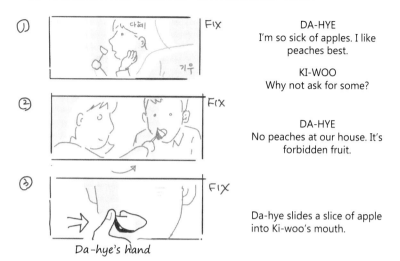

Da-hye's hand

DA-HYE
I'm so sick of apples. I like peaches best.

KI-WOO
Why not ask for some?

DA-HYE
No peaches at our house. It's forbidden fruit.

Da-hye slides a slice of apple into Ki-woo's mouth.

#37. "MARKET PEACH"

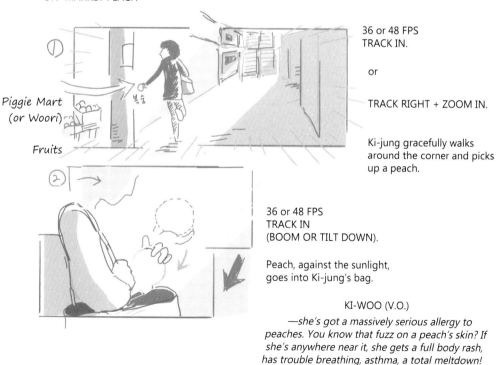

Piggie Mart (or Woori)

Fruits

36 or 48 FPS
TRACK IN.

or

TRACK RIGHT + ZOOM IN.

Ki-jung gracefully walks around the corner and picks up a peach.

36 or 48 FPS
TRACK IN
(BOOM OR TILT DOWN).

Peach, against the sunlight, goes into Ki-jung's bag.

KI-WOO (V.O.)
—she's got a massively serious allergy to peaches. You know that fuzz on a peach's skin? If she's anywhere near it, she gets a full body rash, has trouble breathing, asthma, a total meltdown!

#38. "PEACH FUZZ" SEMI-BASEMENT – FRONT

24 FPS
TRACK IN.

Ki-woo sits in a corner
and shaves off the fuzz
of a peach.

BIG CLOSE-UP.
36 or 48 FPS

Ki-woo scrapes off the fuzz into a
transparent pen cap.

#39. "PEACH PEN" MANSION – GARDEN – LATE AFTERNOON

36 FPS
TRACK OUT.

Ki-woo walks out the front door. He walks
by Moon-gwang, who is giving snacks to
the puppies.

36 FPS
Big CLOSE-UP.

Peach fuzz inside the cap.

#40. "TWILIGHT COUGH" MANSION – GARDEN – NIGHT

Seongbuk-dong

Moon-gwang's VIOLENT COUGHING instantly begins. Ki-woo casually walks down the hill as the coughing echoes throughout the neighborhood and the sound blends in with escalating MUSIC.

#41. "KI-TAEK SELFIE" HOSPITAL

CAMERA (almost) FIXED.
RACK FOCUS.

MOON-GWANG
No, no, there weren't any peaches anywhere. That's what I'm saying! Usually when I get symptoms like this, I run to my room and take my medicine, but it was so sudden, I wasn't sure where I left it.

HANDHELD (on escalator).

KI-TAEK
Madame, this woman behind me, is that...?

TELEPHOTO. CAMERA FIXED ON THE FLOOR
BLOCKING for actors (escalator >> walk the floor).

Tele. Fix on Floor. 인물이동 (에스컬 → Floor)
걷는

HANDHELD:
Yeon-kyo POV.

YEON-KYO
Oh, it's our
housekeeper!

TRACK RIGHT
+ Slightly
ZOOM IN.

Ki-taek, and then Yeon-kyo, FRAME
IN from SCREEN BOTTOM.

Ki-taek walks OUT OF FRAME.

PAN to Yeon-kyo.

KI-TAEK
So it's true. Oh, how sad. I wasn't sure if that was really her. I've only seen her a couple times in the living room.

YEON-KYO
This was in the hospital?

KI-TAEK
A few days ago I went for my annual medical exam. I took a selfie for my wife, and there she was behind me.

YEON-KYO
Is she talking on the phone there?

KI-TAEK
Anyway, I wasn't trying to eavesdrop... I wasn't trying to eavesdrop, but her words came through clearly!

(continues to dialogue from Scene #44)

KI-TAEK
...so I couldn't help but overhear. What I'm trying to say is, it's just that, your housekeeper's voice is quite loud, you know?

YEON-KYO
I understand, it's all right. Just tell me, okay?

#43. "ACTING CLASS" SEMI-BASEMENT – LIVING ROOM - FLASHBACK

TRACK IN
+ PAN RIGHT.
DOWN.

Chung-sook observes
the rehearsal from
behind

TRACK OUT/IN.

KI-TAEK
So I couldn't help but...!

KI-WOO
Cut, cut! Dad, your emotions are up to
here. Bring them down to about there.

Ki-taek rehearses his "scene," holding
a piece of paper with his lines.

CHUNG-SOOK
Action!

KI-TAEK
....so I couldn't help but overhear.

#44. "PHONE CONVERSATION" MERCEDES - DAY

Slight PAN LEFT.
Quick RACK.
FOCUS.

FIX.

KI-TAEK
What I'm trying to say is, it's just that, your
housekeeper's voice is quite loud, you know?

YEON-KYO
I understand, it's all right. Just tell me, okay?

Inside the Mercedes. Ki-taek looks at Yeon-
kyo through the rearview mirror.

Beat.

KI-TAEK
I don't know if I should say...

#45. "ACTING CLASS" SEMI-BASEMENT – LIVING ROOM - FLASHBACK

FIX.

KI-WOO
She said she got diagnosed with active TB.

Chung-sook mops the floor and watches as Ki-woo
gets into the acting.

#46. "ACTIVE TB" MERCEDES - DAY

RACK FOCUS: Ki-taek >> Yeon-kyo.

YEON-KYO
Tuberculosis? Come on...

KI-TAEK
It's true, she phoned someone saying she had active TB.
She seemed very upset, like she was angry at herself.

#47. "ACTING CLASS" – SEMI-BASEMENT - FLASHBACK

KI-WOO
(female voice)
Do people still get TB?

#48A. "OECD" MERCEDES - DAY

①

CAMERA FIXED. FOCUS on Yeon-kyo.

YEON-KYO
Do people still get TB?

②

CAMERA FIXED.

KI-TAEK
Back in the day, people used to buy Christmas seals, right?
Feels like a bygone era. But I saw it on the Internet. Korea
has the #1 rate of TB of all the OECD countries.

③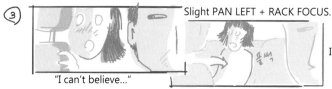

Slight PAN LEFT + RACK FOCUS.

YEON-KYO
I can't believe that Moon-gwang...
How could she not tell me?
I can't...

"I can't believe..."

#48B. "ACTING CLASS" – SEMI-BASEMENT - FLASHBACK

KI-TAEK
But she's still working, as if
nothing's wrong. With a kid like
Da-song in the house.

④

#48C. "OECD" MERCEDES - DAY

KI-TAEK
So you've got a young kid like Da-song
in the house, and a TB patient is doing
dishes, cooking, spraying spittle...

YEON-KYO
Stop it, please!

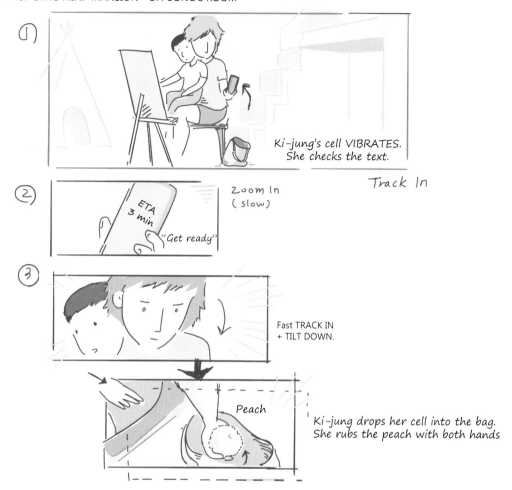

Ki-jung's cell VIBRATES.
She checks the text.

Track In

Zoom In
(slow)

ETA
3 min
"Get ready"

Fast TRACK IN
+ TILT DOWN.

Peach

Ki-jung drops her cell into the bag.
She rubs the peach with both hands

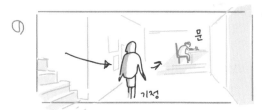

① Track In. 36 or 48 fps

Ki-jung comes down the stairs and heads to the refrigerator in the kitchen.

② Track In. 36 or 48 fps

Ki-jung sprinkles peach fuzz on Moon-gwang's back while she is preoccupied with sorting the receipts.

③ 36 or 48 fps.
(Slight) Track In.

Ki-jung peeps at Moon-gwang as she brings out a beverage from the refrigerator.

④ (Slight) Track In. 36 or 48 fps

Moon-gwang senses that something is wrong.

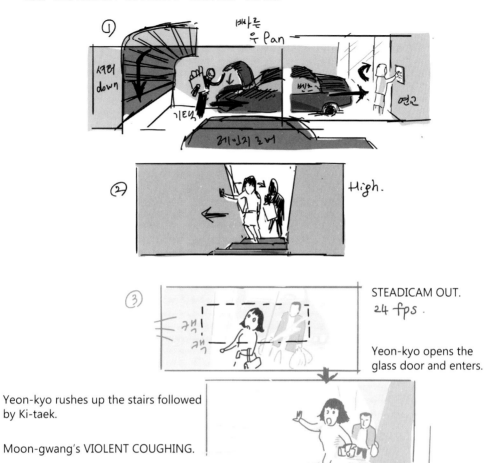

STEADICAM OUT.
24 fps.

Yeon-kyo opens the glass door and enters.

Yeon-kyo rushes up the stairs followed by Ki-taek.

Moon-gwang's VIOLENT COUGHING.

#52. "THE NAPKIN" MANSION – GARAGE STAIRS – ENTRANCE - KITCHEN

Track In
36 fps

Moon-gwang coughs.

Track In + Boom Down.
36 fps

Yeon-kyo is horrified, as if watching
Ebola spread right in front of her eyes.

TELEPHOTO; Ki-taek's POV.

36 fps

Moon-gwang tries to stifle her cough with a
napkin. She throws the napkin in the trash.

#53. "ICING ON THE CAKE" SEMI-BASEMENT – KI-JUNG'S ROOM

CAMERA FIXED; Ki-taek's POV.

KI-WOO
If you get the chance, this'll be icing
on the cake.

RACK FOCUS >> Hot sauce.

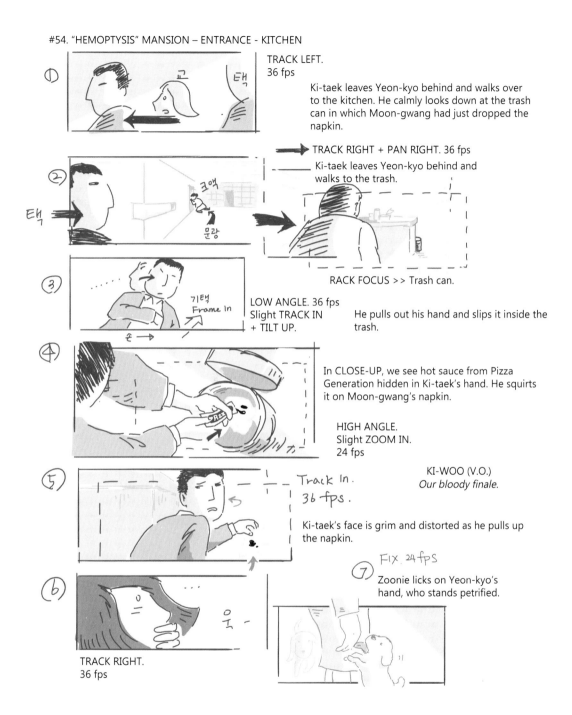

① TRACK LEFT.
36 fps

Ki-taek leaves Yeon-kyo behind and walks over to the kitchen. He calmly looks down at the trash can in which Moon-gwang had just dropped the napkin.

② TRACK RIGHT + PAN RIGHT. 36 fps
Ki-taek leaves Yeon-kyo behind and walks to the trash.

RACK FOCUS >> Trash can.

③ LOW ANGLE. 36 fps
Slight TRACK IN + TILT UP.

He pulls out his hand and slips it inside the trash.

④ In CLOSE-UP, we see hot sauce from Pizza Generation hidden in Ki-taek's hand. He squirts it on Moon-gwang's napkin.

HIGH ANGLE.
Slight ZOOM IN.
24 fps

⑤ Track In.
36 fps.

KI-WOO (V.O.)
Our bloody finale.

Ki-taek's face is grim and distorted as he pulls up the napkin.

⑦ FIX. 24 fps
Zoonie licks on Yeon-kyo's hand, who stands petrified.

⑥ TRACK RIGHT.
36 fps

Ki-taek's cellphone fills the screen. Text messages from Yeon-kyo:
2nd floor sauna room
Don't let her see you

No more music. The house is quiet.
Ki-taek checks the texts. He looks around before quietly climbing up the stairs.

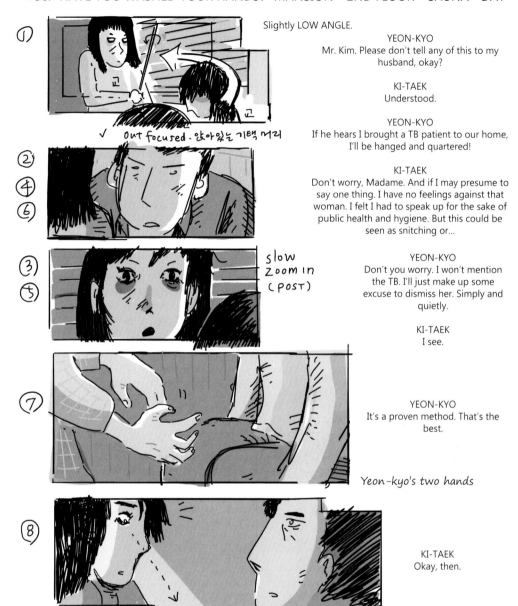

Slightly LOW ANGLE.

✓ Out focused · 앉아있는 기택 머리

slow
zoom in
(POST)

Yeon-kyo's two hands

PAN ..

YEON-KYO
Mr. Kim. Please don't tell any of this to my husband, okay?

KI-TAEK
Understood.

YEON-KYO
If he hears I brought a TB patient to our home, I'll be hanged and quartered!

KI-TAEK
Don't worry, Madame. And if I may presume to say one thing. I have no feelings against that woman. I felt I had to speak up for the sake of public health and hygiene. But this could be seen as snitching or...

YEON-KYO
Don't you worry. I won't mention the TB. I'll just make up some excuse to dismiss her. Simply and quietly.

KI-TAEK
I see.

YEON-KYO
It's a proven method. That's the best.

KI-TAEK
Okay, then.

Ki-taek puts out his hand as if he is sealing a confidential deal.

They share the most awkward handshake in the world.

Yeon-kyo suddenly cringes.

YEON-KYO
Have you... washed your hands?

① CAMERA FIXED. WIDE SHOT.

Da-song looks outside the kitchen window.

② CAMERA FIXED. HIGH ANGLE.
Da-song's POV.

Outside the window:
Yeon-kyo is having a talk with Moon-gwang, who is devastated.

③ CAMERA FIXED.

Bleak late afternoon.
Puppies loiter.
HUSH! - Da-song puts his finger on his lips to silence Zoonie.

EXTENDED VERSION

YEON-KYO: No need to mention your cooking. You're the best out there. You remember how LS Group's vice president wanted you, and because I didn't let you go, our relationship with them soured. Believe me, it's not because of what the bodhisattva says. Kids are older now and I thought I should take care of the house now. Mr. Park and I were talking even this morning. I still don't understand why he bought this gigantic house. Anyhow, thank you so much for everything.

#58. "MOON-GWANG DEVASTATED" MANSION – FRONT GATE – SEONGBUK-DONG – NIGHT

FIX

Moon-gwang, in disbelief, carries luggage in her hands. Her hair dances to the wind. The sky is getting darker.

Moon-gwang keeps looking back. She stops and stares at the firmly shut gate for a long time.

FIX.
빗물흐르는
차유리
바라보는
동익…

Dong-ik stares out the window for a while.

DONG-IK
Mr. Kim, do you know a good braised ribs place? Somewhere close by?

KI-TAEK
Sure. You'll be eating out?

FIX
유연하게
우회전 하는
벤츠

DONG-IK
That's right. Why such a craving for braised ribs today? 'Cause I can't have them at home anymore.

Ki-taek makes a smooth right turn. Raindrops slide against the window to the same direction.

DONG-IK
Our old housekeeper made delicious ribs.

KI-TAEK
The one who quit this week?

DONG-IK
My wife wouldn't even tell me why she quit. Sure, it's easy enough to hire a new one. Still, it's a shame. She was a great housekeeper.

KI-TAEK
I see.

DONG-IK
She kept the house in great shape, and she knew never to cross the line. I can't stand people who cross the line. Perhaps just one weak point? Eating too much. She always ate enough for two. But considering all the work she did…

KI-TAEK
Then you better find someone new. A new housekeeper.

DONG-IK
We're in trouble now. In a week, our house will be a trash can. My clothes will start to smell. My wife has no talent for housework. She's bad at cleaning, and her cooking's awful.

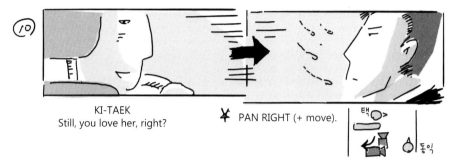

KI-TAEK
Still, you love her, right?

✗ PAN RIGHT (+ move).

Beat. We only hear the RAIN.

Ki-taek's suddenly serious comment catches Dong-ik off guard. Silence. Dong-ik starts laughing. Hard.

Headlights from another car FLASH BY against the front window.

DONG-IK
Of course. I love her. We'll call it love.

KI-TAEK
Then would this help?

OVERHEAD SHOT:
Namecard crosses the line.

On a beautiful ivory-colored stock, only the name "The Care" is printed in elegant typography. No number, no address.

DONG-IK
The Care? What is this?

KI-TAEK
I just recently found out about them. How to describe it? It's like a membership service. The company provides veteran-grade help to VIP customers such as you. For example, maids, caregivers, or drivers like myself.

DONG-IK
You can tell from the card they're high-class.
Cool design. Then how do you know about
this company?

KI-TAEK
They contacted me, as a veteran-grade driver. You
might say they scouted me? But when their call
came I had already arranged to meet with you.

DONG-IK
I see... You turned down this famous
company to work for me. I won't forget that.

KI-TAEK
(laughs) It is pleasure to serve you, sir.

They laugh, but there's a subtle, underlying
tension between the two. Dong-ik all of a
sudden drops his smile.

DONG-IK
Anyway, I can give this card to my wife, right?

KI-TAEK
Yes, that's why I brought it up. No need to
mention me. You can tell her you found the
company yourself.

DONG-IK
Sure. Thanks to you I can play the good
husband.

KI-TAEK
It's membership-only, so they don't
have a website or anything. On the
back, there's a number for
consultations. Tell her to call there.

OVERHEAD SHOT.

VRRRR AND RING – and OLD
FLIP PHONE vibrates AND rings.

Ki-jung's hand FRAMES IN to grab
the phone.

LOW ANGLE.

> KI-JUNG
> Hello, this is Senior Advisor Yeo of
> The Care.

Chung-sook and Ki-taek have
breakfast and watch Ki-jung take
the phone. They are impressed at
how smooth Ki-jung handles
swindling.

> CHUNG-SOOK
> If she wanted, she'd be a fucking
> great con artist.

> KI-TAEK
> Isn't her voice tone great? Takes
> after me.

Continues to Scene #61:

> YEON-KYO (V.O.)
> *From what I've heard, it's a*
> *full membership service?*

> KI-JUNG
> Yes, we are a membership-only
> service. As you are not our current
> member, I can guide you through the
> steps so you could join.

> YEON-KYO (V.O.)
> *Sure, okay.*

> KI-JUNG
> Are you ready to write this down?
> We'll just need to receive
> a few documents from you.

Yeon-kyo is on the phone with kitchen gloves on, floundering in the kitchen, overloading the dishwasher, and sterilizing dirty pans in an oversized pot.

Dishcloth

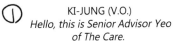

KI-JUNG (V.O.)
Hello, this is Senior Advisor Yeo of The Care.

YEON-KYO
Yes, this is The Care's main office?

KI-JUNG (V.O.)
That's correct.

YEON-KYO
From what I've heard, it's a full membership service?

Mask, disposable gloves

FIX
LOW

steam mod

KI-JUNG (V.O.)
Yes, we are a membership-only service. So you're not currently a member, I assume?

YEON-KYO
That's right. What steps do I need to take?

KI-JUNG (V.O.)
We'll just need to receive a few documents from you. Are you ready to write this down? Your family register, citizenship ID cards, documents to prove your income level, etc.

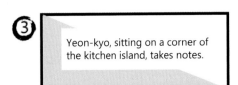

Yeon-kyo, sitting on a corner of the kitchen island, takes notes.

#62. "CHUNG-SOOK JOB INTERVIEW" – MANSION – BACKYARD – LATE AFTERNOON

Chung-sook, with a classy hairdo and tasteful makeup, is sitting at the white patio table.

Yeon-kyo goes through her papers, being especially careful to check her medical record.

A WHITE BUTTERFLY flits by Chung-sook's face, its wings bouncing off the bright summer light. A beautiful ARIA begins.

#63. "STEADICAM" – MANSION – STAIRCASE – JEONJU BACKLOT

As the ARIA continues STEADICAM GLIDES UP the stairs, following Chung-sook's feet climbing up the stairs—

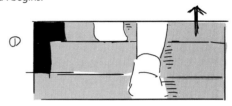

2nd FLOOR HALLWAY – ANSEOUNG DIMA SET

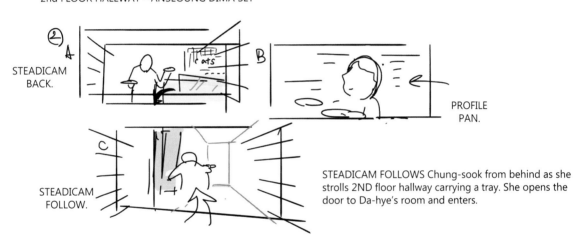

STEADICAM BACK.

PROFILE PAN.

STEADICAM FOLLOW.

STEADICAM FOLLOWS Chung-sook from behind as she strolls 2ND floor hallway carrying a tray. She opens the door to Da-hye's room and enters.

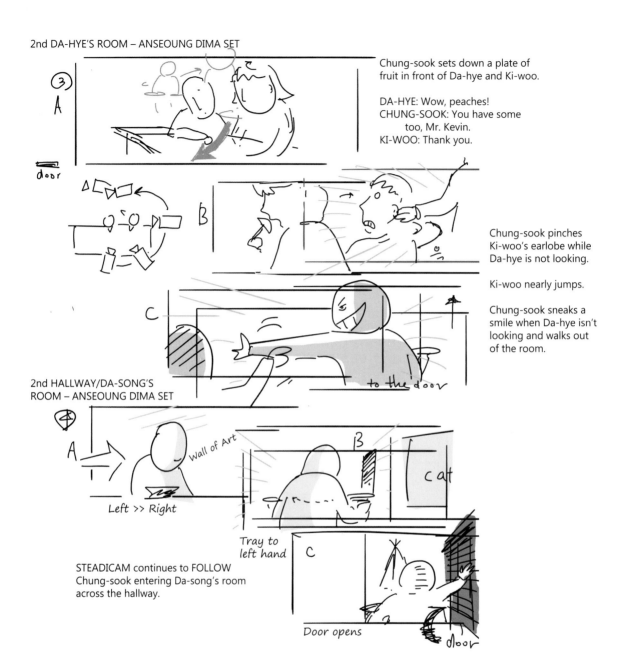

2nd DA-HYE'S ROOM – ANSEOUNG DIMA SET

③
A

door

B

C

to the door

Chung-sook sets down a plate of fruit in front of Da-hye and Ki-woo.

DA-HYE: Wow, peaches!
CHUNG-SOOK: You have some too, Mr. Kevin.
KI-WOO: Thank you.

Chung-sook pinches Ki-woo's earlobe while Da-hye is not looking.

Ki-woo nearly jumps.

Chung-sook sneaks a smile when Da-hye isn't looking and walks out of the room.

2nd HALLWAY/DA-SONG'S ROOM – ANSEOUNG DIMA SET

A
Wall of Art
Left >> Right

B
c a t
Tray to left hand

C
Door opens
door

STEADICAM continues to FOLLOW Chung-sook entering Da-song's room across the hallway.

78

A TEEPEE in the corner. The flap opens and Ki-jung peeks out. Da-song, cuddled up between her arms, is drawing a picture. He looks at Chung-sook, embarrassed.

KI-JUNG
Leave it outside the door next time. And knock!

CHUNG-SOOK
Yes.

KI-JUNG
No entering during my lesson!

Chung-sook scoffs. She mouths "Just eat the damn peaches," handing over the plate.

She looks at the drawings in the picture – not a bit impressed by them.

2nd HALLWAY – ANSEOUNG DIMA SET

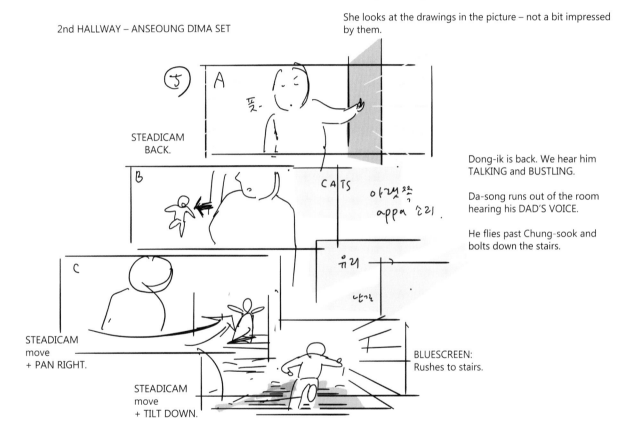

STEADICAM
BACK.

STEADICAM
move
+ PAN RIGHT.

STEADICAM
move
+ TILT DOWN.

Dong-ik is back. We hear him TALKING and BUSTLING.

Da-song runs out of the room hearing his DAD'S VOICE.

He flies past Chung-sook and bolts down the stairs.

BLUESCREEN:
Rushes to stairs.

1st FLOOR – LIVING ROOM – JEONJU BACKLOT

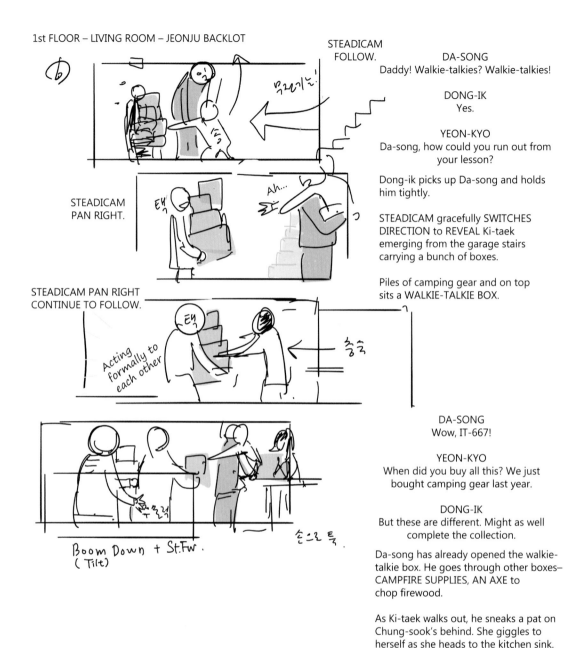

STEADICAM
FOLLOW.

STEADICAM
PAN RIGHT.

STEADICAM PAN RIGHT
CONTINUE TO FOLLOW.

Acting formally to
each other

Boom Down + St.Fw.
(Tilt)

DA-SONG
Daddy! Walkie-talkies? Walkie-talkies!

DONG-IK
Yes.

YEON-KYO
Da-song, how could you run out from
your lesson?

Dong-ik picks up Da-song and holds
him tightly.

STEADICAM gracefully SWITCHES
DIRECTION to REVEAL Ki-taek
emerging from the garage stairs
carrying a bunch of boxes.

Piles of camping gear and on top
sits a WALKIE-TALKIE BOX.

DA-SONG
Wow, IT-667!

YEON-KYO
When did you buy all this? We just
bought camping gear last year.

DONG-IK
But these are different. Might as well
complete the collection.

Da-song has already opened the walkie-
talkie box. He goes through other boxes–
CAMPFIRE SUPPLIES, AN AXE to
chop firewood.

As Ki-taek walks out, he sneaks a pat on
Chung-sook's behind. She giggles to
herself as she heads to the kitchen sink.

The long STEADICAM SHOT shows the Kims' complete and
successful infiltration into the Park mansion. It seems to have come
to a glorious end complete with the ARIA, however—

80

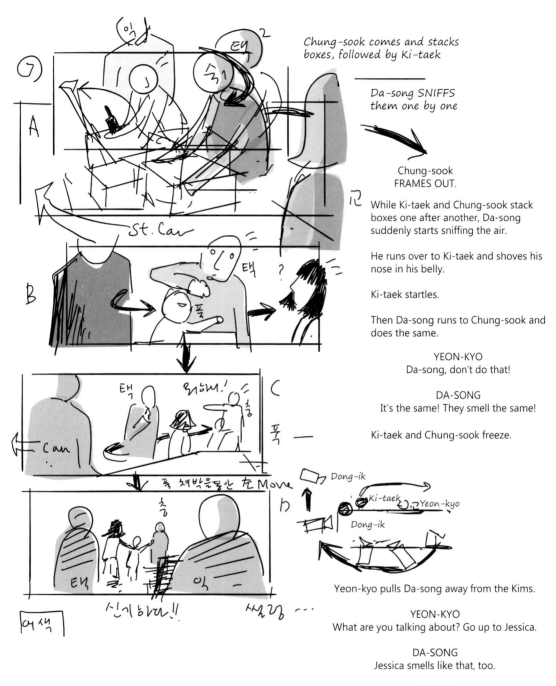

Chung-sook comes and stacks boxes, followed by Ki-taek

Da-song SNIFFS them one by one

Chung-sook FRAMES OUT.

While Ki-taek and Chung-sook stack boxes one after another, Da-song suddenly starts sniffing the air.

He runs over to Ki-taek and shoves his nose in his belly.

Ki-taek startles.

Then Da-song runs to Chung-sook and does the same.

YEON-KYO
Da-song, don't do that!

DA-SONG
It's the same! They smell the same!

Ki-taek and Chung-sook freeze.

Yeon-kyo pulls Da-song away from the Kims.

YEON-KYO
What are you talking about? Go up to Jessica.

DA-SONG
Jessica smells like that, too.

DONG-IK
Sorry, he's a little out there.

They all have a laugh, but there is awkwardness in the air.

#64. "BBQ FEAST" SEMI-BASEMENT

(1) BLACK >> TRACK RIGHT
to REVEAL and FRAME IN:
Ki-taek, Chung-sook,
Ki-woo, and Ki-jung.

SNIFF

KI-TAEK: Da-song, that little punk. So do we all need to use different soap now?
KI-WOO: Dad, we'll need to use different laundry soap, too. And fabric softener.
CHUNG-SOOK: You mean doing four separate loads of laundry each time?
KI-JUNG: That's not it. It's the semi-basement smell.
KI-WOO: ...
KI-JUNG: We need to leave this home to lose the smell.
KI-TAEK: (raises his beer) Anyway...

KI-TAEK
...aren't we fortunate to be worrying about things like this? In an age like ours, when an opening for a security guard attracts 500 university graduates. Our entire family got hired!

KI-WOO
That's right, Dad!

KI-TAEK
If we put our 4 salaries together? The amount of cash coming from that house into ours is immense! Let's offer a prayer of gratitude to the great Mr. Park. And to Min! Ki-woo, that friend of yours turned into such a fine guy, and thanks to him we're all... Fuck, not again!

The Kims all turn to the window to see a DRUNK relieving himself.

OUTSIDE THE WINDOW: DRUNK #2

Ki-woo turns and STANDS UP

PAN + TILT UP.
RACK FOCUS.

Slightly HIGH ANGLE.
PAN + TILT.

KI-WOO
That asshole's dead.

Ki-woo's hand ENTERS behind Ki-taek and grabs the scholar rock.

Ki-taek catches up to Ki-woo and wrests the stone from his hand, handing him a plastic bottle instead.

← TRACK LEFT.

KI-JUNG
Ki-woo's on the rampage!

CHUNG-SOOK
Don't overdo it!

TRACK OUT.

Ki-woo RUSHES, SWINGING the plastic bottle and SPRAYING water at Drunk #2.

Drunk #2, startled, turns around, SPRAYING his urine.

Ki-jung grabs her phone. She opens the HIGH-SPEED CAM APP.

Chung-sook can't care less. She continues to grill meat, happy to finish the food by herself.

Slightly LOW ANGLE.
CAMERA: FIXED.

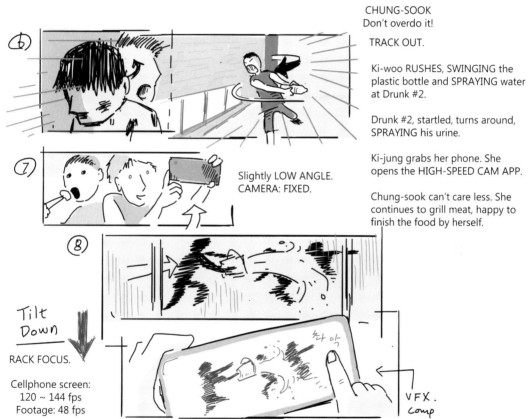

Tilt Down

RACK FOCUS.

Cellphone screen:
120 ~ 144 fps
Footage: 48 fps

VFX.
Comp

UNSETTLING MUSIC plays over the wild, primal thrashing of the threesome. The violent dance DISSOLVES TO --

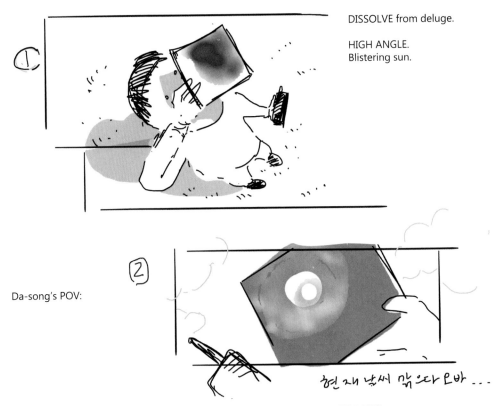

DISSOLVE from deluge.

HIGH ANGLE.
Blistering sun.

Da-song's POV:

DISSOLVE from Scene #64 CONTINUES ONTO –

Sun-drenched garden.

Da-song, with a bow and axe strapped to his back, looks up
at the sky through a piece of soot-covered glass, a
homemade sun-viewer.

He presses his walkie-talkie button.

DA-SONG

Current weather is clear, over. The clouds are moving. But
they're not rain clouds, over.

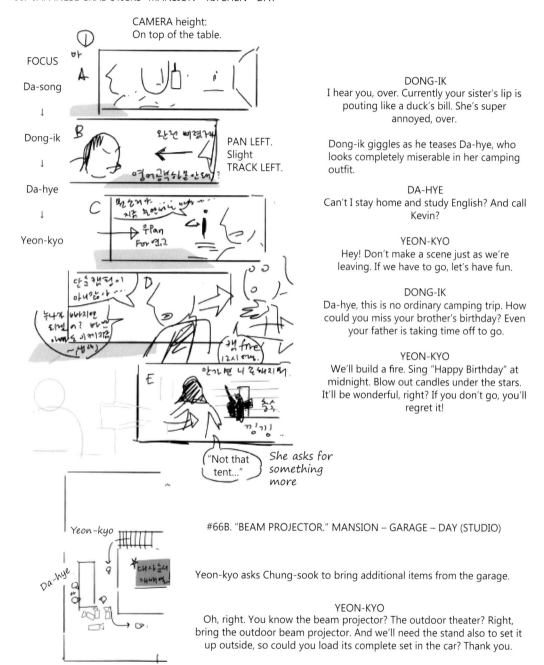

CAMERA height:
On top of the table.

FOCUS

Da-song

↓

Dong-ik

↓

Da-hye

↓

Yeon-kyo

PAN LEFT.
Slight
TRACK LEFT.

"Not that tent..."

She asks for something more

Yeon-kyo

Da-hye

DONG-IK
I hear you, over. Currently your sister's lip is pouting like a duck's bill. She's super annoyed, over.

Dong-ik giggles as he teases Da-hye, who looks completely miserable in her camping outfit.

DA-HYE
Can't I stay home and study English? And call Kevin?

YEON-KYO
Hey! Don't make a scene just as we're leaving. If we have to go, let's have fun.

DONG-IK
Da-hye, this is no ordinary camping trip. How could you miss your brother's birthday? Even your father is taking time off to go.

YEON-KYO
We'll build a fire. Sing "Happy Birthday" at midnight. Blow out candles under the stars. It'll be wonderful, right? If you don't go, you'll regret it!

#66B. "BEAM PROJECTOR." MANSION – GARAGE – DAY (STUDIO)

Yeon-kyo asks Chung-sook to bring additional items from the garage.

YEON-KYO
Oh, right. You know the beam projector? The outdoor theater? Right, bring the outdoor beam projector. And we'll need the stand also to set it up outside, so could you load its complete set in the car? Thank you.

66

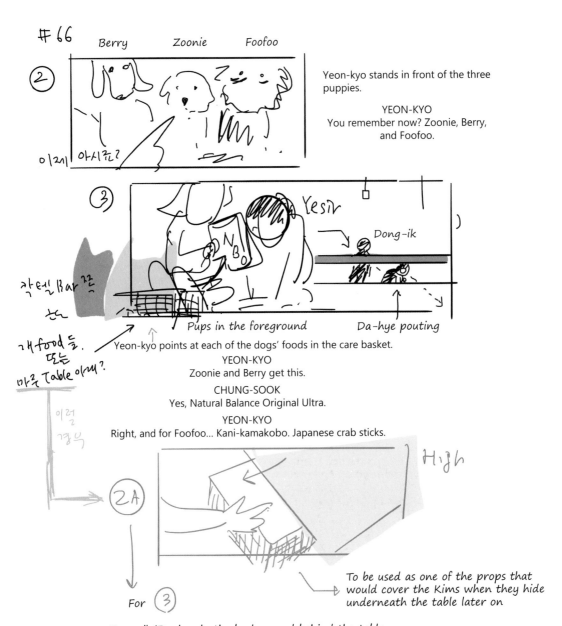

Berry Zoonie Foofoo

② 이게 아시겠2?

Yeon-kyo stands in front of the three puppies.

YEON-KYO
You remember now? Zoonie, Berry, and Foofoo.

③ Yesir

Dong-ik

Pups in the foreground   Da-hye pouting

Yeon-kyo points at each of the dogs' foods in the care basket.

YEON-KYO
Zoonie and Berry get this.

CHUNG-SOOK
Yes, Natural Balance Original Ultra.

YEON-KYO
Right, and for Foofoo... Kani-kamakobo. Japanese crab sticks.

2A   High

For ③

To be used as one of the props that would cover the Kims when they hide underneath the table later on

Dong-ik/Da-hye in the background behind the table

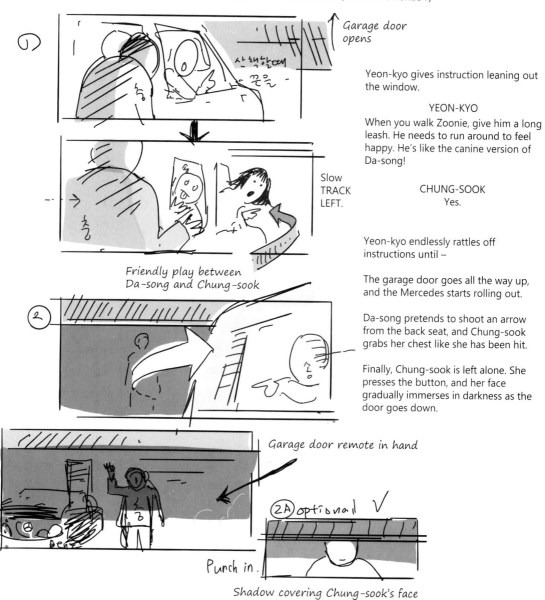

Garage door opens

Slow TRACK LEFT.

Friendly play between Da-song and Chung-sook

Garage door remote in hand

Punch in.

Shadow covering Chung-sook's face

Yeon-kyo gives instruction leaning out the window.

YEON-KYO
When you walk Zoonie, give him a long leash. He needs to run around to feel happy. He's like the canine version of Da-song!

CHUNG-SOOK
Yes.

Yeon-kyo endlessly rattles off instructions until –

The garage door goes all the way up, and the Mercedes starts rolling out.

Da-song pretends to shoot an arrow from the back seat, and Chung-sook grabs her chest like she has been hit.

Finally, Chung-sook is left alone. She presses the button, and her face gradually immerses in darkness as the door goes down.

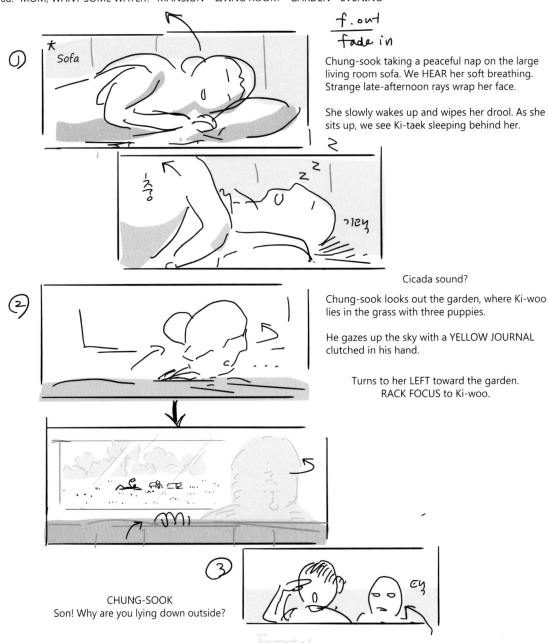

f. out
fade in

Chung-sook taking a peaceful nap on the large living room sofa. We HEAR her soft breathing. Strange late-afternoon rays wrap her face.

She slowly wakes up and wipes her drool. As she sits up, we see Ki-taek sleeping behind her.

Cicada sound?

Chung-sook looks out the garden, where Ki-woo lies in the grass with three puppies.

He gazes up the sky with a YELLOW JOURNAL clutched in his hand.

Turns to her LEFT toward the garden.
RACK FOCUS to Ki-woo.

CHUNG-SOOK
Son! Why are you lying down outside?

88

OUTSIDE THE WINDOW:
Ki-woo takes a deep breath as he gazes up at the sky. He's never been more relaxed.

FIX.
Through Glass

KI-WOO
I'm gazing at the sky
from home. It's so great.

JUMP CUT TO

MANSION – KITCHEN – LIVING ROOM/GARDEN - EVENING

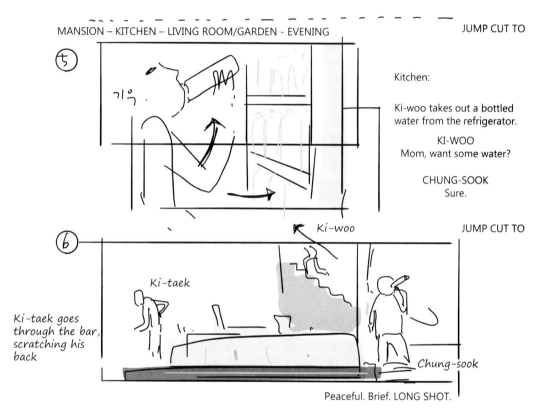

기옹

Kitchen:

Ki-woo takes out a bottled water from the refrigerator.

KI-WOO
Mom, want some water?

CHUNG-SOOK
Sure.

JUMP CUT TO

Ki-woo

Ki-taek

Ki-taek goes
through the bar,
scratching his
back

Chung-sook

Peaceful. Brief. LONG SHOT.

Ki-woo gets a few bottles of imported bottled water and gives one to Chung-sook before heading up the stairs.

Ki-taek, still groggy, gets up from the sofa and trudges over to a cabinet in the corner. A variety of WHISKEYS are on display.

#69. "TELEPATHY" MANSION – 2ND FLOOR BATHROOM – EVENING

TRACK LEFT
(Ki-jung FRAMES IN).

Ki-jung is taking a bubble bath. She picks up the remote and changes the channel on the wall-mounted TV.

KNOCK KNOCK.

KI-WOO
Ki-jung, some water?

KI-JUNG
Telepathy... thank you.

RATTLE...

#70. "DA-HYE'S BED" MANSION – 2ND FLOOR DA-HYE'S ROOM – EVENING

Ki-woo sneaks into the room. He throws himself onto Da-hye's bed.

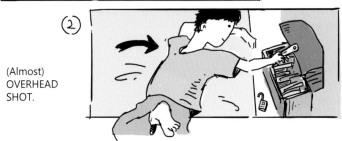

(Almost)
OVERHEAD
SHOT.

Da-hye's
secret box

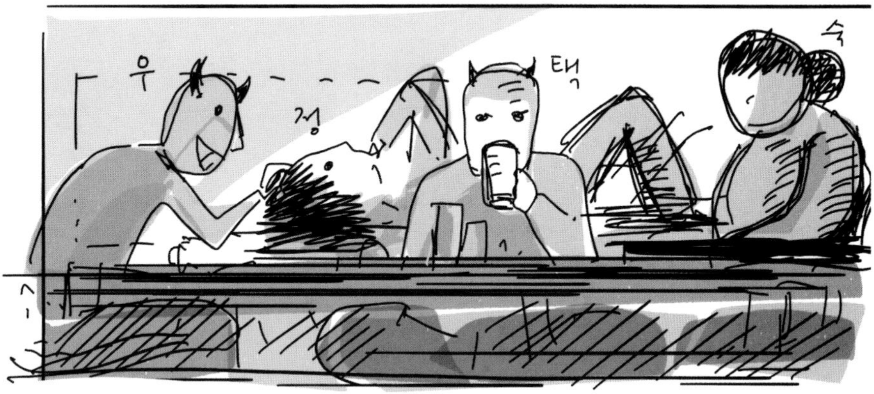
우
정
택
숙

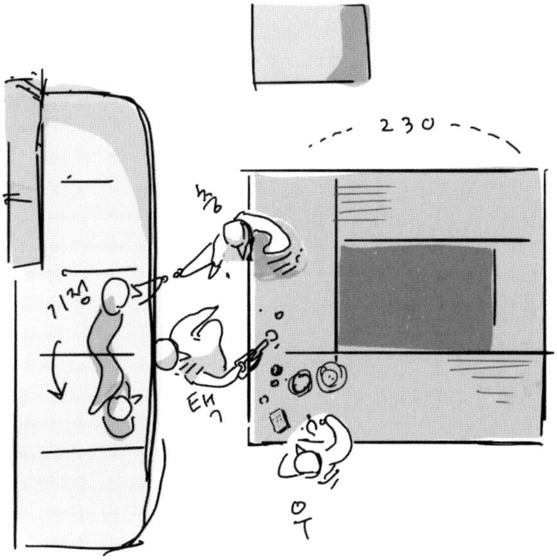
230
기정
택

CAMERA FIXED.

CLINK CLANK - Ki-taek takes several bottles and pours a little of each into his tumbler.

CHUNG-SOOK
Why are you mixing all the booze?

KI-TAEK
So they won't notice. Otherwise, they would find out.

CHUNG-SOOK
How impressive.

KI-JUNG
But you get shitfaced when you mix your drinks, Dad.

KI-TAEK
What do you mean, "shitfaced"? Ki-jung, that's no way to talk to your dad.

KI-WOO
Dad! Let me add another to the mix!

KI-TAEK
This is pretty classy.

CAMERA FIXED or
slight TRACK LEFT + TILT UP.

KI-TAEK
Rain falling on the lawn, as we sip our whiskey...

The Kims are comfortably sprawled across the couch and floor. They sip their drinks and watch rain fall outside the window.

Ki-woo looks out the window, rain pouring.

KI-WOO
It's probably raining at the campsite, too. They must be having a magical time. Raindrops pattering. Playing guitar.

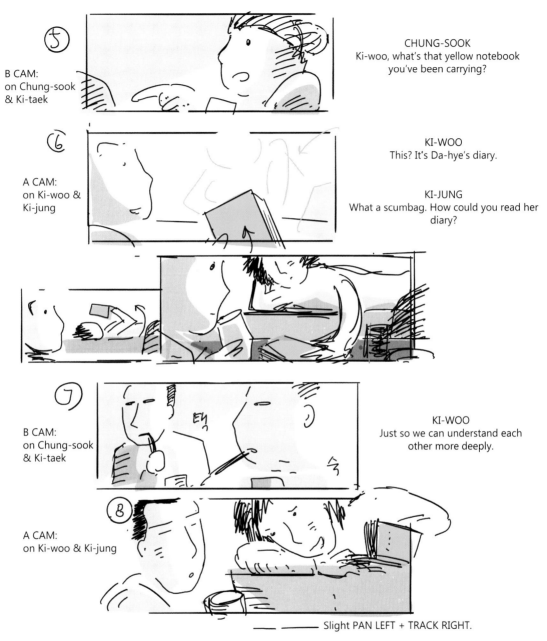

B CAM:
on Chung-sook
& Ki-taek

CHUNG-SOOK
Ki-woo, what's that yellow notebook
you've been carrying?

A CAM:
on Ki-woo &
Ki-jung

KI-WOO
This? It's Da-hye's diary.

KI-JUNG
What a scumbag. How could you read her
diary?

B CAM:
on Chung-sook
& Ki-taek

KI-WOO
Just so we can understand each
other more deeply.

A CAM:
on Ki-woo & Ki-jung

—— Slight PAN LEFT + TRACK RIGHT.

KI-JUNG
Fuck, are you two dating?

KI-WOO
I'm serious. She really likes me, too. When she
enters university, I'll officially ask her out.
Seriously.

CAMERA FIXED. WIDE SHOT.

They all stare at Ki-woo, speechless. Ki-taek
slaps Ki-woo's shoulder.

KI-TAEK
My son! Then this house will be your in-laws' house?

KI-WOO
I guess so.

CHUNG-SOOK
Fuck, then I'm washing dishes at my daughter-in-law's?

KI-WOO
Sure, washing your daughter-in-law's socks!

Ki-taek pretends to wash socks, laughing hysterically,
until he feels Chung-sook staring daggers at him.

Chung-sook downs her shot and calmly turns to Ki-woo.

CHUNG-SOOK
I like her. She's a good kid.

SHOT 13: PAN + TILT UP.

Points to Ki-jung

KI-WOO
Well, now that we're daydreaming... Nowadays in-laws
barely meet each other anyway.

KI-JUNG
Crazy fuck...

KI-WOO
If Da-hye and I marry, we can bring in actors to be my
mom and dad. Look at her. She got so many jobs acting
in weddings last year.

KI-JUNG
I even caught the bouquet from a bitch I've never met.
If you get the bouquet, they pay an extra $10.

KI-TAEK
That's how your acting got so good!

KI-TAEK
Acting is one thing, but this family is so gullible, right?

CHUNG-SOOK
The madame especially.

KI-TAEK
You said it. She's so naïve and nice. She's rich, but still
nice.

B-Cam

Ki-woo   TRACK RIGHT + PAN LT/RT

YELP!

High.
wide

Chung-sook stops mid-sip and stares at Ki-taek.

CHUNG-SOOK
Not "rich, but still nice." "Nice because she's rich." You
know? Hell, if I had all this money, I'd be nice, too! Even
nicer!

Chung-sook gets animated. She kicks when Berry
comes her way.

GULP

whiskey

그건 그래~
네 엄마가 맞이...

대리이~

Pan & Tilt.

기정

으어어 !!

"YEAH!
LIGHTNING!"

45°

KI-TAEK
That's true. Your mom's right. Rich people are naïve.
No resentments. No creases on them.

CHUNG-SOOK
It all gets ironed out. Money is an iron. Those creases
all get smoothed out.

Ki-jung grows agitated listening to her parents.
She tosses back her whiskey.

KI-TAEK
Hey, Ki-woo. You know that driver, Yoon? Was it
Yoon? The driver before me.

KI-WOO
Yeah, Yoon.

KI-TAEK
He must be working somewhere else now, right?

KI-WOO
Sure, he must be. He's young, got a nice physique.
He must've found a better job.

Ki-jung SLAMS DOWN her glass and yells.

KI-JUNG
Fucking hell!

KI-WOO
What's with her now?

KI-JUNG
We're the ones who need help. Worry about us, okay?
Dad! Come on, Dad! Just focus on us, okay? On us! Not
Driver Yoon, but me, please!

Ki-jung looks vulnerable, like a child.

As if on cue, LIGHTNING AND THUNDER strike
outside, followed by heavy rain.

KI-TAEK
Awesome timing, huh?

KI-WOO
She speaks, and the lightning crashes!

Ki-woo brushes her hair as he consoles his baby sister.

KI-WOO
Hey, Jessica. Cheers. Hey, when I went up before,
and you were in the bath...

KI-JUNG
What about it?

KI-WOO
How to put it? You fit in here. This rich house suits
you. Not like us.

KI-JUNG
Fuck off.

KI-WOO
I'm serious! Dad, before... She was lying back in the
tub, watching TV. Like she's lived here for years.

KI-TAEK
Is that right?

CAMERA FIXED. Slightly LOW.

Ki-woo becomes animated, opening his arms wide and pointing at the living room.

KI-TAEK
Speaking of which, if this became our house, if we lived here, which room would you want? What room in this masterwork by the great Namgoong?

Slightly HIGH ANGLE.

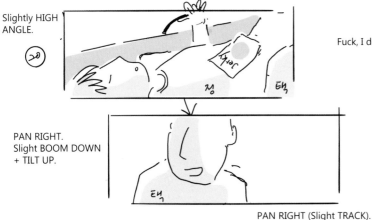

KI-JUNG
Fuck, I don't know. Get me the house first. Then I'll think about it.

PAN RIGHT.
Slight BOOM DOWN + TILT UP.

KI-TAEK
We live here now, don't we? Getting drunk in the living room.

KI-WOO
Right, we live here. Why not?

KI-TAEK
This is our home right now. It's cozy.

PAN RIGHT (Slight TRACK).

Chung-sook, face bulging red, flashes a dirty grin.

CHUNG-SOOK
Cozy? Are you feeling cozy? Sure, but suppose Park walked through that door now. What about your dad? He'd run and hide like a cockroach.

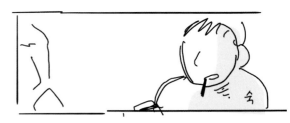

PAN LEFT (Slight TRACK).

CHUNG-SOOK
Kids, you know at our house, when you turn on the light, and the cockroaches scatter? You know what I mean?

Ki-taek stares hard at Chung-sook, who continues to hoot. His eyes are red. Hostile.

KI-TAEK
I'm getting fucking tired of this. A cockroach?

Cut to
→ wide.

Ki-woo looks at Bottles >> Ki-taek & Chung-sook and CUT.

CRASH! Ki-taek SWEEPS the table with his one hand and knocks over the bottle and plates.

Quick PAN LEFT.

96

Quick ZOOM IN (Post).

Ki-taek GRABS Chung-sook by her collar. Chung-sook is absolutely still.

Silence. Tension grows.

Ki-taek stares daggers at Chung-sook.

Ki-woo and Ki-jung are stunned.

KI-JUNG
Huh? What's wrong?

KI-TAEK
(starts cracking) Hee-hee...

CHUNG-SOOK
(snickering) Hahahaha...

KI-TAEK
I fooled you, didn't I?

KI-JUNG
Jesus, Dad.

Chung-sook bursts into laughter. Ki-taek seems pleased with his performance.

KI-TAEK
I fooled you too, Ki-woo? Did it look for real?

CHUNG-SOOK
If it was for real, I'd fucking kill you.

(Twisting Ki-taek's wrist 90°)

KI-WOO
Wow, you totally got me.

CHUNG-SOOK
I didn't believe him for one second.

KI-WOO
Really? It looked so real.

CHUNG-SOOK
Not in a million years. Your dad hasn't a backbone. It's such a pity.

KI-JUNG
What the hell?

Ki-jung holds up a piece of jerky she had been nibbling. It's a dog treat.

KI-JUNG
What is this? Fucking puppy.

KI-WOO
They were pretty good.

72A

KI-JUNG
Gross.

KI-WOO
They're the best.

The DOORBELL buzzes LOUDLY throughout the house.

CAMERA FIXED.

They all freeze and look at each other. Doorbell keeps on BUZZING.

KI-WOO
Who is it at this hour?

KI-TAEK
What is it?

Chung-sook scurries over to the door intercom.

A familiar round face fills the screen.
Standing in the rain, clad in black, is MOON-GWANG

CHUNG-SOOK
What the...?

KI-WOO
What's she doing here?

CHUNG-SOOK
The old housekeeper?

KI-JUNG
What's she here for?

Chung-sook's
hand

Moon-gwang presses the doorbell endlessly. It RINGS LOUDLY throughout the neighborhood.

KI-TAEK
She won't stop ringing it.

KI-JUNG
Raising a racket.

CHUNG-SOOK
(cuts in) Hold on. I'm supposed to be here.

#72A

(31) **Pan + Tilt.**

Before Ki-woo can stop her, Chung-sook presses the "speak" button.

CHUNG-SOOK
Who is it?

MOON-GWANG
Oh, hello! I'm... The madame's not in, right? I worked here for a very long time. Above the monitor there, you see a photo of 3 dogs, right? Zoonie, Berry, Foofoo.

(32)
(34)

TIGHTER than SHOTS #27 & #29.

Moon-gwang's speech is slurred – as if she had a drink or two herself.

CHUNG-SOOK
I get it, but why are you here?

(33)

MOON-GWANG
You're my successor as housekeeper, right?

#72B. "MOON-GWANG RETURNS" MANSION – FRONT GATE – NIGHT
(JEONJU FRONT GATE/GARAGE BACKLOT)

MOON-GWANG
Anyway... I'm very sorry to call on you so late. It's just that... I forgot something in the basement under the kitchen. When I left, they pushed me out so quickly... Would you let me in?

(35)

#72A. "DRINKING PARTY" MANSION – LIVING ROOM - NIGHT

(36)

Chung-sook looks at Ki-woo: *What do we do?* He has no idea.

KI-WOO
This isn't in the plan.

RACK FOCUS >> Ki-woo.

#72B. "MOON-GWANG RETURNS" MANSION – FRONT GATE – NIGHT
(JEONJU FRONT GATE/GARAGE BACKLOT)

Moon-gwang waits with her head down.

CLANG – the gate opens.

CUT TO

(37)

#73. "MOON-GWANG ENTERS" MANSION – ENTRANCE - NIGHT

Chung-sook opens the door to reveal Moon-gwang standing in the rain. She looks grotesque, with one eye heavily swollen, and eerie under the fluorescent motion-sensor light.

MOON-GWANG
Sorry for the trouble. Thank you, thank you.

#74. "WANT TO COME DOWN WITH ME?" MANSION – LIVING ROOM/KITCHEN - NIGHT

Moon-gwang drips water as she walks over to the kitchen. The living room is not visible from her vantage point.

Ki-taek, Ki-woo, and Ki-jung remain in the dark, eavesdropping on their conversation.

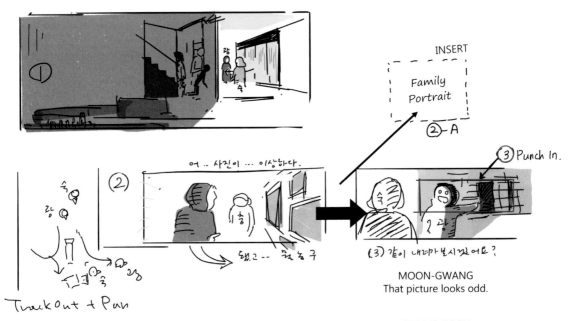

MOON-GWANG
That picture looks odd.

CHUNG-SOOK
But what did you leave below?

SHOT #2 TAIL. SHOT #3 HEAD – PUNCH IN.

MOON-GWANG
Want to come down with me?

CHUNG-SOOK
Well, just go ahead.

100

#75A. "KITCHEN FAUCET" MANSION – FRONT GATE – NIGHT (FRONT GATE/GARAGE BACK LOT)

Front gate
Set

Rain POURS in otherwise silent night. No one is there.

#75B. "KITCHEN FAUCET" MANSION – LIVING ROOM/KITCHEN NIGHT

Slow TRACK RIGHT.

RACK FOCUS:
Ki-woo >> Chung-sook.

PAN RIGHT.
TRACK IN.

CAMERA FOLLOWS Chung-sook until she STOPS and hesitates.

CAMERA CONTINUES to move FORWARD into the darkness.

It's been a while since Moon-gwang went down to the storage room. Chung-sook is worried. She gets up from the dining chair.

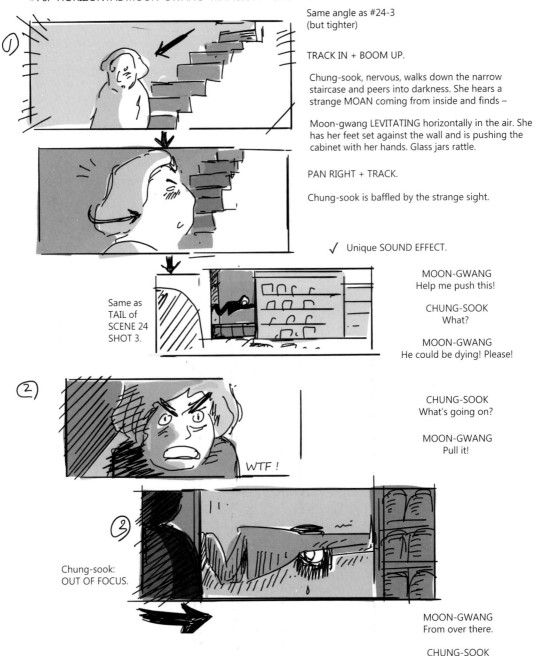

Same angle as #24-3
(but tighter)

TRACK IN + BOOM UP.

Chung-sook, nervous, walks down the narrow
staircase and peers into darkness. She hears a
strange MOAN coming from inside and finds –

Moon-gwang LEVITATING horizontally in the air. She
has her feet set against the wall and is pushing the
cabinet with her hands. Glass jars rattle.

PAN RIGHT + TRACK.

Chung-sook is baffled by the strange sight.

✓ Unique SOUND EFFECT.

Same as
TAIL of
SCENE 24
SHOT 3.

MOON-GWANG
Help me push this!

CHUNG-SOOK
What?

MOON-GWANG
He could be dying! Please!

CHUNG-SOOK
What's going on?

MOON-GWANG
Pull it!

WTF !

Chung-sook:
OUT OF FOCUS.

MOON-GWANG
From over there.

CHUNG-SOOK
What?

④ LOW

ARGHHHHH!
ARGHHHHH...

Moon-gwang hard at work.
Shot from below.

⑤

PAN +
TILT DOWN.

어 이게
끼여서
그런?

배내는 순간 드르륵 – 밀리는
변장

Chung-sook has no idea what's going on but joins Moon-gwang to push the cabinet.

CHUNG-SOOK
Wait. This might be the problem.

PAN RIGHT +
TILT DOWN.

Chung-sook pulls something wedged under the shelf. It smoothly slides to the side.

The shelf rolls and Moon-gwang, who had been pushing it with all her might, CRASHES AND ROLLS onto the floor. PAN LEFT and TILT DOWN to FOLLOW Moon-gwang as Chung-sook FRAMES IN.

CHUNG-SOOK
Are you okay?

TRACK IN to Chung-sook's face.

PAN and TILT to FOLLOW Chung-sook astonished by a DARK STEEL DOOR behind the shelf.

Ki-woo, curious, creeps down the stairs
and is surprised.

⑥A
optional

기우. 놀란다. → 문 보고

⑥
end
⑦

Could be
connected
as a PAN.

CAMERA
TRACK RIGHT
+
RACK FOCUS:
>> Steel Gate.

⑦

꽃들

⑧A

Moon-gwang, staggering, slides
the shelf and then opens a gate.

PAN LEFT and TILT UP to
reveal Ki-jung and Ki-taek
behind Ki-woo, both stunned.

PAN LEFT
+
TILT UP.

Ki-taek   Moon-gwang

STAGGER

"RUSH" – STEADICAM.

We don't know it's STEADICAM until it
FOLLOWS Chung-sook from behind.

Moon-gwang hurries inside. Chung-sook shakes it off and follows down the dark staircase.

Stitch together via VFX.

울며 쓰다듬다가...
절벽 꼭는 문광

MOON-GWANG
Honey!

MOON-GWANG
Honey!

We get a glimpse of Moon-gwang over Chung-sook. She makes a RIGHT and STAGGERS downstairs. Chung-sook continues to FOLLOW.

Chung-sook once down the stairs makes another RIGHT, but then stops. She TURNS AROUND to discover Moon-gwang and Geun-sae.

Moon-gwang strokes CRYING Geun-sae and feeds him a baby bottle.

STEADICAM slowly moves FORWARD in HIGH ANGLE, FOLLOWING Chung-sook who is flabbergasted at the sight.

GEUN-SAE
Honey, I'm fine.

MOON-GWANG
How many days has it been?

Moon-gwang uses light from her cellphone to check up on Geun-sae – checking his pupils and etc.

On Moon-gwang & Geun-sae:
SHOT #10 – TRACK IN
SHOTS #12 & #14 – CAMERA FIXED

MOON-GWANG
It's okay. She's a nice woman. She let me in. There was an iron plate, for grilling meat. It was wedged under the shelf.

GEUN-SAE
So that's why. I couldn't open it from the inside.

CHUNG-SOOK
What's going on here?

MOON-GWANG
I know you must be startled. I would be too in this situation. But as two fellow workers... Right, Chung-sook?

On Chung-sook:
SHOT #9 – TRACK OUT
SHOTS #11 & #13 – CAMERA FIXED

The underground bunker COMES TO FOCUS as Chung-sook turns to her back and takes in the space.

CHUNG-SOOK
How do you know my name?

MOON-GWANG
To be honest, I'm still texting with the boy Da-song. I knew they were going camping, so I came today. I wanted to speak to you alone.

#77

⑮

Same size as
SHOTS 11 – 14.

Tilt Up

⑯

⑰

⑱

P&T

Moon-gwang shows off a pair of wire cutters.

MOON-GWANG
Don't worry, Chung-sook. I cut the wire on the
CCTV by the gate.

CAMERA TILTS UP:

MOON-GWANG
Nobody knows I came. Isn't that good, sis?

CHUNG-SOOK
Don't call me sis!

Ki-taek, Ki-woo, and Ki-jung come down
the stairs, shocked as they look at the space.

CHUNG-SOOK
Aren't you older than me?

MOON-GWANG
74, year of the tiger.

MOON-GWANG
My name is Moon-gwang. This is my hubby, Oh
Geun-sae. Say hello, honey.

CAMERA PAN and TILT to Geun-sae, who
finishes off the bottle and gives it to Moon-
gwang.

MOON-GWANG
Good job.

Moon-gwang takes out a banana from her
pocket. She peels it and feeds it to him.

CHUNG-SOOK
So you'd steal food every day while working in the kitchen. Feeding your husband.

MOON-GWANG
Not at all! I bought all his food with my salary. That's so unfair!

– – – – – – – –

Quick PAN + TILT UP.

Same as TAIL of SHOT #20.

CHUNG-SOOK
But how long has your husband been down here?

MOON-GWANG
Hold on a sec. 4 years?

CHUNG-SOOK
You gotta be kidding me.

slow
Tilt Up.
(RACK FOCUS.)

★ 대사배열 change

GEUN-SAE
4 years, 3 months, and 17 days.

MOON-GWANG
Right, it's June now. Four years ago when Mr. Namgoong moved to Paris, in the time before Mr. Park's family moved in, I brought my husband down here.

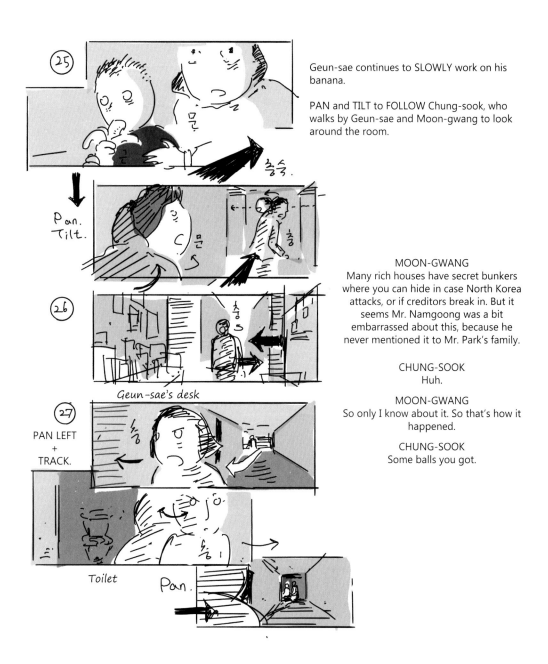

Geun-sae continues to SLOWLY work on his banana.

PAN and TILT to FOLLOW Chung-sook, who walks by Geun-sae and Moon-gwang to look around the room.

MOON-GWANG
Many rich houses have secret bunkers where you can hide in case North Korea attacks, or if creditors break in. But it seems Mr. Namgoong was a bit embarrassed about this, because he never mentioned it to Mr. Park's family.

CHUNG-SOOK
Huh.

MOON-GWANG
So only I know about it. So that's how it happened.

CHUNG-SOOK
Some balls you got.

Geun-sae's desk

PAN LEFT
+
TRACK.

Toilet

Pan.

Slow TRACK IN as Chung-sook
approaches from the end of the hallway.

CHUNG-SOOK
But now that I know, I've no choice but to
call the police!

Moon-gwang drops to her knees.

Geun-sae
still eating
banana

③¹

Moon-gwang starts begging.

MOON-GWANG
No, please, sis! As fellow
members of the needy,
please don't.

SHOT #30

SHOT #31

CHUNG-SOOK
I'm not needy!

MOON-GWANG
But we're needy! We've no house,
no money, only debts!

CHUNG-SOOK
What's that got to do with me?

On underlined line
PAN RIGHT + TILT UP >>
Geun-sae still working on his banana, shaking his legs.

Chung-
sook

Moon-
gwang

Geun-sae

TRACK RIGHT.
RACK FOCUS.

MOON-GWANG
Even after 4 years of hiding, those debt collectors
won't give up. They're still searching for him,
threatening to stab him.

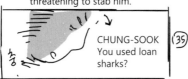

CHUNG-SOOK
You used loan
sharks?

Moon is
embarrassed
to answer

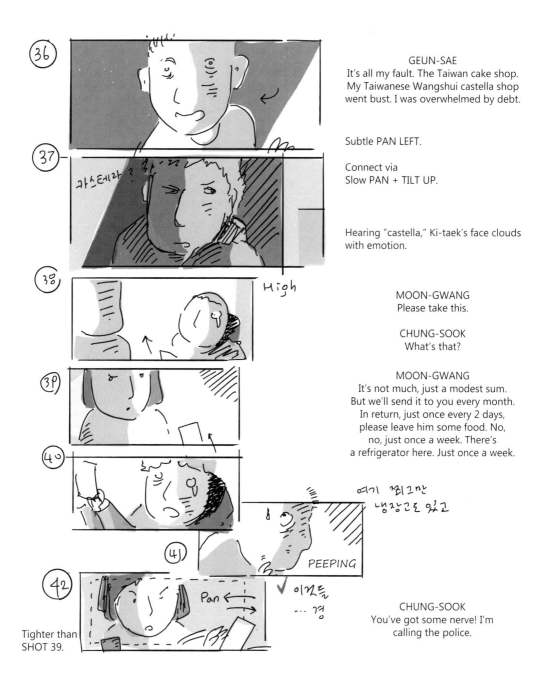

GEUN-SAE
It's all my fault. The Taiwan cake shop.
My Taiwanese Wangshui castella shop
went bust. I was overwhelmed by debt.

Subtle PAN LEFT.

Connect via
Slow PAN + TILT UP.

Hearing "castella," Ki-taek's face clouds
with emotion.

MOON-GWANG
Please take this.

CHUNG-SOOK
What's that?

MOON-GWANG
It's not much, just a modest sum.
But we'll send it to you every month.
In return, just once every 2 days,
please leave him some food. No,
no, just once a week. There's
a refrigerator here. Just once a week.

CHUNG-SOOK
You've got some nerve! I'm
calling the police.

Tighter than
SHOT 39.

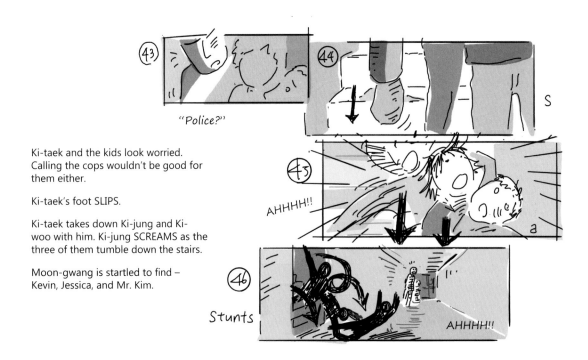

"Police?"

Ki-taek and the kids look worried. Calling the cops wouldn't be good for them either.

Ki-taek's foot SLIPS.

Ki-taek takes down Ki-jung and Ki-woo with him. Ki-jung SCREAMS as the three of them tumble down the stairs.

Moon-gwang is startled to find – Kevin, Jessica, and Mr. Kim.

MOON-GWANG
What's this?

PAN RIGHT.
FOCUS to Geun-sae.

GEUN-SAE
Who is that?

MOON-GWANG
Wait... Jessica? Mr. Kim? What the hell?

Moon-gwang puts the pieces together as she takes out her CELLPHONE.

RACK FOCUS.

As Ki-taek scrambles to get up, he accidentally steps on Ki-woo's foot.

KI-WOO
Dad! My foot.

Ki-woo realizes what he had just done. Chung-sook and Ki-jung freeze. Ki-woo turns his head to find –

Moon-gwang RECORDING everything on her cellphone.

MOON-GWANG
So that's what it is.

Moon-gwang plays back the footage she just shot.

KI-WOO (VIDEO)
Dad! My foot.

The picture and sound are flawless. Ki-woo is done for.

Playback (including the sound).

Everything comes together for Moon-gwang.

MOON-GWANG
Are you some family of charlatans?

Raw RACK FOCUS

SHOT #55

KI-WOO
Let's talk things over.

CHUNG-SOOK
So, sis...

SHOT #57

SHOT #56

MOON-GWANG
I knew something was off when Yoon was fired for no reason.

MOON-GWANG
SHOT #58
Don't fucking call me sis, you filthy bitch! I'm gonna send this video to the madame, how about that?

Moon-gwang's finger hovers over the "send" button.

Pulls up the screen

113

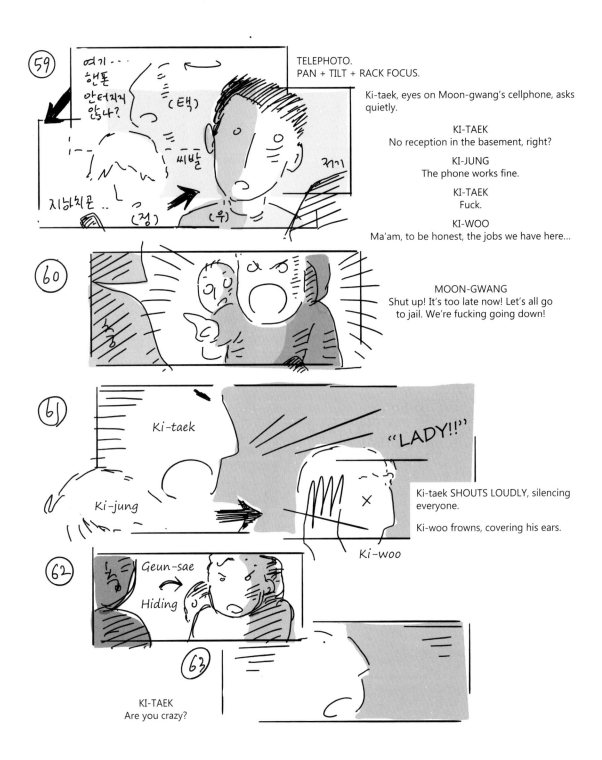

TELEPHOTO.
PAN + TILT + RACK FOCUS.

Ki-taek, eyes on Moon-gwang's cellphone, asks quietly.

KI-TAEK
No reception in the basement, right?

KI-JUNG
The phone works fine.

KI-TAEK
Fuck.

KI-WOO
Ma'am, to be honest, the jobs we have here...

MOON-GWANG
Shut up! It's too late now! Let's all go to jail. We're fucking going down!

"LADY!!"

Ki-taek SHOUTS LOUDLY, silencing everyone.

Ki-woo frowns, covering his ears.

KI-TAEK
Are you crazy?

KI-TAEK
If they see that video, Mr. Park and his wife will be so shocked! What did those nice people ever do wrong? Why do this to them?

MOON-GWANG
What...

KI-TAEK
Erase it! Once you erase it, then I may consider your demands.

Ki-taek seems to be in his own world, as no one buys his performance one bit – his argument fails to convince anyone.

MOON-GWANG
What's wrong with your husband?

CHUNG-SOOK
I apologize on his behalf. Sis, why don't we all calm down.

Moon-gwang pulls out her phone and makes a threat.

MOON-GWANG
Stop right there! Or I'll push the "send" button.

TRACK IN.

The Kims flinch. They slowly back off.

MOON-GWANG
Follow me. Let's go up, honey. Time for you to get some fresh air!

GEUN-SAE
Sounds good.

뒷결음질 춤수 & 식구들

High

MOON-GWANG
Don't try anything funny. If you move an inch out of my sight, I'm hitting the "send" button!

S # 77
End

① CAMERA FIXED.

It's pouring outside. Geun-sae lies facedown on the large couch; on top of him sits Moon-gwang, giving him a massage.

GEUN-SAE
Honey.

② CAMERA FIXED.

GEUN-SAE
Honey, this "send" button is like a missile launcher.

MOON-GWANG
What do you mean, honey?

③ PAN RIGHT.
RACK FOCUS.

GEUN-SAE
If we threaten to push it, those people can't do anything. It's like a North Korean rocket. A North Korean missile button!

④ Moon-gwang, hearing "North Korean" comment, sits up straight like a military cadet.

MOON-GWANG
Today our beloved Great Leader Kim Jong-un, after witnessing the charlatan family video, was unable to contain his shock and fury at their wicked, despicable provocation!

#78

HIGH ANGLE.

GEUN-SAE
I've missed your jokes, honey!

The Kims stare at them incredulously.

MOON-GWANG
Therefore our Great Leader, in this age of denuclearization, has commanded that the nation's last remaining nuclear warhead—

MOON-GWANG
—be driven down the throats of this wicked family!

GEUN-SAE
No one can imitate North Korean news anchors like you!

MOON-GWANG
With their stinking guts serving as the last nuclear graveyard, our Dear Leader's wish to denuclearize and bring world peace can...

She turns to the Kims.

MOON-GWANG
What are you looking at?

SHOTS 7, 9, 11:
Aim same
direction.

MOON-GWANG
Hands in the air, fuckers! Higher!

CELLPHONE SCREEN:
The Kims look down.

Moon-gwang starts recording more,
panning from the Kims to the scattered
food and booze bottles on the floor.

MOON-GWANG
You scumbag family. Is that all you can
think to do, drink yourselves stupid?

MOON-GWANG
In this home suffused with Mr.
Namgoong's creative spirit?

We hear RAIN POURING DOWN
in the background.

GEUN-SAE
It's a great living room. It is so
enchanting when you look out the
garden from here on a sunny day.
Right, honey?

#78B. "ROYAL MILK TEA" MANSION – LIVING ROOM - DAY

Living room. Outside is the garden on a sunny day.

MOON-GWANG
Absolutely. Park would be at work, the kids at the school, Madame would be out shopping. The house would be quiet. You would come up and we would have tea together.

GEUN-SAE
Yes, Royal Milk Tea.

MOON-GWANG
We would enjoy Rachmaninoff in their Bluetooth speaker...

How we'd enjoy the view, and music...

THUMP THUMP

Moon-gwang and Geun-sae turn their heads when they hear HEAVY FOOTSTEPS.

#78A. "NORTH KOREAN MISSILE" MANSION – LIVING ROOM - NIGHT

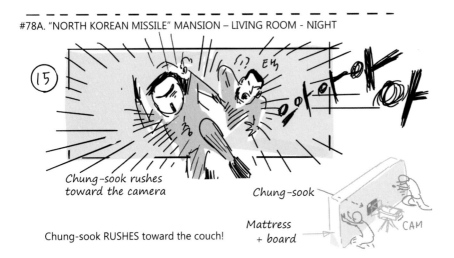

Chung-sook rushes toward the camera

Chung-sook RUSHES toward the couch!

Chung-sook

Mattress + board

CAM

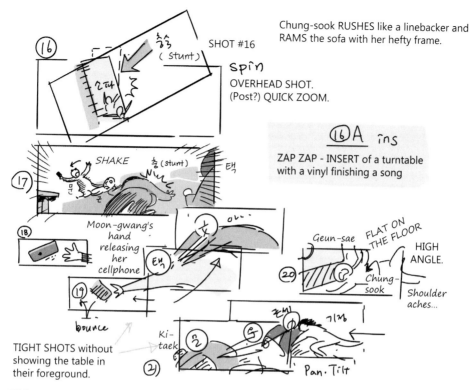

SHOT #16

Chung-sook RUSHES like a linebacker and RAMS the sofa with her hefty frame.

(stunt)

spin

OVERHEAD SHOT.
(Post?) QUICK ZOOM.

16A ins

ZAP ZAP - INSERT of a turntable with a vinyl finishing a song

SHAKE (stunt)

Moon-gwang's hand releasing her cellphone

Geun-sae FLAT ON THE FLOOR HIGH ANGLE.

Chung-sook Shoulder aches...

bounce

Ki-taek

Pan. Tilt

TIGHT SHOTS without showing the table in their foreground.

SHOTS #17 - #22: 48 fps

SHOT #17   Moon-gwang OFF BALANCE.

SHOT #18   Moon-gwang DROPS her phone.

SHOT #19   Ki-taek DIVES after the phone, and so does Moon-gwang.

SHOT #20   Chung-sook sprawled on the floor (her shoulder in pain).

SHOT #21   Ki-woo LUNGES toward Moon-gwang. Geun-sae goes after Ki-woo. Ki-jung goes after Geun-sae.

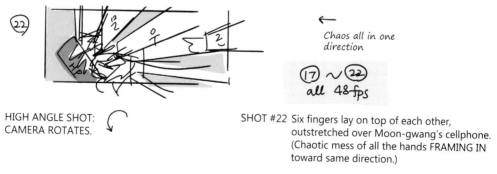

← Chaos all in one direction

17 ~ 22
all 48 fps

HIGH ANGLE SHOT:
CAMERA ROTATES.

SHOT #22   Six fingers lay on top of each other, outstretched over Moon-gwang's cellphone. (Chaotic mess of all the hands FRAMING IN toward same direction.)

#79. "MELEE SEEN FROM THE OUTSIDE" MANSION – GARDEN – NIGHT

The heavy rain DROWNS OUT the sound. OUTSIDE POV:

Through the thick curtain of rain, we see six people, none of whom actually live in the house, chaotically brawling inside.

A surreal sight.

RAIN POURING

Ki-jung rushes to the couch

#80. "PEACH BAG" + #81. "PEACH ATROCITY" MANSION – LIVING ROOM > KITCHEN > LIVING ROOM

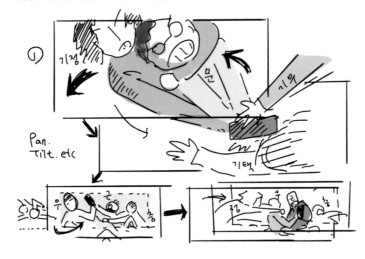

Ki-woo pries the phone away while Ki-jung chokes Moon-gwang from behind.

Geun-sae, despite Chung-sook holding him down, tries to take back the phone.

Moon-gwang swings her elbow to shake off Ki-jung.

Ki-jung rushes to Geun-sae.

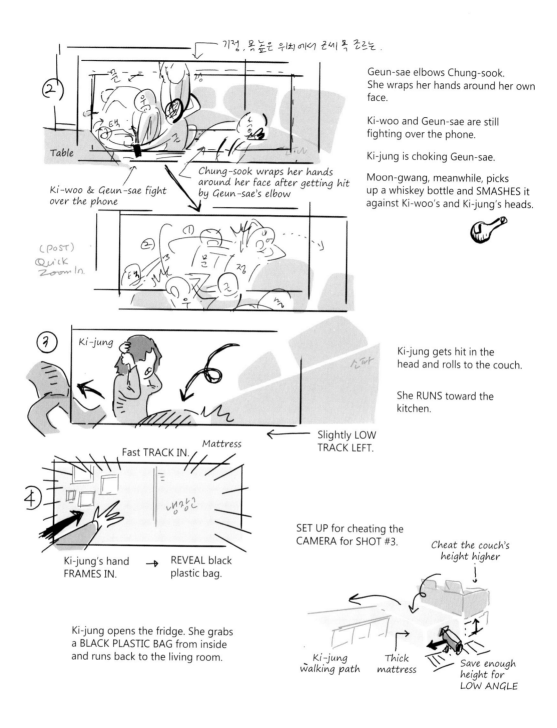

기정, 몸높은 위치에서 근세 목 조르는.

② Table

Ki-woo & Geun-sae fight over the phone

Chung-sook wraps her hands around her face after getting hit by Geun-sae's elbow

Geun-sae elbows Chung-sook. She wraps her hands around her own face.

Ki-woo and Geun-sae are still fighting over the phone.

Ki-jung is choking Geun-sae.

Moon-gwang, meanwhile, picks up a whiskey bottle and SMASHES it against Ki-woo's and Ki-jung's heads.

(POST) Quick Zoom In.

③ Ki-jung

Ki-jung gets hit in the head and rolls to the couch.

She RUNS toward the kitchen.

Slightly LOW TRACK LEFT.

④ Fast TRACK IN. Mattress

냉장고

Ki-jung's hand FRAMES IN. → REVEAL black plastic bag.

SET UP for cheating the CAMERA for SHOT #3.

Cheat the couch's height higher

Ki-jung opens the fridge. She grabs a BLACK PLASTIC BAG from inside and runs back to the living room.

Ki-jung walking path

Thick mattress

Save enough height for LOW ANGLE

CAMERA TRACK LEFT (+ ZOOM OUT in post) FOLLOWING Ki-jung rushing back.

MELEE CONTINUES: Moon-gwang grasping onto the phone; Chung-sook choking Moon-gwang from behind; Ki-woo trying with all his might to pry away the phone; Ki-taek brawling with Geun-sae.

Ki-jung flips the black plastic bag and dumps a dozen PEACHES onto Moon-gwang. She SCREAMS!

TRACK LEFT
+
+ ZOOM OUT in post.

Ki-jung picks up a peach and SQUASHES it against Moon-gwang's face.

AHHH! - Moon-gwang sticks her tongue out and coughs violently, rolling on the floor, clutching her swollen throat.

OVERHEAD SHOT.

SPIN
+
TRACK RIGHT.

Ki-jung's hand + peach

Peaches roll down

Ki-woo's hand comes in, SNATCHING the phone. Ki-woo, finally, gets the phone!

Ki-taek also SUBDUES Geun-sae.

KI-TAEK
Delete it!

Ki-woo is about to delete it when the
PHONE begins to RING throughout
the entire house.

BOOM DOWN + TILT UP.

Chung-sook looks around, following
the sound until she finds a phone
sitting in a corner by the bar.

Quick BOOM UP following
Chung-sook getting up.

BOOM DOWN
+
Slow TILT UP
as the phone rings.

Phone rings set as
audio system in the
background

RING RING

----> Spots the
phone

Chung-sook sits up

Repeat quick
BOOM UP.

Chung-sook heads
to the phone

Bar in the corner

Fast TRACK IN.

Phone

CHUNG-SOOK
Hello?

YEON-KYO (V.O.)
Why didn't you pick up the phone?

CAMERA FIXED.

Rain batters the Mercedes. Da-song has taken Da-hye's Bluetooth headset. He is in the back with his eyes closed and pouting.

Yeon-kyo glances back at her son from the passenger seat.

YEON-KYO
Listen, do you know how to make ram-don?

CHUNG-SOOK (V.O.)
Ram-don?

YEON-KYO
Da-song likes ram-don more than anything. If you boil the water now, the timing will be perfect. There's sirloin in the fridge, add that too.

Slight PAN?
+
RACK FOCUS.

YEON-KYO
My god, what a disaster. The river overflowed and everyone was packing their tents, but Da-song was crying and refusing to go home. Anyway, ram-don as soon as we walk in, okay?

CHUNG-SOOK (V.O.)
Then you're almost here?

YEON-KYO
8 minutes, according to the GPS.

CHUNG-SOOK (V.O.)
You arrive in 8 minutes...

YEON-KYO
Start boiling the water right away! You're the best!

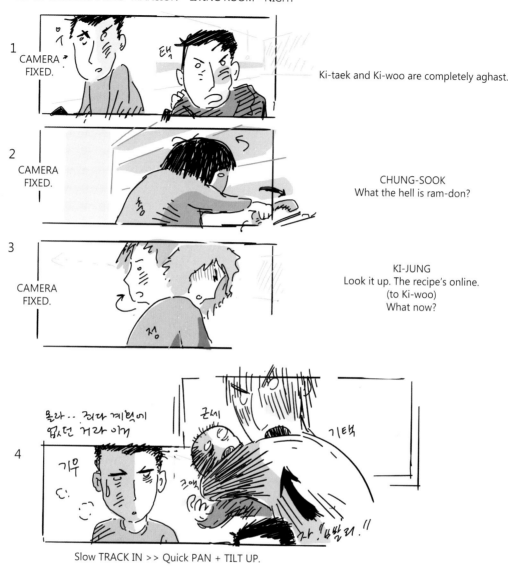

1 CAMERA FIXED.

Ki-taek and Ki-woo are completely aghast.

2 CAMERA FIXED.

CHUNG-SOOK
What the hell is ram-don?

3 CAMERA FIXED.

KI-JUNG
Look it up. The recipe's online.
(to Ki-woo)
What now?

4

Slow TRACK IN >> Quick PAN + TILT UP.

KI-WOO
I don't know. This wasn't part of the plan.

ARGH! - Geun-sae howls as Ki-taek twists his arm.

KI-TAEK
Hurry!

The Kims jump into action upon Ki-taek's order.

Chung-sook heads to the kitchen, cellphone in her hand.

CAMERA TRACKS RIGHT following Chung-sook.

Ki-taek drags Geun-sae toward the basement while Ki-woo helps Ki-jung pull up Moon-gwang.

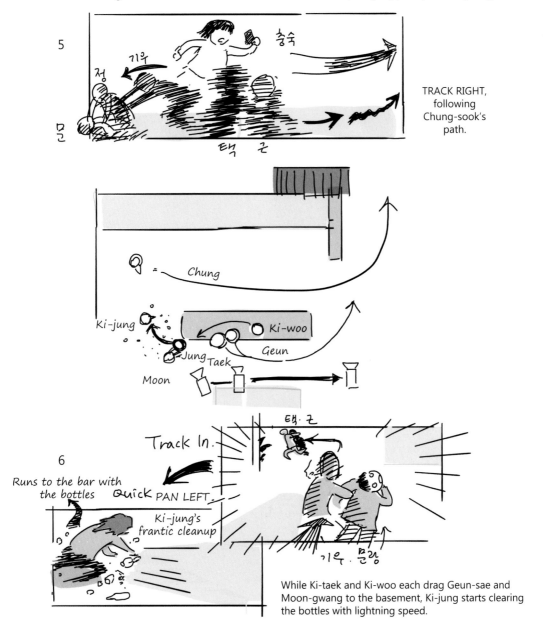

5

TRACK RIGHT, following Chung-sook's path.

Chung

Ki-jung
Ki-woo
Geun
Jung Taek
Moon

6

Track In.

Runs to the bar with the bottles Quick PAN LEFT.

Ki-jung's frantic cleanup

While Ki-taek and Ki-woo each drag Geun-sae and Moon-gwang to the basement, Ki-jung starts clearing the bottles with lightning speed.

Chung-sook is focused on getting the ram-don ready. She looks up the recipe while putting water on the stove. She rips open two packs of noodles – Jajang Ramen and Instant Udon.

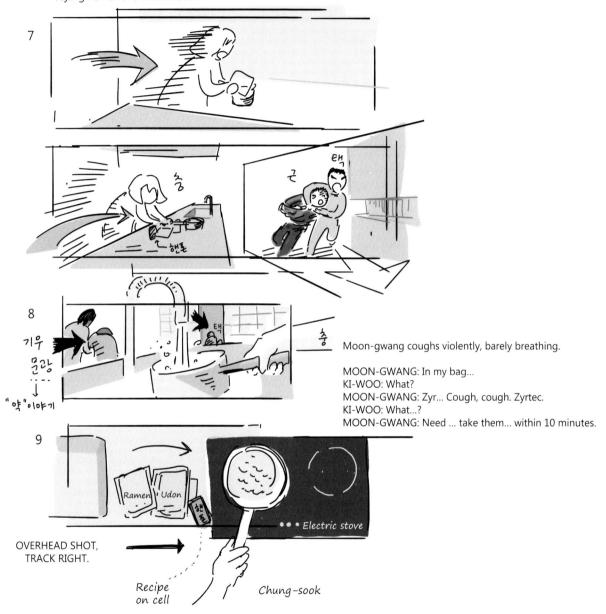

Moon-gwang coughs violently, barely breathing.

MOON-GWANG: In my bag...
KI-WOO: What?
MOON-GWANG: Zyr... Cough, cough. Zyrtec.
KI-WOO: What...?
MOON-GWANG: Need ... take them... within 10 minutes.

OVERHEAD SHOT, TRACK RIGHT.

Recipe on cell

Chung-sook

#84A. "DRAGGING DOWN MOON-GWANG" MANSION - BASEMENT

#84 ①

Jars of plum extract

Ki-woo & Moon-gwang

STEADICAM FORWARD.

#84B. "TIE UP GEUN-SAE" MANSION – SECRET ROOM

1

STEADICAM BACK
(or HANDHELD).

KI-WOO
Dad, I can't drag her any further.

Moon-gwang slumps down. Ki-woo is helpless.

PAN LEFT 90°
on Ki-woo shouting.

Ki-taek wildly drags Geun-sae down the stairs into the secret room.

2

백그라운드 B

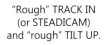

"Rough" TRACK IN
(or STEADICAM)
and "rough" TILT UP.

Ki-taek SLAMS DOWN Geun-sae onto the floor. He RIPS OFF a cable cord from the wall.

GEUN-SAE
You don't have to do this. Why don't we all sit down and talk.

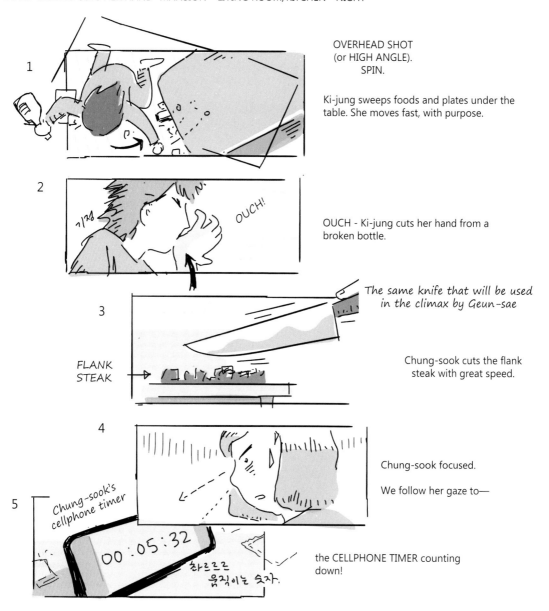

1

OVERHEAD SHOT
(or HIGH ANGLE).
SPIN.

Ki-jung sweeps foods and plates under the table. She moves fast, with purpose.

2

OUCH!

OUCH - Ki-jung cuts her hand from a broken bottle.

3

The same knife that will be used in the climax by Geun-sae

FLANK
STEAK

Chung-sook cuts the flank steak with great speed.

4

Chung-sook focused.

We follow her gaze to—

5

Chung-sook's cellphone timer

00:05:32

the CELLPHONE TIMER counting down!

#84B. "TIE UP GEUN-SAE" MANSION – SECRET ROOM

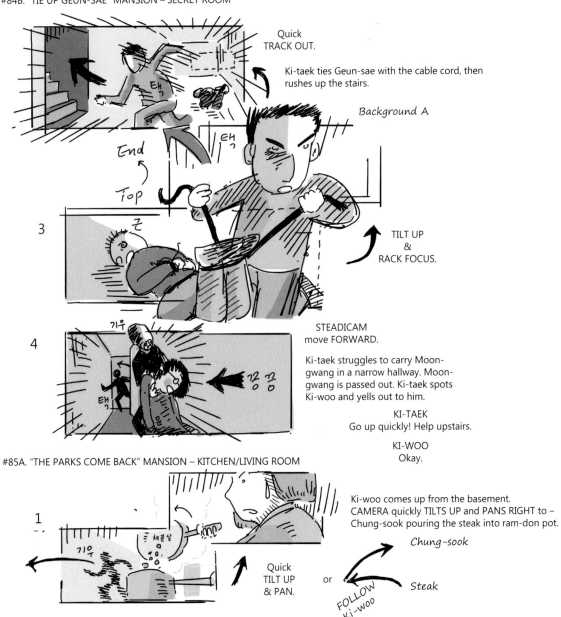

Quick
TRACK OUT.

Ki-taek ties Geun-sae with the cable cord, then
rushes up the stairs.

Background A

End

Top

3

TILT UP
&
RACK FOCUS.

4

STEADICAM
move FORWARD.

Ki-taek struggles to carry Moon-
gwang in a narrow hallway. Moon-
gwang is passed out. Ki-taek spots
Ki-woo and yells out to him.

KI-TAEK
Go up quickly! Help upstairs.

KI-WOO
Okay.

#85A. "THE PARKS COME BACK" MANSION – KITCHEN/LIVING ROOM

1

Ki-woo comes up from the basement.
CAMERA quickly TILTS UP and PANS RIGHT to –
Chung-sook pouring the steak into ram-don pot.

Chung-sook

Quick
TILT UP   or
& PAN.

FOLLOW
Ki-woo   Steak

132

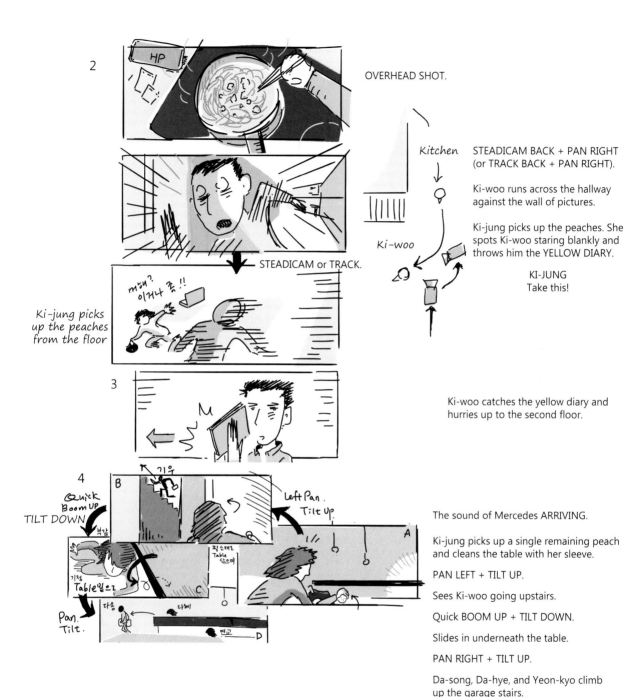

2

OVERHEAD SHOT.

Kitchen

Ki-woo

STEADICAM BACK + PAN RIGHT
(or TRACK BACK + PAN RIGHT).

Ki-woo runs across the hallway
against the wall of pictures.

Ki-jung picks up the peaches. She
spots Ki-woo staring blankly and
throws him the YELLOW DIARY.

KI-JUNG
Take this!

STEADICAM or TRACK.

Ki-jung picks
up the peaches
from the floor

3

Ki-woo catches the yellow diary and
hurries up to the second floor.

4

Quick
Boom UP
TILT DOWN

Left Pan.
Tilt Up.

Pan.
Tilt.

The sound of Mercedes ARRIVING.

Ki-jung picks up a single remaining peach
and cleans the table with her sleeve.

PAN LEFT + TILT UP.

Sees Ki-woo going upstairs.

Quick BOOM UP + TILT DOWN.

Slides in underneath the table.

PAN RIGHT + TILT UP.

Da-song, Da-hye, and Yeon-kyo climb
up the garage stairs.

TRACK IN.

Chung-sook greets the Parks from far inside the kitchen.

> CHUNG-SOOK
> Welcome home!

Yeon-kyo, running after Da-song, points to the kitchen.

> YEON-KYO
> Da-song, look! Let's eat ram-don!

Da-song walks up the stairs.

Da-hye, also pissed, comes up behind and snatches her own headset from her baby brother. She STOMPS ahead of him.

#85B. "MOON-GWANG WAKES UP" MANSION – SECRET ROOM

TRACK IN
+
PAN RIGHT.

Ki-taek fumbles as he tries to tie up Moon-gwang.

> YEON-KYO (V.O.)
> *Da-song! Da-song!*

Moon-gwang suddenly wakes up, hearing the madame's voice from a far distance.

#86. "UNDER THE BED" MANSION – 2ND FLOOR – DA-HYE'S ROOM - NIGHT

HIGH ANGLE

Da-hye FOOTSTEPS
Door OPENING

Quick

PAN RIGHT.

Da-hye's bed

shit
fuck

PAN LEFT again.

Quickly hides
under the bed

Ki-woo closes the box of journals and puts
the combination lock back on.

Da-hye walks inside and THROWS herself on the
bed. Ki-woo quickly hides under the bed.

Da-hye turns up the volume and MUSIC blares out
of her headset.

Music comes out of the headset

#87. "MOON-GWANG GETS UP" MANSION – SECRET ROOM

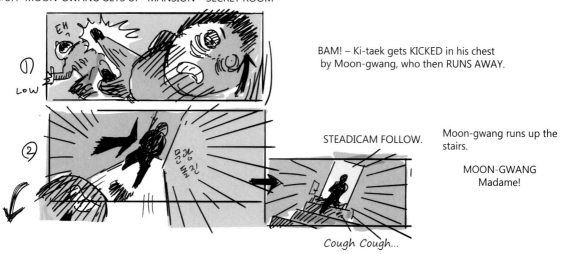

LOW

BAM! – Ki-taek gets KICKED in his chest
by Moon-gwang, who then RUNS AWAY.

STEADICAM FOLLOW.

Moon-gwang runs up the
stairs.

MOON-GWANG
Madame!

Cough Cough...

#88A. "CHUNG-SOOK KICKS" MANSION – KITCHEN

1

FOOTSTEPS!!

Quick Tilt Up.

PAN LEFT.
RACK FOCUS.

Chung-sook pours the finished ram-don into a fancy plate.

CAMERA quick TILT UP
+ PAN LEFT + RACK FOCUS.

FOOTSTEPS! Chung-sook swiftly turns her head to the basement door.

TRACK RIGHT.

2

아...
숙제마 진짜

냉장고

연교

TRACK RIGHT FOLLOWING --

Yeon-kyo, who heads to the fridge. In the background:

Chung-sook kicks
Moon-gwang
down the stairs.

1

Concussion ——
impact

Ki-taek's reaction,
running after her

#88B. "CONCUSSION" MANSION - BASEMENT

Moon-gwang TUMBLES DOWN the stairs and SLAMS her head HARD into the wall at the end of the stairs.

PAN RIGHT to --

Ki-taek is stunned.

#88A. "CHUNG-SOOK KICKS" MANSION – KITCHEN

3

Quick PAN + TILT.

End

Top

Match to the fall →

off

Moon-gwang's fall MATCHES to Chung-sook setting the plate on the table.

PAN RIGHT + TILT UP to --

YEON-KYO: Why don't you just eat the ram-don?
CHUNG-SOOK: Shall I?
YEON-KYO: No, wait. I can give it to my husband. There's sirloin in here.

Chung-sook looks toward the basement.

PAN LEFT + TILT UP to --

YEON-KYO: What's taking him so long?

2   #88B. "CONCUSSION" MANSION - BASEMENT

High Angle

Moon-gwang lies unconscious with her head resting against the wall. Ki-taek drags her.

#89A. "SHUTTING THE VALVE – MANSION - BASEMENT

1

Ki-taek pulls Moon-gwang's body to the staircase that leads to the secret room.

Ki-taek tries to slide the shelf back, to no avail. He spots a valve.

2

Ki-taek turns the valve to slide back the shelf.

He HEARS a SONG coming from down the bunker.

1

#89B. "GEUN-SAE BANGS THE SWITCHES"
MANSION – SECRET BASEMENT

GEUN-SAE
Returning after a day's work... I love you so much, Mr. Park! Home from the office, Mr. Park is off duty now. Returning after a day's work....
I love you so much, Mr. Park!

Geun-sae sings to the tune of "Back from Vietnam..."

PAN RIGHT to --

Geun-sae, arms still tied, stops singing and looks up above.

KI-TAEK: What are you doing?
GEUN-SAE: Shut up!

Geun-sae returns to staring above.

2

Loud DONG-IK'S FOOTSTEPS heard from above

LOW. Zoom In

LOW ANGLE. ZOOM IN to --

Tall open space right above Geun-sae.
It's the stairway that connects from the garage to the living room.

We hear Dong-ik's FOOTSTEPS climbing the stairs and Geun-sae bangs on the switches in front of him with his head.

GEUN-SAE: Mr. Park!

138

#90A. "DONG-IK MOTION-SENSOR LIGHT" MANSION - BASEMENT

1

As Dong-ik walks up from the garage, light #1 right above him LIGHTS UP!

Dong-ik

#89B. "GEUN-SAE BANGS THE SWITCHES"
MANSION – SECRET BASEMENT

Geun-sae BANGS his head on switch #2.

1

Light #2 comes on (cheat their placement)

2

#90A. "DONG-IK MOTION-SENSOR LIGHT"
MANSION - BASEMENT

CAMERA FOLLOWS
Dong-ik climbing up the stairs
(almost as if Ki-jung's POV from
underneath the table).

3

Ki-jung watches the scene from under the table.

#90B. "GEUN-SAE BANGS THE SWITCHES"
MANSION – SECRET BASEMENT

TELEPHOTO.

Geun-sae raises his heel and BANGS his head to switch #3.

GEUN-SAE: Thank you!

He has been lighting them up from the beginning.

2

4

Light #3 comes on.

YEON-KYO
Honey, do you want some ram-don?

DONG-IK
No, I'm tired. I'm going to take a shower.

1

KI-TAEK
What are you doing?

GEUN-SAE
Why are you staring. Shut up!

2

Geun-sae turns his head and looks at
magazine pages with Dong-ik on their
covers pasted on the wall.

GEUN-SAE
Mr. Park, you feed me and house me.
Respect!

3

TELEPHOTO.

KI-TAEK
You do this everyday?

PAN RIGHT (+TRACK?).

4

GEUN-SAE
Sure, I even send whole sentences
to thank him.

5

TELEPHOTO.
RACK FOCUS.

big close up.

TAP TA-TAP. Geun-sae sends "ㄱ" in morse
code using his forehead.

GEUN-SAE
Someone of your age should know it.

MORSE CODE – Geun-sae has written on
the wall most-often-used consonants in his
handwriting

140

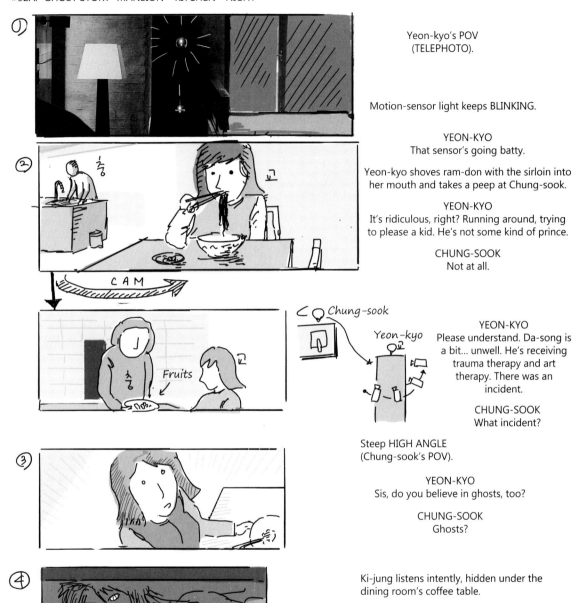

Yeon-kyo's POV
(TELEPHOTO).

Motion-sensor light keeps BLINKING.

YEON-KYO
That sensor's going batty.

Yeon-kyo shoves ram-don with the sirloin into her mouth and takes a peep at Chung-sook.

YEON-KYO
It's ridiculous, right? Running around, trying to please a kid. He's not some kind of prince.

CHUNG-SOOK
Not at all.

YEON-KYO
Please understand. Da-song is a bit... unwell. He's receiving trauma therapy and art therapy. There was an incident.

CHUNG-SOOK
What incident?

Steep HIGH ANGLE
(Chung-sook's POV).

YEON-KYO
Sis, do you believe in ghosts, too?

CHUNG-SOOK
Ghosts?

Ki-jung listens intently, hidden under the dining room's coffee table.

YEON-KYO (V.O.)
Da-song saw a ghost in the house when he was in 1st grade.

Under the dining room's coffee table

141

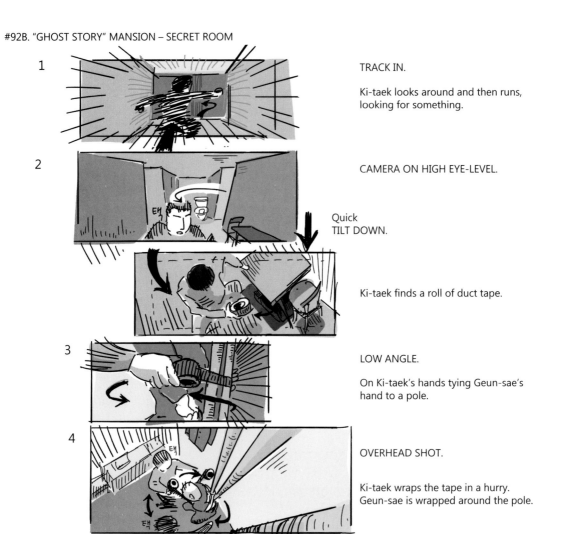

1

TRACK IN.

Ki-taek looks around and then runs, looking for something.

2

CAMERA ON HIGH EYE-LEVEL.

Quick
TILT DOWN.

Ki-taek finds a roll of duct tape.

3

LOW ANGLE.

On Ki-taek's hands tying Geun-sae's hand to a pole.

4

OVERHEAD SHOT.

Ki-taek wraps the tape in a hurry. Geun-sae is wrapped around the pole.

5

Fridge

PAN LEFT.
TILT DOWN.
BOOM UP.

6

FRIDGE
OPENS

Cake
on the
floor

Cake from the
flashback on the floor

Pan. Tilt
(Boom Down)

7

YEON-KYO
He had a birthday party at home that day. Late that night, when everyone was sleeping, Da-song crept down to the kitchen and took the cake out.

YEON-KYO
The whipped cream on that cake was amazing. Even in bed, he couldn't stop thinking about it.

The fridge door opens and on the kitchen floor sits the birthday cake from Yeon-kyo's story.

CHUNG-SOOK
Yes.

YEON-KYO
So Da-song was sitting eating his cake and turned his head toward the staircase...

Yeon-kyo points to the basement entrance.

YEON-KYO
There, his eyes met...

YEON-KYO
...with the Ghost's.

FLASHBACK – From the basement entrance
ascends an EERIE-LOOKING FACE hovering
in an inexplicable position.

FLASHBACK – The ghost's and Da-song's eyes
meet.

Line from #93A OVERLAPS:

KI-TAEK (V.O.)
How can you live in a place like this?

7

8

Background A

1

2

Quick Tilt Up.

#93. "MOLE HUSBAND" MANSION – SECRET ROOM

GEUN-SAE
Well, lots of people live underground.
Especially if you count semi-basements.

Ki-taek scratches profusely, not finding the
opening of the tape.

KI-TAEK
What'll you do? You don't have a plan?

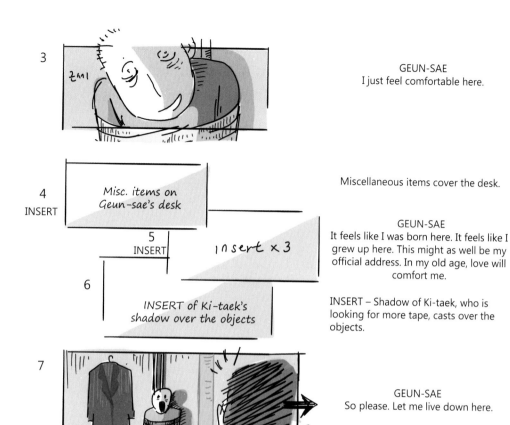

3

GEUN-SAE
I just feel comfortable here.

4
INSERT

Misc. items on
Geun-sae's desk

Miscellaneous items cover the desk.

5
INSERT

Insert × 3

GEUN-SAE
It feels like I was born here. It feels like I
grew up here. This might as well be my
official address. In my old age, love will
comfort me.

6

INSERT of Ki-taek's
shadow over the objects

INSERT – Shadow of Ki-taek, who is
looking for more tape, casts over the
objects.

7

GEUN-SAE
So please. Let me live down here.

#93B. "GHOST STORY" MANSION – KITCHEN - NIGHT

1

SHRIEK

15 min

Slow TRACK IN.

YEON-KYO
He screamed, and I ran downstairs, and he
was all... His eyes rolled back in his head,
convulsions, foam in his mouth.

CHUNG-SOOK
Oh my gosh.

YEON-KYO
Have you ever seen a child have a seizure?
They need 15-minute treatment, or they're
done for. That's the time you have to reach
an emergency room, 15 minutes.

CAMERA FIXED.

YEON-KYO
My husband was away on business, so I had to deal with it all. Since then we've always gone out for his birthday. Last year my mother's house, this year, camping. Now it's all gone to crap.

CHUNG-SOOK
I see...

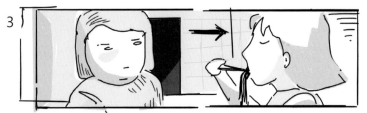

TRACK TO RIGHT to REVEAL the door to the basement behind Chung-sook for a brief second; then it is hidden again behind Yeon-kyo.

YEON-KYO
Da-song's dad says it's just a part of growing up. They say a ghost in the house brings wealth. Actually, the money's been good recently.

CLANK – chopsticks drop into the all-cleared bowl of ram-don.

#93A. "MOLE HUSBAND" MANSION – SECRET ROOM

Tilt Down + Track Out/In

"Honey! Honey!"

Ki-taek steps onto a chair and grabs a sock from a laundry line

Ki-taek picks up a sock from a laundry line while Geun-sae rambles on.

GEUN-SAE
Please talk to my wife. We don't have to fight. Where did my wife go? She didn't mean what she said. The woman really has a heart of gold. She stood by me the whole time I was in here. For four years.

Ki-taek rushes to Geun-sae and shoves the sock into his mouth.

#93C. "BLOOD ON MOON-GWANG'S HEAD" MANSION – SECRET ROOM (PLUM EXTRACT BASEMENT SET)

1

Fast TRACK OUT
on horizontal hallway.

Midway between the basement and the secret bunker.
Ki-taek runs the horizontal hallway, holding another
sock in his hand.

2

TRACK OUT +
BOOM DOWN.

Ki-taek rushes up the stairs to where
Moon-gwang is.

Ki-taek gags Moon-gwang's mouth with
a sock. He feels something wet behind her
head – BLOOD!

Ki-taek's head spins when he sees the blood
on his fingertips. Horrified, he turns the valve
to the entrance.

#94. "LOCKDOWN THE BASEMENT" MANSION - BASEMENT

①

Ki-taek, BREATHING HEAVILY, takes
a peep through a tiny opening.

②

WIDE SHOT.

All is quiet except for
Ki-taek's HEAVY BREATHING.

③

④

Ki-taek grabs the valve before shutting the door.

A GLIMPSE of Moon-gwang right before the door closes.

⑤

WIDE SHOT.
CAMERA FIXED.

HEAVY SOUND
of shelf sliding.

Ki-taek completely
LOCKS DOWN the door
to the underground
world.

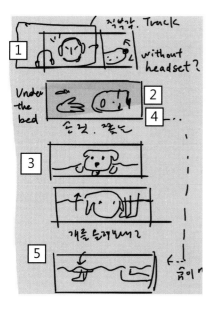

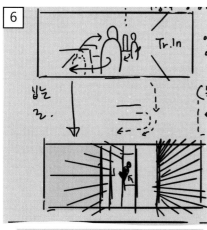

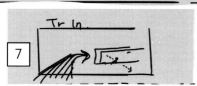

SHOT #1: OVERHEAD SHOT; TRACK RIGHT

Da-hye lies on the bed and takes off the headset (or no headset). She senses something, and CAMERA moves to reveal Zoonie poking its head under the mattress.

SHOT #2

Ki-woo, hiding under the bed, SHOOS AWAY Zoonie with his hand.

SHOT #3 (Ki-woo's POV)

Zoonie poking its head inside. Da-hye's feet as she picks up the dog.

SHOT #4

Ki-woo holds his breath.

SHOT #5 (Ki-woo's POV)

Da-hye gets down on all fours to take a look underneath the bed. She is about to flip open the bed skirt when we HEAR her MOM climbing the stairs. Da-hye picks up Zoonie and walks out to the hallway.

SHOT #6: TRACK IN (Da-hye's room in the background)

Yeon-kyo climbs the stairs and heads toward the master bedroom. Da-hye comes out of the room and makes a corner chasing Yeon-kyo. Da-hye confronts her mother.

DA-HYE: Mom!
YEON-KYO: Yeah?
DA-HYE: How could you?
YEON-KYO: What?
DA-HYE: I like ram-don too! How could you not even ask me?!
YEON-KYO: Well...
DA-HYE: Da-song didn't want it, so you asked Dad, then ate it yourself. You didn't ask if I wanted it?

As CAMERA TRACKS we see Ki-woo emerge from the bed and peep from the door.

SHOT #7: TRACK IN (from Da-hye's room >> stairs)

While mother and daughter bicker, Ki-woo tiptoes down the stairs.

YEON-KYO: You're on a diet. You shouldn't eat something at night.
DA-HYE: All I had today was salad for lunch.
YEON-KYO: I'm sorry. Want her to make one?
DA-HYE: No thank you.
YEON-KYO: Thought so. That's why I ate it.
DA-HYE: That's not the point! Why didn't you even ask me?
YEON-KYO: That's why I'm asking you now. Do you want one?
DA-HYE: No, I'm fine.
YEON-KYO: Da-hye. You know you're being unreasonable?
DA-HYE: Talk about unreasonable when I had to go camping?
YEON-KYO: So are you going to eat it or not?
DA-HYE: No, I'm not going to eat it!
YEON-KYO: *What the*... Just stop it.
DA-HYE: *WHAT THE WHAT?* Dad, Mom is swearing in English!

#95B. "KI-TAEK & KI-WOO JOIN" MANSION – LIVING ROOM - NIGHT

SHOT #1: STEADICAM (Chung-sook & Ki-taek come toward the camera, then CAM follows back of the two)

Chung-sook stands in the corner of the kitchen, pointing to the front entrance. Ki-taek joins her, and the two head toward the living room. Ki-woo joins them from upstairs, and they reach the living room.

CHUNG-SOOK: Garage, to the garage!

#96. "SEX ON THE COUCH" MANSION – LIVING ROOM - NIGHT

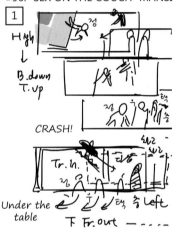

SHOT #1: HIGH ANGLE >> BOOM DOWN + TILT UP >> TRACK IN

Ki-woo arrives at the middle of the living room and helps Ki-jung out from under the table.

BOOM DOWN + TILT UP.

FOOTSTEPS run across the 2nd floor hallway and descend the stairs. Ki-jung hides under the table again.

TRACK IN while Ki-jung, Ki-woo, and Ki-taek FRAME OUT to screen bottom.

Chung-sook turns to see.

Chung-sook is seen on the left side of the screen.

Da-song, in a raincoat, runs down the stairs wearing a backpack AND a teepee strapped across his shoulders.

SHOT #2

Rain POURS DOWN and bamboos SWAY outside the window. Da-song dashes through the living room dangling all kinds of camping gear.

CHUNG-SOOK: Da-song, slow down!

SHOT #3

The rest of the Kims are trapped underneath the living room table. Behind them, Da-song opens the glass door and heads to the garden.

He starts building the teepee in the middle of the garden. Like a true Scout, he's quick and efficient.

YEON-KYO: Da-song?

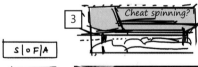

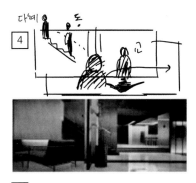

SHOT #4: TELEPHOTO

Yeon-kyo and Dong-ik rush down the stairs.

YEON-KYO: Da-song?
DONG-IK: Hey, Park Da-song! What a monster.
YEON-KYO: He's gone crazy! Get an umbrella.

Chung-sook FRAMES OUT to bring one umbrella from the front door. Yeon-kyo and Dong-ik head to the garden.

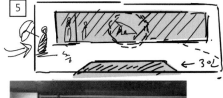

SHOT #5: Same angle as "What a view" moment from Drinking Party scene

Chung-sook passes the umbrella to Dong-ik and Yeon-kyo.

DONG-IK: Who do you take after to be so stubborn! Look at this rain!
DA-SONG: You're supposed to camp when it rains!
YEON-KYO: Do something. His cellphone will get wet.
DA-SONG: You don't need your smartphone in the wild. What you need is walkie-talkie!
DONG-IK: I'm impressed.
DA-SONG: The weather doesn't look too good, so why don't you wait inside.
YEON-KYO: You gotta be kidding...
DONG-IK: Hey, enough. Channel 3 for emergencies!

SHOT #5: TRACK IN + TRACK LEFT

Chung-sook leaves the scene to get another umbrella.

Da-hye watches her parents pleading with Da-song out in the rain. She shoots a video with her cellphone and sits down on the coffee table.

DA-HYE
(In English)
What the fuck is going on here...

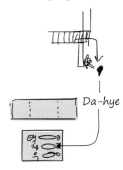

SHOT #7: TILT UP

Da-hye sits on top of the coffee table. She fiddles with her phone.

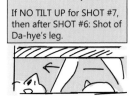

optional 6A

If NO TILT UP for SHOT #7, then after SHOT #6: Shot of Da-hye's leg.

SHOT #8

Da-hye sends the video to "Mr. Kevin" a.k.a. Ki-woo.

SHOT #8A

Tighter than SHOT #8.

SHOT #9

Phone VIBRATES from under the table.

SHOT #10

Da-hye seems to have heard it, too. Confused, she looks around.

Chung-sook COUGHS to cover the sound as she carries a huge towel and heads to the garden while she peeps at Da-hye.

SHOT #11 (LOW ANGLE)

Ki-woo silences his phone.

Change phone setting

SHOT #12

CHUNG-SOOK: Here are towels.

Chung-sook hands towels to Yeon-kyo and Dong-ik, who return after much bickering. Da-hye checks her texts.

SHOT #13 (Da-hye's WhatsApp screen)

DA-HYE: SMH Da-song's crazy rain dance
KI-WOO: LMAO
DA-HYE: Totes saw this coming. Started losing his shit
      at camp.
KI-WOO: LOL Da-song!!
DA-HYE: I miss you
KI-WOO: Me too

WhatsApp screen

SHOT #14

Ki-woo looking at his cellphone from under the table.

SHOT #15

DA-HYE: Selfie please
KI-WOO: No
DA-HYE: Plzzz.
KI-WOO: We are always together
DA-HYE: But not right now
KI-WOO: Always

WhatsApp screen

SHOT #16 (SWING RIGHT + PAN LEFT)

> DONG-IK
> Hey, Da-hye! Stop using your
> phone. Go to bed.

Dong-ik and Yeon-kyo return to the living room. Chung-sook follows them. (CAM MOVE!)

> YEON-KYO
> Go sleep in your room. We'll
> take care of things.

Dong-ik and Yeon-kyo head to the couch, and Da-hye goes upstairs. Chung-sook heads to the kitchen.

Yeon-kyo and Dong-ik sit down on the couch in front of the coffee table, under which the three Kims are hiding.

> DONG-IK
> This is the living room, do
> you copy? Daddy is standing by
> for emergencies, over.

> DA-SONG
> Got it, over.

Dong-ik lets out a weak laugh as he hears Da-song's excited voice from the walkie-talkie.

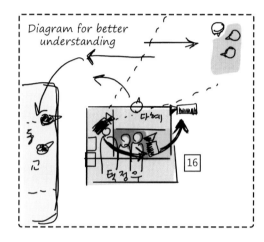

SHOT #17

> DONG-IK
> Is that tent going to leak?

> YEON-KYO
> We ordered from the U.S.
> It'll be fine.

Outside, the teepee lanterns light up one after another.

As the RAIN POURS, the teepee emits a pleasant orange glow against the backdrop of trees. It's picturesque.

SHOT #18 (BOOM DOWN / FOCUS IN)

Yeon-kyo turns off the light. Dong-ik places a few cushions on Yeon-kyo's side.

> DONG-IK
> Should we sleep here? We've got
> a full view of the tent.

> YEON-KYO
> Good idea. I'll feel much better.

CAMERA BOOMS DOWN to REVEAL the Kims under the table. They're FUCKED.

(Yeon-kyo turning off the light – by switch?)

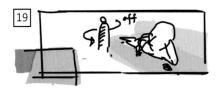

Walkie-talkie

다송이가

Tilt Up

25

OVERHEAD SHOT.
Tighter than SHOT #22.

Under the
table

SHOT #19

DONG-IK: Wait a minute. Where's that smell
            coming from?
YEON-KYO: What smell?
DONG-IK: Mr. Kim's smell.
YEON-KYO: Mr. Kim? Not sure what you mean.

Dong-ik and Yeon-kyo sniff the air.

SHOT #20

Ki-taek under the table. Nervous, he smells his T-shirt.

SHOT #21 (Post ZOOM IN)

Dong-ik puts the walkie-talkie on the table.

DONG-IK: I guess you don't know. I sit
            behind him and smell this every day.
YEON-KYO: Bad smell?
DONG-IK: No, it's subtler. It kind of seeps
            in the air.
YEON-KYO: An old man's smell?
DONG-IK: No, no, it's not that. Like an old
            radish? You know when you boil a rag? It smells
            like that.

SHOT #22 (OVERHEAD SHOT; Post ZOOM IN)

Ki-taek tries his best to keep a straight face under the table.

SHOT #23 (Post ZOOM IN)

DONG-IK: Anyway, the man can drive for sure,
            and even though he always seems
            about to cross the line, he never does cross it.
            That's good. I'll give him credit. But that smell
            crosses the line. It powers through right into the
            back seat.

SHOT #24 (TILT UP)

YEON-KYO: You think that's what Da-song was
            talking about?
DONG-IK: I don't know. It's hard to
            describe. But you sometimes smell it
            on the subway.
YEON-KYO: It's been ages since I rode a
            subway.
DONG-IK: People who ride the subway have a
            special smell.

SHOT #25 (OVERHEAD SHOT; tighter than #22)

Ki-taek's, Ki-jung's, and Ki-woo's faces as they hear Dong-ik
rant about the smell. Ki-taek's face remains expressionless,
hard to read.

Yeon-kyo's eyeline

SHOT #26

Dong-ik slowly slides up his hand and caresses Yeon-kyo's breasts over her pajama top.

DONG-IK: Isn't this like the car's back
          seat?
YEON-KYO: What if Da-song comes back in?

SHOT #26A (Yeon-kyo's POV)

The teepee stands in the pouring rain.

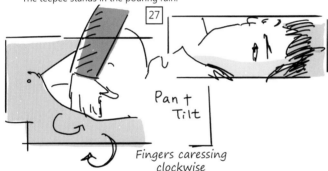

Pan + Tilt

Fingers caressing clockwise

SHOT #27 (PAN & TILT)

DONG-IK: I can just pull my hand back.
YEON-KYO: We shouldn't... Do it clockwise.

Dong-ik moves his finger as instructed.

Dong-ik's wrist comes down from the couch

box

SHOT #28

Under the table. Dong-ik's wrist slips down the couch.

Dong-ik's pants

Yeon-kyo's hand

SHOT #29

Yeon-kyo's hand slips into Dong-ik's pants.

SHOT #30 (POST ZOOM)

Dong-ik's hand starts slipping below Yeon-kyo's navel.

Their bodies grow closer.

Breathing becomes labored.

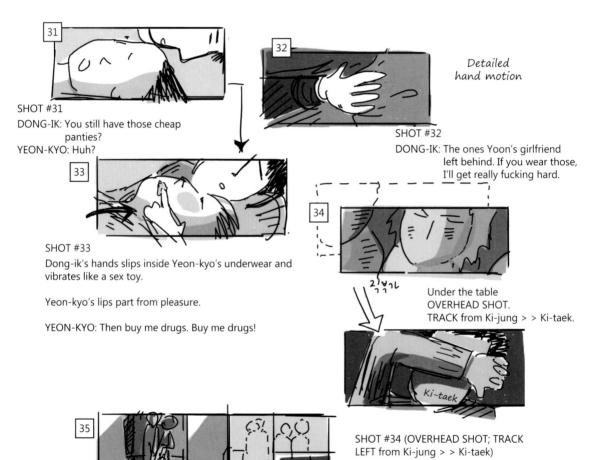

SHOT #31

DONG-IK: You still have those cheap
panties?

YEON-KYO: Huh?

Detailed
hand motion

SHOT #32

DONG-IK: The ones Yoon's girlfriend
left behind. If you wear those,
I'll get really fucking hard.

SHOT #33

Dong-ik's hands slips inside Yeon-kyo's underwear and vibrates like a sex toy.

Yeon-kyo's lips part from pleasure.

YEON-KYO: Then buy me drugs. Buy me drugs!

Under the table
OVERHEAD SHOT.
TRACK from Ki-jung > > Ki-taek.

Ki-taek

SHOT #34 (OVERHEAD SHOT; TRACK
LEFT from Ki-jung > > Ki-taek)

Ki-jung tries to keep cool.

Ki-taek seems more uncomfortable than Ki-jung herself.

SHOT #35 (OVERHEAD SHOT)

Yeon-kyo and Dong-ik push closer toward climax.

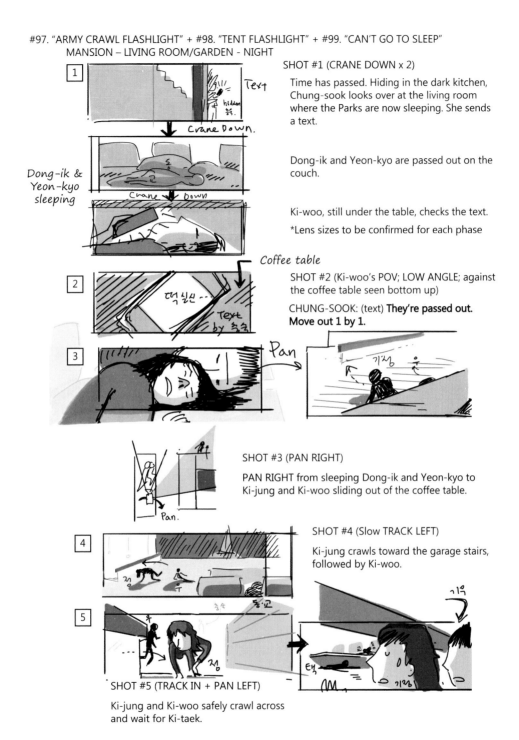

SHOT #1 (CRANE DOWN x 2)

Time has passed. Hiding in the dark kitchen, Chung-sook looks over at the living room where the Parks are now sleeping. She sends a text.

Dong-ik and Yeon-kyo are passed out on the couch.

Ki-woo, still under the table, checks the text.

*Lens sizes to be confirmed for each phase

SHOT #2 (Ki-woo's POV; LOW ANGLE; against the coffee table seen bottom up)

CHUNG-SOOK: (text) **They're passed out. Move out 1 by 1.**

SHOT #3 (PAN RIGHT)

PAN RIGHT from sleeping Dong-ik and Yeon-kyo to Ki-jung and Ki-woo sliding out of the coffee table.

SHOT #4 (Slow TRACK LEFT)

Ki-jung crawls toward the garage stairs, followed by Ki-woo.

SHOT #5 (TRACK IN + PAN LEFT)

Ki-jung and Ki-woo safely crawl across and wait for Ki-taek.

157

SHOT #6 (Quick PAN RIGHT)

Living room is silent except for the HEAVY RAIN. Ki-taek slowly makes his way when –

FLASHLIGHT searches the room before settling on Yeon-kyo and Dong-ik on the couch. Ki-taek lies flat on the floor to avoid the light.

Da-song: "Emergency! Emergency, over!"

SHOT #7

Ki-taek freezes and shuts his eyes. Dong-ik wakes up and picks up the walkie-talkie.

DONG-IK: What is it, over!
YEON-KYO: Da-song, what's wrong?

SHOT #8

Yeon-kyo and Dong-ik are too concerned with Da-song to notice Ki-taek hunched over in the dark.

DA-SONG: I can't sleep, over.

SHOT #9

Dong-ik and Yeon-kyo can't help but laugh. He raises the walkie-talkie.

DONG-IK: So stop it and come in, okay? Go sleep in
        your soft bed, over.
DA-SONG: I don't want to, over.

Da-song TURNS OFF the flashlight.

SHOT #10

The teepee stands in the heavy rain. Da-song's shadow dances against the teepee light.

OVERHEAD
SHOT.

SHOT #11

All is quiet again. Ki-taek lies still like a freeze frame, then begins to move again.

A bug quickly crawls across in front of Ki-taek.

158

#100. "SHUTTER 40CM" MANSION – GARAGE – NIGHT (GARAGE/FRONT GATE BACKLOT)

Glass door

Track Out · 좌Pan · 붐다운

Door switch

Mercedes

**SHOT #1
(TRACK OUT + PAN LEFT +
BOOM DOWN)**

Ki-jung and Ki-woo open the glass
window and enter the garage. Ki-taek
presses the door switch.

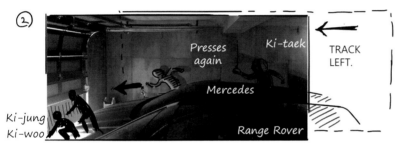

Ki-taek

Presses
again

Mercedes

Ki-jung
Ki-woo

Range Rover

TRACK
LEFT.

SHOT #2

Ki-taek presses it again and
then runs.

CAMERA TRACK LEFTS to REVEAL

Ki-jung and Ki-woo, who crawl
through the narrow opening.
Ki-taek slips through the crack
before it closes.

Track Out

Ki-woo, Ki-jung,
Ki-taek all dash
through the rain

SHOT #3

Ki-woo, Ki-jung, and Ki-taek
come out of the garage and
dash through the rain.

159

#101A. "RAINY DOWNHILL" MANSION – ROAD (GARAGE/FRONT GATE BACKLOT)

SHOT #1 (TRACK RIGHT + PAN;
RACK FOCUS: CCTV >> Ki-taek)

The surveillance camera's wires are severed.

RACK FOCUS to REVEAL –

Ki-taek finally sneaks out of the house and makes his way down the winding road in the HEAVY RAIN.

#101B. "RAINY DOWNHILL" MANSION – DOWNHILL (SEONGBUK-DONG HILL LOCATION)

Track In
(crane)

When Ki-taek passes the CAMERA
Quick Tilt Down.

(Almost) OVERHEAD SHOT
Massive amount of rain spurts out of a sewer

160

Extreme LONG SHOT.

Ki-woo, Ki-jung, and Ki-taek descend, a bit apart from each other as they take in the neighborhood.

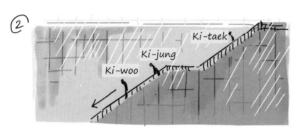

Down and down.

The Kims enter the tunnel, brushing the water off their heads.

A car PASSES, and the Kims slightly turn their heads away from it.

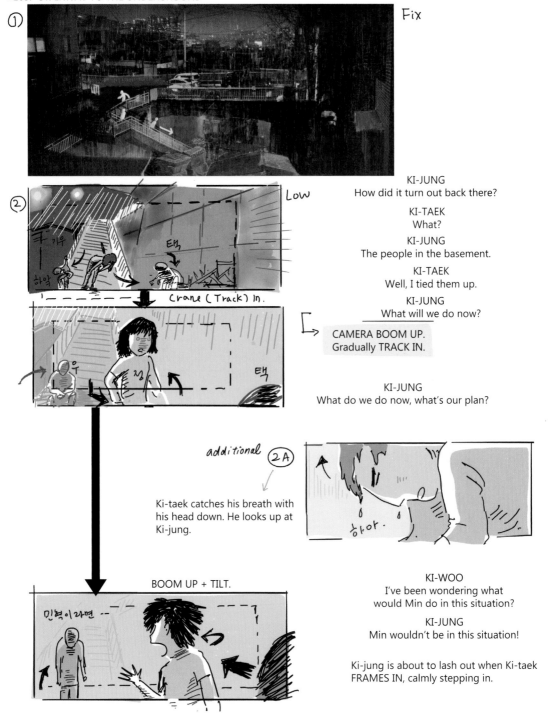

① Fix

② Low

Crane (Track) In.

KI-JUNG
How did it turn out back there?

KI-TAEK
What?

KI-JUNG
The people in the basement.

KI-TAEK
Well, I tied them up.

KI-JUNG
What will we do now?

→ CAMERA BOOM UP.
Gradually TRACK IN.

KI-JUNG
What do we do now, what's our plan?

additional ②A

Ki-taek catches his breath with his head down. He looks up at Ki-jung.

BOOM UP + TILT.

KI-WOO
I've been wondering what would Min do in this situation?

KI-JUNG
Min wouldn't be in this situation!

Ki-jung is about to lash out when Ki-taek FRAMES IN, calmly stepping in.

(3)

KI-TAEK
Calm down, both of you. Look, we made it
out of there safely, right? And besides us,
nobody knows what happened there. Right?

Begin TRACK IN slowly.

KI-TAEK
So nothing happened. You understand? I've
got my own plan. So you two just forget
about it, okay?

Slow TRACK IN continues (+ PAN LEFT) >> to Ki-taek.

Let's go home.

KI-TAEK
Let's go home.

With that Ki-taek steps back into the
rain, followed by Ki-woo and Ki-jung.

UNSETTLING MUSIC creeps in over the rain.

#104A. "PIGGY MART RAIN" ALLEYWAY – POOR NEIGHBORHOOD (FRONT OF PIGGY MART)

(1) TRACK IN.
Slightly PAN LEFT once Ki-jung,
Ki-woo, and Ki-Taek FRAME OUT.

#104B. "CHANGSHIN RAIN" ALLEYWAY – POOR NEIGHBORHOOD (CHANGSHIN-DONG)

(2) CRANE (TILT) DOWN.

Ki-woo stops in his tracks in the HEAVY
RAIN.

Ki-taek, already far ahead of his son,
stops and turns around.

(3) Slight CRANE MOVE.

Ki-taek calls after his son, but
Ki-woo stares at the tops
of his feet.

(4) Ki-woo's POV.
CAMERA FIXED; OVERHEAD SHOT.

RAIN cascades down the stairs,
streams splitting in between Ki-woo's
feet.

#104C. "NORTH AHYEON RAIN" ALLEYWAY – POOR NEIGHBORHOOD (NORTH AHYEON-DONG)

North Ahyeon-dong

TELEPHOTO; CAMERA FIXED.

The three Kims hurry against the HEAVY RAIN.

SHOUTING and HONKING can be heard from a distance.

#104D. "WATER TANK RAIN" ALLEYWAY – POOR NEIGHBORHOOD – NIGHT
(GOYANG WATER TANK SET)

STEADICAM; FORWARD.

Ki-jung stands in front of the FILTHY WATER. She stops in her tracks and folds up her pants.

> KI-TAEK
> (yelling)
> You stay there. This is all
> sewage water.

Ki-taek DASHES through the water toward his house.

STEADICAM; BACK.

Ki-taek runs forward and spots their house window.

> KI-TAEK
> Was our window open?

Water POURS from nowhere.

> KI-TAEK
> Damn it!

Ki-woo runs past Ki-taek and dashes into their house.

> KI-TAEK
> Ki-woo! Be careful!

Ki-woo FRAMES OUT, passing right against the CAMERA.

STEADICAM; FORWARD
PAN RIGHT.

YOUNG MAN NEXT DOOR climbs
up carrying a makeshift raft.

YOUNG MAN: Bro!
KI-TAEK: You got a bloody nose!
YOUNG MAN: Help me out, Ki-taek!

STEADICAM; LOW ANGLE.

RAIN pouring down seen from
in between the buildings.

+ TILT DOWN.

Ki-taek comes to the alleyway to his
semi-basement home. He runs around
the corner.

+ PAN RIGHT.

Ki-woo struggles to open the front
door before entering.

166

#105. "ORANGE KING CRAB" SEMI-BASEMENT

Ki-taek uses all his strength to open the door. Brown floodwater pours in through the window.

> KI-TAEK
> Ki-woo! Close the window!

CAMERA quickly PANS RIGHT to Ki-woo in the living room.

> KI-WOO
> Oh, shit!

Ki-taek dashes through the water FRAMING IN.

> KI-TAEK
> You got shocked? Don't touch anything.

Ki-taek's hand FRAMES IN

MASTER BEDROOM:

Ki-taek grabs a picture of young Chung-sook from when she was an athlete. His foot touches something, and he reaches into the filthy water to pick up an orange KING CRAB.

Ki-taek stares flummoxed at the crab flailing its legs. He chucks it away.

We see Ki-jung crossing behind the door.

Quick Pan

PAN RIGHT.

#106. "KI-JUNG SITS ON THE TOILET" SEMI-BASEMENT - BATHROOM

①

CAMERA FIXED.

Ki-jung pries the door open and trudges toward the toilet SPEWING sewage water.

②

HIGH ANGLE.

Ki-jung struggles to reach out and closes the lid.

③

LOW

Pan + Tilt follow.

Ceiling

Ki-jung's hand FRAME IN

Ki-jung opens a square panel on the ceiling and reaches to find A PACK OF CIGARETTES AND A LIGHTER that she had hidden. There also are a few folded bills stashed inside the wrap.

jump

④

FIX.

- Lighter "spark"
- Fluorescent lamps blinking
- (Ki-jung blowing) smoke
- Sewage water spurting out

#107. "MURKY SCHOLAR ROCK" SEMI-BASEMENT

①

CAMERA FIXED; OVERHEAD SHOT.
Ki-woo's POV. (48 fps)

It looks as if the scholar rock FLOATS UP by itself.

②

Slightly LOW ANGLE.

Ki-woo is looking down at the scholar rock. Ki-taek shouts at Ki-woo and Ki-jung to hurry.

KI-TAEK
We gotta leave! Hurry!

①

"Shit, I'm dizzy."

SHOT #1 (Slight TRACK IN)

Moon-gwang, with the sock hanging on her neck, staggers and hops toward Geun-sae. She looks like a ghost with her hands and feet tied up as she hops up and down.

> MOON-GWANG
> I'm dizzy. But I'm okay.

②

SHOT #2

Geun-sae still has the sock in his mouth. He whimpers, struggling hard to free himself.

Moon-gwang FRAMES IN and rips off the tapes around Geun-sae with her teeth.

> MOON-GWANG
> Shit, I'm dizzy. I feel like throwing up.

③

Tr In.
slow.

SHOT #3 (Slow TRACK IN)

Moon-gwang sits in front of the toilet.

> MOON-GWANG
> Vomiting is a symptom of... Concussion...

④

SHOT #4 (TELEPHOTO?)

Geun-sae shakes violently as if the tapes have come off. Toilet FLUSH.

Moon-gwang falls flat on the floor.

⑤ ⑦

⑥

SHOTS #5 & 7 (#5 is tighter)

Geun-sae struggles violently.

SHOT #6

> MOON-GWANG
> Honey, that woman Chung-sook...
> She kicked me down the stairs.

#109A. "SEWAGE OCEAN" SEMI-BASEMENT

OVER GEUN-SAE'S WAILING:

Sewage water, now up to their chin, fill the Kims' semi-basement house.

Ki-taek is the last to come out of the house, like the captain of a sinking ship.

Out the window we see Ki-woo and Ki-jung. Sewage water inside the house and out the window all connect into one vast ocean of sewage.

UNNERVING MUSIC continues. A dark, black water rolls over the screen.

#109B. "SEWAGE OCEAN RAFT" SEMI-BASEMENT – MAIN ALLEY

OVERHEAD SHOT; HORIZONTAL MOVE.

Residents evacuate the deluge.

The street is completely submerged.

#110. "GEUN-SAE DRIPS BLOOD" MANSION – SECRET ROOM - NIGHT

① FIX
(POST) Zoom In.

Geun-sae SMASHES his
forehead against the switch.
Blood drips on his forehead.

② FIX
(POST) Zoom In.

JAM! JAM!

Frightening sound

③ (Geun-sae's shadow)
Wall of Fame:
Cans and pictures
look as if they are (slightly)
shivering or maybe it's just
an illusion?

#111. "DA-SONG MORSE CODE" MANSION – GARDEN - NIGHT

① Da-song

② Over the rain we
see light flickering

⑥ Zoom in.
To use zoom lens

③ **⑤** Da-song opens the Scout note to
check on Morse Code >> Looks
at the living room

④ MORSE CODE

OVERHEAD SHOT

⑦ Big CLOSE-UP;
(Post) ZOOM IN

SHOT #1 - Da-song pulls down the teepee zipper and looks at the living room.

SHOT #2 – (ZOOM IN – to use zoom lens) Front door's fluorescent lights keep FLICKERING.

SHOT #3 - Da-song checks the Morse Code in his notebook and checks the living room.

SHOT #4 - He times the blinking and transcribes them as dots and dashes on his note.

SHOT #5 (TIGHT SIZE) Da-song looks at the living room.

SHOT #6 - (ZOOM IN – to use zoom lens) Lights flicker even more FRANTICALLY.

SHOT #7 (Big C.U. post ZOOM IN) – Da-song attempts to decipher the code but fails.

CAMERA FIXED; WIDE.

Packed gym.
Evacuees fill the 1st
and 2nd floors, attempting to sleep.

Cellphone screens flicker like
fireflies.

Slow CRANE DOWN.

KI-WOO: Dad.
KI-TAEK: Yeah?
KI-WOO: What was your plan?
KI-TAEK: What are you talking about?
KI-WOO: Before, you said you had a
plan. What will you do? About... the
basement.

OVERHEAD SHOT.

Ki-taek is silent for a long moment.
His face shows no emotion, and yet,
there's coldness.

Extremely slow (post) ZOOM IN or CRANE DOWN.

KI-TAEK
Ki-woo, you know what kind of plan never
fails? No plan at all. *No plan*. You know
why? If you make a plan, life never works
out that way. Look around us. Did these
people think, "Let's all spend the night in a
gym"? But look now. Everyone's sleeping
on the floor, us included.

Slow ZOOM IN; OVERHEAD SHOT.

KI-TAEK
That's why people shouldn't make plans. With no plan, nothing can go wrong. And if something spins out of control, it doesn't matter. Whether you kill someone, or betray your country. None of it fucking matters. Got it?

CAMERA FIXED.

Ki-taek talks quietly with fatigue and hostility in his voice. Ki-woo is scared to see his father like this for the first time. He tightly holds onto the scholar rock.

KI-WOO: Dad. I'm sorry.
KI-TAEK: For what?
KI-WOO: All of it. I'll take care of everything.

CAMERA FIXED; OVERHEAD SHOT.

KI-TAEK: Why are you hugging that stone?

CAMERA FIXED; OVERHEAD SHOT.

KI-WOO: This? It keeps clinging to me.
KI-TAEK: What?
KI-WOO: It's true. It keeps following me.
KI-TAEK: I think you need some sleep.

CAMERA FIXED; OVERHEAD SHOT.

KI-WOO: I knew it was a sign when Min gave it to me. It's metaphorical...

Ki-woo stares blankly ahead. We have no clue what he is thinking.

173

#113. "MARVELOUS MORNING" MANSION – LIVING ROOM - MORNING

Glass
window

The teepee reflected
on the glass

✓ FOCUS stays on
Yeon-kyo's 2nd mark.

Sunlight fills the living room. Yeon-kyo walks up
to the window and looks up at the marvelous sky
and the tent in the garden.

Dong-ik slowly rises from the sofa behind her.

#114. "DONG-IK LOOKS IN THE TEEPEE" MANSION – GARDEN - MORNING

Dong-ik walks over to the teepee covered in
raindrops and carefully peeks inside.

Dong-ik's POV.

Da-song fast sleep inside the tent.

Dong-ik smiles and gives the okay sign to
Yeon-kyo in the living room.

174

#115. "YEON-KYO'S DRESSING TABLE" MANSION – 2ND FLOOR – DRESSING ROOM - MORNING

YEON-KYO
Miss Jessica! Sorry to call on Sunday morning. Are you free for lunch today? We're having a birthday impromptu for Da-song.

Yeon-kyo sits at her vanity, chatting excitedly into her iPhone, which is on speakerphone.

#116. "BIRTHDAY PARTY?" SCHOOL GYM - MORNING

Slightly LOW ANGLE; CAMERA FIXED.

A groggy Ki-jung answers the phone. Rows of people sleep behind her.

KI-JUNG: A birthday party?
YEON-KYO: If you come too, Da-song will be so happy.

#117. "THUMBS-UP" MANSION – 2ND FLOOR – DRESSING ROOM/BEDROOM - MORNING

Reflected Da-hye comes in

Track.

PAN RIGHT.

SHOT #1

YEON-KYO: And have as much pasta, gratin, and salmon steak as you want. You know I'm an excellent chef, right? You have to come.

KI-JUNG: Sure...

YEON-KYO: Please come by 1PM, and I'll count today as one of your lessons. (In English) *You know what I mean?* See you soon!

SHOT #2

MIRROR: Da-hye approaches Yeon-kyo. TRACK IN + PAN LT.

DA-HYE: Mom. For the impromptu, should we invite Kevin too?
YEON-KYO: Great idea! (In English) *Why not?* Will you call him?
DA-HYE: On it!

Da-hye, ecstatic, runs to her room.

YEON-KYO: Get some more sleep, honey. You must be tired after yesterday.

Dong-ik crawls back into the bedroom.   PAN RT.

DONG-IK: Thank you. If we have a party, won't you need to do the rounds?

SHOT #2

YEON-KYO: Right, the wine shop, supermarket, bakery, florist... But I already told Mr. Kim to hurry over. I'll pay him overtime.
DONG-IK: *Perfect.*

Dong-ik gives her a thumbs-up with his eyes closed.

Yeon-kyo smiles, pleased with Dong-ik's approval. She opens the closet.

Slightly HIGH ANGLE.

(wider than drawn on the board)

Evacuees surround a pile of secondhand clothes, looking for something salvageable. Donations from a local organization.

Ki-jung looks frustrated, seeing nothing appropriate for the party. She looks at Ki-taek, who is also frantically digging through the pile with bloodshot eyes.

Ki-jung looks back where Ki-woo is still lying on the floor. He opens his eyes and looks at his phone – "7 MISSED CALLS FROM DA-HYE." Ki-woo sits up and goes through the messages. He puts the scholar rock in the gray bag.

← PAN LEFT, following Ki-jung.

Slightly LOW ANGLE.

"Women's clothes should be over there."

CAMERA FIXED.
Ki-woo's POV:
Cellphone screen.

Chung-sook, wearing clear disposable gloves, prepares ingredients for the party.
Yeon-kyo FRAMES IN:

YEON-KYO
Sis, in the basement we have 10 outdoor tables.

CHUNG-SOOK
Yes.

YEON-KYO
First take them all out, clean them. We'll set them up with Da-song's tent in the middle.
No, come to the window, I need to show you.

Yeon-kyo waves her hand, calling Chung-sook out to the living room.

YEON-KYO
With Da-song's tent in the middle, curve
the table's outward... A crane's wing
formation!

(slow) Track In

Slow TRACK IN.

YEON-KYO
Like Admiral Yi used, you know? The Battle of
Hansan Island! Think of the tent as the Japanese
warship. And our tables will make a semicircular
crane's wing formation. Then near the tent will
be the barbecue grill, firewood, and such.

#120. "CHUNG-SOOK LOOKS AT THE WALL" – MANSION –
    STORAGE BASEMENT - MORNING

SHOT #1 (Quick PAN RIGHT)

Chung-sook struggles to pull out the party tables from the faintly lit basement. She stops to take a breath. A chilling silence envelops the basement.

Chung-sook looks at the shelf covering the secret door.

She stares at the shelf for a long time, as if she can almost hear Moon-gwang and Geun-sae's breathing coming out from the other side.

Slightly HIGH ANGLE.
Slow TRACK IN - with the
secret door in the center.

SHOT #2 (Slightly HIGH ANGLE, Slow TRACK IN)

Slow TRACK IN with the secret door in the center.

Chung-sook brings out the tables.

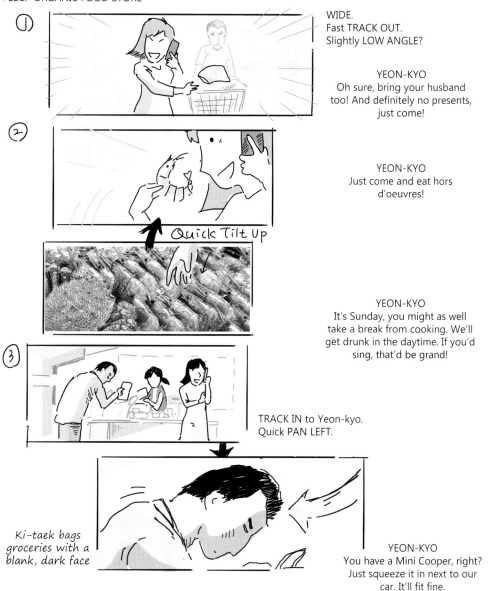

1

WIDE.
Fast TRACK OUT.
Slightly LOW ANGLE?

YEON-KYO
Oh sure, bring your husband
too! And definitely no presents,
just come!

2

YEON-KYO
Just come and eat hors
d'oeuvres!

Quick Tilt Up

YEON-KYO
It's Sunday, you might as well
take a break from cooking. We'll
get drunk in the daytime. If you'd
sing, that'd be grand!

3

TRACK IN to Yeon-kyo.
Quick PAN LEFT.

Ki-taek bags
groceries with a
blank, dark face

YEON-KYO
You have a Mini Cooper, right?
Just squeeze it in next to our
car. It'll fit fine.

179

STEADICAM

YEON-KYO
What dress code? It's an impromptu. You can wear sweatpants! And definitely no presents! Just come and eat hors d'oeuvres!

A wine store full of pricey wines. Yeon-kyo, walking in front of the rack, picks one after another and hands them to Ki-taek behind her. Ki-taek follows her, carrying a rack full of wines. He seems dizzy.

LOW ANGLE; TRACK RIGHT.

Chung-sook is setting up the tables in the crane formation around the teepee.
Da-song is still sleeping inside.

She is sweating and grunting away all by herself when she sees –

A pajama-clad Dong-ik walking toward the tent. He smiles awkwardly at Chung-sook before checking inside the tent.

He turns to Chung-sook and puts a finger on his lips – SHHH.

DONG-IK
(quietly)
He's still sleeping.

Chung-sook nods and proceeds quietly. It's hard to set up the bulky tables without making a noise.

Dong-ik scratches his belly as he returns to the house.

Fast TRACK RIGHT + PAN; RACK FOCUS.

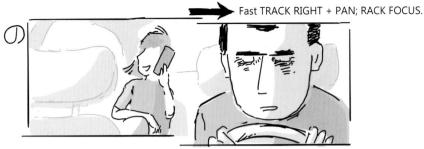

YEON-KYO: Today the sky's so blue, and no pollution! Thanks to all the rain yesterday.

PAN RIGHT to Ki-taek.

YEON-KYO: Right. So we traded camping for a garden party.

CAMERA FIXED.

YEON-KYO: Lemons into lemonade. Right, that rain was such a blessing!

Yeon-kyo is jabbering away when she suddenly smells something and holds her nose. Ki-taek's scent must have drifted her way.

She rolls down the window slightly.

CAMERA FIXED.

YEON-KYO: And definitely no presents, I mean it! Right, just squeeze your Mini Cooper into the garage.

Ki-taek sees her cover her nose through the rearview mirror. SNIFF - He sniffs his donated clothes.

①

extra shot → 박사장. 욕조에.

slow
트랙 인

"믿음의 벨트" sequence 중에.

#126A. "DO I FIT IN?" MANSION – 2ND FLOOR – DA-HYE'S ROOM

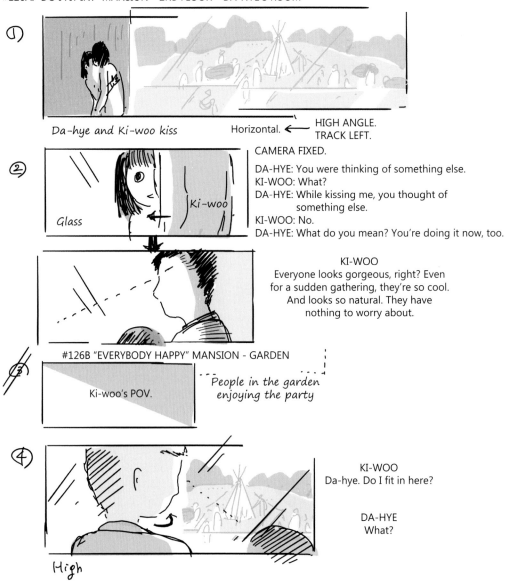

① Da-hye and Ki-woo kiss   Horizontal. ← HIGH ANGLE. TRACK LEFT.

② Glass   Ki-woo

CAMERA FIXED.

DA-HYE: You were thinking of something else.
KI-WOO: What?
DA-HYE: While kissing me, you thought of something else.
KI-WOO: No.
DA-HYE: What do you mean? You're doing it now, too.

KI-WOO
Everyone looks gorgeous, right? Even
for a sudden gathering, they're so cool.
And looks so natural. They have
nothing to worry about.

③ #126B "EVERYBODY HAPPY" MANSION - GARDEN

Ki-woo's POV.   People in the garden enjoying the party

④ High

KI-WOO
Da-hye. Do I fit in here?

DA-HYE
What?

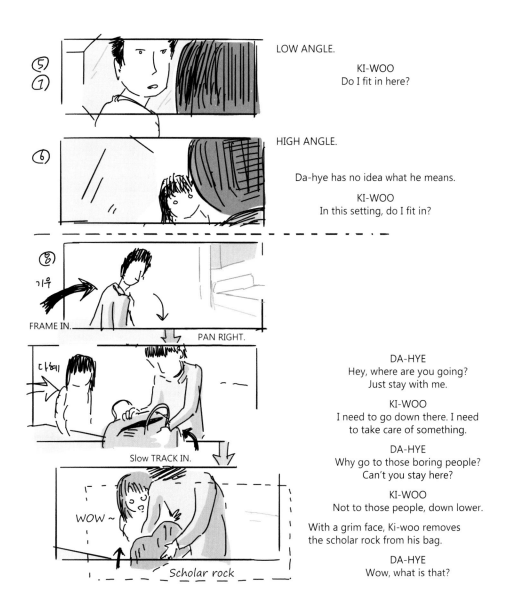

LOW ANGLE.

KI-WOO
Do I fit in here?

HIGH ANGLE.

Da-hye has no idea what he means.

KI-WOO
In this setting, do I fit in?

FRAME IN.

PAN RIGHT.

DA-HYE
Hey, where are you going?
Just stay with me.

KI-WOO
I need to go down there. I need
to take care of something.

DA-HYE
Why go to those boring people?
Can't you stay here?

KI-WOO
Not to those people, down lower.

With a grim face, Ki-woo removes
the scholar rock from his bag.

DA-HYE
Wow, what is that?

Slow TRACK IN.

WOW ~

Scholar rock

①

E랙아웃. 화Pan. Boom Down

SHOT #1 (TRACK OUT + BOOM DOWN) ~ SHOT #6

We get a glimpse of party guests and tables behind the trees. CAMERA MOVES to REVEAL Dong-ik and Ki-taek.

DONG-IK: God, I can't believe I'm doing this at my age. It's so embarrassing. I'm really sorry, Mr. Kim.
KI-TAEK: It's fine...
DONG-IK: Da-song's mom insisted, it can't be helped. But the concept is simple. There'll be a parade with Jessica carrying a birthday cake. Then we jump out and attack Jessica. Swinging our tomahawks! You know, we're the bad guys.
KI-TAEK: Right.
DONG-IK: Just then, Da-song the good Indian will jump out and we'll do battle. Finally, he'll save Jessica the cake princess, and they'll all cheer. Something like that. Silly, isn't it?

②
④

③
⑤

KI-TAEK: I guess your wife likes events and surprises.
DONG-IK: Yeah, she does. But she's particularly into this party.
KI-TAEK: You're trying your best, too. Well, you love her, after all.

⑥

DONG-IK: Mr. Kim. You're getting paid extra.
KI-TAEK: Yes...
DONG-IK: Think of this as part of your work, okay?

SHOT #7

Ki-taek slowly pulls up his hands and either grasps Dong-ik's face or his Indian headband. Dong-ik is alarmed.

KI-TAEK: Your strap...

The two men's faces come close. It seems as if Ki-taek is sniffing and checking out Dong-ik's smell.

SHOT #8 (PAN LEFT)

DONG-IK: What are you doing?
KI-TAEK: ...

Dong-ik, irritated, pushes away Ki-taek's two hands. There is strange tension between the two. They look at each other for a moment.

Track In + Pan

SHOT #1

Chef and his assistant carry the foods and head out to the garden.

Ki-jung looks around before approaching Chung-sook inside the kitchen.

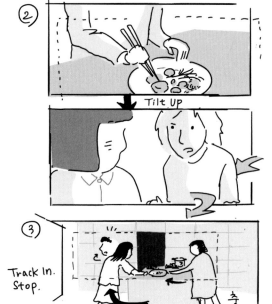

Tilt Up

SHOT #2

KI-JUNG: Did you go down below?
CHUNG-SOOK: Not yet.
KI-JUNG: Shouldn't we talk to them? Reach an understanding?
CHUNG-SOOK: Exactly. We all got too fucking worked up last night.
KI-JUNG: Where is Dad? Dad was going on about some plan. I'm just going down there.

SHOT #3

CHUNG-SOOK: Take this down to them. I made them just in case. Let them eat first and see if they'll talk.

Ki-jung approaches the basement entrance, then turns around and adds one meatball and places it on top of the plate.

She hears YEON-KYO'S LAUGHTER coming from the SCREEN LEFT and TRACKING STOPS to reveal Yeon-kyo on the phone.

Track In.
Stop.

SHOT #4

Yeon-kyo finishes her call.

YEON-KYO: Here you are, Jessica.
KI-JUNG: This is so amazing.
CHUNG-SOOK: Isn't it great? Another one?

Chung-sook grabs a serving tray and quickly escapes to the garden.

SHOT #5

YEON-KYO: This is... how to describe it? Da-song's trauma recovery cake? So it needs to be you who does it.

Yeon-kyo and Ki-jung FRAME OUT heading to the garden.

RACK FOCUS to the back to reveal Ki-woo coming down with the scholar rock.

#129. "KI-WOO TO THE BASEMENT" MANSION – STORAGE BASEMENT - DAY

SHOT #1 (Slow TRACK IN)

Ki-woo comes down the stairs.

GRRR – Ki-woo has barely enough strength to push the shelf.

189

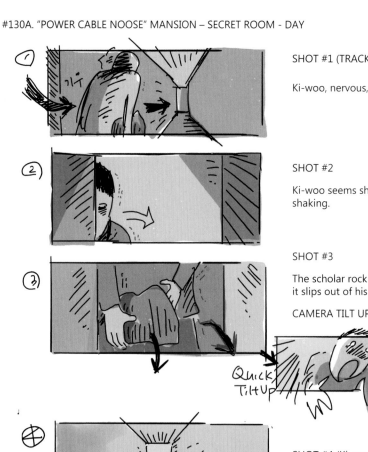

SHOT #1 (TRACK IN)

Ki-woo, nervous, glances back.

SHOT #2

Ki-woo seems shell-shocked and scared. He is shaking.

SHOT #3

The scholar rock in Ki-woo's hands trembles. OOPS – it slips out of his hands.

CAMERA TILT UP to catch Ki-woo's reaction.

SHOT #4 (Ki-woo's POV)

The scholar rock tumbles down the stairs, making a LOUD NOISE in the otherwise quiet basement.

SHOTS #5, #7 (#7 to be tighter)

Ki-woo, scared, goes down the stairs one step at a time.

SHOTS #6 & #8 (Ki-woo's POV)

CAMERA slowly goes down.

Darkness surrounds the scholar rock.

We HEAR Ki-woo's HEAVY BREATHING.

SHOT #9 (Slow ZOOM IN; TELEPHOTO?)

Ki-woo's head pops out. He looks around the pitch-black hallway.

SHOTS #10 & #12 (Ki-woo's POV starts to MOVE; #12 – advance to the toilet)

A figure seems to be there in the dark – perhaps it seems to be Moon-gwang.

SHOTS #11 & #13 (Slow TRACK OUT > STOP)

Ki-woo approaches the figure.

Slow TRACK OUT comes to a stop and Ki-woo stops in his tracks, too.

A white ring slowly forms above, behind Ki-woo.

SHOT #14 (Slow TRACK IN)

Ki-woo's trembling hand is just about to reach a wet raincoat* over what looks like Moon-gwang.

*Maybe somebody had put the raincoat over her?

SHOT #15

A white power cord wraps around Ki-woo's neck and his neck SNAPS BACK. He is dragged across the floor.

SHOT #16 (Fast TRACK OUT)

Geun-sae pulls a metal handle, dragging Ki-woo across the floor.

OVERHEAD SHOT.

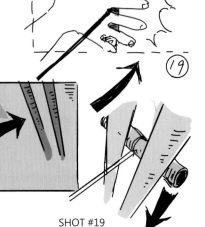

SHOT #17

Ki-woo gets dragged across the floor and bumps against the scholar rock.

SHOT #18 (Rough TRACK IN)

Geun-sae brings the metal handle that is connected to the power cord against the pipes standing at the very end of the hallway.

SHOT #19

Geun-sae's hand clasping the metal handle into the pipes.

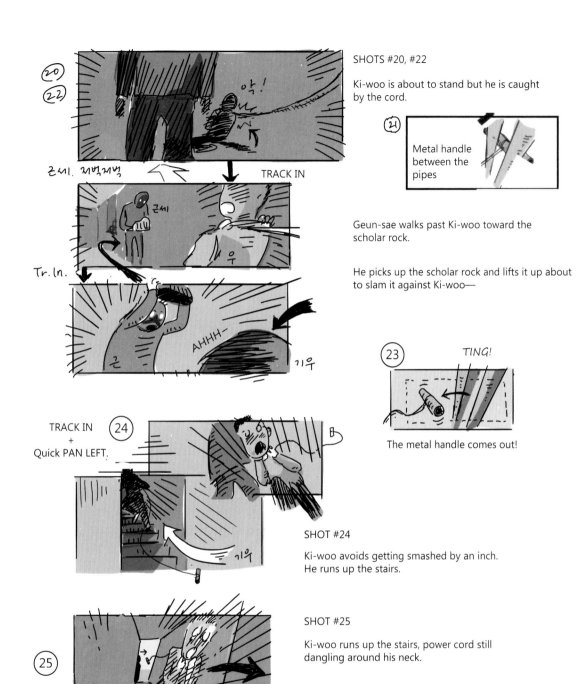

SHOTS #20, #22

Ki-woo is about to stand but he is caught by the cord.

Metal handle between the pipes

Geun-sae walks past Ki-woo toward the scholar rock.

He picks up the scholar rock and lifts it up about to slam it against Ki-woo—

TING!

The metal handle comes out!

TRACK IN
+
Quick PAN LEFT.

SHOT #24

Ki-woo avoids getting smashed by an inch. He runs up the stairs.

SHOT #25

Ki-woo runs up the stairs, power cord still dangling around his neck.

#130B. "KI-WOO IN THE AIR" MANSION – SECRET ROOM - DAY

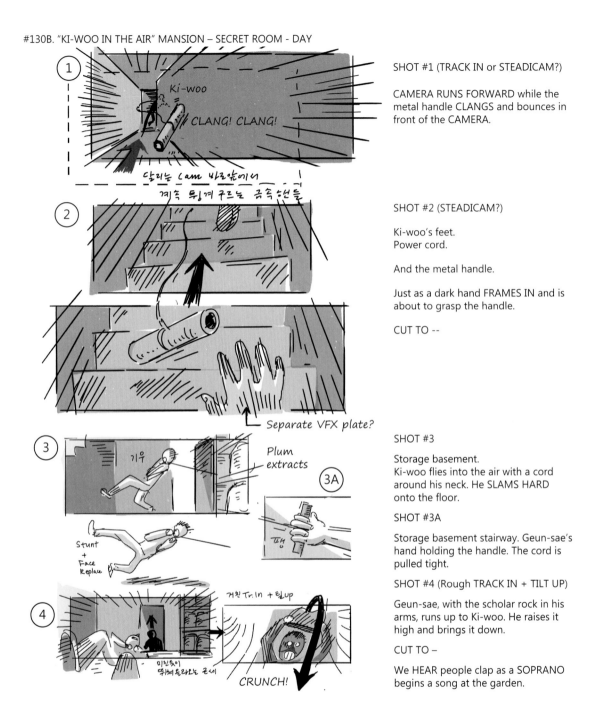

SHOT #1 (TRACK IN or STEADICAM?)

CAMERA RUNS FORWARD while the metal handle CLANGS and bounces in front of the CAMERA.

SHOT #2 (STEADICAM?)

Ki-woo's feet.
Power cord.

And the metal handle.

Just as a dark hand FRAMES IN and is about to grasp the handle.

CUT TO --

SHOT #3

Storage basement.
Ki-woo flies into the air with a cord around his neck. He SLAMS HARD onto the floor.

SHOT #3A

Storage basement stairway. Geun-sae's hand holding the handle. The cord is pulled tight.

SHOT #4 (Rough TRACK IN + TILT UP)

Geun-sae, with the scholar rock in his arms, runs up to Ki-woo. He raises it high and brings it down.

CUT TO –

We HEAR people clap as a SOPRANO begins a song at the garden.

A high-end Bluetooth speaker. Someone presses the button and piano accompaniment begins.

CAMERA moves as the cello joins.

A soprano begins Hendel's "Mio caro bene" in her beautiful voice.

As the music begins, Yeon-kyo lights up ten candles on top of the cake held by Ki-jung.

SHOT #1 (Extremely subtle TRACK IN)

Geun-sae GULPS DOWN a bottle of plum extract then chucks it away.

Geun-sae slides the shelf and closes off the entrance to the secret room. He turns toward the camera.

(Extremely subtle TRACK IN.)

There's dried BLOOD on his face and he looks horrendous.
He looks down.

SHOT #2 (Geun-sae's POV; HIGH ANGLE)

Two pools of liquid - Ki-woo's blood and the puddle of plum extract – refuse to blend together.

SHOT #3

Geun-sae picks up the scholar rock and throws it down on Ki-woo.

We faintly hear CLAPPING and OPERA from the garden.

Geun-sae climbs upstairs.

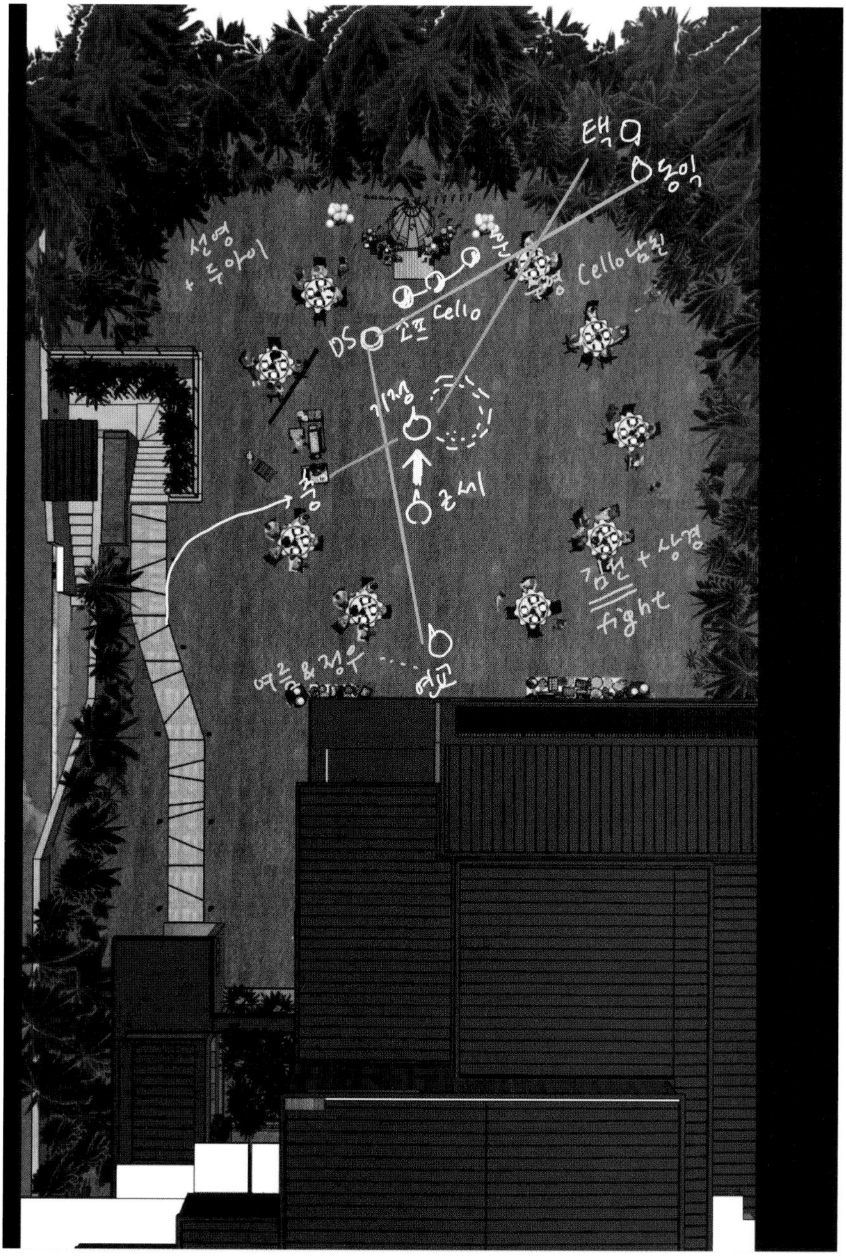

택
동익
Cello 남친
DS
Cello
기정
근세
fight
여름 & 정우
연교

#133. "GEUN-SAE AND KNIVES" MANSION – KITCHEN - DAY

TRACK LEFT.

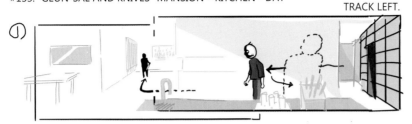

Geun-sae trudges up the stairs and walks past the kitchen. He goes back to grab a KITCHEN KNIFE. He passes the shiny living room and heads to the garden.

대비

FRAME OUT.

Mumbles: "Bug-like... cook..."

If deleting SHOT #2, have Geun-sae walk out the door and stand staring blankly ahead at the TAIL of SHOT #1.

Everybody is looking at Ki-jung and the cake.

#134. "CLIMAX" MANSION – GARDEN - DAY

Everybody is excited, CLAPPING at the cake, Ki-jung, and the birthday boy.

Geun-sae looks quite embarrassed, perhaps overwhelmed by all the people after years of estrangement.

He comes to his senses and looks for Chung-sook and rest of the Kims.

198

PAN RIGHT.

Da-song puts his head out of the teepee and sees Jessica with the cake. SCREAM! – Quick PAN and just as we see Geun-sae dash out of the crowd CUT TO—

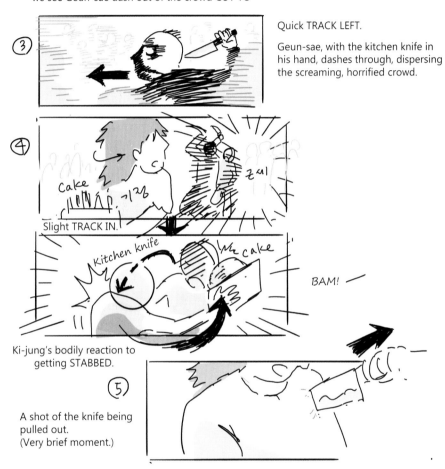

Quick TRACK LEFT.

Geun-sae, with the kitchen knife in his hand, dashes through, dispersing the screaming, horrified crowd.

Slight TRACK IN.

BAM!

Ki-jung's bodily reaction to getting STABBED.

A shot of the knife being pulled out.
(Very brief moment.)

199

Slightly LOW ANGLE.

⑥

Geun-sae's face is covered in whipped cream.

Blood SPRAYS as he pulls out the knife.

⑦

Tilt
Down

Ki-jung slumps down

Da-song

Ki-jung

PEOPLE SCREAM
& SHRIEK!!!

⑧

LOW ANGLE:
Da-song's POV.

Geun-sae looks at the boy for a second.

⑨ SHRIEK!!!

TELEPHOTO.
Yeon-kyo's profile.

⑩

36 or
48 fps

Da-song's eyes roll back (VFX)
before he falls back.

← shot 7 extend

Ⓑ A

Ki-taek ↑ Dong-ik

Quick
Zoom In.

Ki-taek and Dong-ik jump
out of the trees.

⑪

⑫

HUFF

Tastes like cream?

Track or
Zoom In.

WHOOSH

Geun-sae

SHRIEK!!!

DON'T MOVE!

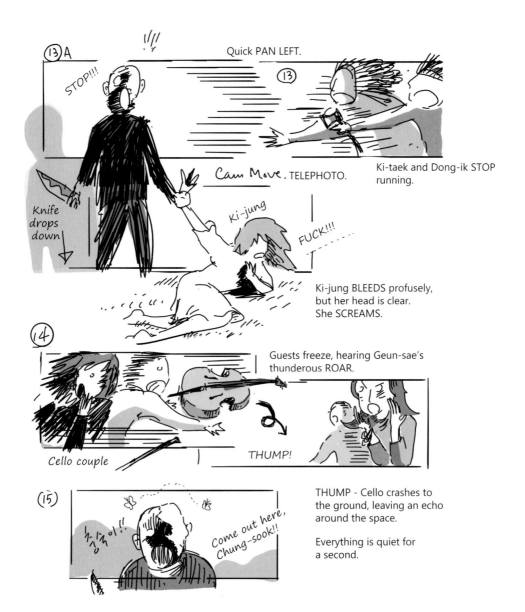

Quick PAN LEFT.

STOP!!!

⑬A

⑬

Ki-taek and Dong-ik STOP running.

Cam Move. TELEPHOTO.

Knife drops down

Ki-jung

FUCK!!!

Ki-jung BLEEDS profusely, but her head is clear. She SCREAMS.

⑭

Guests freeze, hearing Geun-sae's thunderous ROAR.

Cello couple

THUMP!

⑮

Come out here, Chung-sook!!

THUMP - Cello crashes to the ground, leaving an echo around the space.

Everything is quiet for a second.

(16) Chung- sook

Tilt Up. RACK FOCUS.

"Stop the blood!
Push down on the wound!"

Smoke rises from
BBQ skewers

(17) Ki-jung

Ki-jung is bent over, her forehead
almost touching the ground. She is
holding onto her wound.

KI-JUNG
Fuck. I'm okay. I am.

But her voice is faint.

Quick
Pan. Tilt Up.

Geun-sae tosses Ki-jung's hand
and charges to Chung-sook.

Chung-sook bumps into STUNT
and he knocks down the grill

BBQ skewers, firewood, axe spilled
all over the lawn

(18) stunt

"KI-JUNG!!!"

Tr. Out
Pan.

(steady cam)

(18A) OVERHEAD
SHOT.

Dong-ik

Da-song

Ki-taek

Ki-jung

Dong-ik, face white as a sheet, picks up Da-song and turns his head to check Yeon-kyo.

Track Out. Tilt Down (Rough)

Dong-ik jumps over Ki-jung's face and runs to Yeon-kyo.

Plastic axe

Dong-ik

Quick Pan & Tilt Down

Dong-ik

PAN RIGHT + TILT UP.

Two fight for their lives with Chung-sook on the bottom

The stairway is jammed with everyone trying to escape.

Change into 36fps

48 fps

Ki-taek's POV.

Mom with two kids   SCREAM!!

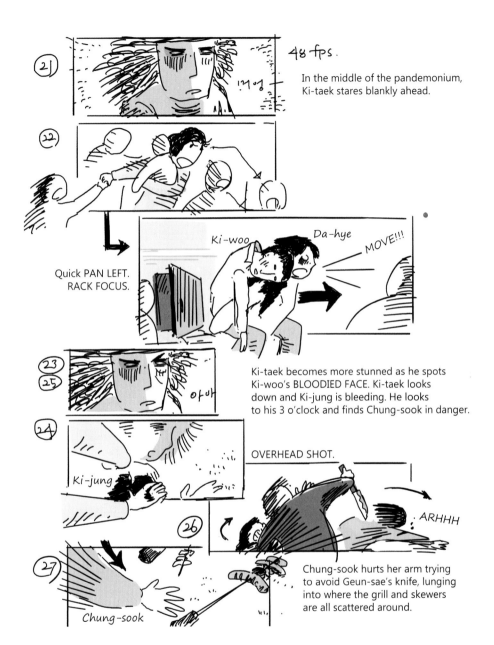

21 48 fps.

In the middle of the pandemonium, Ki-taek stares blankly ahead.

22

Quick PAN LEFT. RACK FOCUS.

Ki-woo   Da-hye   MOVE!!!

23
25

Ki-taek becomes more stunned as he spots Ki-woo's BLOODIED FACE. Ki-taek looks down and Ki-jung is bleeding. He looks to his 3 o'clock and finds Chung-sook in danger.

24

Ki-jung

OVERHEAD SHOT.

ARHHH

26

27

Chung-sook

Chung-sook hurts her arm trying to avoid Geun-sae's knife, lunging into where the grill and skewers are all scattered around.

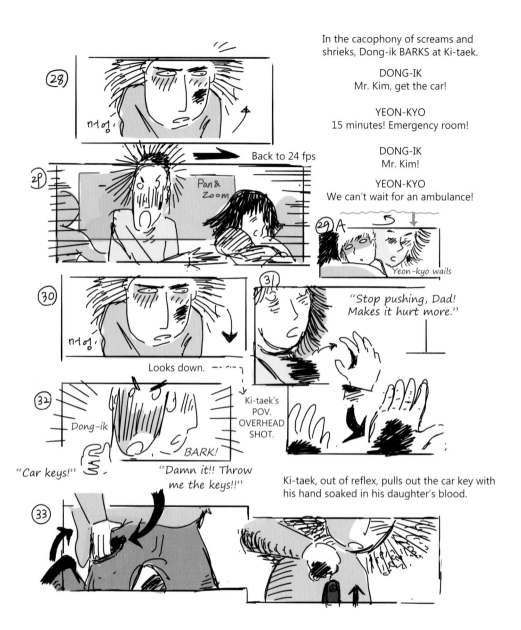

(28)

In the cacophony of screams and shrieks, Dong-ik BARKS at Ki-taek.

DONG-IK
Mr. Kim, get the car!

YEON-KYO
15 minutes! Emergency room!

DONG-IK
Mr. Kim!

YEON-KYO
We can't wait for an ambulance!

Back to 24 fps

(29) Pan & Zoom

(29)A Yeon-kyo wails

(30) Looks down.

(31) "Stop pushing, Dad! Makes it hurt more."

Ki-taek's POV. OVERHEAD SHOT.

(32) Dong-ik BARK!

"Car keys!"

"Damn it!! Throw me the keys!!"

Ki-taek, out of reflex, pulls out the car key with his hand soaked in his daughter's blood.

(33)

206

34

36 fps ↓

Ki-taek

Geun-sae

Chung-sook

PAN RIGHT

Mercedes key flies to where Chung-sook and Geun-sae FRAME IN. She overpowers him.

35

Mercedes key bounces off Geun-sae's head

OVERHEAD SHOT. **36**

Key drops to the lawn. Chung-sook and Geun-sae roll on top of the key.

37

Yeon-kyo

FREEZE

Dong-ik runs to the key, all a sudden, stops in his tracks.

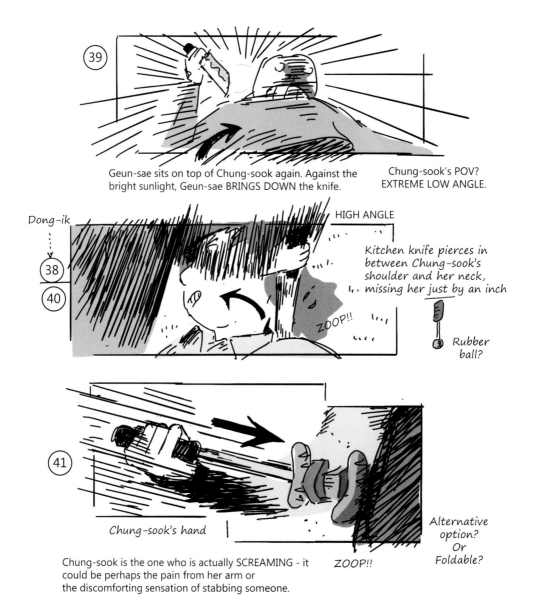

39 Geun-sae sits on top of Chung-sook again. Against the bright sunlight, Geun-sae BRINGS DOWN the knife.

Chung-sook's POV?
EXTREME LOW ANGLE.

Dong-ik

38
40

HIGH ANGLE

Kitchen knife pierces in between Chung-sook's shoulder and her neck, missing her just by an inch

ZOOP!!

Rubber ball?

41 Chung-sook's hand

Alternative option?
Or
Foldable?

Chung-sook is the one who is actually SCREAMING - it could be perhaps the pain from her arm or the discomforting sensation of stabbing someone.

ZOOP!!

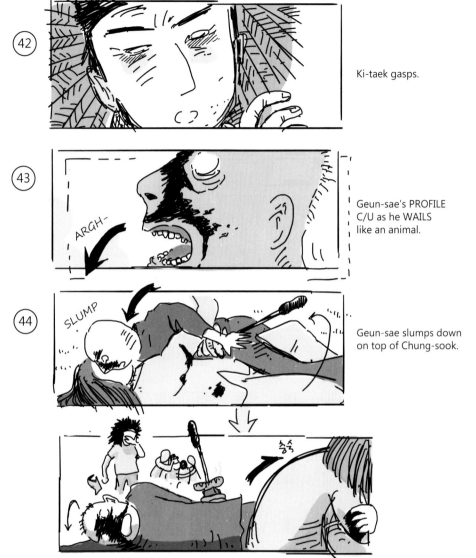

42 Ki-taek gasps.

43 Geun-sae's PROFILE C/U as he WAILS like an animal.

ARGH—

44 SLUMP

Geun-sae slumps down on top of Chung-sook.

RACK FOCUS. Dong-ik, horrified, rushes in. Behind him Yeon-kyo's friends cover her eyes for her.

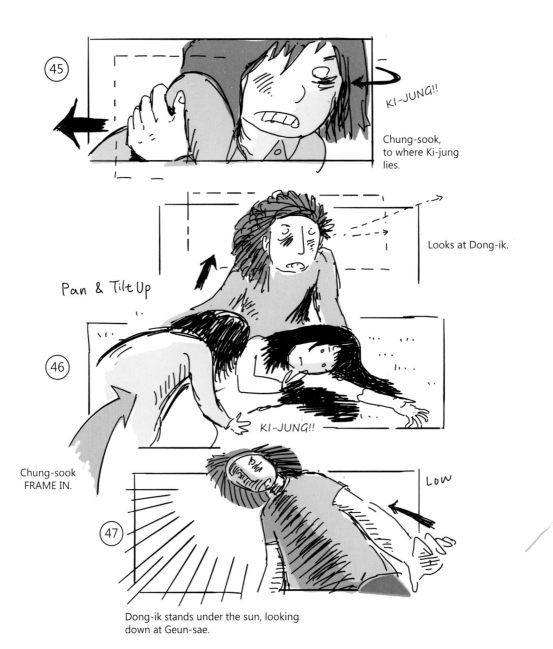

(45)

KI-JUNG!!

Chung-sook,
to where Ki-jung
lies.

Looks at Dong-ik.

Pan & Tilt Up

(46)

KI-JUNG!!

Chung-sook
FRAME IN.

Low

(47)

Dong-ik stands under the sun, looking
down at Geun-sae.

"Hello, Mr. Park. RESPECT!"

48 — Steep HIGH ANGLE.

49

Dong-ik is baffled by Geun-sae's "greeting."

He crouches down.

Tilt Down

50 — HIGH ANGLE.

Geun-sae

Dong-ik's POV.

Dong-ik lifts Geun-sae's body. Underneath is the key to the Mercedes.

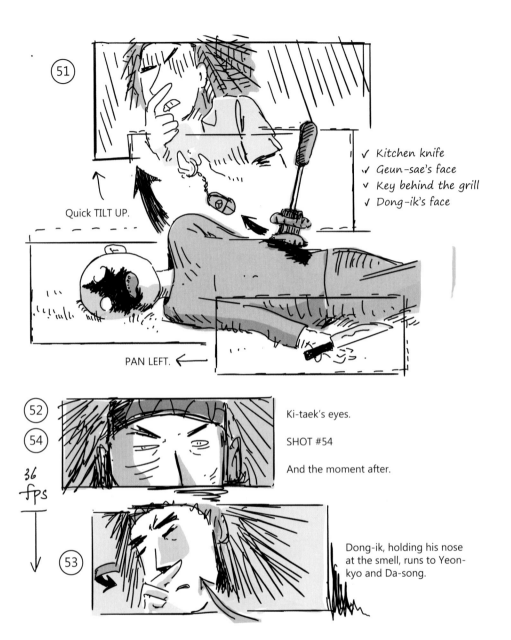

(51)

Quick TILT UP.

PAN LEFT. ←

✓ Kitchen knife
✓ Geun-sae's face
✓ Key behind the grill
✓ Dong-ik's face

(52)
(54)

Ki-taek's eyes.

SHOT #54

And the moment after.

36 fps

(53)

Dong-ik, holding his nose at the smell, runs to Yeon-kyo and Da-song.

212

55
Geun-sae
Ki-taek
24 fps
56
Dong-ik
Yeon-kyo
Ki-taek
Ki-taek finally takes off the headband
57
59
?!
JAM
end
Ki-taek's face
end
57

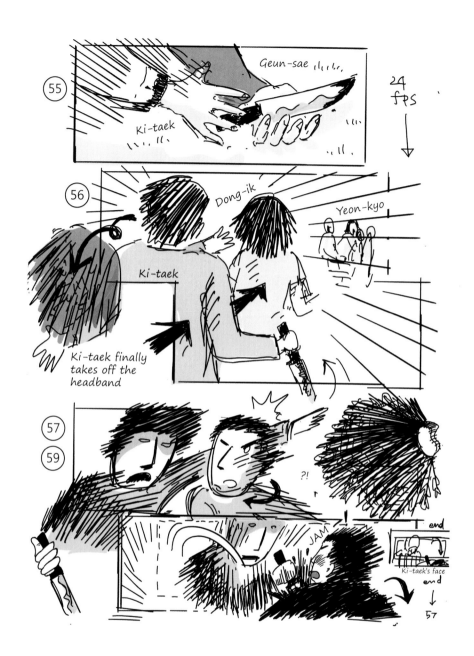

(58) Geun-sae lies still – he finally seems to be dead.
RACK FOCUS + PAN LEFT from his empty hand to face.

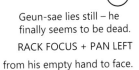

focus 이동 + 좌PAN

TRACK RIGHT.

(60)

THUD

Dong-ik

(61)

all 24fps

Yeon-kyo

Da-song

AHHH!!!

Yeon-kyo's friends standing next to her SHRIEK.
Yeon-kyo, however, is rather calm, as if her brain has actually stopped working.

(62)

Chung-sook
Ki-jung

Ki-taek

Ki-taek, still stunned, looks around.

Dong-ik

63 | Chung-sook   HIGH ANGLE.

Ki-jung

PAN + TILT.

64

Ki-taek, at last, seems
to have come to his senses,
and he looks to Yeon-kyo.

65

Yeon-kyo, with Da-song
in her arms, falls flat onto
the ground. Her friends
spot her.

66

Ki-taek closes his eyes for a
second, then he runs.

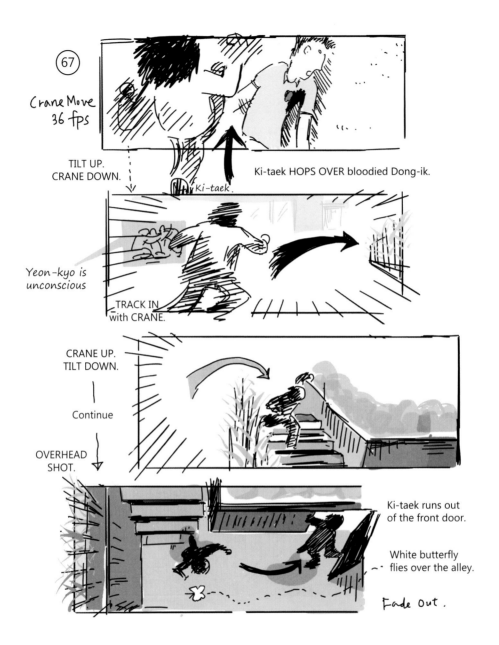

(67)

Crane Move
36 fps

TILT UP.
CRANE DOWN.

Ki-taek

Ki-taek HOPS OVER bloodied Dong-ik.

Yeon-kyo is
unconscious

TRACK IN
with CRANE.

CRANE UP.
TILT DOWN.

Continue

OVERHEAD
SHOT.

Ki-taek runs out
of the front door.

White butterfly
flies over the alley.

Fade Out.

#135. "MIRANDA WARNING" SOMEWHERE (HOSPITAL WARD)

CAMERA FIXED; LOW ANGLE.

The screen is PITCH BLACK. Complete darkness has debilitated any sense of geography.

We hear faint NOISES before slowly FADING IN –

A MAN stares into the CAMERA.

> KI-WOO (V.O.)
> Opening my eyes for the first time in a month, I saw a detective. Who looked nothing like a detective.

> DETECTIVE
> You have the right to an attorney... the right to make an appeal... The right to ask for the review of legality for confinement... Is he laughing?

> DOCTOR
> Just a sec.

A doctor examines Ki-woo's pupils (CAMERA).

> KI-WOO (V.O.)
> Then a doctor who looked nothing like a doctor spoke.

> DOCTOR
> That happens sometimes after brain surgery. They keep laughing.
> For no reason.

> DETECTIVE
> ...
> DOCTOR
> Do you hear me? Can you hear me?

> DETECTIVE
> Then do I have to do it again?

> DOCTOR
> Do what?

> DETECTIVE
> The Miranda thing.

CAMERA FIXED; HIGH ANGLE.

CAMERA FIXED; TELEPHOTO.

> KI-WOO (V.O.)
> Just like the doc said, I couldn't stop laughing. Even when I heard how much Ki-jung bled that day...

#136. "HE-HE-HE" HOSPITAL – HALLWAY

Ki-woo chuckles, holding onto his stomach, as he pushes an IV pole down the hall. The guards look at him strangely.

#137. "TRIAL" COURT

TRACK IN + PAN LEFT.

Ki-woo can't stop giggling as the JUDGE hands down the sentence. Chung-sook and his lawyer give him a look.

KI-WOO (V.O.)
Even when I heard the words forgery, trespassing, foul play, self-defense and we were lucky to get away with probation...

#138. "BUS"

CAMERA FIXED; Slightly LOW ANGLE.

Chung-sook and Ki-woo bounce in their seats as the bus speeds away. They sit next to each other looking at the view outside.

KI-WOO (V.O.)
Even when I finally got to see Ki-jung's face.

#139. "CINERARIUM" CINERARIUM

CAMERA FIXED.

Ki-jung in the picture of the cinerarium is smiling. The picture must be from few years back. Ki-jung seems happier and more innocent. She is radiant and adorable.

KI-WOO (V.O.)
I kept laughing.

CAMERA FIXED.

Ki-woo stares at his sister's picture and smiles back. Chung-sook sobs behind him.

CAMERA FIXED.

Countless white urns line the shelves inside the cinerarium.

218

#140A. "KI-JUNG'S ROOM"

Everything is still there just as Ki-jung had left it.

Chung-sook is on the floor scrubbing every inch of the floor to get rid of mud stains.

CAMERA MOVES to REVEAL Ki-woo sitting on the toilet, watching a month-old news report.

TRACK RIGHT + BOOM UP: Ki-jung's room >> Restroom

① Ki-jung's room

Chung-sook

TRACK.

Ki-woo sits on the stairs
looking at his cellphone

② News.

(Post) slow Zoom-in

③ Low

slow Z-m.

④

News
Live Report

#140B "LIVE ONSITE REPORTER"

REPORTER YOON
Kim, after exiting this door and descending the stairs, disappeared into
the neighboring alleys. Police searched the CCTVs of nearby homes to
no avail, and they have yet to find any witnesses. Given the situation,
it's not an exaggeration to say that Kim vanished into thin air.

Use generic background, unrelated to the actual news, such as night cityscape.

①

②

To be prepped by production

③

Back double to be played by production

Not to use background image showing information related to the incident

*** To shoot Mr. Seo and Ms. Shim, respectively, at the news room studio in above three sizes
(though it is actually 2 sizes)
*** Rewritten dialogues to be delivered to the reporters before 5/7

REVISED VERSION

REPORTER SEO

People are shocked that the CEO of a well-known tech company was killed in his own residence in the middle of the day. This kind of coldblooded murder rarely happens, especially right in the center of luxurious residential neighborhoods. Police are having difficulty solving the case as they struggle to figure out the motive or the purpose behind such a killing. Evidently, a homeless man who was responsible for the knife rage had been killed at the site as well.

REPORTER SHIM

Apparently, Mr. Kim, the driver, had been cordial with Mr. Park prior to the murder. Police have yet to find any financial motive. They continue to search for the whereabouts of Mr. Kim. As they have yet to find any evidence at the site, where Mr. Kim's cellphone had been recovered, using GPS to locate the fugitive isn't an option.

#141. "DECTECTIVE TRIPS" RESIDENTIAL AREA – ALLEY - NIGHT

Low.
Fix.

Ki-woo's hand
posting the ads

TRACK RIGHT (+ CRANE DOWN).

KI-WOO (V.O.)
Actually Mom and I had no idea where
Dad was.

Ki-woo goes around different apartments, posting promotional
flyers as a part-time gig.

He turns around and catches a DETECTIVE who had
been tailing him twist his ankle and tumble down the stairs.

Ki-woo feels bad for the guy.

KI-WOO (V.O.)
But those detectives still wore themselves
out tailing us.

CAMERA FIXED.

It is now winter. Ki-woo, bundled in a parka, climbs a hill in the middle of Seoul city.

> KI-WOO (V.O.)
> But I did have an intuition of where Dad would be.

Ki-woo's head arises from the trees.

CAMERA FIXED.
RACK FOCUS as Ki-woo FRAMES IN.

Ki-woo walks through gray, lifeless trees, breathing mist in the air.

CAMERA FIXED.

Ki-woo checks his back and the houses below as he climbs.

High up on the hill.

CAMERA FIXED; HIGH ANGLE.

Ki-woo's hand brings out a pair of BINOCULARS from his backpack.

> KI-WOO (V.O.)
> Eventually the news went quiet, and after the tails stopped, I started going up that mountain.

Late afternoon.

Ki-woo looks through the binoculars.

CAMERA
FIXED.

KI-WOO
From up there, you get a great
view of the house.

Beyond the mansion's trees and
garden inside the living room:
German family relaxing

Jeonju Backlot + Neighborhood CG plate
Slight PAN + TILT.

BINOCULARS' POV:
MAGNIFIED VIEW of the Parks' mansion and the garden.

Evening > Night

DISSOLVE TO – night has come. Ki-woo,
shivering in the cold, still looking through
the binoculars.

KI-WOO
That day, despite the cold, I felt like
staying longer.

The family members have gone
to bed. The living room is empty.
All of a sudden, MOTION-SENSOR
LIGHTS blink at varied intervals.

Night.
The MOTION-SENSOR LIGHTS by the
entrance blink – they are Morse code sent
by Ki-taek!

Same as SHOT G.

Ki-woo's eyes grow wide through the lens.
Blinking lights continue as if somebody is
sending Morse code. Ki-woo starts to record
the pattern in his cellphone. Wind howls as
Ki-woo continues to rattle off in a
trembling voice.

High

Ki-woo is on the last train of the night listening to the recording from the hill through his earphones. He uses a permanent marker to transcribe the dots and dashes on a prescription bag. When he runs out of room, he starts writing on his jeans.

Slight TRACK IN.

The WOMAN sitting next to him looks at his jeans and his face, perturbed.

HIGH ANGLE.

MORSE CODE TRANSLATOR

Pan
(spin?)
+ Zoom.

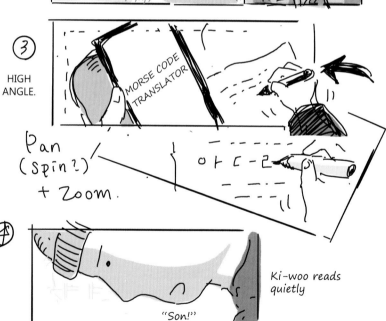

Ki-woo reads quietly

"Son!"

Ki-woo stops the playback and starts to decipher.
Series of dots and dashes become words. Ki-woo reads quietly –

KI-TAEK (V.O.)
Son!

SHOT #1 (TRACK OUT + PAN RIGHT)

CAMERA MOVES to REVEAL Ki-taek sitting at the desk in the dark chamber.

KI-TAEK (V.O.)
Perhaps you, if no one else, will be able to read this letter.

TRACK OUT + PAN RIGHT.

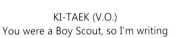

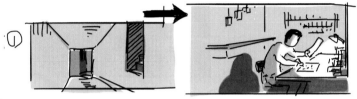

SHOT #2

On the desk is a densely written letter by Ki-taek. Next to the letter is a MORSE CODE CHART.

KI-TAEK (V.O.)
You were a Boy Scout, so I'm writing this just in case.

SHOT #3

Ki-taek looks inside the toilet as he flushes.

KI-TAEK (V.O.)
Have your injuries healed? I'm sure your mom is plenty healthy. I'm doing fine in here. Though thinking of Ki-jung makes me cry.

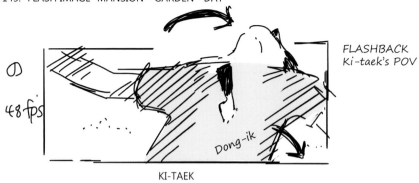

① 48 fps

FLASHBACK
Ki-taek's POV

Dong-ik

KI-TAEK
Even now, what happened that day doesn't seem
real. It feels like a dream, and yet it doesn't.

② 48 fps

Zoonie

Geun-sae

OVERHEAD SHOT.

③ 48 fps

OVERHEAD SHOT >>
Ki-taek's POV:
Looking at his own
bloodied hand.

KI-TAEK (V.O.)
That day as I went out the gate,
I suddenly knew. Where I needed to go...

#146. "KI-TAEK TO GARAGE" MANSION – FRONT GATE – DAY (FRONT GATE/GARAGE BACKLOT)

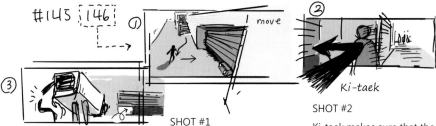

SHOT #3 (Ki-taek - OUT OF FOCUS)

Over the surveillance camera that Moon-gwang had cut the cords, Ki-taek enters the garage.

SHOT #1

Ki-taek runs down the stairs. The front of a Mini Cooper juts out of the half-open garage. Ki-taek ducks through the opening and enters the garage.

SHOT #2

Ki-taek makes sure that the party guests are fleeing the mansion, then he enters the garage.

#147. "KI-TAEK CROSSES THE LIVING ROOM" MANSION – LIVING ROOM > KITCHEN – DAY

SHOT #1

Garage stairway leading to the living room. Ki-taek pokes his head out.

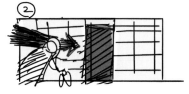

SHOT #2

Ki-taek, holding shoes in his hands, quickly crosses the kitchen heading to the storage basement entrance.

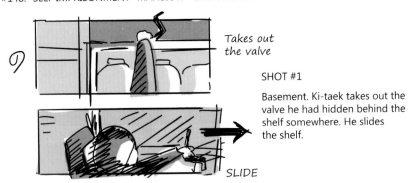

Takes out
the valve

SHOT #1

Basement. Ki-taek takes out the
valve he had hidden behind the
shelf somewhere. He slides
the shelf.

SLIDE

SHOT #2

Ki-taek turns the valve with fury.
The shelf SLIDES open.

SHOT #3

Behind the shelf. Ki-taek turns
the valve.

#149A. "VACANT HOUSE" MANSION – STORAGE BASEMENT

SHOT #1

Empty storage basement. Gone are plum extracts. The shelf is empty.

#149B. "VACANT HOUSE" MANSION – KITCHEN + LIVING ROOM - EVENING

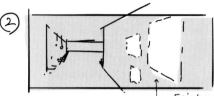

✓ **SHOT #1 (Evening)**

Vacant kitchen and the living room. White rectangles remain on the wall where there used to be paintings and portraits.

└─ Faint marks where the frames used to be

KI-TAEK (V.O.)

A house where such a grisly crime took place would surely not be easy to sell. I struggled to hold out like that in an empty house.

#149C. "TUNA RATIONING" MANSION – SECRET ROOM - NIGHT

HIGH ANGLE

SHOT #1 (HIGH ANGLE)

Secret basement area. Ki-taek picks at a can of tuna using Geun-sae's fork.

한조각. eat
그거 뭔가 close

SHOT #2

Over Ki-taek, alley extends into darkness.

SHOT #2A

Ki-taek comes out of the dark carrying Moon-gwang on his back. He has a small shovel in his hand.

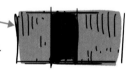

KI-TAEK (V.O.)

Still, thanks to the house being empty, what was her name? Moon-gwang? I was able to give her a proper send off.

#150. "TREE-SIDE BURIAL" MANSION – KITCHEN > LIVING ROOM > GARDEN - NIGHT

┌─ Empty shelf with lights off

M.S 식 dissolve

Ki-taek with Moon-gwang on his back

엎으 눈가 .
Looks around
>> Digging ②
MS 식 dissolve →

심장생드...
엎으 두리υ

SHOT #1 (PAN LEFT)

Ki-taek, carrying Moon-gwang on his back, walks across the basement and crosses the living room.

KI-TAEK (V.O.)

I hear tree-side burials are trendy, so hell, I did my best.

SHOT #2

Ki-taek looks around then digs a hole.

#151A. "MOMENT OF SILENCE" MANSION – SECRET ROOM - DAY

SHOT #1

Ki-taek has a moment of silence in front of Dong-ik's photo that still remains on the wall.

SHOT #2

Ki-taek raises his head, hearing FOOTSTEPS come from above.

Ki-taek crying(?)

SHOT #3

Over Ki-taek, we see the bottom surface of the garage stairs.

FOOTSTEPS.

#151B. "GERMAN ON THE OTHER SIDE" MANSION – SECRET ROOM - DAY

SHOT #1

Ki-taek puts his ears on the back of the shelf to listen to the other side. He hears lively chatter on the other side. Someone has come to see the house. They speak German.

KI-TAEK (V.O.)

But those real estate sharks sure are clever. They hoodwinked some people who had just arrived in Korea and managed to sell the house.

TRACK RIGHT.

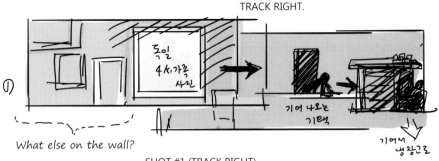

What else on the wall?

SHOT #1 (TRACK RIGHT)

A portrait of the newly moved German family of four.
CAMERA TRACK RIGHT to –

Ki-taek walks up from the basement entrance and
crawls over to the refrigerator.

KI-TAEK (V.O.)

With the parents working, and the kids
attending school, the family is usually out.
But the goddamned housekeeper stays
there 24 hours a day. Each time I go
upstairs, I take my life in my hands.

SHOT #2

More magnet pictures on the refrigerator.

One shows a maid with her arms around the
family's kids.

Refrigerator door OPENS.

SHOT #3

Cool shaft of light from the refrigerator. All kinds
of foods inside.

Ki-taek takes a little of various foods in the
plastic container that Geun-sae had been
using. He heads back to the basement entrance.

KI-TAEK (V.O.)

It turns out Germans eat more
than just sausage and beer. What
a relief.

SHOT #1

Ki-taek lies motionless on Geun-sae's cot.

> KI-TAEK (V.O.)
> Passing the time down here,
> everything starts to go hazy.

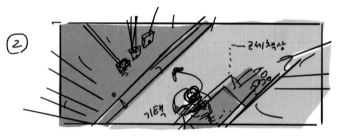

SHOT #2 (HIGH ANGLE; Slight SPIN)

Ki-taek gets up from his desk and walks over to the light switches with the letter written in Morse code in his hand.

> KI-TAEK (V.O.)
> Today at least I was able to
> write you a letter.

SHOT #3

Ki-taek stands in front of the light switches.

With the coded letter in his hand, he flips on and off the switches with the other hand.

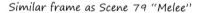

└─ Letter in Korean & Morse code

SHOT #4

Motion-sensor lights seen from the garden outside. They turn on and off according to Ki-taek's pressing.

> KI-TAEK (V.O.)
> *So long.*

Similar frame as Scene 79 "Melee"

SHOT 5

Ki-taek rereads his own letter.

#154. "KI-WOO DASHES THROUGH AN ALLEY" NEIGHBORHOOD ALLEY - NIGHT

Slightly LOW ANGLE.

TRACK or STEADICAM.

Ki-woo runs the alley as fast as he can, chest bursting with excitement. His breath creates a trail of mist as he passes the lights coming out of nearby semi-basement apartments.

#155. "KI-WOO WRITES A LETTER" SEMI-BASEMENT - NIGHT

Ki-woo, out of breath, rushes into the apartment and immediately picks up a scratch paper still with his jacket on. He sits at the kitchen table and starts writing furiously.

CAMERA MOVES IN on Ki-woo's hand with a pen busily going about writing a letter. And begins SENTIMENTAL MUSIC.

Quick TRACK IN.
PAN RIGHT.
TILT DOWN.

#156. "KI-WOO DREAMING" SEMI-BASEMENT – EARLY MORNING

OVERHEAD SHOT.
CRANE DOWN.

CAMERA goes down to Ki-woo's face.

CAMERA MOVES IN on Ki-woo's face sleeping. He looks happy holding the letter that he just finished.

His eyelids flutter. He seems to be in deep sleep.

VOICEOVER of Ki-woo reading the letter begins:

> KI-WOO (V.O.)
> Dad, today I made a plan.

#157. "STREAM" UNKNOWN MOUNTAIN - STREAM

OVERHEAD SHOT.
CAMERA FIXED.

The moment when the scholar rock was first discovered. From a beautiful stream, A PAIR OF HANDS pick up the pristine rock.

KI-WOO (V.O.)
A fundamental plan.

#158. "KI-WOO IN SUIT" RICH NEIGHBORHOOD – HILL – DAY (SEONGBUK-DONG HILL)

CAMERA FIXED.

Ki-woo walks up the hill of a wealthy neighborhood. He is older, dressed in a nice suit, sporting a tie.

KI-WOO (V.O.)
I'm going to earn money. A lot of it.

#159. "REAL ESTATE AGENTS" MANSION – FRONT GATE – DAY
(JENONJU FRONT GATE/GARAGE BACKLOT)

Ki-woo

Ki-woo is at the mansion – the one that once belonged to the Parks, the German family, and Namgoong Hyunja. Ki-woo walks up the stairs with REAL ESTATE AGENTS.

KI-WOO (V.O.)
University, a career, marriage, those are all fine, but first I'll earn money.

TRACK IN & CRANE UP.

OVERHEAD SHOT.
CRANE DOWN.

EXTENDED VERSION:
Ki-woo is at the mansion – the one that once belonged to the Parks, the German family, and Namgoong Hyunja. Ki-woo walks up the stairs with REAL ESTATE AGENTS.

REAL ESTATE AGENT
Pierre Namgoong is a famous architect who studied in France. He was also a Pritzker Architecture Prize nominee in 2008. And this is one of his! He always dreamed of living in a mansion ever since he was 5. *"Dream come true"* for the master architect, right? You'll see once you go in, but it's very spacious. Actually, we don't show this house to just anyone. But since we have a VIP with us today, I'll let you have a look at it.

MOVING BOXES fill the screen to BLACK.

TRACK RIGHT to –

We see Ki-woo and Chung-sook in the sunny yard.

KI-WOO (V.O.)
We'll move in on a sunny day.

KI-WOO (V.O.): All you'll need to do is walk up the stairs.

(Slight) TRACK LEFT.

CAMERA set inside the living room.

Ki-woo sees Ki-taek. He walks away.

Ki-taek walks toward the garden. Ki-woo walks into the living room. Chung-sook joins them. Far in the distance, under the bright sunshine, Ki-taek and Ki-woo reunite.

#161A. "HILL ENDING" WINTER HILL

Cold and windy hill. Sun is about to go down.

Ki-woo is looking through the binoculars despite the chilling wind. He puts the binoculars down and looks into the distance.

#161B. "HILL LAST" RICH NEIGHBORHOOD - NIGHTSCAPE

Ki-woo's nose is red and eyes watery, most likely from the cold

Night. Last.
Ki-woo looks into the distance.
The air is chilly

Residential nightscape. WIDE SHOT.

KI-WOO (V.O.): But I have no idea how to get this letter to you.

We see the Park Mansion far away surrounded by countless other wealthy mansions. Lights come on and off as if each of them is sending signals. Wind blows sharply, dispersing Ki-woo's misty breath and engulfing the screen.

FADE TO BLACK.

OVER BLACK – Bright and yet subtly dim music begins to play.

#162. VERSION A

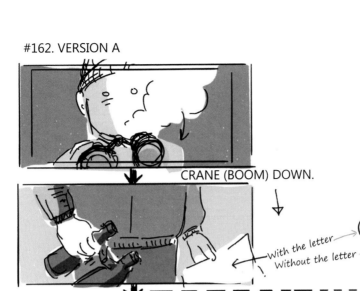

CRANE (BOOM) DOWN.

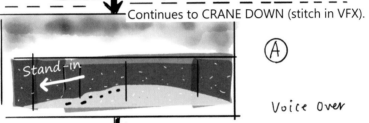

With the letter
Without the letter

Continues to CRANE DOWN (stitch in VFX).

Ⓐ

Stand-in

Voice Over

#162. VERSION B

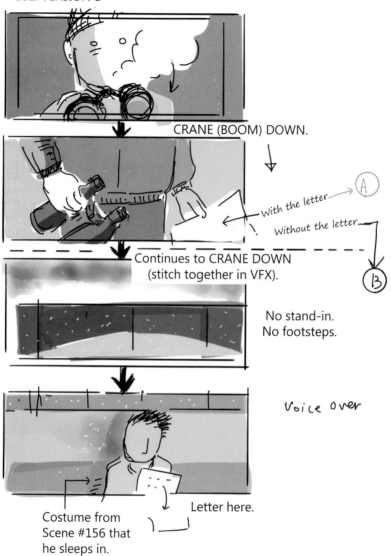

CRANE (BOOM) DOWN.

With the letter →Ⓐ

Without the letter ─

Continues to CRANE DOWN
(stitch together in VFX).

Ⓑ

No stand-in.
No footsteps.

Voice over

Letter here.

Costume from
Scene #156 that
he sleeps in.

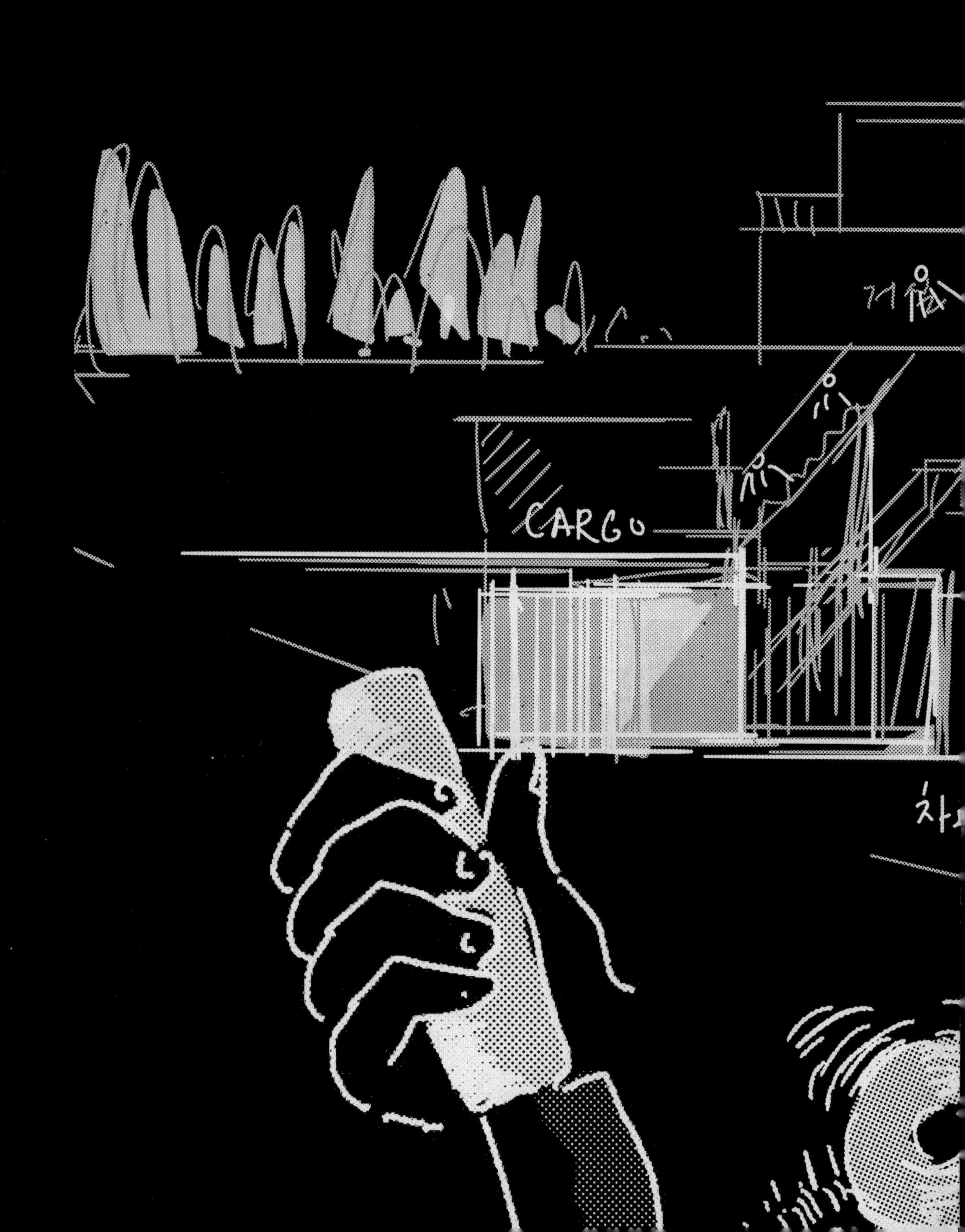
CARGO

Part 2. Early Drawings

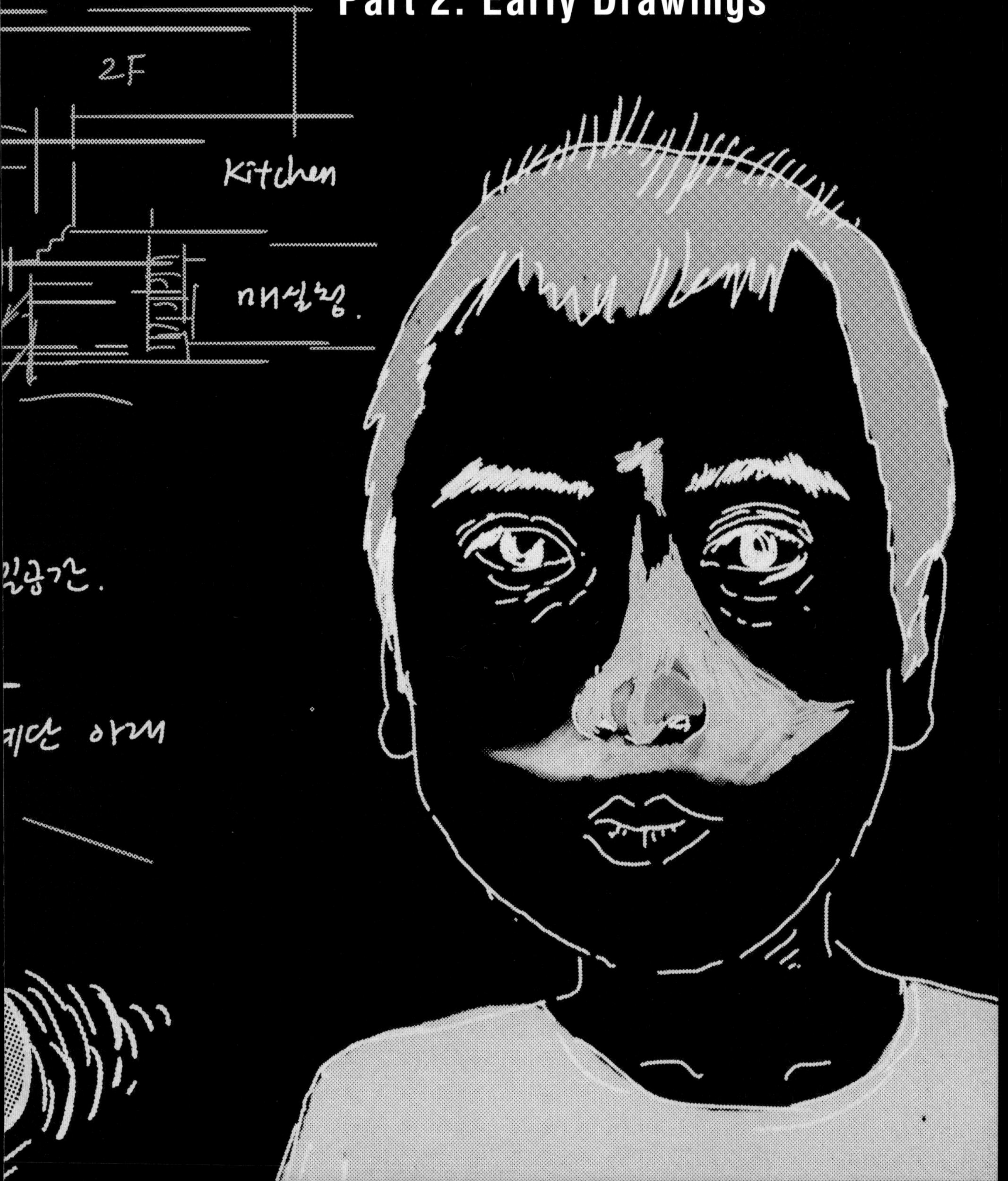
2F
Kitchen
매실청.

정은

긍 긍

Brief
encounter.

정은 + 홍숙

같은 일하는 사람끼리.
한번만 봐줘요 ... 우리 ...   어쩌다 이렇게 된거에요.

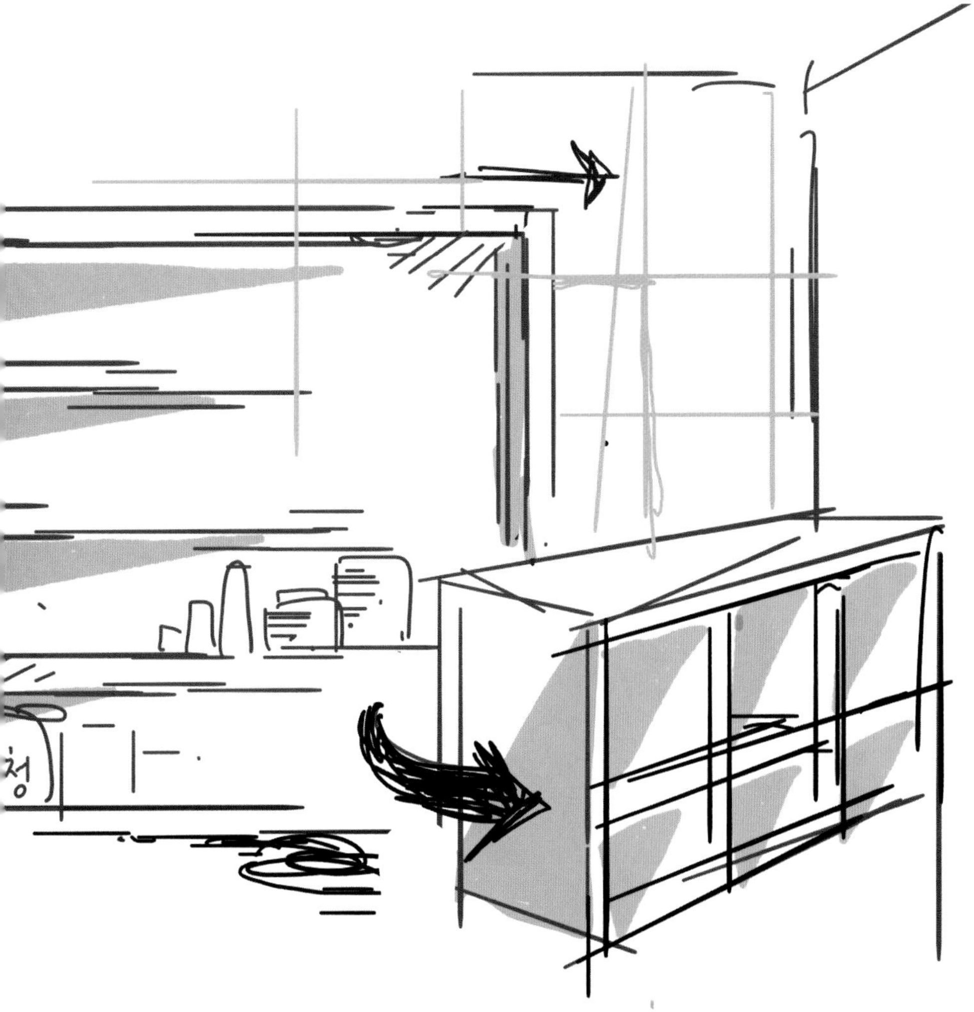
청

먹었던
캔 마다

전 세계 위인. 유명인 사진 (정
오려진것. 꽂혀있다. why ?

Finantial Times 나 economy

박롱익 인터뷰 사진도 꽂혀있다

"남궁변자 선생님
빈껍은 없지만...

오르스

- 종이 7역

명예의
전당

연가보전 해러잡지
또는 LUXURY 류의
매거진들

개미집.

Books

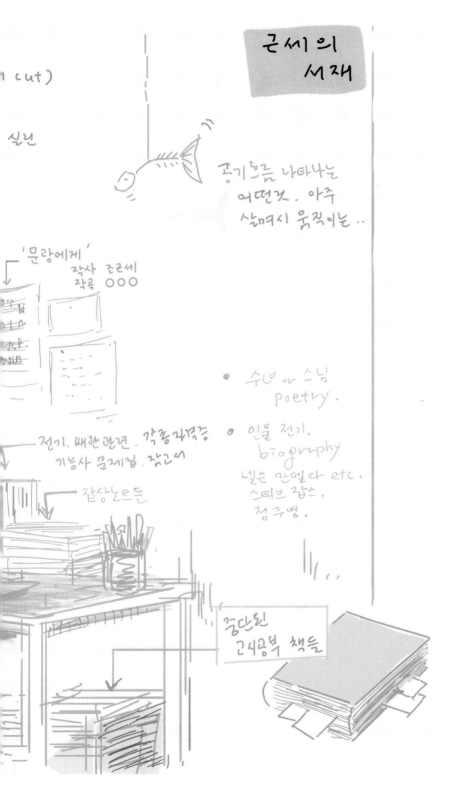

근세의 서재

(cut)

실내

공기흐름 나타나는 어떤것. 아주 살며시 움직이는..

'문랑에게'
작사 근로세
작곡 ○○○

● 수녀 or 스님
　poetry.

● 인물 전기.
　biography
　넬슨 만델라 etc.
　스티브 잡스.
　정주영.

전기. 배관 관련. 각종자격증
기능사 문제집. 참고서

잡상노트들

끔단된
고시공부 책들

245

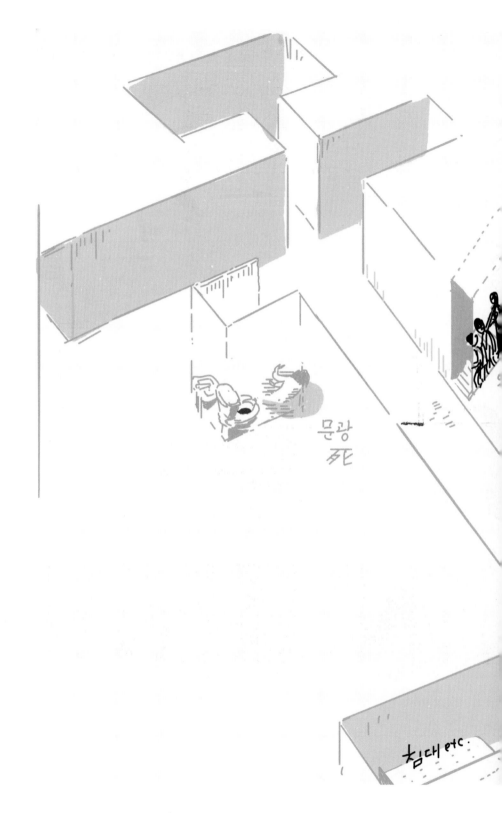

문광
死

침대 etc.

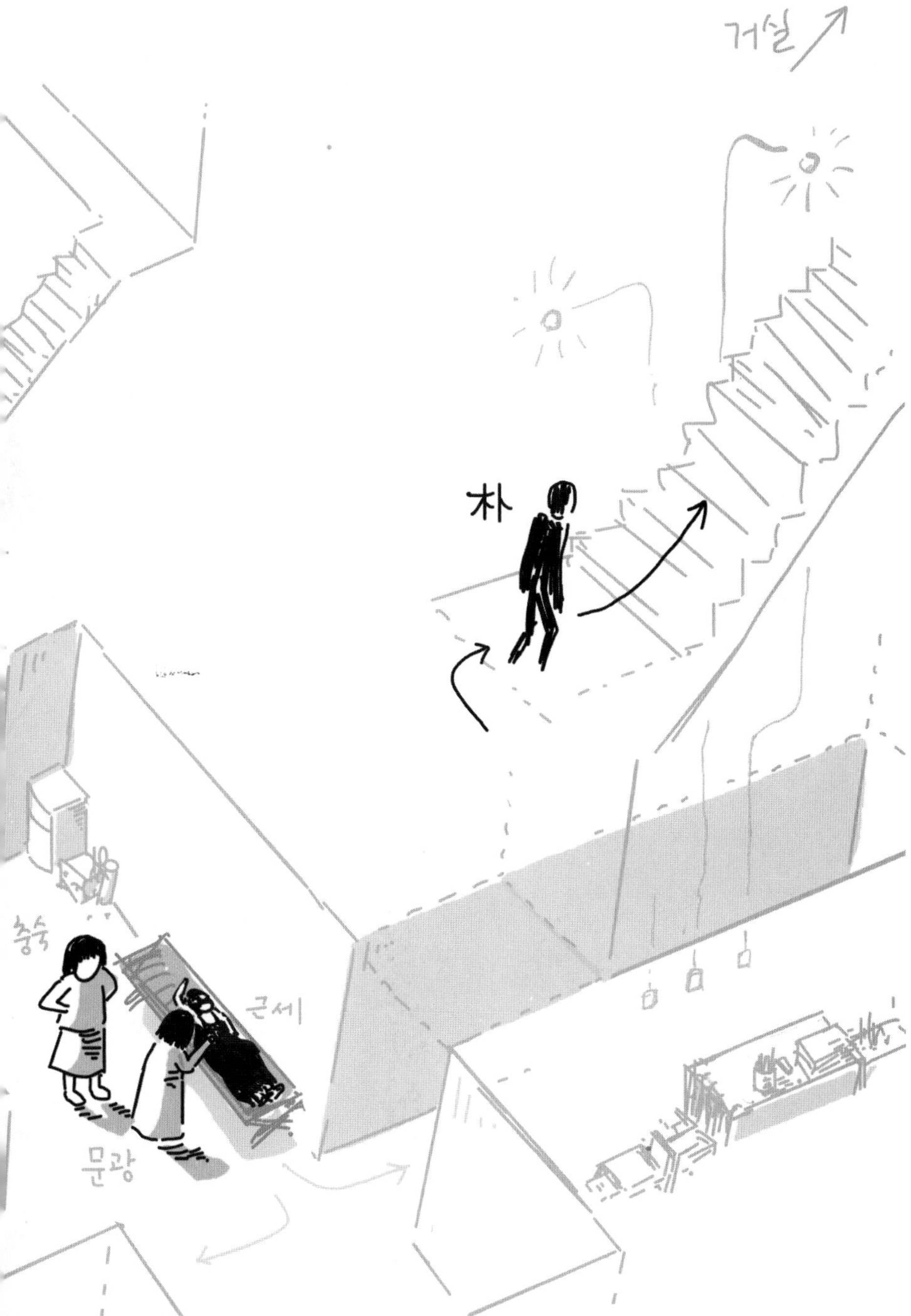
거실
朴
충숙
근세
문광

인디언 텐트

동익 .. 인디언
연교 .. 엄마 인디언
다혜 .. 죽도록 저항,
다솜 .. Trauma Again.
　　(또는 도끼 공격?)

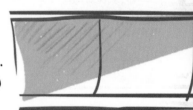

충숙 ... 칸에 찔린 딸
　　　주하며. 도끼 fight?

✳ 산수경
● 장난감

기택의 Choice 는?

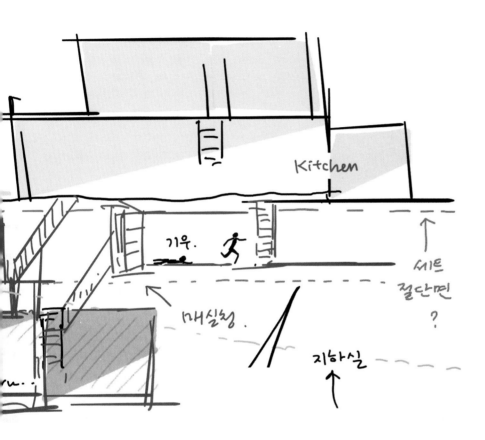

Kitchen

기우.

세트
절단면
?

매실청.

지하실

진짜도끼.

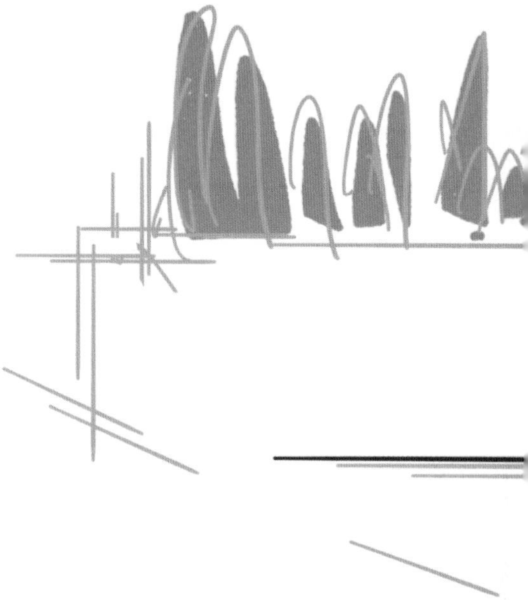

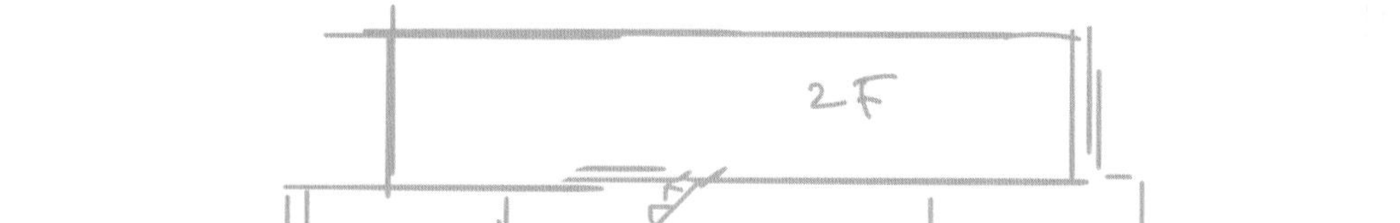
2F
1F
← 매실청
스위치

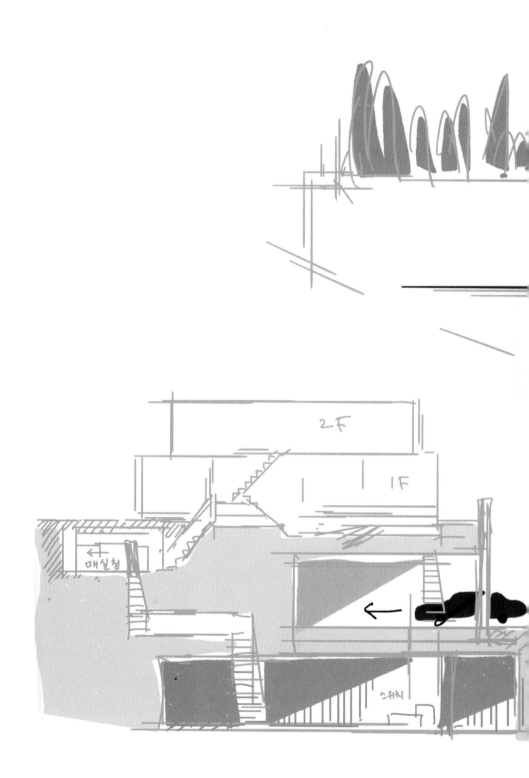

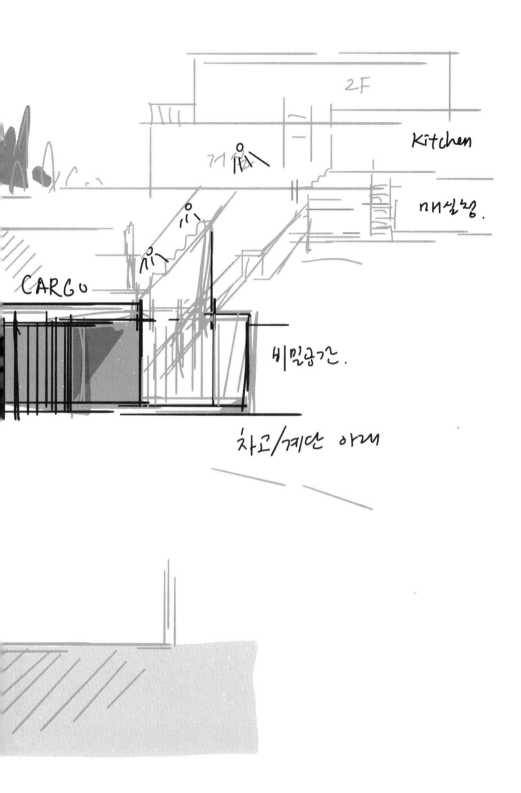

2F

Kitchen

계단

매실력.

CARGO

비밀공간.

차고/계단 아래

기피

케이크

가든파티.

다용.
기정. Cake ← 쫌쫌
푸욱 ... "생크림귀신"

∨ 근세라 흉측 뒤엉킴.
"저열한" 칼부림. 몸싸움

⤴ 흉흉 die. 근세. killed b

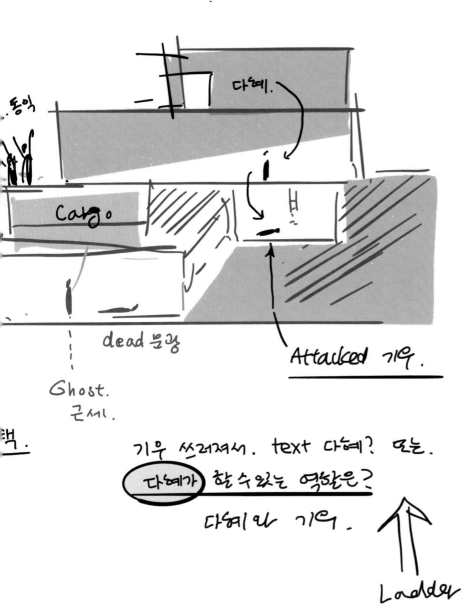

동익

다혜.

Cargo

dead 붕괴

Attacked 기우.

Ghost.
근세.

객.

기우 쓰러져서. text 다혜? 또는.
다혜가 할 수 있는 역할은?
다혜와 기우.

Ladder

two pipeline

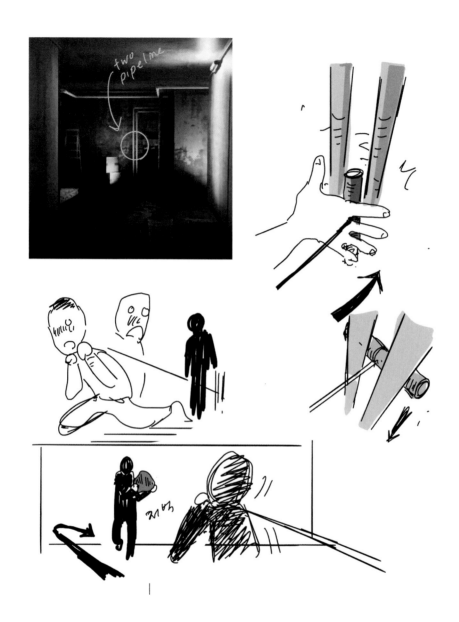

VFX
Practical
어!
wire
크악!
Quick
Stone
광!
뭔가 strange
금속. 파이프 도막?

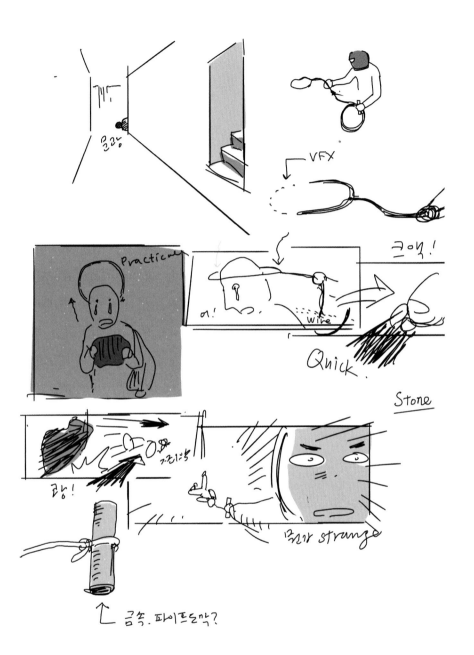

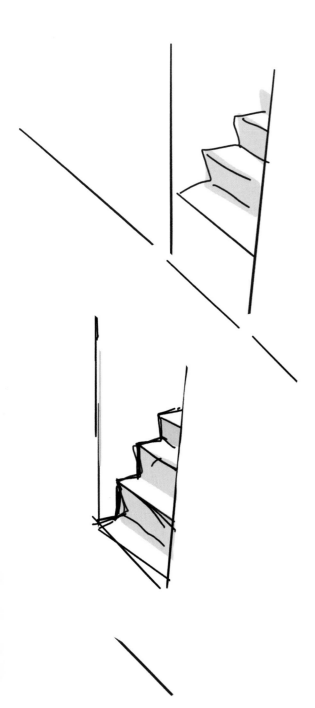

박사장
기택
다송
기정
BBQ
충숙
잔류 손님
약 20여명.
CA

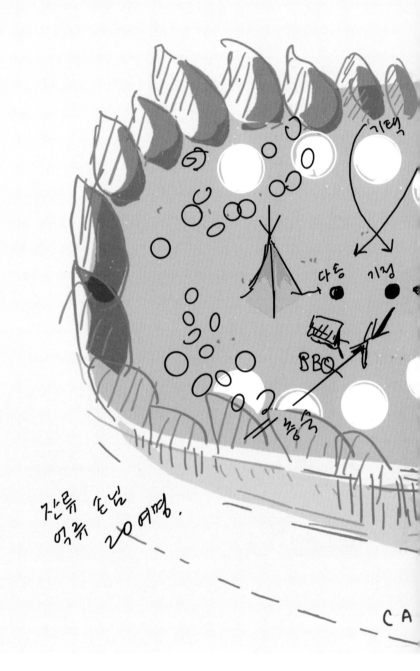

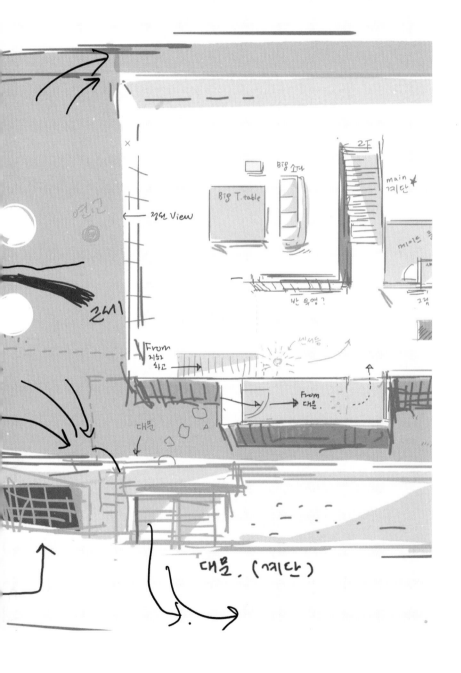

정원에서.

✓ 언덕 주택가의 가장 위. ㄴ

정원 View

그새

Big T.table

Big 쇼파

2F

main 계단 ★

miple 길

반 투영?

From 지하 창고

센서등

From 대문.

대문

대문. (계단)

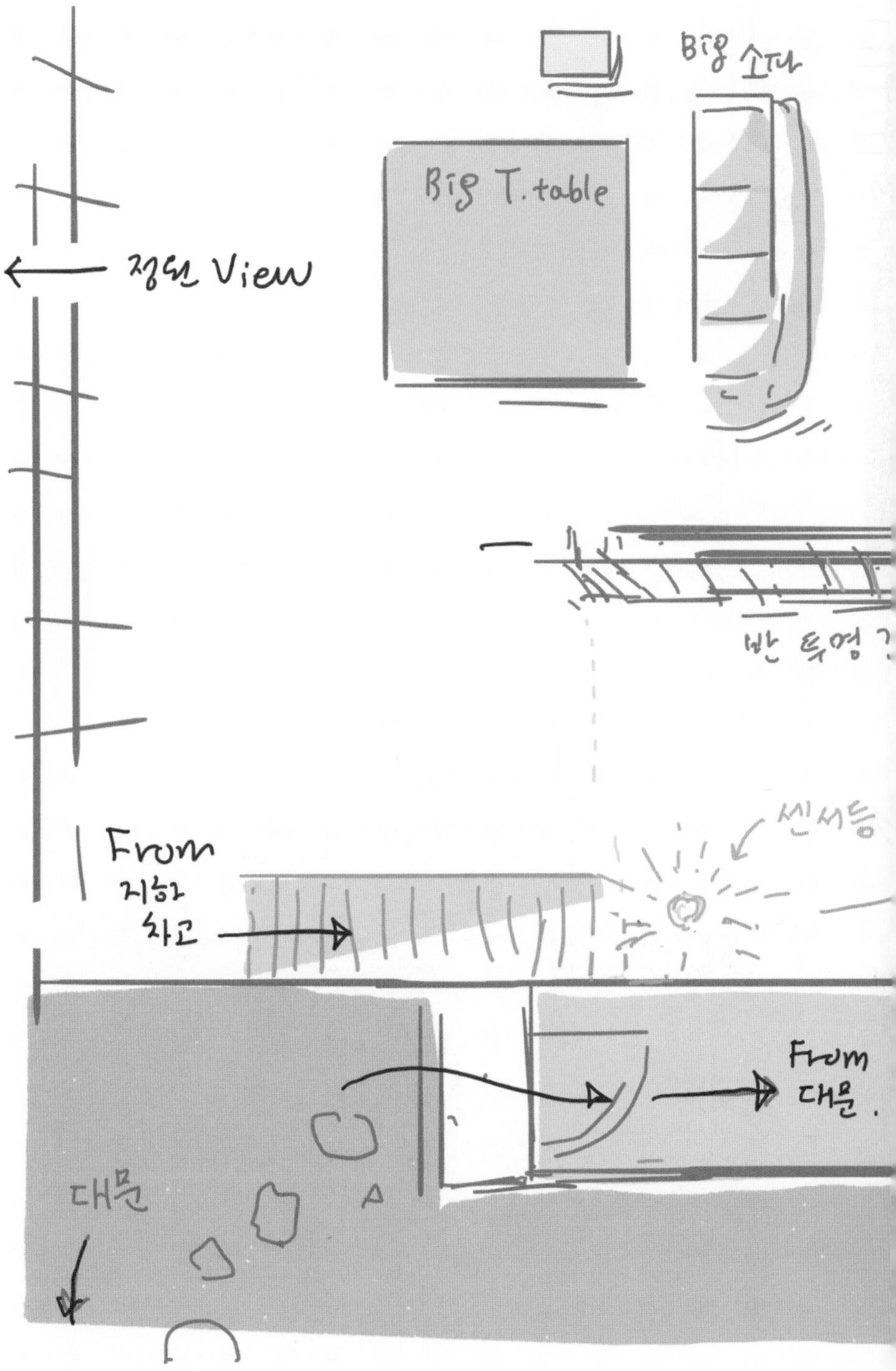

Big 소파
Big T.table
정원 View
반 투명 ?
센서등
From
지하
차고
From
대문.
대문

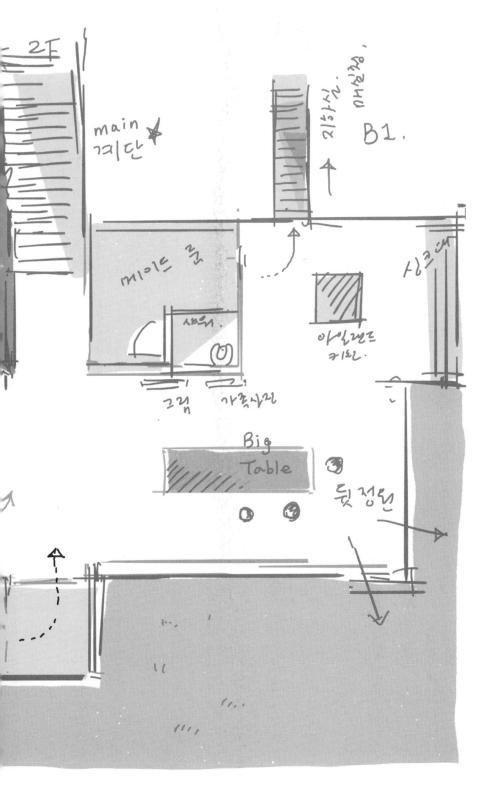

2F

main 계단

메이드 룸

샤워

그림   가족사진

리스너. 어릴때. B1.

선큰뜰

아일랜드 키친.

Big Table

뒷 정원

263

Wifi zone
Stanway to
더 길게
Wifi
기정.
MB
충숙
기택.
crawl
tracks.
Camera Angle
" must be

VR · Simplest.

Pee Watcher 역순

기우

SOFA 겸
쉼대

table

→ POOP
~ame 연결 쉽다.

↑ mainy
detached.

침수되었을때. 우리 싯수크라
음라라스 북쉬늘은 ...

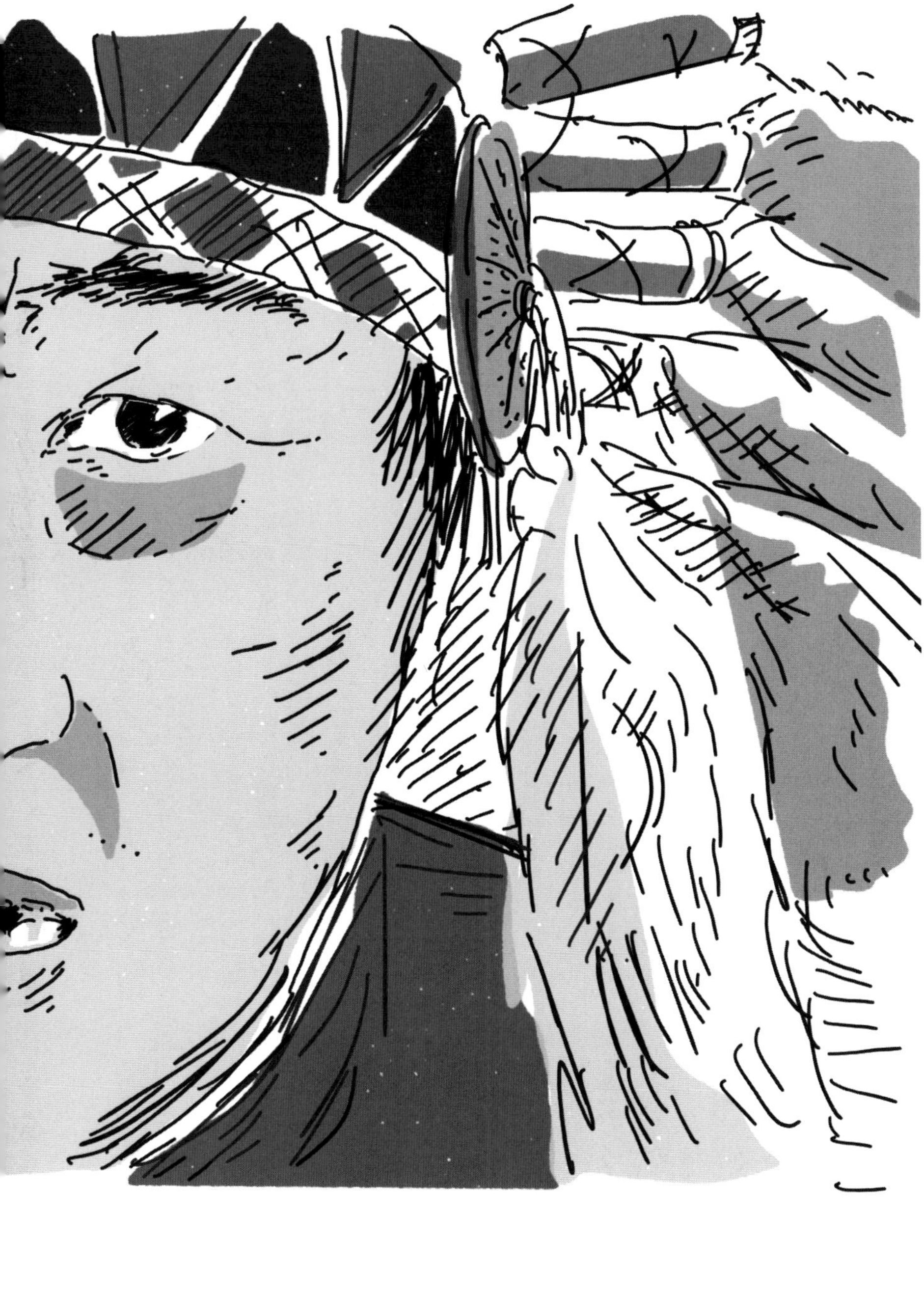

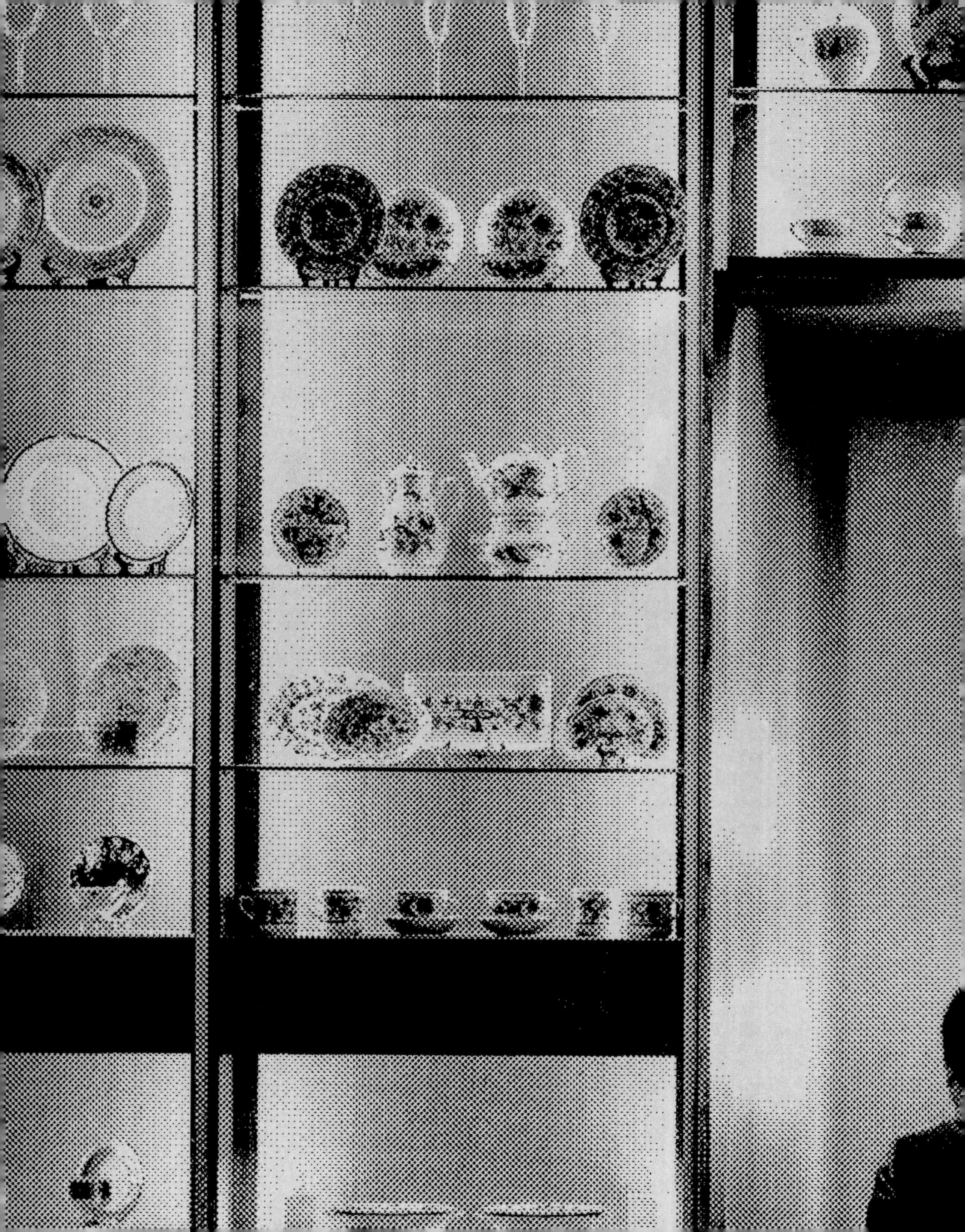

Part 3. Production Stills

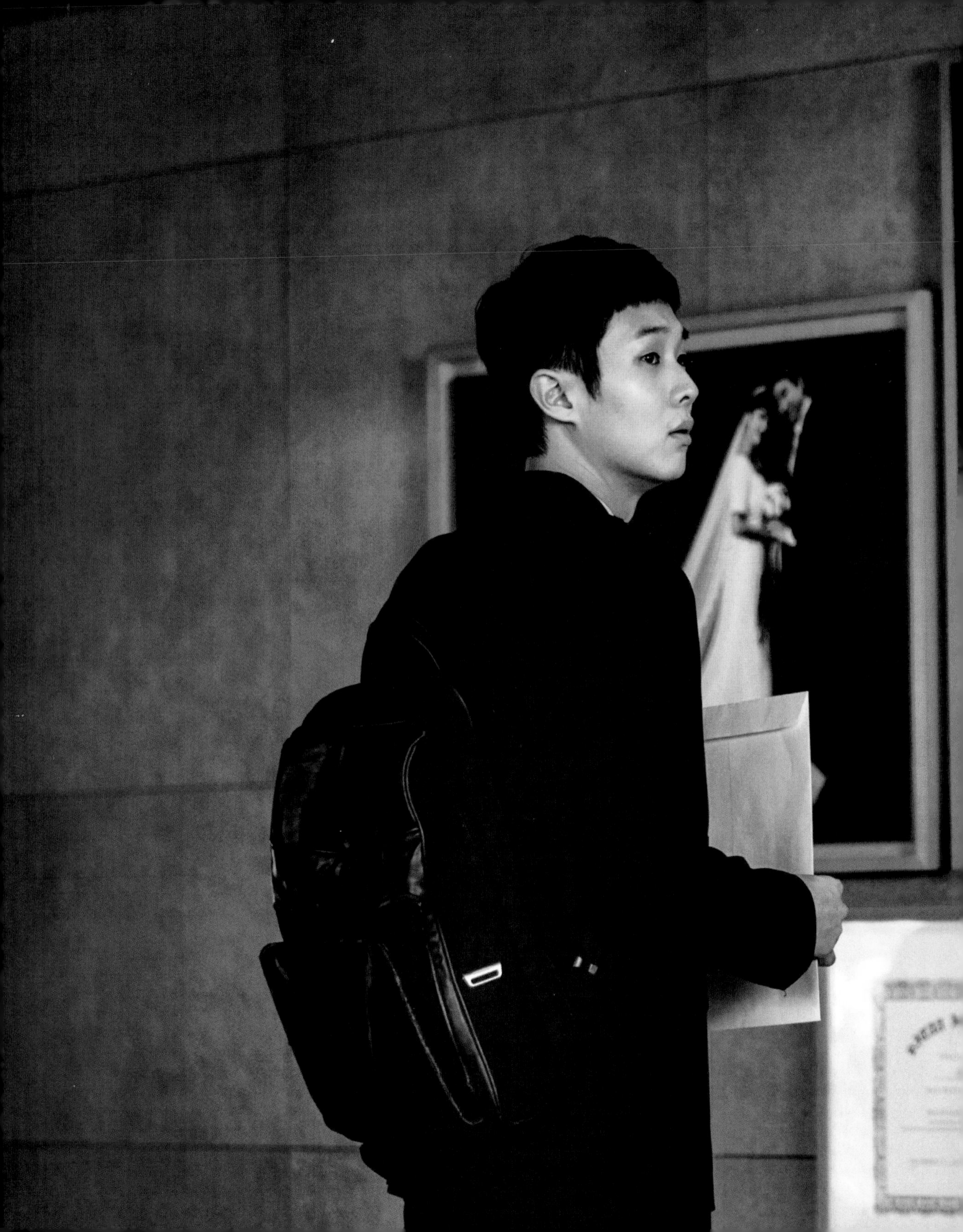

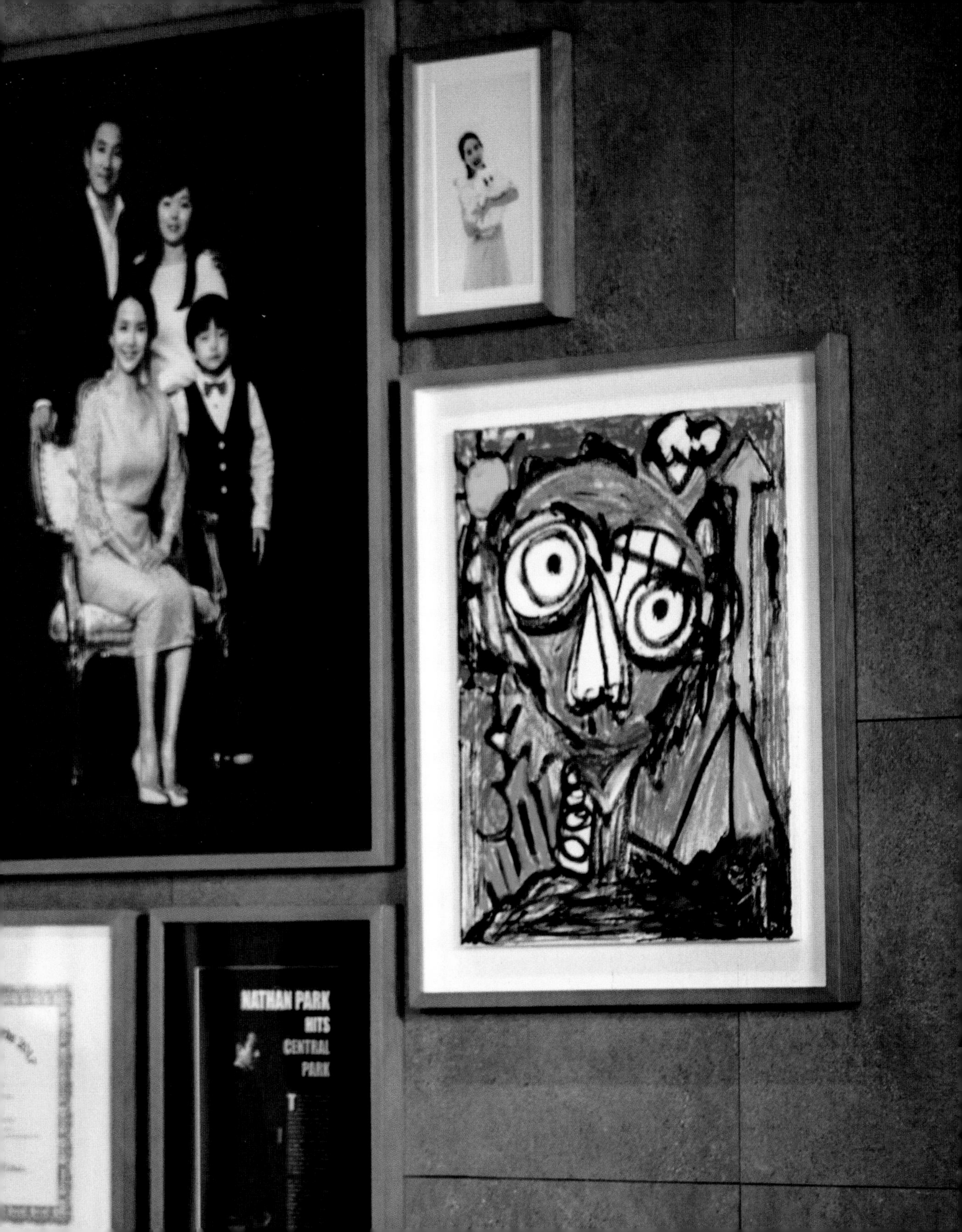
NATHAN PARK
HITS
CENTRAL
PARK

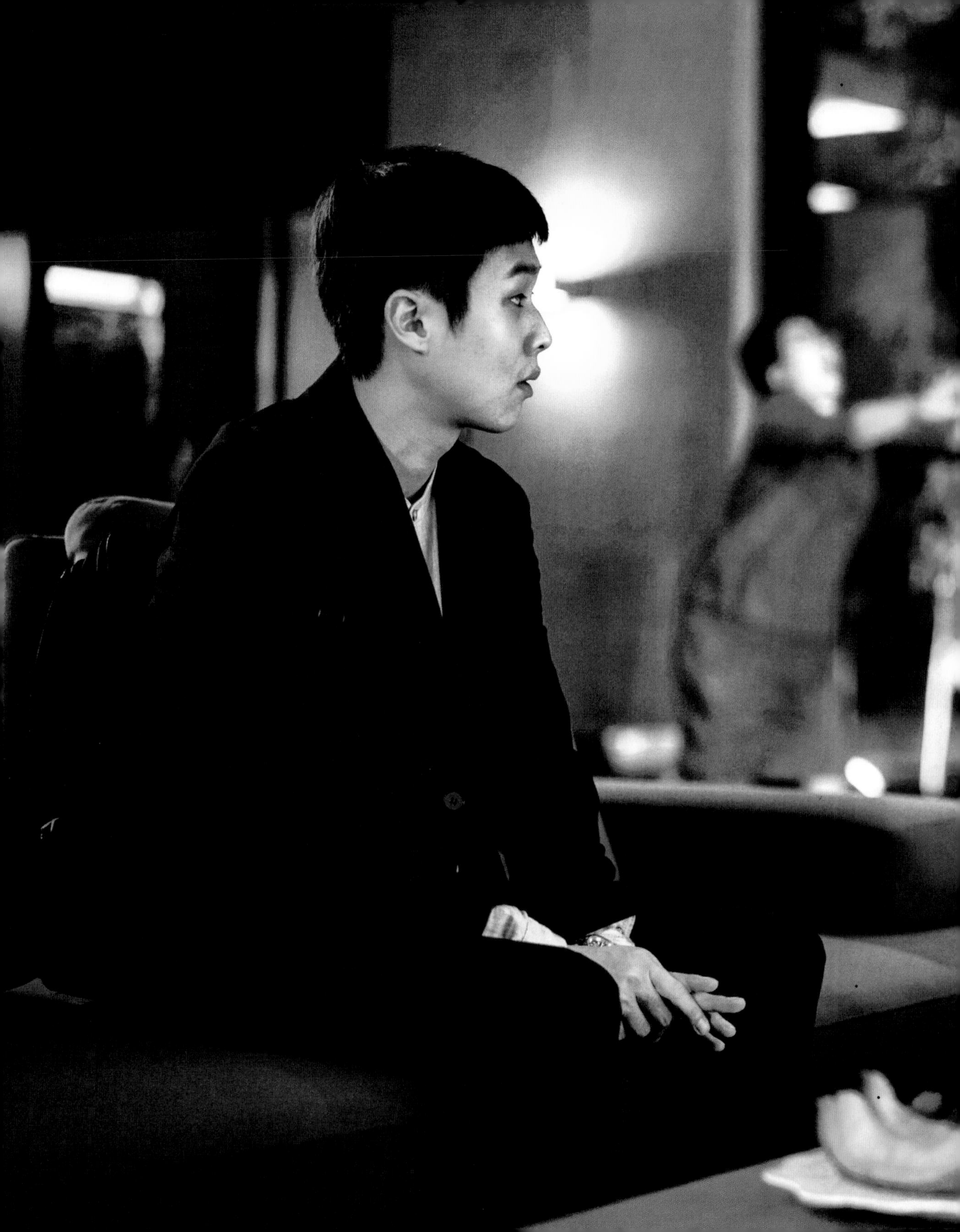

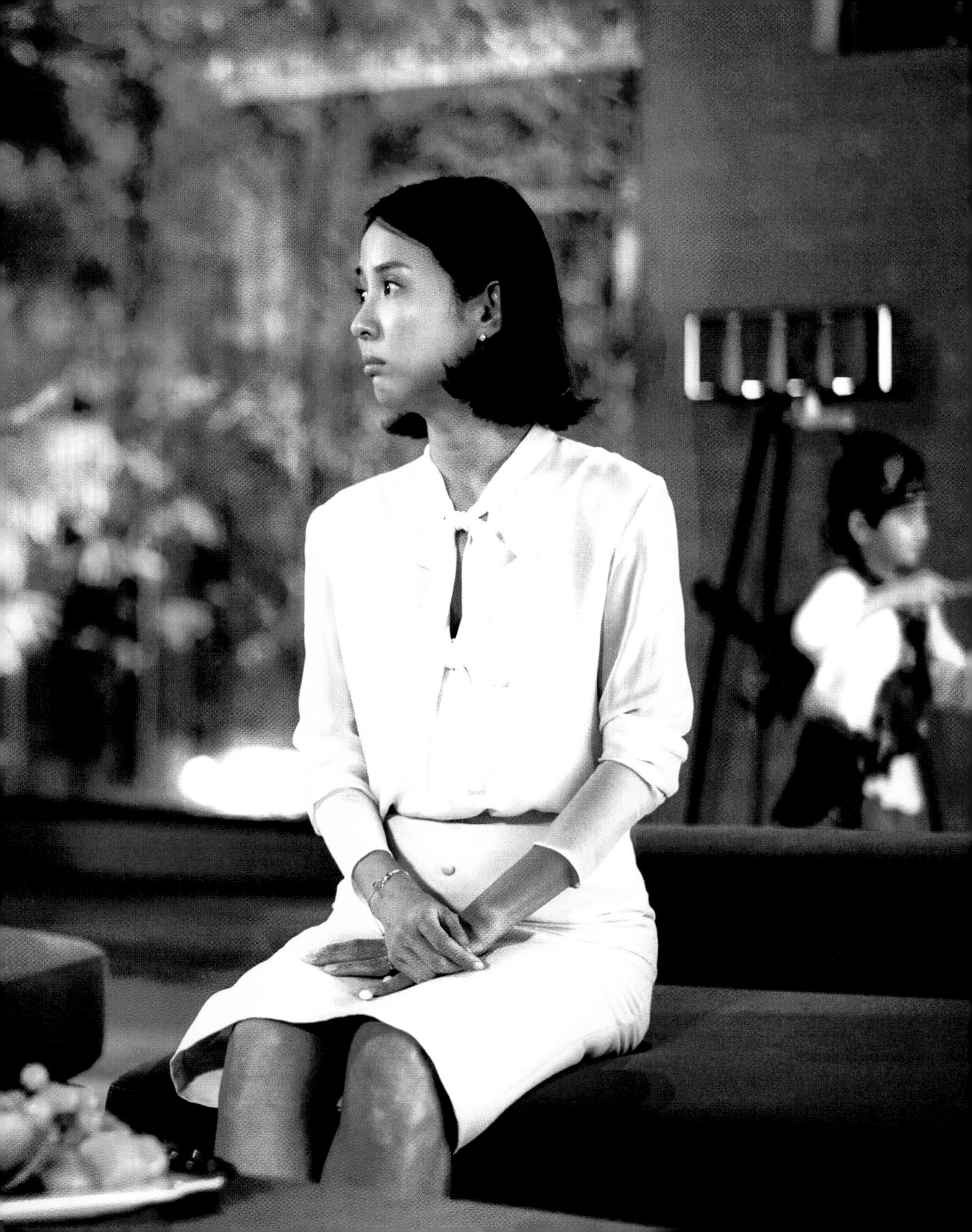

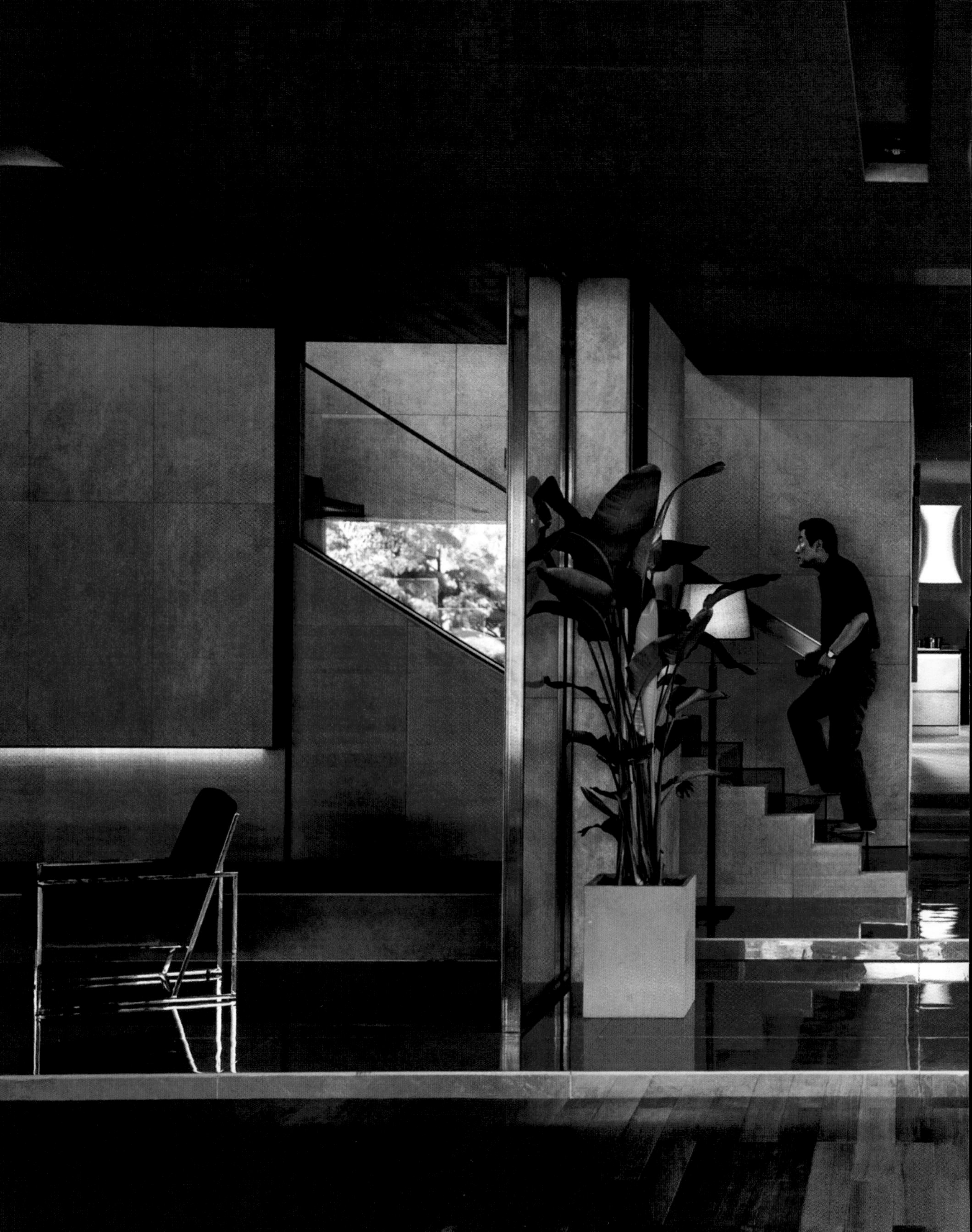

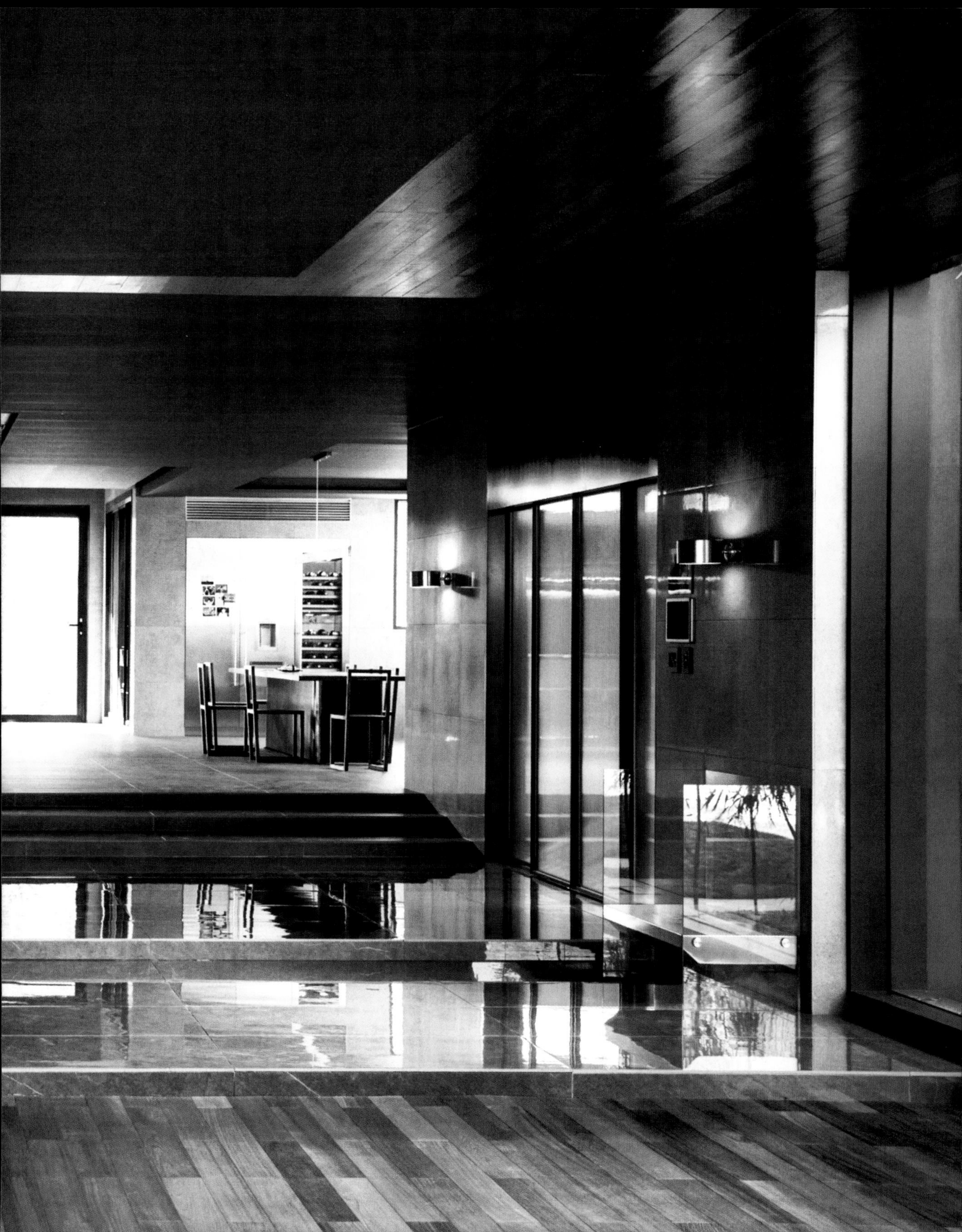

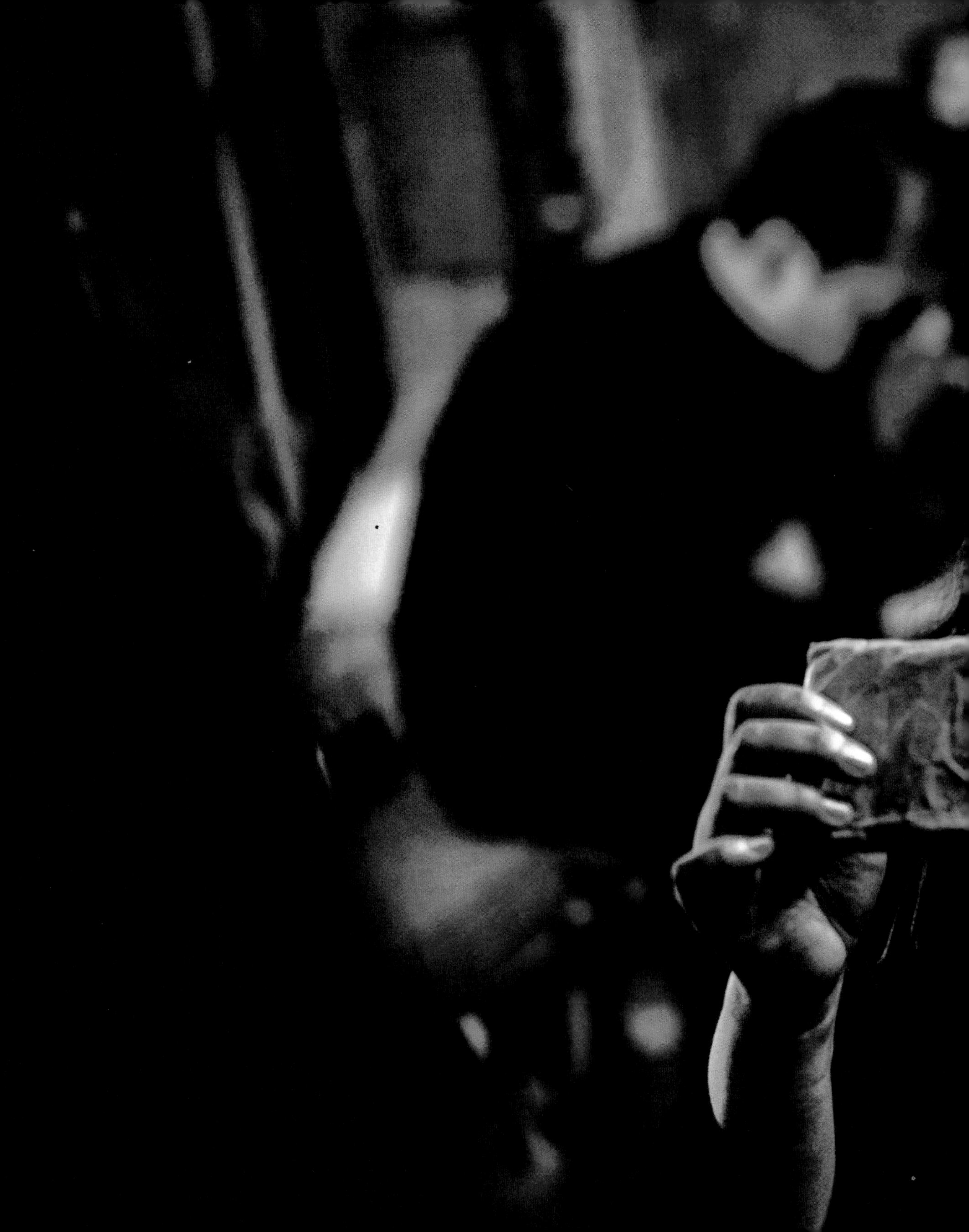

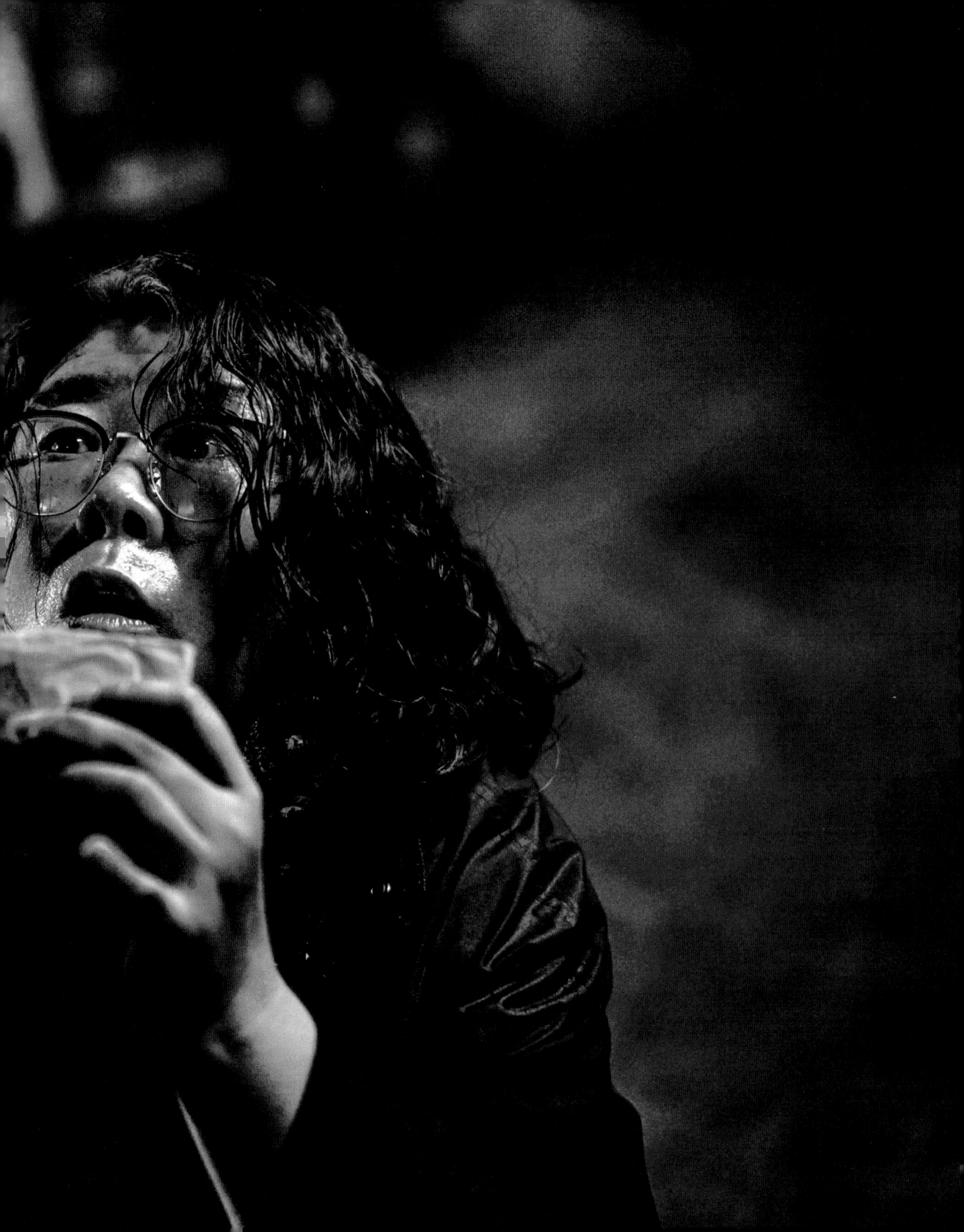

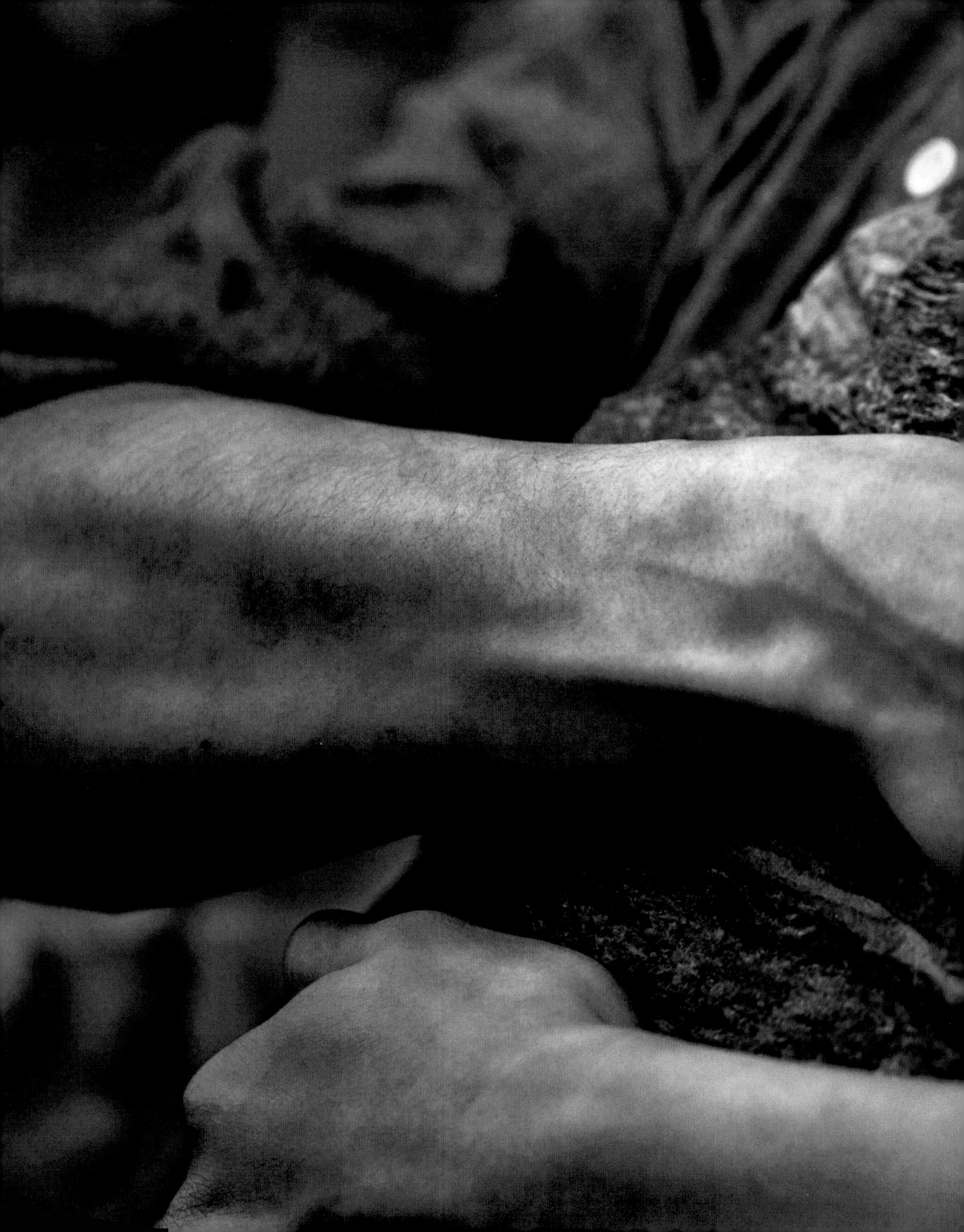

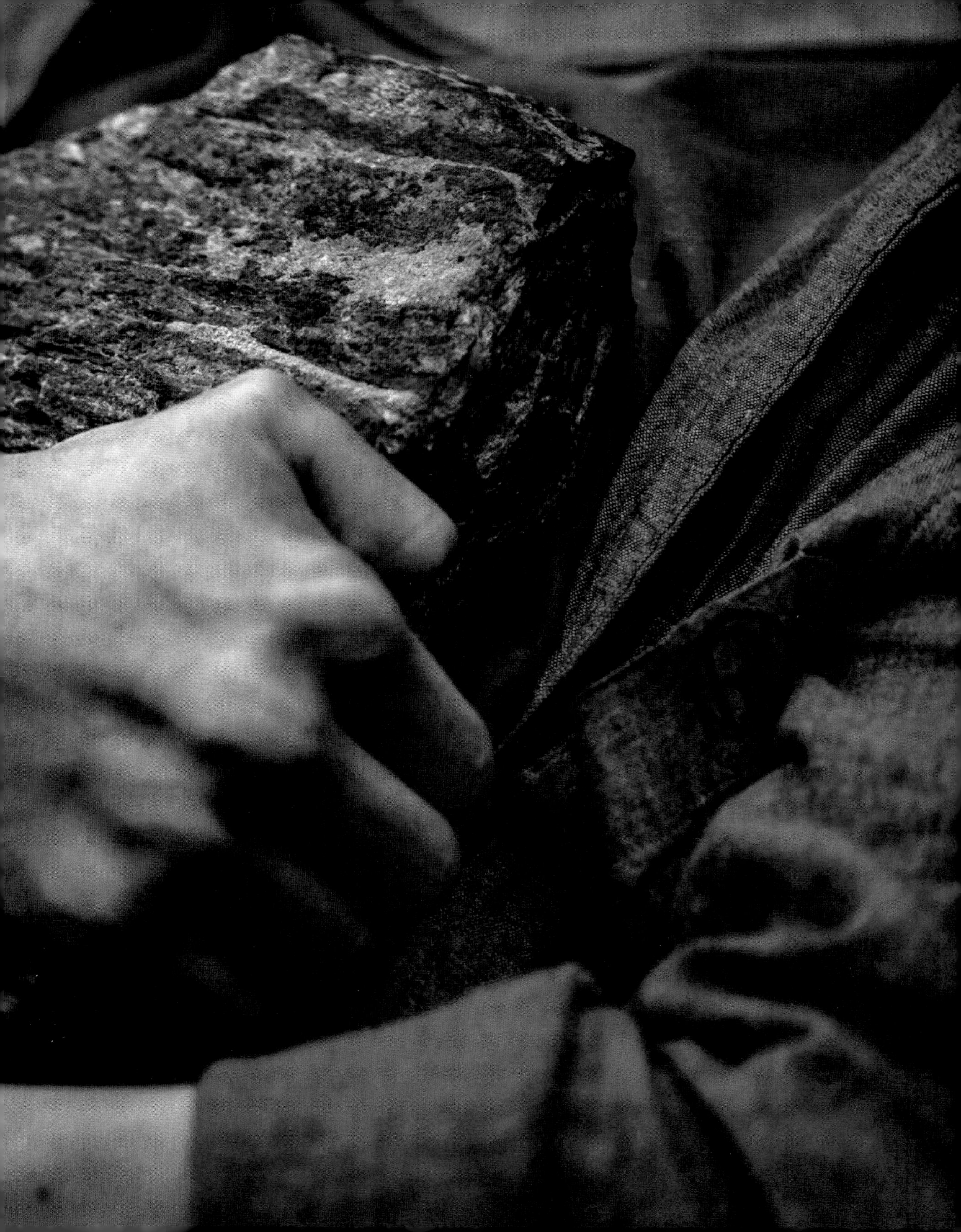

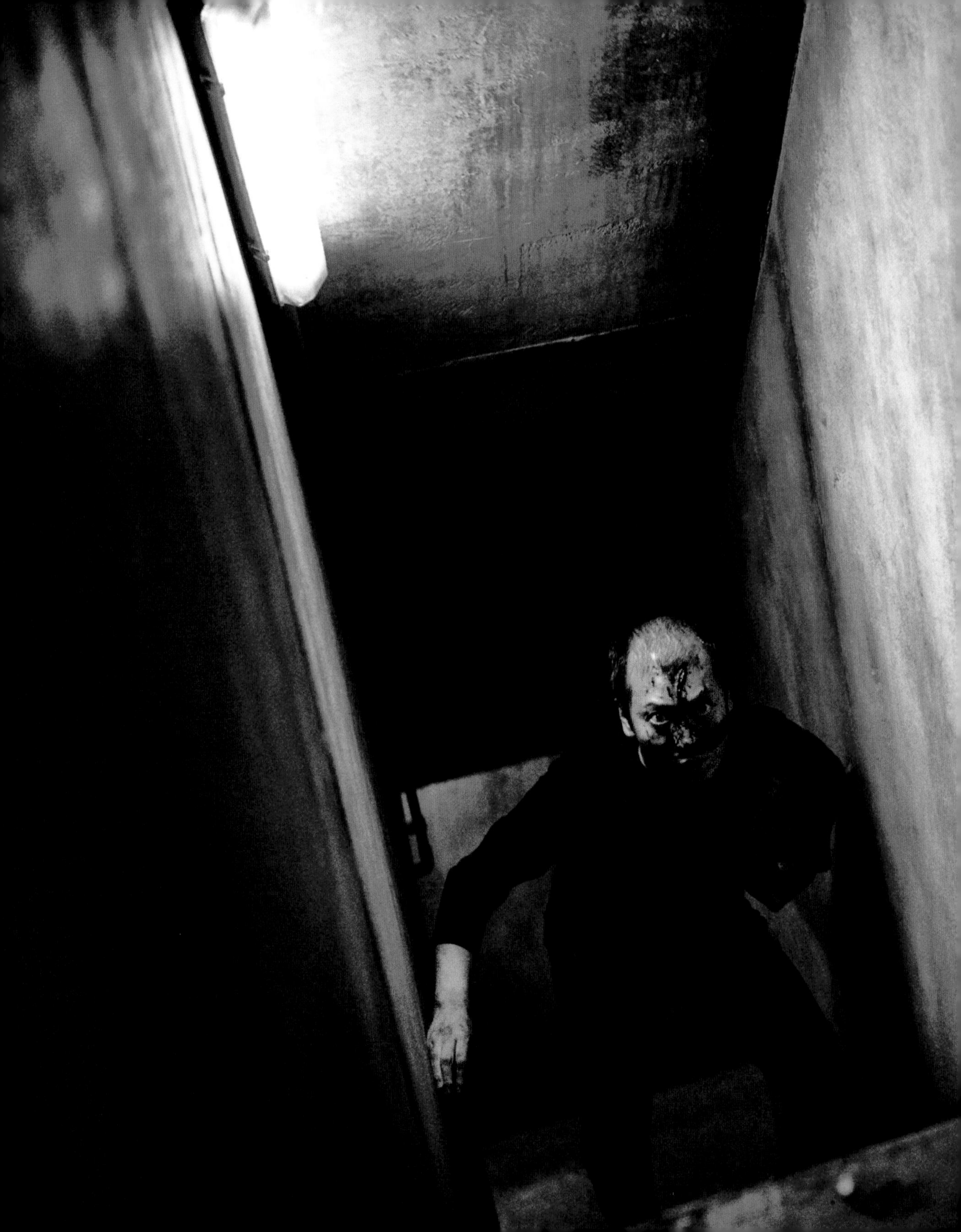

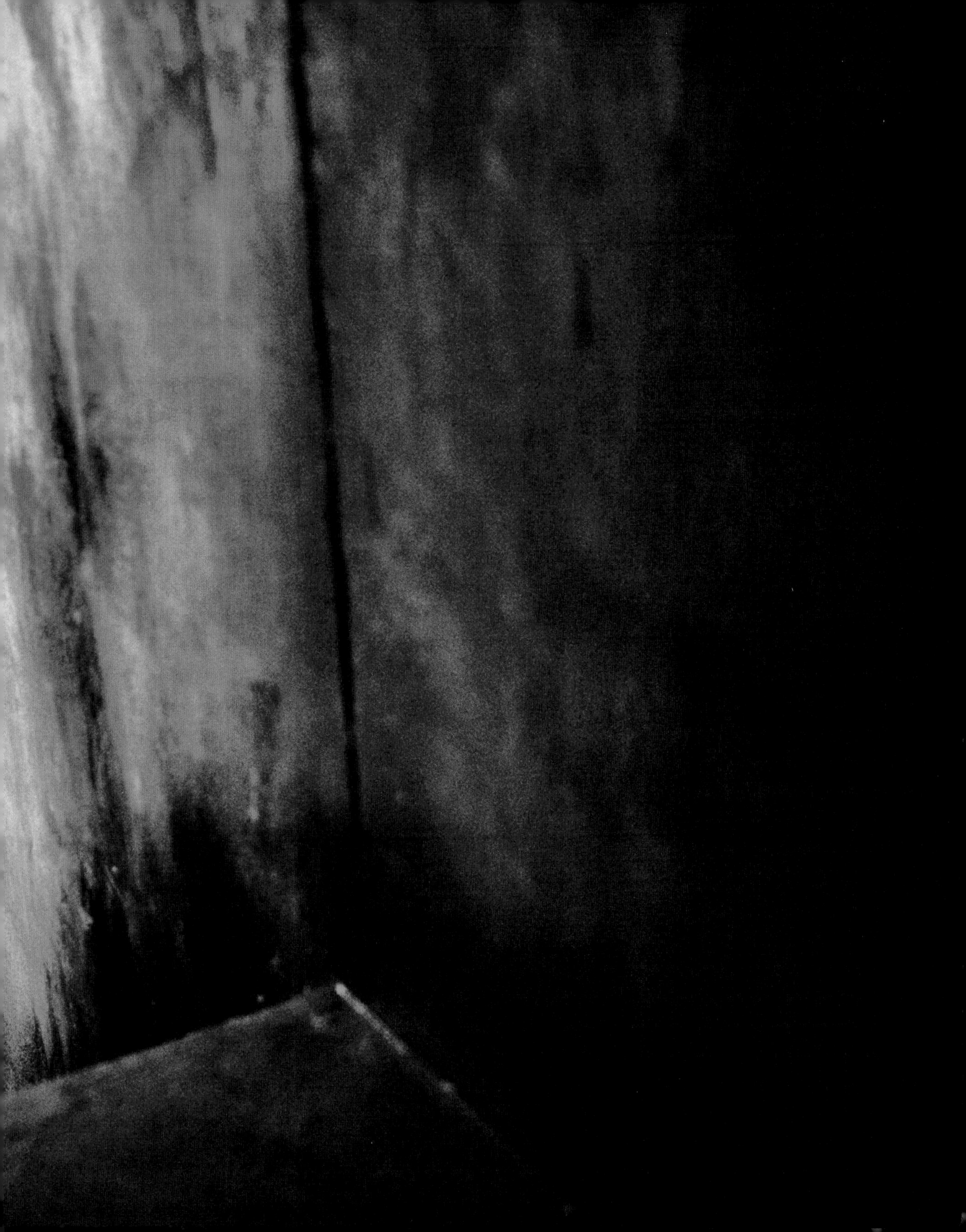

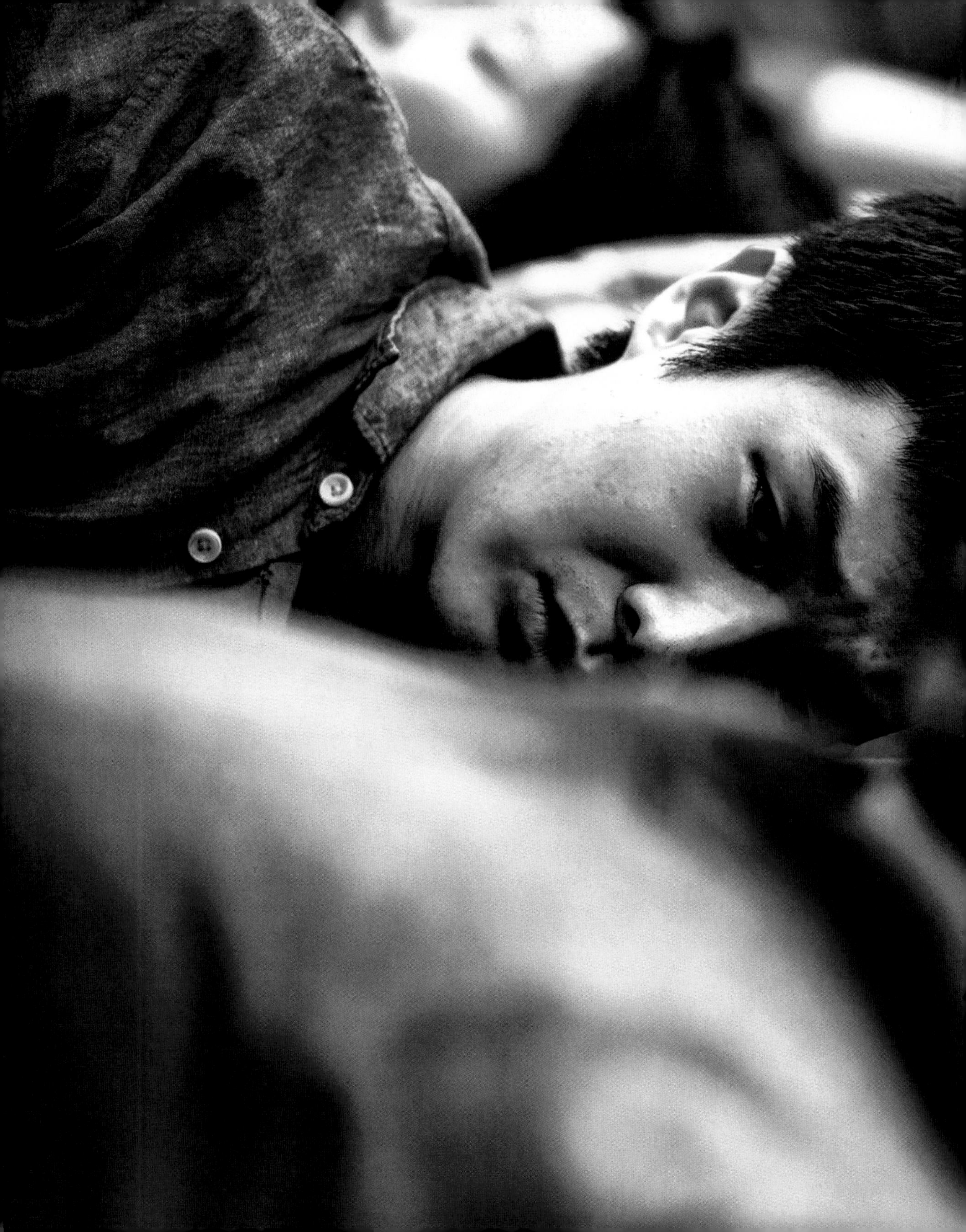

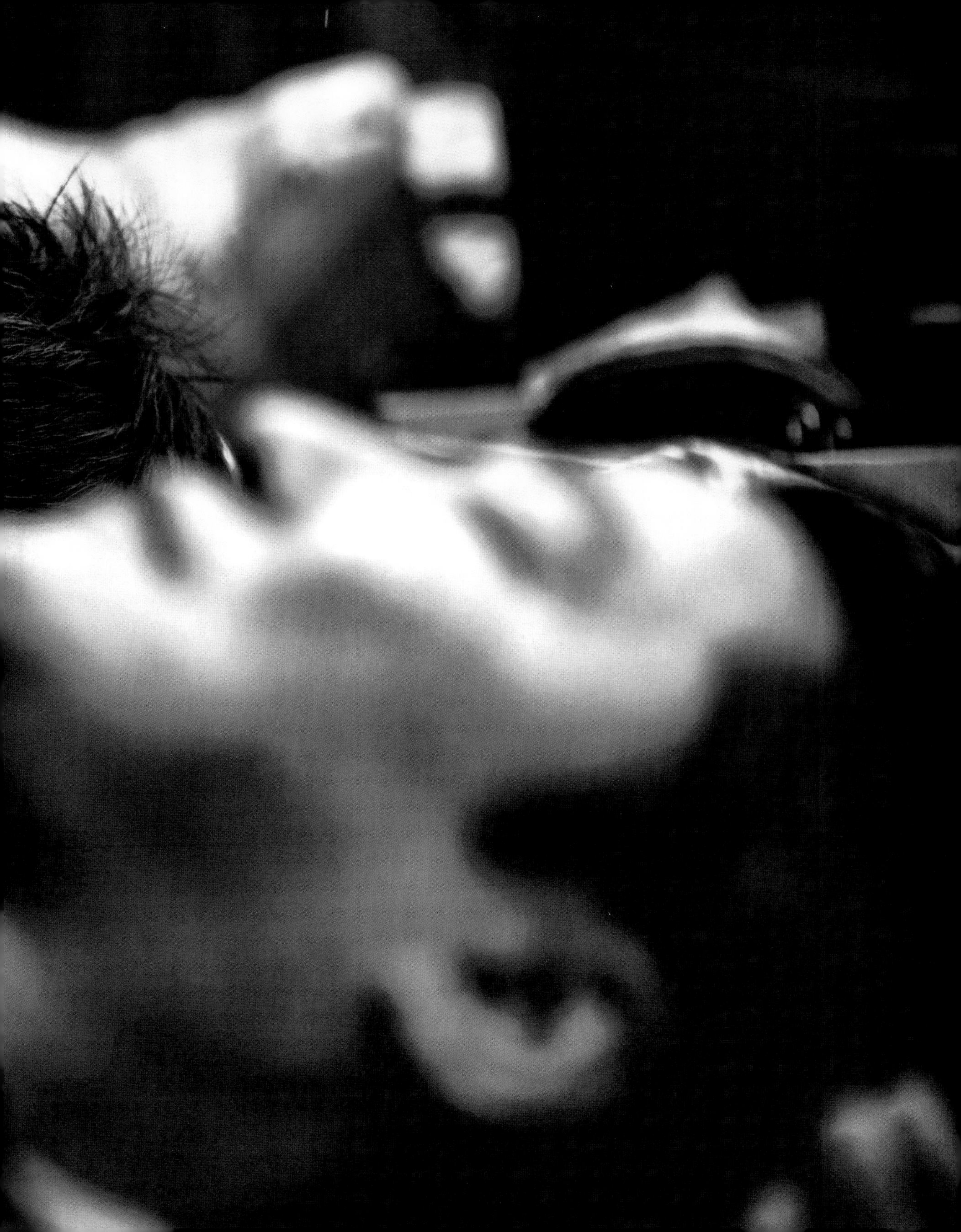

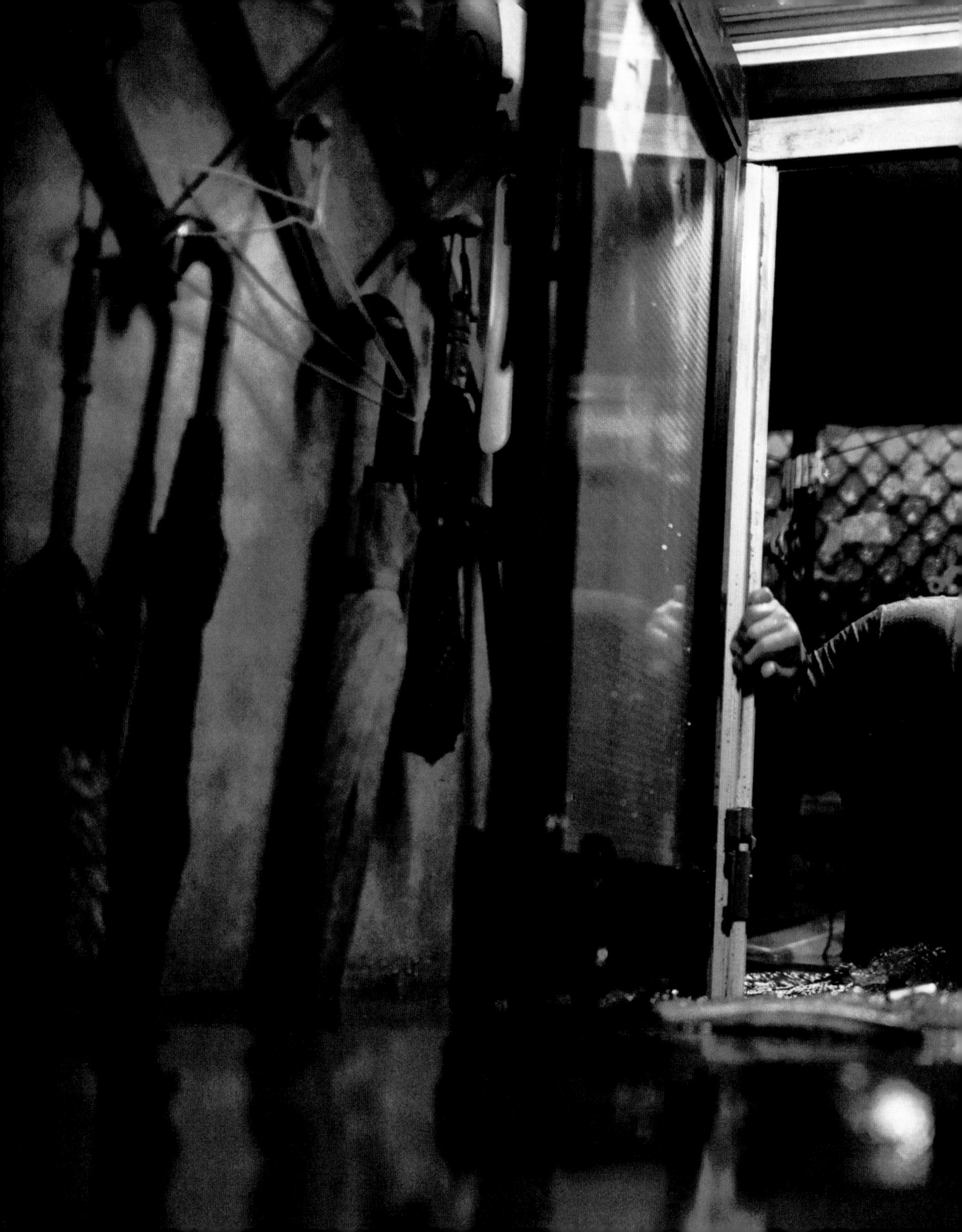

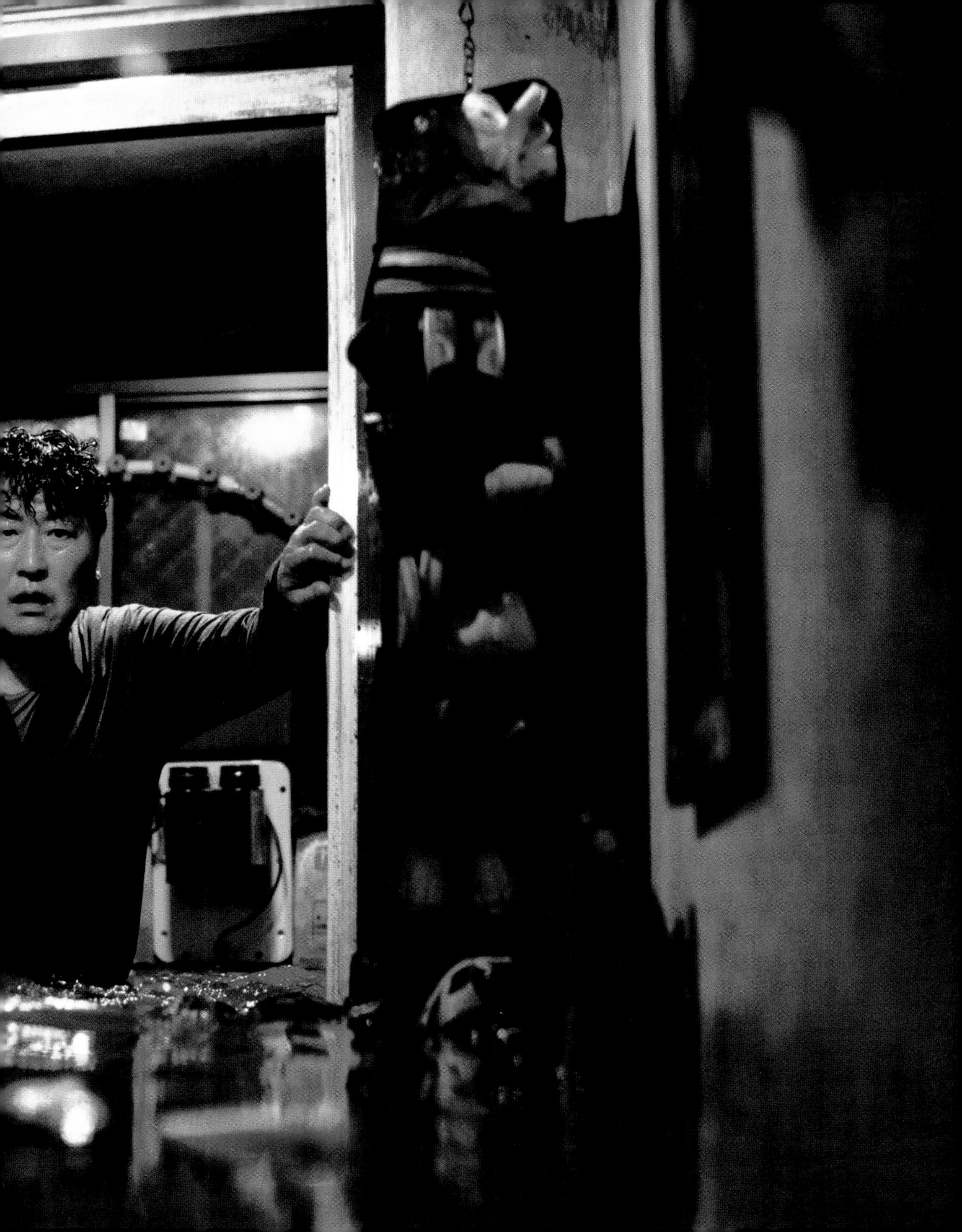

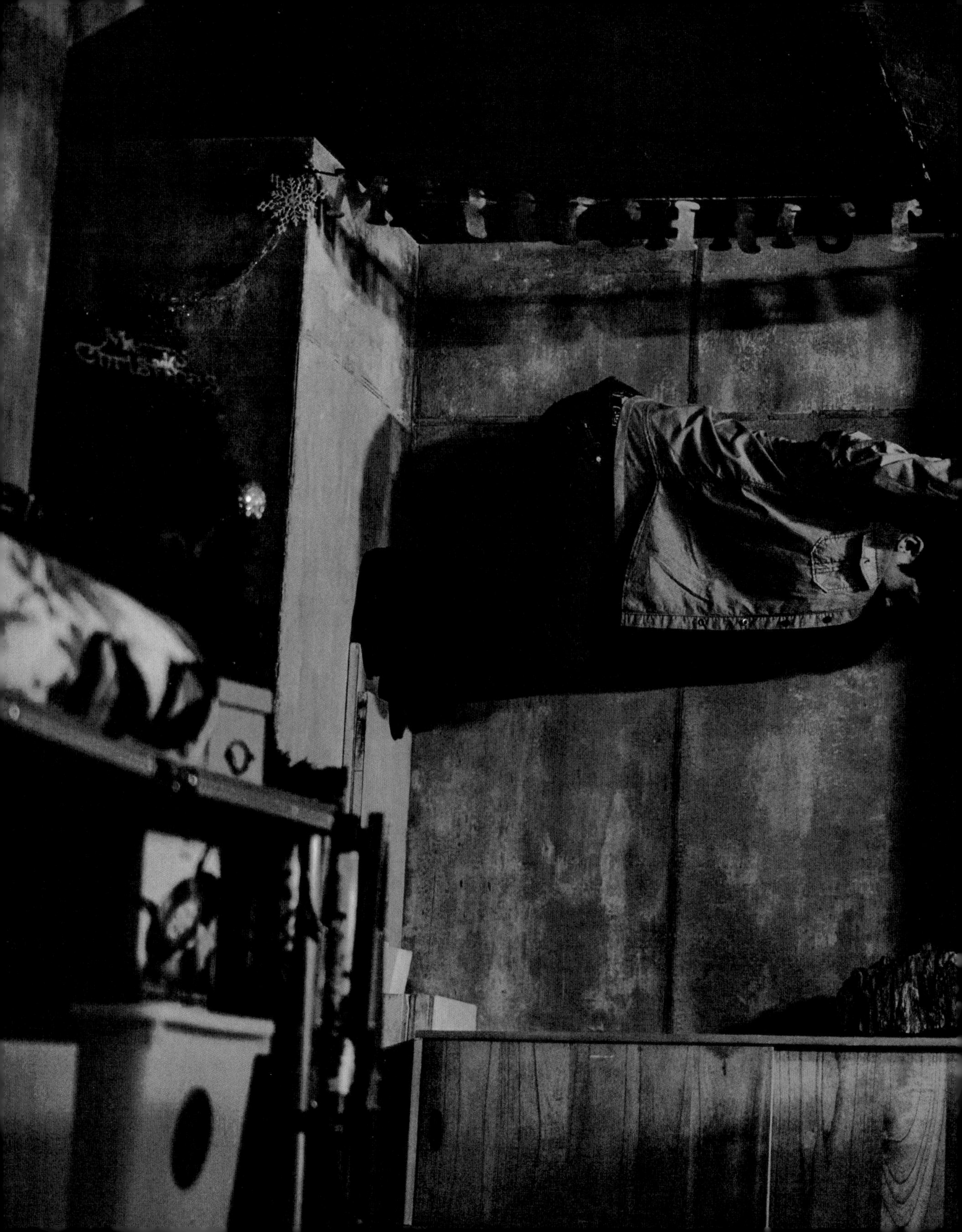

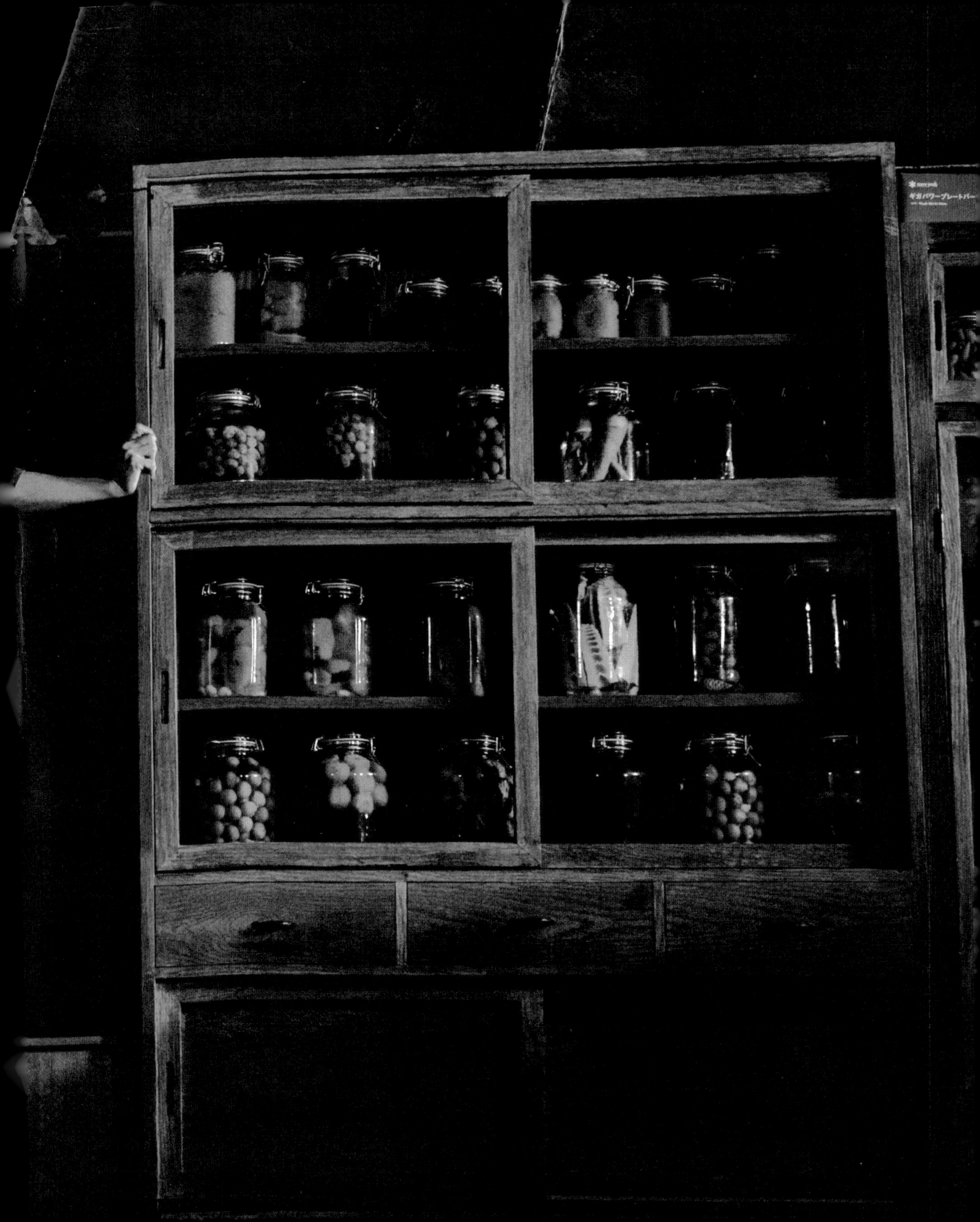
ギガパワープレートバー

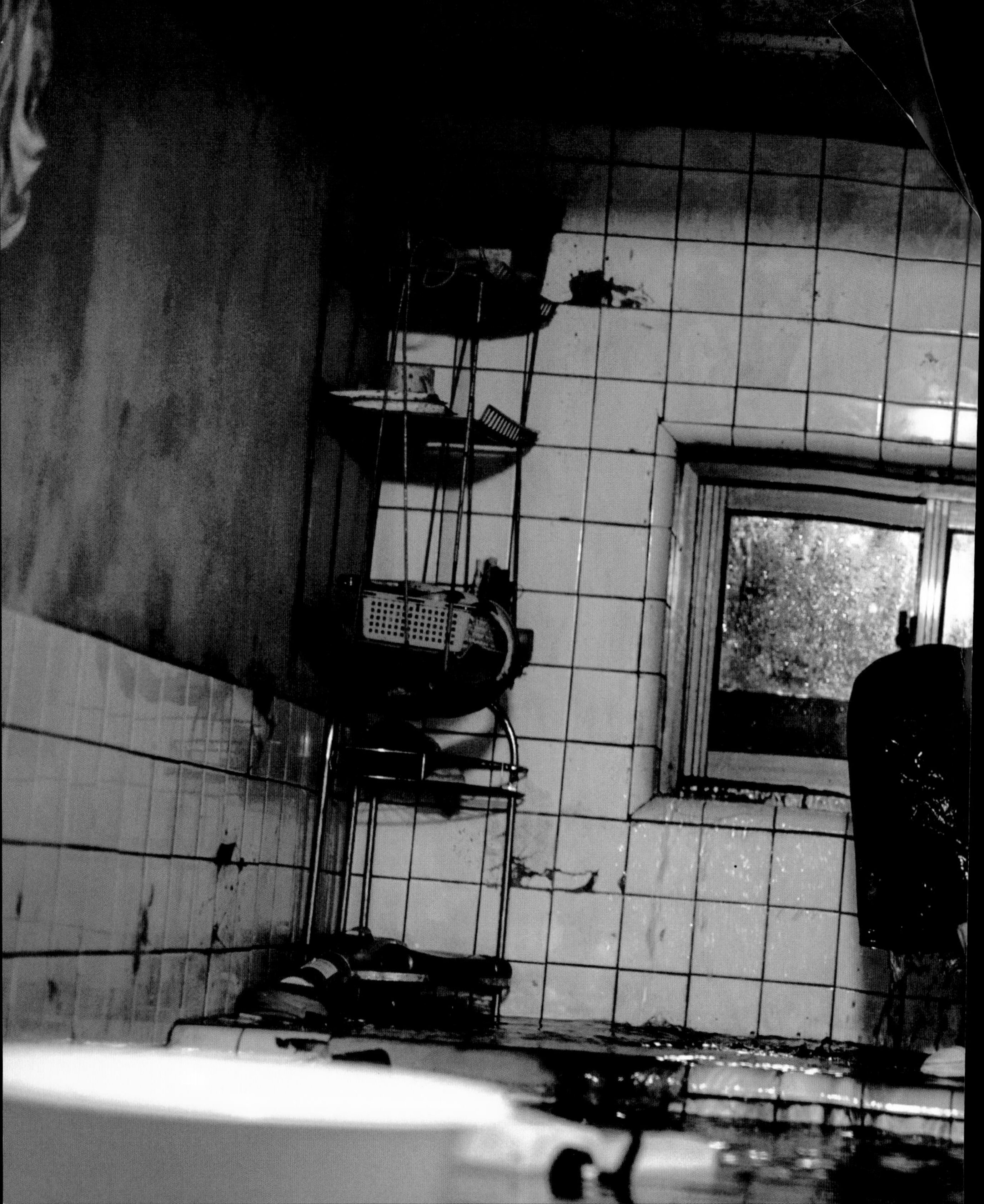

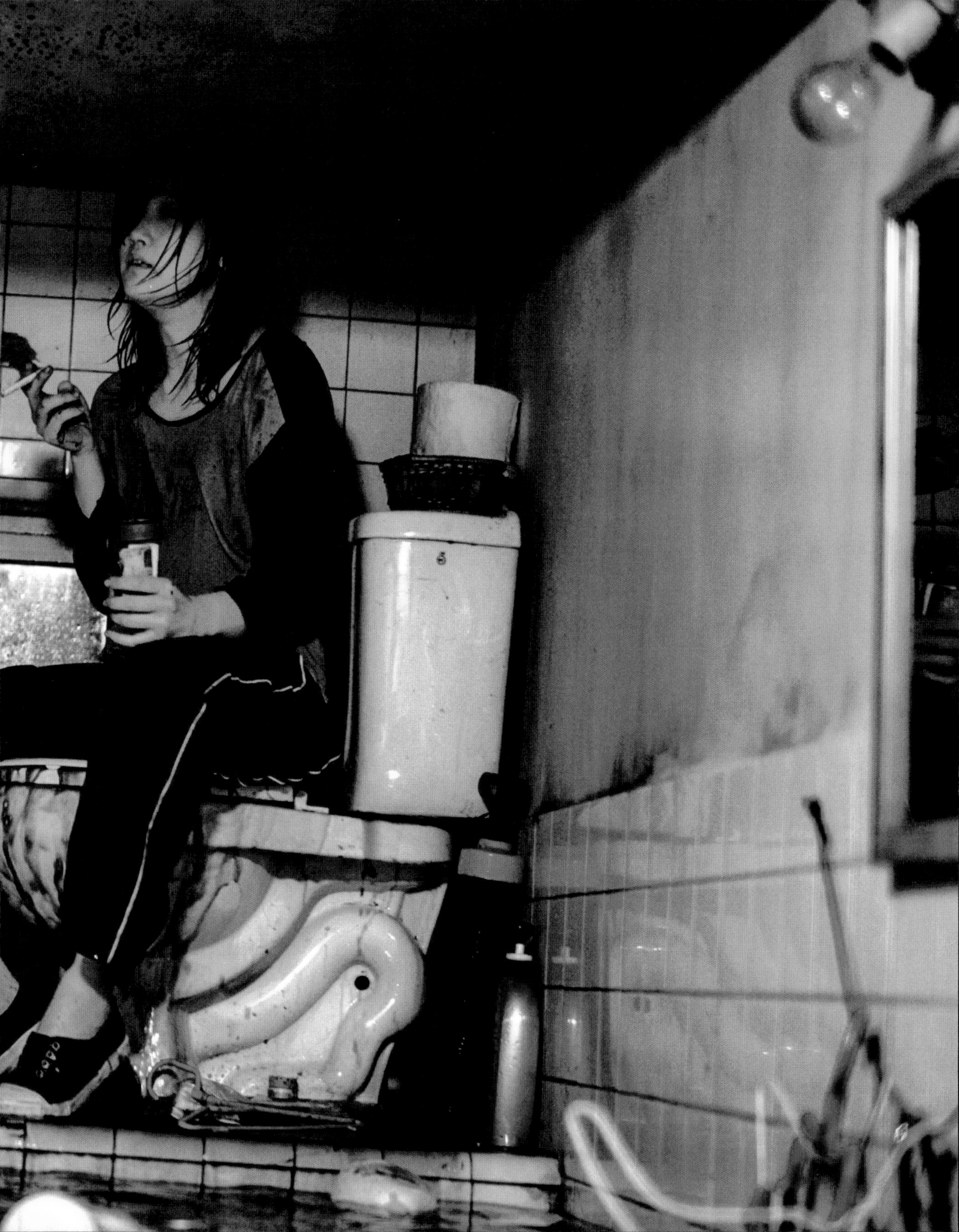

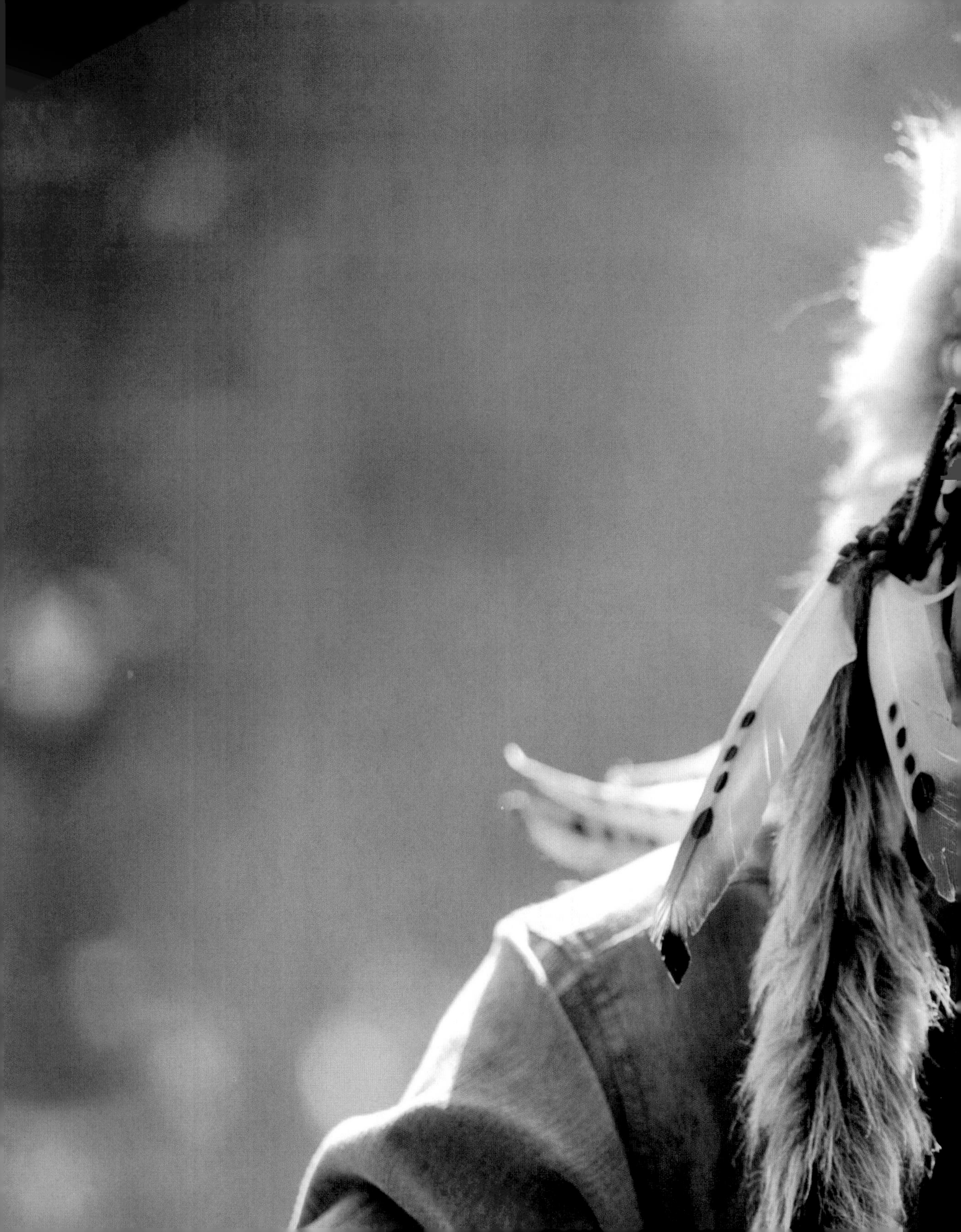

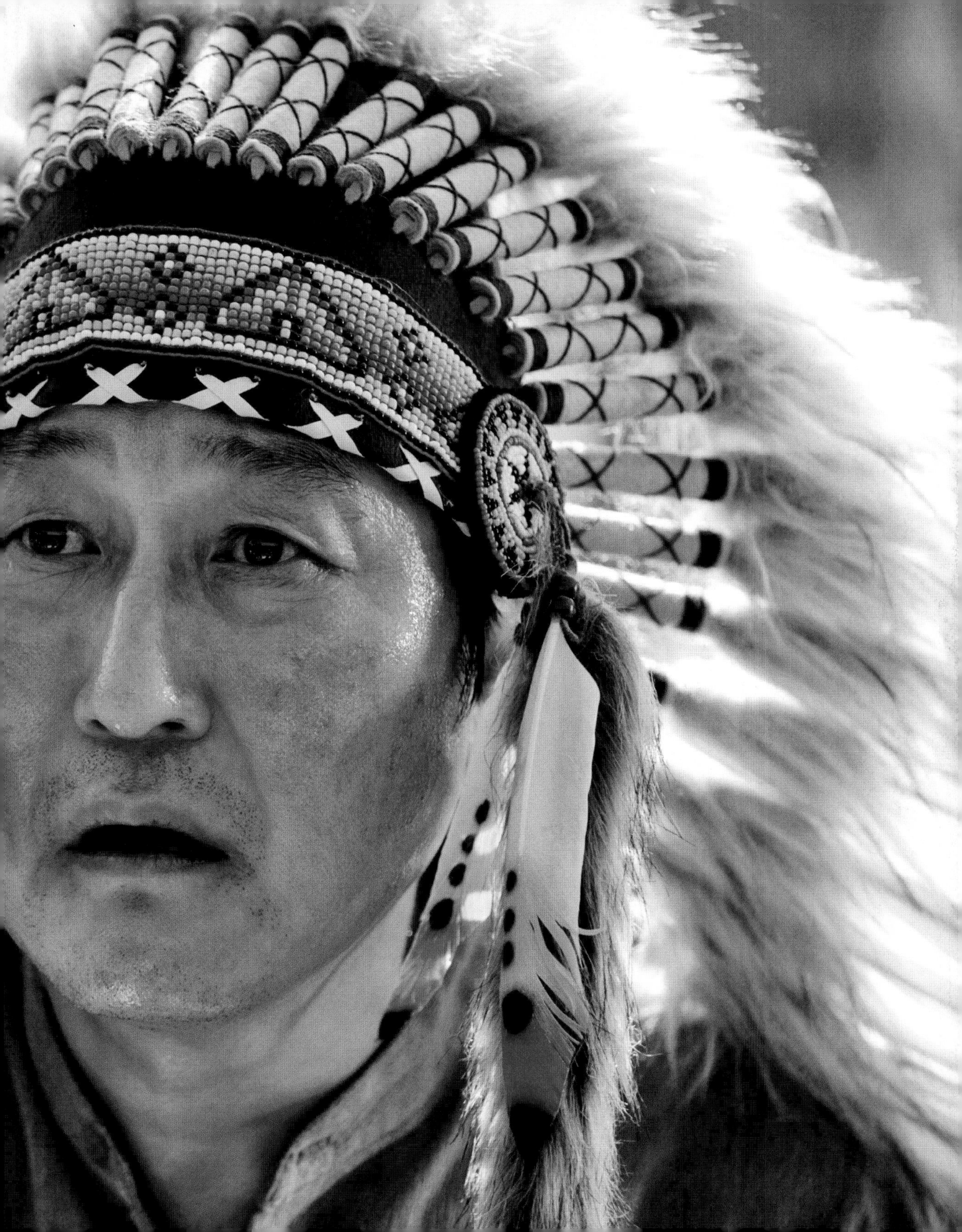

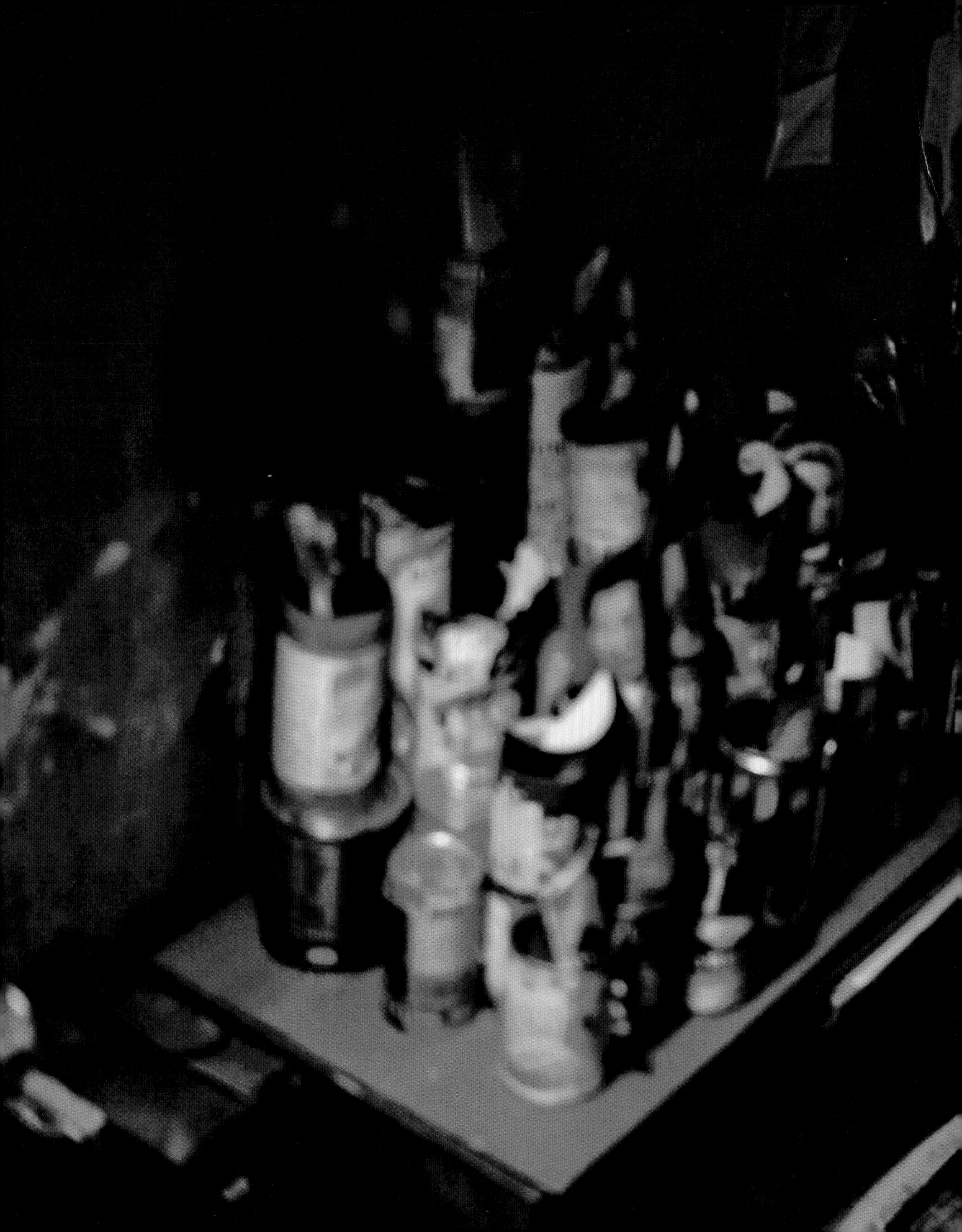

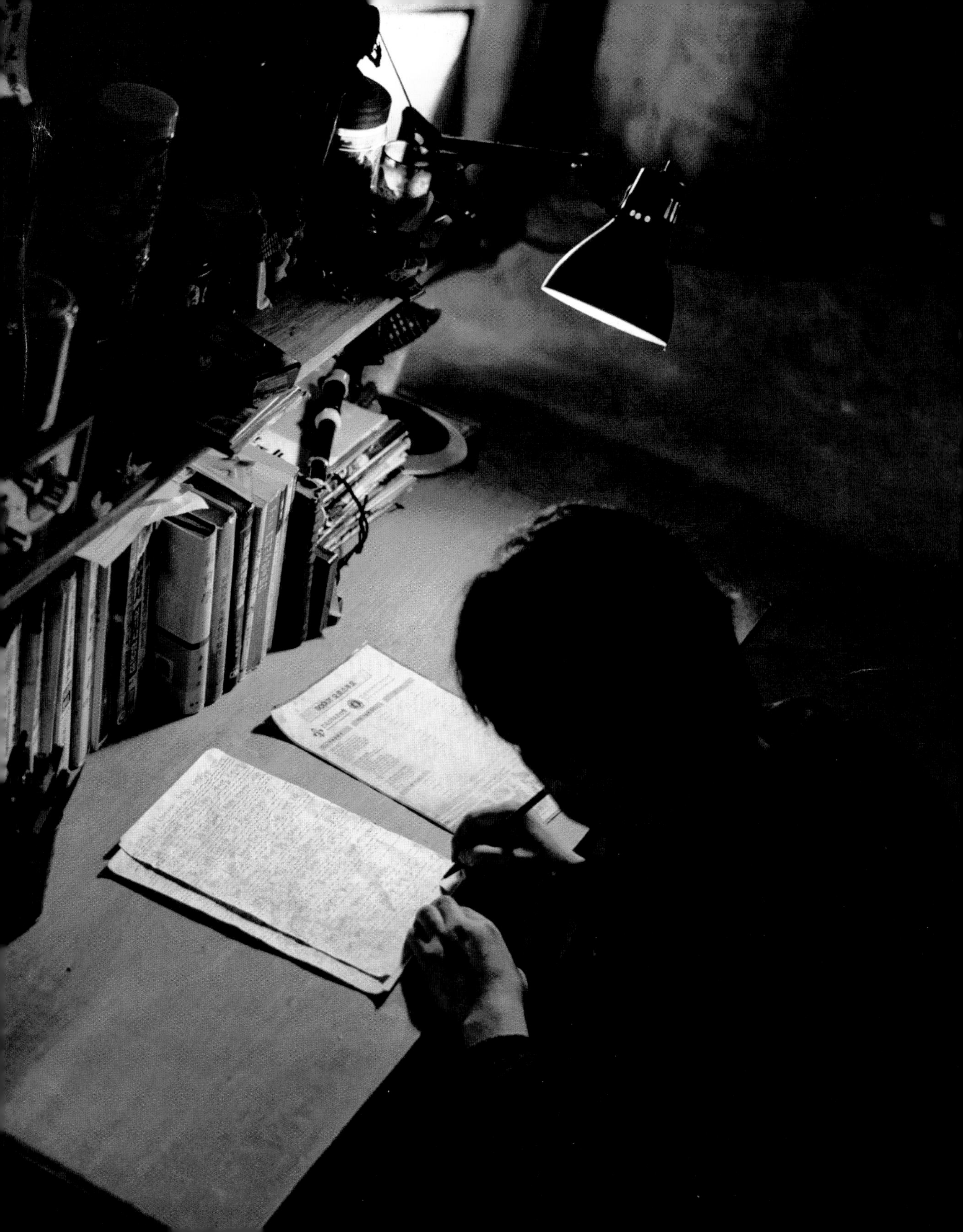

②

스카우트 수첩 펼쳐서
모르스부호품 ... 다시 거실쪽
         보는 다솜

\# extra shot → 박사장. 욕조에.